The Perfect Affair

Also by Lutishia Lovely

The Hallelujah Love Series
Sex in the Sanctuary
Love Like Hallelujah
A Preacher's Passion
Heaven Right Here
Reverend Feelgood
Heaven Forbid
Divine Intervention
The Eleventh Commandment

The Business Series
All Up in My Business
Mind Your Own Business
Taking Care of Business

The Shady Sisters Trilogy
The Perfect Affair
The Perfect Deception
The Perfect Revenge

Published by Kensington Publishing Corp.

LUTISHIA LOVELY

The Perfect Affair

KENSINGTON PUBLISHING CORP.
www.kensingtonbooks.com

DAFINA BOOKS are published by

Kensington Publishing Corp.
119 West 40th Street
New York, NY 10018

Copyright © 2014 by Lutishia Lovely

All Kensington titles, imprints, and distributed lines are available at special quantity discounts for bulk purchases for sales promotion, premiums, fund-raising, and educational or institutional use.

Special book excerpts or customized printings can also be created to fit specific needs. For details, write or phone the office of the Kensington Special Sales Manager: Kensington Publishing Corp., 119 West 40th Street, New York, NY 10018. Attn. Special Sales Department. Phone: 1-800-221-2647.

Dafina and the Dafina logo Reg. U.S. Pat. & TM Off.

ISBN-13: 978-0-7582-8665-9
ISBN-10: 0-7582-8665-1
First Kensington Trade Paperback Printing: June 2014

eISBN-13: 978-0-7582-8667-3
eISBN-10: 0-7582-8667-8
First Kensington Electronic Edition: June 2014

10 9 8 7 6 5 4 3 2

Printed in the United States of America

With loving gratitude, I dedicate this book to YOU.

Acknowledgments

I am grateful, thrilled and rather amazed to be penning the acknowledgments for the first novel of yet another exciting series, The Shady Sisters Trilogy. I can hardly believe it! When I started this journey less than ten short years ago I had three books in mind. Between me and my alter-ego BFF, Zuri, this is book number twenty-five! Time flies when we're having fun, right? Well, I'm having a blast and while Spirit has blessed me with the gift to write, I didn't reach this milestone alone. I've had help, lots of it, from more people than I can adequately name or this book can contain. There are a few, however, who I must recognize and give a special thank you for their huge participation in my literary journey to this point and beyond.

Selena James, my editor, angel, and dear friend. Thank you so much for allowing my voice to reach the masses, for entertaining my crazy story ideas and for being my partner in "rhyme" for most of the ride!

Natasha Kern, my agent, angel, and spiritual sister. Thanks for allowing this woo-woo chick the space to be herself, the room to share my wild and lofty dreams and the support and belief in knowing that they can all come true!

Kensington Publishing, my literary home. I am blessed to be a part of such a wonderful family. From the bottom of my heart and to all on Team Lutishia (sales and marketing, publicity, and amazing editorial) . . . thank you.

Kristine Mills-Noble, for the absolutely perfect cover. Girl . . . you did that!

Future movie makers, thank you for seeing the vision and helping to put these printed pages on the big screen!

To my literary sisters and brothers, you know who you are and you know what you do . . . lift me up on wings of encouragement, support, and mutual respect. To have gained such valuable friends in this business is an unexpected yet treasured blessing. I heart you all.

To my family, who have supported me from the time I kept company with imaginary friends as a child, until now. I love you more than there are stars in the sky!

Last but not least, Lovely readers. There are no words for how much you are loved and appreciated. Some of you have been with me from the beginning. Some just came on board with my last book. Others stumbled across me in the library. Still more were given a Lovely novel as part of a book club read. However it happened, I'm happy we've met, and delighted that after that first book you decided to continue with me on this incredible journey. Every reader who's ever turned my page and spread the buzz by word of mouth, every book club who's discussed a unique character or plot twist, every blogger or sponsor who's mentioned my name in your post, everyone who's had anything at all to do with my reaching book number twenty-five, I appreciate you more than that word means, and hope that all of you stay with me through, let's see, twenty-five hundred more!

This one . . . is for you.

CHAPTER 1

"Let's toast to Jacqueline!"

A group of five fashionably dressed and vivacious women, seated in a trendy Toronto eatery, lifted their champagne flutes in the air. The atmosphere was festive. Even the April showers had paused, allowing bright, warm sunshine to surround them.

"To you, Jacqueline Tate," Rosie, the speaker, continued. "A woman who has finally gotten what all of us want."

"A good man?" The plus-size cutie with dimples and curves kept a straight face as she asked this. The others laughed.

"No, Kaitlyn, money. The next best thing."

"Or the best thing," Jacqueline countered, "depending on how you look at it."

"We wish you tons of success on this new venture. Go get 'em, girl!"

"Cheers!"

The ladies clinked their glasses and took healthy sips of pricey bubbly before questions rang out.

"What, exactly, will you be doing?"

"Is this full-time or freelance?"

"How did you get this job?"

Jacqueline laughed as she raised her hands in mock surren-

der. "All right, already! I'll tell you everything." She took another sip of her drink, eyes shining with excitement. "First of
all, it's a freelance writing contract—but," she continued when
the other writer in the group moaned, "it's for three months
and . . . it's with *Science Today!*"

"What's that?" Kaitlyn asked, looking totally unimpressed.

"It's the magazine for scientists like *Vogue* is for models,"
Jacqueline replied.

Kaitlyn cocked a brow. "Really? That big, huh?"

"It's a huge deal," Molly, the other writer, commented.
"Doing articles for such a prestigious journal will look great
on the résumé."

"Wow, that's wonderful!" Rosie said. "Will you work from
an office or from home?"

Jacqueline sat straighter, barely containing her excitement.
"That's the best part, guys. I'll be spending most of this assignment in America, traveling to events and interviewing the
movers and shakers in the science world."

Kaitlyn reached for the champagne bottle. "Somehow
'mover,' 'shaker,' and 'scientist' sound weird in the same sentence."

"That's because your world revolves around Hollywood,"
Jacqueline countered. "And you consider tabloids real reading
and their content true fact."

"It isn't?"

This elicited more laughter from the group, and more
questions. Finally, the successful-but-shy one in the group,
Nicole, spoke up. "I'm really happy for you, Jacqueline. After
what you've gone through, you deserve to have some good
stuff come your way."

It was true. Last year had been a doozy. On top of losing a
high-paying job due to downsizing, she'd found out that the
love of her life was someone else's love too. Walked in on them
in her house, in her bed. Guess he'd not counted on the fact
that the interview she'd been called out to do might wrap up

early. It did, and so did the relationship. They'd been dating for months. Jacqueline had even confided to her friends that he might be "the one." The one to break her heart, maybe, but not the one for lifetime love.

Rosie sensed Jacqueline's sadness, and placed a hand on her arm. "At least he's out of your life."

"I wish."

Kaitlyn cringed. "He's not?"

"Occasionally we'll cover the same event. You guys remember that he's a photographer, right?"

"I remember he's a jerk," Kaitlyn replied.

"And an asshole," Molly added.

Jacqueline laughed, and it was genuine. "Thank you, guys. You sure know how to make a girl feel good."

Kaitlyn peered at her friend of more than five years. She began shaking her head.

Jacqueline noticed. "What?"

"I don't get it. You're smart, funny, and the most beautiful woman I've ever seen in person."

"Oh, girl . . ."

"Seriously? If it weren't for you, I'd think those chicks posing on the magazine covers were make-believe."

"They are," Molly said. "It's called Photoshop."

"My point," Kaitlyn continued, "is I can't understand why you're not married. I'm with my third husband and I look like a whale!"

Jacqueline frowned. "You do not. Stop exaggerating and putting yourself down like that."

"That analogy may have gone a bit overboard. But I don't look like you."

No one would argue that Jacqueline was a natural beauty. Tall, slender, with creamy tan skin, long, thick hair and perfectly balanced features, she was often thought to be a model when out on assignment, and once had even been mistaken for the pop star Rihanna.

"Maybe Kaitlyn's right," Rosie offered. "Maybe in addition to finding great stories, you might find love."

"Oh no. I'm not even going to think like that, and set myself up to be disappointed. I'm going to stay focused and disciplined, never forgetting the reasons for why I'm there. I'll be going to some great places—LA, Vegas, New York—so, sure, I plan to have fun. But guys? Not interested."

"You say that now." Kaitlyn was obviously not convinced.

"True. Anything can happen. So if I do see a hottie and want a good time, I'll view it as just that, a good time, nothing more. For me, when it comes to men and relationships, using words like 'love' and 'forever' only leads to a broken heart."

Rosie gazed at Jacqueline with compassionate eyes. "You've been through a lot and you're still smiling. You deserve to be happy and to find true love. I, for one, will be rooting for that happiness to come your way."

Kaitlyn reached for the champagne bottle and, noting it empty, flagged down the waiter to bring another one. Already outspoken and boisterous, the bubbly loosened her tongue even further and made her talk more loudly. "I'm with you, Jacqueline," she said, trying to further drain her already empty glass. "I say get wined, dined, and screwed out your mind, then tell the muthafuckas to kiss your ass. Don't even give them your phone number if they can't pass the shoe."

Every face showed confusion. "The shoe?" Jacqueline asked.

"That's right. The shoe. Y'all haven't heard of that? It's a test." Noting her very interested audience, including some from surrounding tables, Kaitlyn lowered her voice as if she was about to drop secrets from Camp David. "Okay, here's what you do. Have him take you out, buy you dinner, and then, after a night of partying, when he's trying to get in the panties, take off your stiletto, pour a drink in the shoe, and tell him to drink it. If he can't do that, then he's not a coochie connoisseur."

Ms. Shy, Nicole, was suddenly not shy at all. "A what?" When the waiter brought out the second bottle, hers was the first glass raised.

"Coochie con-no-sir. One who'll lick it, kiss it, nip it, and flick it before he fucks it."

Rosie's cheeks turned as red as her hair. "Oh my," she whispered with a hand to her mouth.

Molly pulled out her phone to take notes.

"Thanks anyway," Jacqueline responded. "But the last man I'd give my phone number is one who'd drink out of my shoe. That's just foul."

"Whatever." Kaitlyn's countenance was one of pure confidence. "I'm just sayin' . . ."

Jacqueline sat back and crossed her arms. "And you know this because?"

"Because when I met the man who drank out of my shoe? I married him!"

This comment sent the table into another vocal frenzy.

"You're lying."

"No, he didn't!"

"Sounds like a wild and crazy date!"

"Geez! I'll never look at good old Harry the same way again."

Jacqueline sat back and took it all in. These were her girls; some she'd known for years and others a few months. Their sisterhood and support were genuine. Only one of her besties was missing. Kris. Her ride-or-die BFF who'd been there forever. She couldn't wait to share this great piece of news with the main one who'd been beside her during both good times and bad.

"Okay, maybe asking him to sip from your heels is a bit extreme."

You think? Jacqueline's raised brow seemed to imply.

"But there are still good men out there. I finally found one, though it took me three tries."

"Evidently my radar on good men is in need of repair."

"My mother always told me that when you meet him, you'll know." Kaitlyn sat back, thoughtful. "I have to admit, it wasn't until Harry came along that I knew what she meant."

Intrigued, Jacqueline eyed her. "How was he different?"

"It was natural, easy," Kaitlyn said with a shrug. "He felt like an old shoe."

"Ha! What is it with you and shoes?" Rosie asked.

Kaitlyn laughed. "I don't know. Probably time for a new pair." Her voice became serious as she looked at Jacqueline. "I didn't have to try with Harry. I was just myself. He felt right, and good, from the beginning. That's how I knew it. Maybe that's how you'll know it too."

"Sounds easy, but again, with the bad luck I've been having, I'm just not sure."

"I understand your being cautious. Just don't shut totally down. Leave a little space in your heart open to love. A little light, so the right man can find it."

They toasted to that and once the entrées arrived, the conversation moved around to other things. Later, however, Kaitlyn's words still echoed. Jacqueline wanted to find love, really hoped that it would happen. But during this assignment and over the next three months, at least? She wouldn't go looking for it.

CHAPTER 2

Award-winning biologist Randall Atwater walked toward the baggage claim area of Los Angeles International Airport envisioning green palm trees, blue skies, and fluffy white clouds. Instead, looking out the windows, he saw rain. Lots of it. Pouring out steadily and heavily from a dark gray sky.

I thought they said it never rained in California. Randall was sure he'd heard those words in a song. April showers were common in Virginia, where he lived and unfortunately where he'd left his umbrella. *Sheesh.* Looking down at the expensive outfit he'd just purchased for the trip, he lamented, *So much for this brand-new, tailored designer suit.*

He retrieved his bag and, using the *USA Today* he'd been given on the airplane for cover, made a dash for the taxi stand across from the passenger pick-up area. So focused was he on trying to stay dry and not getting hit, he didn't recognize the long line until he'd arrived at his destination, where only two taxis waited.

First the rain and now no taxis? Randall had enthusiastically boarded the plane back home, excited about coming to one of his favorite cities to meet some of his most esteemed colleagues and to learn the latest discoveries and innovations in his chosen field. He was still happy to be here, but so far the visit hadn't gotten off to a terrific start.

"Hey, excuse me," he said to the young man standing in front of him, whose thumbs were flying all over his iPhone screen. "Do you know what's going on, and why there are no taxis?"

"Accident," the man answered without looking up. "Traffic is having a hard time getting through."

"How long have you been standing here?"

"About thirty minutes."

Randall looked at the twenty or so people in front of him and his scowl increased. He looked at his watch and the crease in his brow deepened. The conference didn't start until the next morning, but he'd made plans to meet a talented colleague and good friend for drinks at six. It was now four thirty. Getting from the airport to downtown, where the conference was being held, could sometimes take forty-five minutes. Waiting a half hour for a taxi wasn't going to work for him. He turned and looked around, thinking of possible alternatives. And that's when he saw her.

Jacqueline gripped her full-sized umbrella in one hand while pulling her carry-on with the other. Organized and prepared to the point of what some would consider obsessive, she'd known about the 70 percent chance of rain hovering over Los Angeles and the seasonably cooler weather and had dressed and packed accordingly. She placed one Bebe-pump-covered, French-manicured foot in front of the other, thankful that she'd tightened the belt on her Burberry raincoat and donned a matching hat. Jacqueline was more self-conscious than conceited, but she knew how to highlight her best assets, and right now the best parts of what she was working with—breasts, legs, classically pretty face—were on full display.

She strode to the taxi stand, coyly smiling at the unabashed appreciation on Randall's face.

"Hello," he said with emphasis as soon as she joined the line.

"Hello," she replied. "Perfect California weather we're having, wouldn't you say?"

Randall smiled back. "I'm glad to be seeing a little sunshine now." He looked at her umbrella and then down at her rainy-weather attire. "I see someone checked the Internet."

"I like to be prepared."

"I'll remember that the next time I travel." He stuck out his hand. "Randall Atwater."

"A pleasure to meet you. *Doctor* Atwater, correct?"

Randall's brow rose. "Forgive me if I've forgotten but . . . have we met?"

Jacqueline's laugh was melodic. "No," she said, holding out her hand. "Jacqueline Tate." Their hands touched and something happened: a magnetic electricity unlike anything she'd ever felt before. The way his eyes darkened as he continued to gaze at her, Jacqueline was sure he felt it too. And just as quickly as the absurd idea came to her head, she forced its exit and reclaimed her hand. "I'm a freelance writer with *Science Today*," she explained, working to forget the undeniable jolt she'd just experienced. "I'm well aware of your research and groundbreaking work."

"It's a pleasure to meet you. I take it you're also here for the conference?"

"Yes, I'll be conducting interviews and attending workshops. Along with your talk on progressive changes in the technology regarding stem-cell research, I'm looking forward to covering Dr. Darshana Chatterji and his rather unorthodox position on spiritual healing." She looked at her watch. "In fact, I was hoping to get to the hotel quickly—get organized for the pre-conference breakfast happening in the morning." Looking over his shoulder, she asked him, "Where are all the cabs?"

Randall relayed the information he'd been given. "I don't

want to wait for a taxi either, and was just thinking about try-ing to find a car service. If so, you're welcome to ride as well."

"Oh no, Dr. Atwater. I wouldn't want to be a bother." She also didn't want to be in quarters as close as a car, not with a magnet like him. In town less than an hour, and already she was battling with her vow to stay focused on business. If she rode with this doctor, she felt it was a battle she'd lose.

But he persisted. "Call me Randall."

"Thank you, Randall, but I couldn't impose."

"Nonsense. We're going to the same place, right? Are you staying at the conference site?"

"Yes. I'm at the Ritz."

"Then it's no trouble at all." Randall placed a hand on her elbow. "Come on, let's go inside. I believe I have a contact who can help us out quickly."

"If you insist." She relented, justifying it by deciding to use the opportunity to learn more about the scientist and gather information for an article.

"I do."

Ten minutes later, Randall and Jacqueline were dry and comfortable, riding in the back of a cushy town car and chat-ting as if they'd known each other far longer than fifteen min-utes. "The article on bone regeneration," he said, nodding with recognition. "That's where I've heard your name."

"I've written dozens of articles, but I must admit . . . that one definitely made my name more recognizable."

"Forgive me, but it also had some people thinking you were certifiable!"

"Ha! That's not nice."

"Well, when you tell the scientific community that it's pos-sible to regrow limbs and other body parts . . ."

"Hey, I did the research and stand behind that story."

"If you say so," Randall conceded with a shrug.

"I do, and at least a dozen of your noteworthy, award-winning cohorts agree with me."

"A dozen? You sure?"

"I am. Four were named in the article. But I can recall the names of all twelve."

"Right now? From memory?"

Jacqueline quickly recited the names of the scientists and doctors who'd backed the research.

"Impressive. You do like to be prepared." Randall leaned back so he could take a good look at her. "You're obviously as smart as you are beautiful. I like that."

The conversation flowed much more easily than LA's rush-hour traffic. Their journey took almost an hour. By the time they reached the Ritz, however, they were chatting like old friends.

"Thanks for the ride," Jacqueline said to Randall after the doorman had helped her out of the car. Reaching into her purse, she asked, "How much do I owe you?"

Randall dismissed her question with a wave of his hand. "Don't worry about it. We were both coming to the same place."

"Thanks again. I look forward to hearing more from you during this week."

"Perhaps you can join me for dinner."

His words stopped her cold. They weren't at all what she'd expected. Given the self-talk she'd continued throughout the ride, she hadn't expected anything. Not from someone like Dr. Randall Atwater. While not exactly star-struck, she was indeed impressed with not only what she'd read but what she'd seen. He was highly intelligent, totally engaging, and blessed the heck out of a tailored suit. *Which is exactly why you shouldn't dine with him. Totally professional, remember?*

How could she forget? Totally professional and absolutely determined is how she'd conduct herself this week, she'd vowed. But she remembered something else. What Kaitlyn had said about finding Mr. Right, how Kaitlyn had known the man she met at a friend's office party would become her husband. *He felt right, and good, from the beginning. That's how I knew it. And that's how you'll know it too.*

This man felt good, and right. Their conversation had been easy, had flowed like water. So after taking a deep breath and throwing caution to the wind, Jacqueline answered him. "I'd like that too."

CHAPTER 3

Randall reached his room, set down his luggage, and continued straight to the bathroom. Having bypassed the airport restaurant selections, he was more than ready for a tasty meal. But first he knew he needed to return e-mails, check phone calls, and freshen up. So he stripped and hit the shower, all the while thinking about the beautiful and fascinating woman with whom he'd just shared a car.

He stopped, suds dripping as he remembered her name: *Jacqueline Tate.*

Stepping out of the shower to the sound of a ringing phone, Randall hastily wrapped a towel around his lean hips and crossed over to the counter, where he'd left it. He smiled at the name on the ID, and answered after putting the call on speaker phone. "James! What's happening, brother? Are you here yet?"

"No."

"But you are in LA."

"You didn't get my message?"

"I saw that you'd called, but, no, I didn't listen. Figured you were checking on my whereabouts. Where are you?"

"In Phoenix."

"As in Arizona?" His friend's deep chuckle floated around the room. "What the heck are you doing there?"

"Air travel nightmare: mechanical failures, overbooking. Even with first class and my frequent-flyer upgrade status, a connecting flight originating out of Newark was the only way I'd get from Long Island to LA before midnight."

"You had to drive to New Jersey from Long Island to catch a flight? What time will you arrive?"

"Nine o'clock. With the early breakfast meeting that's scheduled . . . too late to meet for drinks."

"No worries, man, I've made other plans. We'll find time to catch up."

Before hanging up, the two men chatted a few more minutes and made plans to meet for breakfast. Randall hated that James was stuck at the airport but was glad he'd called. Given his impromptu dinner plans, all had worked for the best. He reached for his leather garment bag and, after hanging up its contents, chose a casual outfit, dressed, and sat at the desk in the tastefully appointed suite. His stomach growled its annoyance, but because of the three-hour difference between LA and the East Coast, Randall was determined to handle e-mail and telephone business before leaving the room. If nothing else, there were at least three very important calls that he needed to make. One was to his assistant back at his company, Progressive Scientific Innovations, or PSI. The second was to the administrator of the nonprofit organization he'd founded, the one that tutored grade- and high school students in science and math. The third was to someone who probably wouldn't go to sleep until she'd heard from him.

Her room looked like someone was studying for a college exam. Books and magazines were strewn across her bed. An iPad lay atop that mess while a laptop occupied the nightstand. The most recent newspapers from five major cities were stacked on the table that doubled as desk and eating area, and the television was turned to CNN. People who met Jacqueline considered her extremely knowledgeable and academically above average. Some had even labeled hers a photographic memory. It was true, she was no dummy. But few would believe how fiercely hard she worked to make intelligence look so easy. For the past two weeks she'd read all of the information she could find about the careers of the people she wanted to interview. She'd stayed up late and gotten up early. She'd made phone calls, sent e-mails, and now felt totally prepared to deliver informative articles.

So why did she feel so nervous? *Because of Randall Atwater, that's why.* "Don't do anything stupid," she mumbled, even as just thinking about sharing the car ride with him gave her heart a thrill. "If you play your cards right, this three-month contract can turn into full-time employment." She laughed as she imagined mother-hen Rosie's voice in her head. *Don't trade a short-term BMW for a long-term J.O.B."*

A short while later, after organizing her information for the following morning and putting her room back in a semblance of order, Jacqueline dressed to go downstairs. She studied herself in the mirror. Far from being conceited, she looked at her reflection with a hypercritical eye, making sure that every part of her being was perfect, from the long, silky hair, which most mistook for a weave, to her designer-clad, size-seven feet.

Turning this way and that, she noted the way the simply-designed Calvin Klein dress she'd chosen fit her body to a tee, as if it had been tailored, though it hadn't. The neckline exposed just the right amount of her 36Ds, and the dress clinched her twenty-four-inch waist and hugged her thirty-six-inch hips. Falling just an inch above her knee, the dress color was a perfect complement to her creamy caramel skin, and the strappy red-bottomed heels she wore highlighted her toned thighs and calves, evidence of the time she spent on the StairMaster. Her jewelry was simple: a cross dangling just above her cleavage on a thin gold chain, a slender tennis bracelet, and diamond stud earrings. With a nod to the fact that her attire passed muster, she turned and walked into the bathroom, sprayed on a subtle perfume, and gave a final fluff to her hair. After calling the elderly neighbor whom she treated like a grandmother, the woman who'd graciously agreed to babysit her Siamese cat, Jacqueline took a last look around the room, made sure she had her room card, and left.

Randall exited the elevator and entered the lobby. Even in a pair of simple, tailored black slacks, a white button-down shirt, and loafers, he looked exceptional. Even so, he wasn't vain. Far from it. His journey had been that of an ugly duckling turning into a prince. So even though his lanky teenage frame had finally filled out, his smooth chocolate skin became all the rage, and stylish black-rimmed glasses or contacts replaced his thick specs, and even though he was one of the most acclaimed and respected scientists in the country, if not the world, vestiges remained of that shy, awkward boy growing up in the inner city streets of Washington, D.C.

For this reason, he was aware of the appreciative glances, the blatant stares, the subtle nods offered by one female after another . . . but a part of him refused to believe their adoration was really for him.

Randall reached the WP24 lounge and took a seat. Within seconds a server approached with a menu. He ordered a pinot noir from the Drake vineyards of Temecula. The cute, petite redhead smiled. "Good choice," she said with a wink. "I'll be right back to take your order."

He was staring at the menu when he smelled it, a subtle floral odor with citrus accents that floated across the table and tickled his nose.

"Fancy meeting you here."

The unexpected whiff of goodness, and a sexy sounding voice, caused him to look up.

"Ah, yours must be the perfume I'm smelling."

Jacqueline smiled and held out a delicate wrist. "Could be."

Randall sniffed it. "Yes, it's you. Very nice." He stood to pull out her chair. "Allow me."

"Such a gentleman," she cooed as she sat down. "Thanks."

"My mama raised me well."

"She did, and it shows."

"Thank you."

"With all of the education and accolades and awards you've received, you still appear to be humble and down-to-earth. It's refreshing." She placed her chin in her cupped hand and gazed at him. "Tell me about that upbringing."

Randall chuckled slightly as his mind went back to obviously good memories. He leaned back and looked out the floor-to-ceiling windows at the tableau that was downtown LA. "Barbara, my mother, single-handedly raised three rough-and-tumble hardheads in a very challenging part of Washington, D.C."

"You grew up in the hood?" Jacqueline used air quotes to emphasize the last two words.

"I did, the Anacostia projects." He stopped the waiter. "Would you like something to drink while we wait for our table?"

She ordered. He continued. "So where was I? Oh yes, growing up in the hood."

"And coming out a world-class scientist, specifically, biologist, one of the best in his field. Kudos to Barbara."

"Indeed."

"How did she do it?"

"Lots of love and even more discipline."

"You required lots of discipline, did you?"

"Let's just say I saw my share of the famous black belt, and I'm not talking karate."

"Corporal punishment?" Jacqueline's brow raised in surprise.

"Oh yeah. There was no time-out in my neighborhood. Those mothers and fathers were strictly old-school."

"So your dad was around."

Randall shook his head. "He died when I was fourteen."

"How did you cope with such a terrible loss at such a young age?"

"Buried myself in books. I'd always loved reading; in fact, it was often my sanctuary in those turbulent times. My mentor, a science teacher named Mr. Brunner, saw my talent early on and encouraged me every chance he got. He'd pick me up from home, take me to science fairs and technology conferences. He was young himself, not more than thirty-five, and became a big brother, almost a surrogate dad."

The server approached their table. "Dr. Atwater, your table is ready." He motioned to their drinks. "Shall I take these there for you?"

Randall looked at Jacqueline. "Are you ready to eat, beautiful lady?"

"Yes, I'm starved."

His expression changed, eyes narrowing ever so slightly behind his black rims. Aside from that, his demeanor remained totally professional as he told her, "Let's assuage our appetites."

CHAPTER 4

Once they had settled into their dining room chairs and placed their orders, Jacqueline lifted her glass. "To a successful doctor and a successful conference."

Randall nodded. "Cheers."

Jacqueline sat back. "So, Doctor . . ."

"Please. Just Randall is fine, remember?"

"Randall . . ." She paused as his name rolled off her tongue. "How does it feel to be you?"

"What do you mean?"

"You're this acclaimed, award-winning, progressive soul who is the darling of the scientific community. Not to mention you just won the Albert Einstein World Award for Science, which follows on the heels of the John J. Carty award you received last year. I'd say for a man not yet forty, very well done."

Randall took a small sip of wine. "Believe it or not, when it comes to all of the awards and acclaim, I'm more amazed than anybody."

Jacqueline cocked her head. "Why's that?"

"It feels like being applauded for simply being who I am. I've always loved figuring out how things work. It started as a kid, tinkering with a broken computer, wondering how it worked. Then came Dr. Brunner and a trip to a science museum where the wonders of the human body were being highlighted. I was fascinated, totally enthralled with how all of this muscle and tissue and nerves and fibers worked together. So I mixed my love of fixing things that were operating improperly with my love for the human anatomy, and here I am."

"That's a rare passion for a boy growing up in the inner city."

"True."

They continued small talk but paused as the waiter delivered their appetizers. When he left, Randall nodded toward Jacqueline, and she took a bite.

"Yum," she said, closing her mouth and chewing with pleasure. Obviously her crisp lettuce cup filled with tempura shrimp, pickled ginger, and chili vinaigrette had hit her hunger spot. Her eyes zeroed in on Randall's lips as they wrapped around his food choice. "How are your baby bao buns?"

Randall nodded his approval as he finished the luscious combination of slow-braised pork belly with a honey-garlic glaze. He reached for his napkin, making sure that none of the dough remained in his tidy goatee. "Absolutely delicious."

"I'm glad you chose this restaurant."

"Me too."

After a few moments, Randall reached for the wine and sat back in his chair. "It seems you know quite a bit about me, Ms. Tate. But I know next to nothing about you."

"My story isn't near as glamorous as yours," she responded.

"I'd still like to hear it."

She took a sip of the lemon water that had been placed on the table shortly after they sat down. "For starters, I was born and raised in Toronto."

"A true Canadian, eh?"

Jacqueline laughed. "I guess you could say that."

"Is your degree in journalism or did you just stumble into this job?"

"I've always loved words, and writing. Grew up fancying myself as a best-selling author like Terry McMillan. But after several proposals and even more rejections, I decided to try another track into the literary world and began freelancing wherever I could find the work. I covered a few conferences for *Science Today* and they liked what I wrote. So they put me on contract."

"Does that mean you are no longer a freelancer?"

"I have the ability to write for other magazines, so in that sense, yes, I am. But regarding scientific and medical research, for the next three months, the right of first refusal goes to *Science Today*."

"How did you become interested in science?"

Jacqueline finished her lettuce cup and after wiping her mouth, placed her elbow on the table and her chin in her palm. "Under all this makeup and designer wear . . . I'm a geek."

"No way!"

"Oh yes. Straight-A student, even with all the moving around I did as a child. With a bit of ADD thrown in, I might add; nothing holds my interest for too long. Fortunately, for me, this boded well. I'd tackle a couple of subjects, English and geography, for instance, and then turn to another challenge, like science and math."

"Where did you graduate college?"

Jacqueline hesitated. "I didn't."

Randall didn't try to hide his surprise. "You're writing in-depth articles on science and medical technology for *Science Today* without a degree?"

"Talent, skill, and determination made up for any education I didn't possess."

Randall's eyes shone with admiration. "Impressive."

"Thank you."

Their entrées arrived and over scrumptious servings of "angry"—translated, "spicy"—Maine lobster with noodles and Alaskan halibut with rice, Randall and Jacqueline became better acquainted. They passed on dessert, left the restaurant, and headed to the bank of elevators.

Randall yawned.

"Tired?" Jacqueline asked him.

"I am. It's been a long day." He looked at his watch. "It's one o'clock in the time zone where my day started."

"That's too bad."

"How's that?" Randall asked with a curious look.

"Because I have a feeling your schedule will be crazy, and I'd love to finish the interview with you that began in the car." An elevator door opened. "Just fifteen minutes?"

Randall looked at his watch. "And not one minute more."

"Great! I'll go get my iPad and be right back."

"Let's go upstairs, if you don't mind. I have a suite. We can talk in the living room."

After a brief pause, Jacqueline responded, "Are you sure that's okay? It's a little loud in the lobby, but I can make it work."

"I've been going nonstop since five this morning and have had only three hours' sleep. If you want this interview, it will have to be in my room. Don't worry, I'm too exhausted to do anything but talk. You'll be safe."

Twenty minutes later Jacqueline returned to her room, tired but happy. She'd kept her promise of interviewing the doctor for only fifteen minutes, and he'd kept his promise about her being absolutely safe in his room.

She didn't know how she felt about that.

Yawning, she pulled out her notes for the next day's interviews. Try as she might to stay focused, her mind kept drifting. When she realized she'd been staring at the same page for the last five minutes, she stood, stretched, and walked over to the window. The large square panes offered a sweeping, unob-structed view of downtown Los Angeles, with lights that twin-kled and stretched for miles. Jacqueline leaned against the glass as a myriad of diverse thoughts fought for dominance in her head, thoughts of the wild roller-coaster ride that had been her life last year—the job that had fooled her, the man who had failed her. Her face turned hard as she remembered her last employer. The official reason for her termination had been downsizing. The truth was that she wouldn't sleep with her boss. If he'd been fine and packing, she might have entertained the idea. It probably hadn't helped matters when she informed him that she didn't do trolls.

And now here she was with someone like Dr. Randall At-water, someone who seemed like a good, kind, upstanding man. She remembered how his eyes lit up when he mentioned his children. She remembered how her heart soared when he didn't mention a wife. He wasn't wearing a ring either. Didn't mean he wasn't married. But she could hope.

"Doesn't matter to me one way or the other," she mum-bled as she crossed the room to the bathroom and began her bedtime preparations. "I've never blurred the lines between professional and personal and I'm not going to start now!"

She'd said it with conviction, even repeated it silently as she washed her face and brushed her teeth. By the time she lay down, she'd almost convinced herself that she really had ab-solutely no interest in a personal relationship with Dr. Randall Atwater. But just before sleep claimed her, the truth flitted through her mind. She was attracted, impressed, and quite taken with the man she'd met just hours ago. A man who was definitely not a troll.

Fire.
Lots of it.
All around her, and hot, scorching her skin as she tried to enter the hallway where she'd heard the voices. Two were not a

surprise to her but the third voice should not be coming from that room.

"Jackie . . . help!"

With an arm covering her nose and mouth, she crept forward. "Where are you!"

"In here," the little girl shrieked, her voice raspy, filled with smoke and terror.

"Walk towards me!"

"I'm scared!"

Jacqueline took tentative steps, following the sounds as speaking gave way to coughing.

"Can you see me? Reach out your hand!"

A small, outstretched arm burst through the smoke.

Jacqueline trudged forward, smoke and flames impeding her desire to rush toward the hand. "I see you!"

She was almost there.

So close she could almost touch her, could almost grab the hand that reached out in desperation.

She grabbed the hand, which grew larger as a contorted face came into view.

"Mom? No!"

She was instantly, harshly pulled into the flames, her mother's brash, maniacal laugh surrounding her.

Jacqueline awoke with a start, gasping for breath, covered in sweat.

The nightmare had returned.

CHAPTER 5

The ringing iPhone alarm woke Randall from a deep sleep. Six a.m. had come way too soon. He went one round with the snooze button, rolled out of bed and hit the shower, shifting the water temperature from hot to cold to help wake him up, and then donned a suit. After quickly checking his e-mails and making the required phone calls, he grabbed what he'd need for the morning activities and left the room.

Stepping off the elevator, he entered the quiet chaos of over one thousand medical- and science-minded professionals descending upon a space. Small groups of two to six individuals stood clustered in conversation, or sat sipping coffee and comparing career notes. Randall nodded this way and waved another, knowing many of the faces dotting the lobby on this sunny Tuesday morning. He spoke, but did not stop to chat. The welcome breakfast was about to begin and as one of the featured guests, he needed to be in the banquet hall at least fifteen minutes in advance.

He made it there with five minutes to spare and immediately spotted his best friend standing on the speaker platform.

"James!"

A nice-looking man, well dressed in a navy pin-striped

suit, stark white shirt, and a winning smile, turned around. "Well, if it isn't the brainy biologist." He stepped forward, hand outstretched. "How are you, Randall? Look like life's treating you well."

"Can't complain, doctor," he answered, returning the handshake. "Can't complain at all. How are you doing?"

"Good, man. Real good."

"The wife?"

"Debbie is one of the best decisions I've ever made. She's made me believe in love again."

"She must be handling her business! You sound like a whipped brother if I ever heard one."

"The sex is great, no doubt. But believe it or not, that isn't the best thing I love about her. It's her compassion, her generous nature, the way that she not only cares about me but takes care of me and the family. I wish I'd given these traits more consideration the first time around. Divorce is an ugly business. I want me and Debbie to last a lifetime."

Randall placed a hand on his friend's arm, touched by his words. "If you want it, then it will happen," he responded. "You know I'm pulling for you both, and wishing you the best."

Their conversation was interrupted as other panelists mounted the dais and the room quickly filled with conference attendees. James and Randall took their seats at the head table and soon were enveloped in tasty dishes, welcoming speeches, and an outline for the trends-and-technology-filled week ahead. Those on the panel were there to offer a brief description of their workshop and to contribute to the discussion of the conference theme: Old Science in a New World. He'd always been confident in front of a crowd, so when it was Randall's turn to speak, he stood, approached the podium, and delivered his prepared spiel flawlessly. The audience listened with rapt attention, and all of the women and several men noted that he looked as good as he spoke.

"Good morning, my fellow professionals. My name is Dr. Randall Atwater. As most of you know, I recently received an award for my research on the use of plant stem cells to heal human diseases." He waited while the spontaneous applause that broke out at this announcement died down. "I appreciate that," he said with a grin way too sexy for this time of morning and this type of crowd. "And I am honored. However, I mention it only to let you know that I'm much more excited about how many medical problems can be appropriately addressed by the focus of said award, how many sick people can be healed, and how many lives can be changed than I am for any type of award or honor that can sit on a shelf or be hung in my office. My workshop will expound on what you've already read about this groundbreaking work, as well as get you up-to-date with the work I've done since receiving that acknowledgment.

"In my workshop, I'll be sharing all that I've recently discovered with you. But know that I also want you to come prepared to share with me. I and my partner in this research, James Sullivan, will be picking your brains and engaging you in lively and hopefully meaningful discussions about how we can continue on our path toward finding cures for debilitating brain diseases and all types of cancer. Come to learn, but just as importantly, come to share. I look forward to seeing and meeting all of you. Thank you."

Jacqueline sat at a table near the back of the room, fingers flying over iPad keys, recorder immortalizing the moment, mind racing with how to turn all she was hearing into articles that were educational, informative, and concise. She really did love hearing all of this cutting-edge information and got excited that she was a part of disseminating it to the masses. Her concentration on precisely gathering said information kept her focus away from the man she'd become aware of as soon as he'd entered the room—Randall, whose body once again blessed a navy suit, and all of those who watched him wearing it.

"Jacqueline?" One of her tablemates, a serious-minded college student covering the event for his college paper, looked at her with an adoring smile. Jacqueline returned it with a patient one of her own. He was cute but had zero chances, even though he'd been flirting since she'd arrived. "Are you planning to attend Dr. Atwater's workshop?"

"Absolutely. What about you?"

"I hope so, but I'll have to try to get one of the general spaces reserved for attendees. I couldn't get a media pass."

"Good luck. They're very limited. His and Dr. Sullivan's workshop is being touted as the top draw for what normally doesn't attract this much mainstream attention."

"Yes, unfortunately, that's what I found out."

"Here's my card, which includes my cell number. There's going to be a great deal of information disseminated this week. Let's keep in touch. Perhaps we can trade notes on what the other might have missed."

Jacqueline and Evan engaged the other attendees at their table as they listened to the remaining speakers' introductory presentations. By the end of the breakfast it was clear to Jacqueline that her early hunch had been correct: Getting an exclusive interview with Randall Atwater had been a major coup, one that might not only ensure her continued presence at *Science Today*, but also one that could open doors to any number of opportunities. After this week, she realized, she'd have to step back, regroup, and decide which direction she wanted life to take her in.

Where she wanted to go right now was not in question. The introductory breakfast over, she made a beeline for her intended target and was not at all daunted that he was surrounded by a crowd of reporters, scientists, and adoring fans.

She pushed her way through, looking as stern and professional as her black conservative pant suit—well, except for the girls, a bit discreetly yet deliciously spilling out of the sleeveless floral blouse that she'd paired with precision. "Excuse me, Dr.

Atwater!" She watched as Randall looked in her direction, gave her a nod, but continued to chat with the reporter standing before him while a cameraman filmed it all. Inching forward, she was able to snag Randall's partner, James, just as he finished with a TV reporter.

"Dr. Sullivan," she began, her tone serious and ultraprofessional. Even so, she didn't miss the appreciative once-over James gave her, or the way he bypassed other reporters to step to her mike. "Jacqueline Tate with *Science Today*. Can you tell me how your contribution to this week's workshop will differ from Dr. Atwater's?"

"Ms. Tate, our involvement in this project is like two halves of the same coin. My background as a medical doctor provides a hands-on analysis of the problem. Dr. Atwater's expertise in the scientific field provides a hands-on approach to the solution. That he too has a medical background puts him in a position to accurately assess the problem and understand both my concerns and my confidence in what we are trying to do to treat illness in general and brain diseases in particular . . . find a cure."

Just as she finished with James, Randall passed by her. "Excuse me, Dr. Atwater."

"Sorry, Jacqueline," he said forcibly but not unkindly. "Not now."

"Of course," she mumbled, her eyes holding admiration and more as she watched a host of hangers-on and wannabes scramble behind Randall as he left the room. She calmly looked around for some lesser known yet equally interesting attendees to interview. She didn't have to run behind Randall Atwater to get what she wanted. She'd held a one-on-one, in-depth interview with him in the comfort of his suite. With that, the notes from his talk, and research on the Internet, she already had enough for a great cover story. Keeping a distance the rest of the week was probably best.

The better choice, perhaps. But not meant to be.

As soon as the workshop was over, he approached her. "Jacqueline?"

"Yes?"

"Forgive me for having to rush off earlier. I didn't mean to be rude."

"It's okay, Randall. I know you're busy."

"I was preoccupied, but that's not an excuse. I insist you let me make it up to you."

"No way, Randall. You've already done so much. I won't let you buy me dinner again."

"Fair enough, but would you care to join me for tonight's concert?"

In all of her studying last night, she'd merely glanced at the attendee packet and its contents. She'd seen something about a concert, and she loved opera. But since tickets were only discounted, not free, and she didn't have an escort, she hadn't given the outing a second thought.

"I don't have anything to wear," was the lame excuse that came to mind.

"Don't worry about that." He gave her the once-over. "The concert starts at eight. Meet me in the lobby at seven thirty. Okay?"

"Sure."

"All right, beautiful. See you then."

CHAPTER 6

For the rest of the afternoon, Jacqueline walked on air. At five o'clock she returned to her room, ordered room service, and transcribed some of the tapes she'd recorded. At six o'clock someone knocked on her door.

Randall?

She peered through the peephole to see a hotel employee standing next to a bellman's cart. On it were a couple garment bags and several boxes. She opened the door.

"I didn't send anything to be cleaned. You have the wrong room."

"Ms. Tate?"

"Yes?" Jacqueline replied with a scowl.

"These are for you, compliments of Dr. Atwater."

Jacqueline was speechless. She stepped back so that the employee could pull the cart into the room. "Here, let me get you a tip."

"Already taken care of, ma'am," the employee said with a slight bow. "Enjoy your evening."

Jacqueline watched the employee leave, then turned toward the cart before her. She gingerly touched the plastic covering, almost afraid to lift it and see what was inside. Below were shoe boxes. She reached for one, opened it up, and saw one of the prettiest pairs of shoes she'd ever seen. The sandals were covered in iridescent crystals, with straps that came up around the ankle. Always a sucker for a great high heel, she walked to a chair, kicked off her house shoes and slid on the sandal.

Perfect fit. *How did he know?*

Curiosity effectively piqued, she walked back over to the rack and lifted the first bag. A gasp escaped her mouth before she could stop it. Before her was a stunning gown in burgundy satin, a strapless creation made to fit like a glove. The second bag held a gown made of emerald-colored raw silk. The halter neck and trim waistline gave way to a ruffled skirt with an uneven hem that created a modest train. Jacqueline held her breath as she unzipped the final bag. She pressed her hands to her cheeks in wonder. She reached out, her hand brushing against the stark white fabric that had been sprinkled with Swarovski crystals in a haphazard way. Another body hugger, the dress's straps were made of crystal and the neckline was designed in such a way as to accent one's cleavage. Blinking back tears as she took away the bag and removed the dress from the hanger, Jacqueline had no doubt which dress she would wear. If only it fit.

It did. Perfectly. As if measurements had been taken and patterns drawn. Without even pulling the sandals back out, she knew they would pair just right with the white dress, and after checking the remaining five boxes she realized she was right. She was overwhelmed with Randall's kindness. He had changed her world in a matter of minutes, and her head spun.

"What does all this mean?" she asked the empty room.

That he likes you of course. Duh.

"I want to believe it. But I'm so afraid of getting my heart broken again."

She looked at the clock, and with only forty-five minutes

until the time she was supposed to meet Randall in the lobby, she headed for the shower.

"Today wasn't bad. I'm not as tired as I thought I'd be."

Randall sat in the lobby listening to his friend James spout on about the day's activities. "I love what I do," James finished. "But sometimes I agree with Debbie. I need to slow the pace."

"I hear you, man. When I established the Atwater Achievement Module five years ago, I planned on being totally hands-on. But for the past several months, I've basically had to leave it in the hands of the mentors."

"How is your tutor program going?"

"Excellent, really. Right now we have twenty-five students from surrounding universities who are helping with science and math. Because of its integral part in our modern world, we're getting ready to add computer technology as well. When I last attended the monthly roundup three months ago, I was overjoyed. The kids are smart, excited, and determined to succeed. That's all I can hope for."

James watched as Randall's face took on a somber appearance. "Still feeling guilty, huh?"

"I know I shouldn't but yes, I do."

"You tried to save him, man; did more for him than the father he never knew. You tried to keep him out of the streets. At the end of the day, it was his choice and his alone that brought about deadly consequences."

Both were quiet a moment, remembering the horror five years ago when Randall learned that his nephew had been gunned down. "If anything," Randall said, finally breaking the silence, "Joshua's death reminded me of the lifestyle I barely escaped, one all too familiar among African-American males. That man wasn't a news story or a statistic in the newspaper that I read. He was alive and breathing. He was my nephew; someone I knew, someone I loved. If I can save just one kid from meeting the same fate as he did . . ."

"I'm sure you already have," James softly replied. "You're doing good things, bro. Makes me want to step up my game as well."

"You're being a good stepfather to Debbie's son. We all do what we can where we are."

"Damn!"

Randall's eyes traveled to where James was now staring.

"Is that the same woman who interviewed me this afternoon?"

"Yes, that's Jacqueline Tate."

James looked at him. "I thought she was attractive then but . . ." The sentence died as he stared at her.

"Now you think she's stunning."

"Exactly."

"I think you're right."

"Wonder where she's going?"

"You haven't checked your packet? The opera is tonight."

Both men watched—as did everyone in the lobby—as Jacqueline came toward them.

"Good evening, gentlemen," she said as Randall and James stood to acknowledge her presence.

"Good evening, Jacqueline," James said, reaching out for a handshake and smiling broadly when it was accepted.

"You look incredible," Randall said, his hand stuck out as well.

And when she pushed it away and went in for a heartfelt hug that melded her body to his . . . he didn't complain.

CHAPTER 7

Jacqueline sat next to Randall, admiring the beauty of the Walt Disney Concert Hall. "This place is amazing," she whispered, reverently looking around the brilliantly constructed room. "Beautiful is too small a word to describe it."

"It pales in comparison to you."

Randall squeezed her hand, and Jacqueline felt butterflies. He looked so handsome in his black tuxedo with stark white shirt. All eyes had been on them as they'd walked from the lobby into the auditorium, the crystals on her white dress catching the light and bathing them in a subtle glow. From the moment the dresses had arrived at her room, she'd felt like Cinderella on her way to the ball. Now here she sat, with her prince, listening to the LA Philharmonic and LA Opera perform Mozart's *Così fan tutte*. From the time she'd slipped on the dress to find that it fit perfectly, she'd stopped trying to talk herself out of her growing feelings for Randall. She knew it was foolish, something once started would probably not last, but she couldn't help it. He was wonderful, thoughtful, perfect. He paid attention to detail. How else could he have known her dress and shoe sizes? He was intelligent and engaging but still down-to-earth and humble. And the most amazing part?

He was obviously interested in her! Why else would he invite her to share this evening, when any number of colleagues, especially the female ones, would have been more than delighted to be his guest?

Is it my imagination or did Randall just brush his leg against mine? So far, aside from adoring looks and desire-filled eyes, he'd been the perfect gentleman. Now that Jacqueline was allowing truthful thought to reign, she'd admit that images of Randall not being so gentlemanly had flitted through her mind. Thoughts of how it would feel to be hugged, kissed, loved by this man. Thoughts of how his body, hard and naked, would feel against hers. Thoughts of how much she wanted to find out the answers to the questions now plagued her, along with a desire so strong it ached.

Yes, he'd definitely moved his leg. She pressed hers back against it. He looked over, his eyes questioning, searching. She hoped the desire in her eyes matched what she now saw. They both looked to the stage, but the air around them had shifted. It had become intense, expectant. What would come next? After the orchestra performed their encore, would Randall and Jacqueline perform one of their own?

After two hours of exceptional music, the performance ended. The patrons filed out to town cars, luxury vehicles, and limousines. Jacqueline got into the stretch limousine that awaited their arrival and scooted over so that Randall could enter as well. No sooner had he got in the car than he turned to her.

"Jacqueline . . ." His eyes were fastened on her lips.

"Yes . . ." Her lips were parted slightly, wet from a nervous lick. Her eyes were bright yet hooded, anticipating what was to come.

"I'm very attracted to you," he said.

"Me too."

He ran a tentative finger over her lips. "You're so beautiful."

Jacqueline said nothing, just kept peering into his eyes.

"I want to kiss you."

"Then do. Please." She closed her eyes, waited for the moment, felt his breath against her chin as he lowered his head. Their lips touched and a familiar jolt—strong, electric—pierced her body. His kiss was soft at first, but quickly deepened and became more intense. She opened her mouth. His tongue slid home, as if it had been there before, as if her mouth was the only place it should be. She turned to him, her breasts crushed against his hard chest. One of his arms wrapped around her neck, the other ran lazily up her arm, leaving a trail of goose bumps in its wake. Their breath mingled along with their desire, their passion grew with each second that passed. Time stood still, and they had no awareness of the car carrying them through the streets of downtown LA. All Jacqueline was aware of was this moment, this man, the feel of his essence around her. In this instant she believed that she'd very much enjoy feeling it for the rest of her life.

"Um, excuse me," the driver said, after clearing his throat. "We're here."

As they stood in front of Jacqueline's hotel room door, holding hands, looking into each other's eyes, Randall brushed an errant strand of hair behind her ear. "Thank you for a wonderful evening."

"It's me who should be thanking you." Jacqueline's eyes fell from his eyes to his lips. "This has been one of the most amazing evenings of my life."

"Yes, the opera was exceptional."

"Indeed. But I wasn't talking about the performance."

Silence fell, and Jacqueline could hear her own heartbeat. She knew she shouldn't. Good girls never gave it up on the first night. But she was grown, the time between lovers had been too long, and the desire for this man was overwhelmingly strong. If he asked, pronouncing the word "no" would probably be too hard.

"Tomorrow's another early morning," Randall said into a

silence where their mutual desire was palpable. "I should probably say good night."

"That's probably a good idea."

Perhaps it was. But neither moved.

Randall leaned forward and pressed a tender kiss against Jacqueline's temple. "Good night, my princess."

Jacqueline was so full of emotion she could barely breathe. Was she dreaming? She had to be. Wonderful moments like these didn't happen to her. But then she felt his lips press ever so gently against her lips.

"Sleep well," he whispered against them. "May I have your card?"

It took a couple of seconds for Jacqueline to understand his question. Her head was in a yearning-induced fog. "Oh, card. Right." She fumbled in her small clutch and pulled out the hotel key.

He pulled it from her grasp and opened the door. "There you are. Safely delivered back to your room." He leaned forward for one last kiss. "Thanks again, Jacqueline." He held out the card. "Good night."

Jacqueline looked at the card, and then at him. "Keep it," she said in a brazen move. "It just might come in handy."

Within minutes she was in her room, out of the dress, and talking with her best friend, Kris.

"I can't believe the night I just had," she said dreamily. "I'll spill all the juicy details later, but I just came back from a date with an award-winning scientist, the same man with whom I had dinner last night."

"Tell me more."

"His name is Randall Atwater—intelligent, handsome and a perfect gentleman—everything I could wish for in a man. But this is an important assignment. I don't have time to get sidetracked, Kris," she finished. "Please say that you agree."

"Agree that you shouldn't enjoy yourself? No can do."

"That I don't have time to be falling in love!"

"Jack, you just met the man."

Hearing her nickname, one used solely by this best friend, Jacqueline calmed down. A little. "I've been telling myself the same thing all day, have given myself every sound reason in the book to keep this professional. But there's something between us, Kris. Randall feels it too. At first I thought it was just my imagination, but after tonight? I can no longer deny it. This magic I'm feeling is real."

A pause and then Kris asked her, "You do know magic is *not* real, right? They don't really saw the girl in two. And the rabbit was in the hat all along."

Jacqueline sighed.

"I'm not trying to burst your bubble. Well, I am, but only if it's as tenuous as one that's made from the soapy solution for kids. You're my best friend, Jacqueline. I want your happiness as much as you want it. But I'm the one who's nursed you through your last few heartbreaks, been there to dry the tears and help pick up the pieces. That last fool devastated you, had you feeling you were losing your mind. You had me worried too. That's why I'm trying to be your voice of reason, and coming down on the side of caution. If he's the one, he'll still be the one a week from now. Just take your time, okay?"

Jacqueline ended their conversation without making any promises. Though it was late and she'd gotten up early, she still tossed and turned in search of sleep. She fluffed her pillow, flopped on her back, and stared at the ceiling. Kris's opinion mattered. Everything her bestie said made sense. Still, she'd given Randall her hotel key. If he decided to use it, Jacqueline knew she would not turn him away.

He was big, a monster; smelling of beer and disappointment. His pot belly, the texture of raw chicken skin covered in sweat, jiggled when he walked. Like now, as he came toward her, a mere shadow in a room lit by a single streetlight at the end of the block.

She cowered on the bed, against the wall, a thin sheet covering knees pulled up to a quivering chin.

Two words pushed through her fear and revulsion. "Please. No."

Her protector lay just down the hall, cradling gin and tucked under a blanket of feigned ignorance. Lying on a pillow of complicity and shame.

The monster towered over her, so close now that she felt his labored breathing.

A nightmare, this time with eyes wide open, happening again.

CHAPTER 8

The next night, Jacqueline passed on Evan's invitation to join him and a couple other writers for drinks. Instead, she went back to her hotel room. She told herself it was to go over the notes for the next day's interviews. But that wasn't the only reason. She was hoping for something else. She pulled out her iPad and looked over the information for the next day's speakers. But her mind kept returning to Randall and the look on his face when she'd told him to keep the key. Just the thought of how his eyes had narrowed before dropping to her cleavage made her wet with longing.

I'll never be able to concentrate without some relief. She headed for the bathroom.

Moments later, Jacqueline eased into the hotel room's soaking tub, filled to the rim with hot, bubbly water. The mixed fragrance of lilies and musk enveloped her as richly as the water, teasing the tendrils of hair that had escaped her hastily created bun. Leaning against the bath pillow, she opened her legs, allowing the water to soak her clit before she ran a tentative finger between her feminine folds, down and back again.

Ah!

Repositioning her head against the bath pillow, she reached for the loofah and washed her body in a slow, leisurely fashion. All the while she thought of Randall, and wondered if he would take her up on her offer and use the key. *He's probably downstairs with his friend James. Or maybe another woman?* Jacqueline shook the thought out of her head. The last thing she needed to be was possessive. She had no claims on the handsome scientist and set her heart to the fact that even if they connected, it would more than likely be a short-term fling. That thought wasn't too appealing, but she'd have to cross that good-bye bridge when she came to it.

Letting the loofah fall into the water, Jacqueline reached down, cupped her breasts, and held them above the suds. *I wonder if he'll be surprised to learn that these are real?* She ran her finger around the areola and, feeling a squiggle travel from there to her heat, ran her hand across her flat stomach, down between her legs, and back. Picking up the sponge once more, she ran it lightly over her nipples until they stood at rapt attention. She grazed the firm nubs with the tips of her French-manicured nails. Her nether muscles clenched as the sensation of tweaking her own nipples once again ran through her body. Her hand moved beneath the water, and again, a finger eased between her lower lips. She touched her nub as lightly as she had her nipples, closed her eyes, and imagined it was Randall's hand between her legs, and his finger making her harden with each delicate stroke. She'd had a full bikini wax just days before leaving home, along with a spa treatment that consisted of a sugar scrub followed by a shea butter body soufflé. The result? Skin that was smoother than a baby's bottom and blemish-free.

She lifted one long, toned leg out of the water, and then the other. *I wonder how it would be to wrap these around your waist, Randall. How would it feel to hold on tight while you screw my brains out with what I'm sure is a big, thick appendage!*

She closed her eyes. And heard a click. Her eyes flew open.

She sat up, heart pounding as fiercely as a drum being played in a marching band. *Could that be him? Is he here?* She listened intently but heard nothing else. *You want him so badly you're imagining him here. Chill out, girl. The minute you stop getting your hopes up is the minute they stop getting dashed.* She slid down farther into the tub, resting her head on the bath pillow and closing her eyes.

"Jacqueline."

Clearly, the noise hadn't been her imagination. He had come to her! She remained still, with her eyes closed, wanting to savor the moment just in case she opened them to find that this was all a dream.

She heard him kneel, felt him staring at her body. Slowly, ever so slowly, she opened her eyes. "You came."

A wisp of a smile ran across his face at the double entendre. "You thought I wouldn't? If you've changed your mind, just say the word and I'll—"

"I haven't changed my mind." The words came out in a breathless rush. Jacqueline closed her eyes, hoping against hope that she hadn't just come off sounding like a desperate fool.

"Look at me." She opened her eyes. "You are a vision of loveliness, my dear."

He reached for the sponge, dipped it in the soapy water, then held it up and squeezed. Rivulets of water cascaded down her body and bounced off her nipples. He ran the loofah over her breasts and across her stomach before lifting one of her legs out of the water and running the sponge from her calf to her inner thigh.

She lay back and watched him, smelling the musky cologne that for the past two days—from the car ride to the concert—had driven her wild. Her smile was slight, her breath catching in her throat as she watched his eyes devour her body. She knew that tendrils of hair had escaped her upswept ponytail and now lay wet and clingy on her long, exposed neck. Her eyes remained fixed on his as he replaced the sponge with his hands and traced lazy circles across her stomach, her nipples hard and glistening as they protruded out of the water.

"Simply beautiful."

His voice was low and husky with desire. Without looking, she knew he was already hard for her, ready for her, wanting her. *Ditto.*

Finally she turned her head toward him and whispered, "I'm glad you're here."

"I hoped you would be."

His touch was tentative. He took a strand of wet hair away from her face and gently placed it behind her ear, then ran his forefinger down her cheek and neck and across her weighty breasts. He cupped one of them in his hand and gave it a squeeze.

"They're real."

This comment brought out an amused smile. "Surprised?"

"I am. These days most generous cleavage is courtesy of a surgeon's deft hand. Very rare to find a woman who's been so . . . naturally blessed."

"Do you like them? Big breasts?"

"I love yours." This as he used his finger to tease her already erect nipple. First one, and then the other. "You're even lovelier than I imagined."

"Oh, so you have been thinking about me."

"I've thought of little else from the moment you joined me at the taxi stand."

"Then I'm glad I went outside of my comfort zone and gave my spare room card to you."

"Me too."

She watched him as he stood, a nice-sized bulge clearly evident at the front of his slacks.

"That water must be getting cool. Let's get you dried off."

Jacqueline pulled the stopper and stood—looking much

like a water nymph or goddess—as water and bubbles slid down her silky, hairless skin. She stepped out of the soaking tub and into the fluffy white towel that Randall held for her. In other words, she stepped into his waiting arms.

For a moment he simply held her, his nose against her neck, breathing in her freshly bathed scent. He nuzzled her neck. She wrapped her arms around his, marveling at how well they fit together. Her five foot eight was a perfect complement to his height of six feet; a simple tilt and her mouth would be aligned with his.

One small tilt and she could claim the succulent lips she'd eyed each time they'd met She eased back her head. He raised his. Their eyes met, both pairs dark with desire, glistening with the excitement that comes with illicit, daring adventures, with spontaneous delights. She lowered her eyes to his mouth and slowly leaned forward. Their lips touched. She shivered, giddy with the knowledge of what was happening: Randall, live and in beautifully living color, here, with her, in her room. Just like she'd envisioned.

She pressed her soft, slightly thick lips against his much fuller ones, loving the way his neatly clipped mustache tickled her upper lip. He smelled so good. He felt amazing, his body toned but not overly muscular, his close-cropped, curly hair soft to the touch. When she ran her tongue against the crease of his mouth it immediately opened. His tongue met hers— softly searching, expertly exploring—even as he pressed the towel against her body, drying her off and making her wet at the same time.

The kiss deepened. She pressed her body against his, moving her head along with her tongue, an oral exchange that was sensuous and promising. His hands left the towel and became entwined in her hair. Still kissing her, he reached for the clip that held up her silky locks. He made quick work of freeing her hair from its bondage and tossed the clip aside. She stepped back, allowing one of the barriers to their being skin-to-skin to fall away.

They both watched the towel slide to the floor. Randall quickly wrapped his arms around her and drew her close. The kiss was different this time: intense, scorching hot, ravaging. His hands ran up and down her body, cupping her butt cheeks and pushing her against his rock-hard erection. Her hands were busy too, spanning the width of his shoulders, running down his waist to his hips and back. She pressed herself against him, her breasts flush against his chest as their tongues dueled and danced together. Randall eased a hand between them and— much as she'd imagined mere moments before—slid a finger between her sticky wet lips.

She gasped, her hot breath escaping into his mouth before her head fell back. She placed her hand over his, willing him to go harder, deeper. It was only one finger, but it had unleashed a madness to have all of this man. Shaky hands reached for his belt buckle, impatient to free the beast that she'd felt against her pelvis. It wasn't happening fast enough. The buckle, the belt loops, the lack of experience at undressing a man in a hurry. *Damn you, belt buckle. Come loose!*

"Whoa, baby," Randall drawled after ending the kiss. "No need to rush. We've got all night. Here, let me help you with this. In fact, this bathroom is beautiful, but I think the bed will serve a much better purpose for what I have in mind."

They left the bathroom with Randall unbuttoning this and removing that as they went. By the time they reached the bed, he was down to tee and boxers, having removed his shoes as soon as he'd arrived. Jacqueline eased onto the bed, naked and available, poised on one elbow with her head resting against her hand. She watched as he removed his T-shirt. Their eyes locked as he slid the Calvin Klein extra-large from around his hips.

"Are you ready for this?" he asked, looking at his dick standing at attention.

She didn't speak; only nodded. What she saw made her pussy clench and her mouth water. For two days she'd wondered how it would be to fuck the successful scientist. Now, she was getting ready to find out.

CHAPTER 9

It was Friday afternoon. The conference had ended. Randall and James sat at a table for ten in Kerry Simon's restaurant, LA Market. They were joined by esteemed doctor Darshana Chatterji—the Western-trained Indian MD who was boldly and somewhat controversially presenting modules on using Eastern spirituality to facilitate healing—along with six other world-renowned guests.

"Who's missing?" one of the colleagues asked when everyone had been seated and an empty chair remained.

"A person from the media will be joining us," Dr. Chatterji explained. "Wait," he continued, holding up his hands to ward off their protests. "She comes as my personal guest, not as a reporter. She will not bring a microphone and notepad but rather will simply listen to our table talk. She herself is quite intelligent and I believe might add beneficially to our conversation." He looked up, standing as he did so. "Ah, here she is now."

Eight pairs of eyes followed Dr. Chatterji's. What they saw was perfection personified. Jacqueline fairly floated to the table, simply arrayed in a dress of turquoise silk, with simple silver high-heeled sandals and understated jewelry. Makeup was

minimal and her hair was in a conservative ponytail, emphasiz-
ing her almond-shaped eyes, pouty mouth, and long, kissable
neck. Every man's thoughts were exactly alike. She looked
magnificent. As one, the table stood as she reached them.

"Hello, gentlemen," she said, making eye contact with each
man as Dr. Chatterji pulled out her seat. "I hope I haven't kept
you waiting."

"Not at all," Dr. Chatterji said, his sixty-plus-year-old eyes
bright with admiration. "We only just arrived. Gentlemen, I
present to you Ms. Jacqueline Tate, whose article on holistic
healing was recently recognized by the Harvard Medical
School and debated as a class project."

Appreciative comments went around the table. Jacqueline
heard them, but her eyes settled on Randall, whose brow
arched in speculation as if to say, "You didn't tell me that."

Her eyes shifted in response. *A smart girl never reveals all of
her secrets.*

Their conversation moved from technology to taste buds
as the waiter approached with their drinks and waited for their
orders. The men deferred to Jacqueline, who acknowledged
their manners in asking her to choose first. "Thank you, guys,
but really. I just arrived. Please place your orders and by the
time it gets back to me I will have decided."

They did, their choices ranging from decadent orders of
crispy pork belly, prime fillet, and lamb tagine to the more
health-conscious Dr. Chatterji, who ordered a haricot vert
salad with citrus vinaigrette. All eyes were on Jacqueline as she
voiced her choice.

"I probably should choose the salad, Dr. Chatterji, as you
have. But I must admit, I have a ravenous appetite." She let that
double entendre hang in the air for just a moment before she
looked at the waiter and said, "I'd like the Angus burger with
extra bacon and mayo and, oh, could I get a side of mashed
potatoes?"

"Excellent choice," the waiter responded, clearly smitten with Jacqueline's flirty nature. "I didn't get your drink order. Could I take that as well?"

"Sparkling water, please."

With all of the meal orders placed, the conversation meandered back to the conference and which topic would dominate both attendee conversation and media coverage. Most of those around the table felt that Randall's forward-thinking idea of using plant stem cells for human healing would be at the forefront, while a few felt that Dr. Chatterji's concept of holistic healing, specifically integrating the power of the Divine, would prove more newsworthy in the news climate of today.

"What do you think, Jacqueline?" James asked with the merest hint of daredevil glee in his eyes.

She'd been quiet the entire conversation, taking in and mentally recording everything that was said. Along with her high IQ, she had a near-perfect photographic memory, and when it came to conversations, almost total recall. But now, since asked directly, she was more than happy to contribute to the conversation.

"Both topics are quite important," she began, her voice low but firm. "Stem cell research has been at the forefront of medical research for quite some time, and while the use of plants has always been a part of the equation, I think you"— she turned to him—"Randall—excuse me, Dr. Atwater—have approached this possibility in a whole new way.

"That said, I am totally enthralled with the possibilities expressed by Dr. Chatterji." She looked at him with a warm, admiring smile. "The concept of holistic living predates modern medicine by thousands of years, doesn't it?" Dr. Chatterji nodded. "What is now deemed alternative was yesteryear's standard medical practice, administered with a respectable degree of success. To my knowledge, issues such as Alzheimer's and

Parkinson's did not exist. Did they?" While glancing at the others at the table, she'd mostly focused her attention on Dr. Chatterji, and did so now as she asked the question.

"Diseases come and go," Dr. Chatterji explained, sitting back and placing steepled hands on the table. "Many, in fact most, are created by lifestyle and diet. If you look to countries where people live the longest, you will see that theirs is a mostly vegetarian diet with a lifestyle filled with exercise, usually in the form of work. There is also some type of spiritual component to their existence, an entity or deity that fills them with faith, lowers their stress levels, and increases their overall happiness. We make it hard, but actually it's quite simple to live a healthy life."

"That is well said, Doctor." Jacqueline paused as the waiter delivered her sparkling water. "But if what you're saying is true and what you want to do is effective, aren't you liable to put yourself out of business?"

"If I could lessen health problems through prevention, then having to change my occupation would be an easy sacrifice, and I believe that all of my colleagues around the table would agree."

"Speak for yourself," James said, his face a mask of skepticism even as he smiled to show that he teased. "I need my money! And as long as there are sick people, I will have a job."

Dr. Chatterji did not join in the laughter. "Unfortunately, Dr. Sullivan, you are absolutely right."

Their food arrived and conversation lessened as they ate. Jacqueline made a big show of taking the first bite of her large, juicy burger. "Oh my goodness," she said, still chewing. "This is delicious!"

Darshana responded. "It looks very good. Maybe I should have ordered it after all. At the very least I would have enjoyed a good meal, and at most I could help Dr. Sullivan earn more money!" His eyes twinkled with humor. Those around the table laughed at this rare joke from a very serious man. They all declined dessert, and one of the doctors, a top neurologist who practiced at Johns Hopkins, insisted on paying the check.

Jacqueline stood, and the men followed suit. "I hear that the view from the ION Rooftop Patio is amazing. Anyone want to join me there for coffee or tea?" The question was general but her eyes were on Randall.

"I'm afraid I'll have to pass. The conference is over, but I and a few colleagues still have work to do."

"I'm one of the colleagues he's talking about," James said, stretching. "Besides, I need to check in with the chief."

"The chief?" the neurologist queried.

"His wife," Randall explained.

"Ah yes. I have one of those."

There was laughter around the table. Jacqueline turned to the Indian doctor. "What about you, Dr. Chatterji?"

He looked at his watch. "I have some reading to do, but my flight doesn't leave until tomorrow. I guess another half hour won't hurt."

"Anyone else?" Various nays abounded. She hooked her arm through the doctor's. "Looks like it's just you and me."

"Oh goodness, don't tell my wife." His smile was mischievous. "She doesn't know about my girlfriend."

"His wife is his girlfriend," Randall said as he passed. "And has been for the past forty years."

"Forty-two years, thank you very much."

"That's quite a milestone," James slapped him on the back as he too walked by, just behind Randall. "Congrats."

Jacqueline and Dr. Chatterji fell into step behind Randall, James, and the rest of the group who'd been at the table. She furtively watched Randall's long strides as he and James chatted. He laughed at something James said and Jacqueline noted his nice, white smile, his succulent lips and trimmed mustache. She remembered the way that mustache had felt as it tickled the top of her v-spot, and allowed herself the merest of smiles.

He'd said no to meeting her on the rooftop. She refused to let herself "go there" and feel bad about it. She'd been wined, dined, and screwed out of her mind, as Kaitlyn had put it. Just a good time girl, as she'd said she wanted. Perhaps their hook-up was a one-time thing. But a few times during dinner, she'd caught him looking. And if what she read in his eyes was any indication, she'd be with the doctor again.

CHAPTER 10

Randall strolled to the hotel gym, actually looking forward to the workout. The early morning meetings of the past week had left him little time to exercise. But the conference had ended and today, Saturday, he had a couple hours to do what he wanted before being picked up to spend a day in Malibu, meeting with like-minded souls on ways they could positively impact the world. Later on, he would join James and a team of doctors from UCLA who specialized in brain malfunctions for a two-day pow-wow on how his research could help their cause in finding cures.

He entered the exercise room, turned the corner, and saw two perfectly round, nice and firm cheeks. The woman wasn't facing him. Her butt did the greeting. One more second of checking out the toned calves, nice thighs, small waist, smooth skin, and long hair secured in a ponytail and he knew who was running on the treadmill. He hadn't planned on running; was more interested in weights. But on second thought, a little cardio never hurt nobody.

"Fancy meeting you here," he said, mimicking the greeting she'd used earlier in the week, when they met in the restaurant's lounge. He mounted the treadmill next to her and began pushing buttons to set his workout. "I thought you'd be packed and headed back to the border."

"No, I'm going to be stateside a while," she said, not even breathing heavily even though a thin sheen of sweat coated her skin. "When not attending conferences, I'll be based in D.C.."

This got Randall's attention. "Really? That's right next door to where I live."

"Which is?"

"Alexandria, Virginia."

"How far is that from downtown D.C.?"

"A half hour or so, depending on traffic."

He started running, setting a pace that matched Jacqueline's strides. For a few moments, only the sound of rubber slapping rubber was heard between them. A few more early risers broke sweat while using the elliptical machines, stationary bicycles, and weights; mostly with earbuds erasing the sound of the outside world.

After he'd settled into a comfortable stride, Randall resumed the conversation. "What will you be doing in D.C.?"

"A friend of mine is starting up an online publication. I'm helping him set up the website, write copy, provide moral support."

"So you design websites, too? Is there anything you're not good at?"

"Plenty, but I told you I'm a geek. That includes embracing the sciences *and* having a love for tinkering with computers and computer programs."

Jacqueline increased the pace on the treadmill. Randall put in his earbuds and concentrated on his workout. Fifteen minutes later, she brought the machine to a stop and stepped off of it. "It's all yours, guy."

"You're out of here?" Jacqueline nodded. Randall slowed his machine from a run to a walk. "When are you checking out?"

"Tomorrow. What about you?"

"Monday."

"Great! We'll both be here this evening, so I'll get the chance to pay you back."

Randall stopped his machine and reached for the towel draped over its handles. "For what?"

"Taking me out to dinner, for starters. And granting me the exclusive about your latest research. That alone is enough to increase the length of my contract, or have my superiors sit up and take notice at the very least."

"No payback needed. We're always trying to find ways to get our information out there. It was my pleasure to share."

"I insist," Jacqueline said, stepping around the treadmill until she faced him.

The offer was tempting, and so was the woman. There was no cleavage showing, but the tight cotton across her 36Ds left no doubt as to her generous mounds. He stepped down from the treadmill. "I have thoroughly enjoyed your company, but we're here in the City of Angels, filled with bars, fast cars, and movie stars. I'm surprised you don't have . . . I don't know . . . someone like Denzel Washington or what's that other guy's name?"

"Idris Elba."

"Ha! I knew you'd know who I was talking about. It's Saturday night. I'm surprised you don't have a date with someone like that."

"Seriously?" Jacqueline laughed. "Doctor, you underestimate yourself. Besides, it's just dinner, and no matter what else you've planned for the day . . . you have to eat. Am I right? We've enjoyed a whirlwind week, and tonight will be my last opportunity to show you how much I've appreciated all of your help and . . . our time together. I even have the perfect place, a hidden gem I discovered three years ago, tucked away in Topanga Canyon."

"Topanga? Sounds like a jungle."

"It's enchanting, and the food is divine. You'll love it, I promise." When Randall continued to hesitate, she added,

"Have you even seen any other part of Los Angeles besides this hotel? Come on, it's one last dinner. I'll make the reservations and hire a car."

She flashed him an irresistible smile and he caved like an ice cream addict at Coldstone. "I'll have to meet you there," he said, crossing his arms and offering up his own simple smile. "In a little while, I'll be leaving the hotel for an all-day meeting in Malibu."

"I don't think that's far at all from the restaurant, so that's perfect. It's an outdoor setting with a wonderful ambiance, so if your schedule will allow it, I'll make our reservations early, before the sun goes down. How does six thirty sound?"

"Our meeting will go until six. What about seven?"

"Seven sounds great. Listen, I'm going to do a little shopping and may not be in my room. So let me give you my cell number."

"Just call me and I'll lock it in."

Jacqueline retrieved her phone from the treadmill cup and Randall recited his cell phone number. She keyed it in and when his voice mail came on she said, "Dr. Atwater, this is Jacqueline Tate, confirming our appointment for later today. I look forward to seeing you. Thank you. Good-bye."

"Very professionally stated," Randall said, warming to this woman's unique mix of beauty, intelligence, and quirkiness. "I look forward to seeing you too."

She walked away. Randall was sure that the extra sway in her hips was for him.

Little vixen, he thought with a smile as he restarted the treadmill. He liked the way she made him feel: handsome and important. A couple times, when he saw the way she looked at him, he felt a little guilty as well. He wasn't in the mood or in the market for a longtime love. But spending time with the freelance writer had definitely had its benefits. One never knew who was reading what publication. Some billionaire could stumble across an article and decide to fund his research.

That alone was worth the few hours he'd spend with Jacqueline tonight. That she was as beautiful as she was talented and that they'd been able to enjoy each other's company—well, he wouldn't hold that against her.

Several hours later, after hours of talking, listening, and planning strategies, a slightly weary but mentally invigorated Randall stood and shook hands with the men who'd gathered. He'd declined their dinner invitation, citing a previous commitment. He and James walked out together.

"So what do you have going tonight?" James asked as they reached the driveway where several town cars awaited.

"Dinner with Jacqueline."

James stopped walking, almost in midstride. "Just you two?"

"Yes."

"Are you sure that's a good idea?"

"Why wouldn't it be?" Randall asked with a shrug.

"You can't be that naïve, man. Anybody with eyes and close proximity to her could tell how much time she spent checking you out. I think she attended every workshop you conducted, every speech and every meeting where she could go and you showed your face."

"She's very interested in our research."

"Then why didn't she come to any of *my* talks?"

"I think the world focus on stem cell research makes what I'm doing quite marketable right now. Plus"—he rubbed his chin and struck a GQ pose—"I'm better looking." From James, a deadpan stare. "Look, you can even join us if you want. We're meeting at a restaurant that's not too far from here."

"You definitely could use a chaperone. But my frat brothers have the night all planned. I'm headed over to see one of them, who just purchased a home in the Holmby Hills."

"The name means nothing to me. I don't know much about LA."

"Let's just say it's Beverly Hills, only better."

The two men shook hands. "Well, all right then. Enjoy yourself. I'll see you tomorrow."

"Bright and early. We're starting at nine. Maybe we can end early enough for me to fly out tomorrow night instead of waiting until Monday."

"Shoot me that flight info. Since we're both heading east, I might be able to get out too."

The men got in separate cars and left the home of the brain surgeon, which boasted modern architecture and ocean views. During the scenic ride from Malibu to Topanga Canyon and the Inn of the Seventh Ray, the restaurant that Randall had viewed online, he thought about his friend James, and his not-too-subtle warning about spending time with Jacqueline. Concluding that all of his rhetoric was much ado about nothing, he decided to sit back, relax, and enjoy the evening. Because even though she'd be in D.C. and the science community was a small one, chances were that he wouldn't see much of Jacqueline Tate.

CHAPTER 11

Jacqueline entered her room and fell on the bed. She was giddy with happiness; so far her plans had gone perfectly. Dinner had been amazing: the ambiance perfect, the food superb. And the night? She giggled like a schoolgirl dreaming of her first crush. She had no doubt that tonight—their last together before leaving LA—would be sweeter than the berry panna cotta that they'd shared at the Inn. Tonight she'd do more than warm his bed; she vowed to give Randall the type of loving that he wouldn't forget.

After a quick shower, she donned the provocative design purchased at Frederick's of Hollywood, in her opinion a precursor to the nationally popular Victoria's Secret. One look at herself in the dressing room mirror, and she knew this sheer black catsuit that covered everything yet left nothing to the imagination would be just the image to imprint upon Randall's mind; just the memory for him to take back to Virginia. Now giving herself a front-and-back perusal, she knew that tonight would be their hottest yet! After sliding her slender feet into five-inch stilettos, her look was complete. She wore nothing else: no makeup, no jewelry, not even a tie to hold back her hair. She'd washed it and, after doing a flash dry with the hair dryer, let the slightly damp curly locks cascade down her back. All week she'd sported a flatiron-straight style; tonight he'd see her hair wild and untamed—just like her.

Just like she wanted this night to be: wild, untamed, unforgettable.

She'd barely laid her head on the pillow when the door opened and he walked in. Easing up on her elbow, she turned her body toward him and struck a pose, laughing as he stopped dead in his tracks. "Well, hello there."

"Wow."

She laughed again, sitting up completely and tossing her thick curls away from her face. "You like?"

His eyes devoured her, much as his mouth had the filet mignon earlier in the evening. He took a step toward her. "Just . . . wow . . ."

She slid off the king-size bed, with an agenda. All week he had taken the lead; tonight, she planned to do a Janet Jackson and take control. Walking over to the iPod and speakers and selecting the song she'd preset for his arrival, she turned to him. "Have a seat. There's something I want to show you."

As the lyrics from Beyoncé's "Halo" filled the room, so did Jacqueline's sensuality. She moved her hips—slowly, sensually—knowing that the black mesh made her butt cheeks stand out even more than they normally did. Rubbing her hands across them she bent down, hips in rhythm, and touched her toes as if she'd been born on a pole and weaned on the rain that showered the dancers. Using muscles she'd only recently read about, she caused her cheeks to wink at him, finally opening her eyes to view him from between her legs.

She liked what she saw.

He was lying back on the bed, his eyes at half-mast—slowly, sensually, massaging his dick. It was something she planned to do in the not-too-distant future. But not yet. She wanted him harder, thicker, and longer than he'd ever been, almost ready to explode upon contact. She wanted him so excited that he felt his balls would combust. When he came, she wanted it to be deep inside her, his love flowing into her womb.

She turned around. Her eyes never wavered from his. He seemed powerless to do anything but stare. *Yes, baby. I know what you want. And I'm going to give it to you.* She took her middle finger, placed it in her mouth, and began sucking it. All the while she ground her hips standing up, the way she planned to later while lying down. She took her wet middle finger and began tracing the miniature dots the mesh of her catsuit created, along her breasts and stomach, vagina and thighs. She worked her way to the floor, still keeping her butt in time to the rhythm. She licked her fingers again, playfully tapped the top of her punanny, becoming aroused as the mesh rubbed against her hardening nub. She tweaked her nipples. They popped like headlights against the mesh, lighting up Randall's awareness of what she was working with. And then back down again, dropping it like it was hot. Even hotter than Randall looked right now.

Uh-huh. I'm going to make you need this, Randall. I'm going to turn you into a real-life mad scientist. Mad about me.

Playtime was over.

Striding purposefully over to the bed, she stayed him with a hand to the chest when he would have risen. "Lie back," she whispered huskily. "This is my show."

She undid his tie, pulled it from around his neck. Then she reached for his wrist and tied one end of the tie around it. The other end was secured to the leg of the nightstand.

"What are you doing?"

"Shh. I'm tying you up so that I can have my way with you." Using a scarf that had been draped over the headboard, she secured his other hand, straddled him, and began to unbutton his shirt. Her fingers were nimble. It was quick work.

He'd never done this, gone outside the sexual box. She could tell. His eyes showed that perfect mixture of fear, curiosity, and excitement that she'd expect from someone like him. Someone in a conservative field with a conservative countenance, but with a streak of freak beneath the surface.

She leaned into him until her face hovered above his, and after staring deeply into his eyes, plunged her tongue into his mouth. "Kiss" was too tame a word to describe this maneuver. She assaulted his mouth, attacking his well-defined lips with licks and nips before swirling her tongue into his mouth again. All the while her hips never stopped, and her pelvis joined the dance, grinding into his rock-hard shaft, making him strain against his bonds the way she knew he would.

Rising up just enough, she pressed her breasts against his mouth and was rewarded with a nipple being quickly sucked in. He arched his back to try to take the lead, but with his hands bound, that was not happening. She sat back, her laugh throaty and victorious as she reached for the lone zipper that kept the mesh around her.

It was time to up the ante. It was time to release the weapon from its holster and stick it somewhere else. For safe keeping, you might say.

After removing the mesh garment in one fell swoop, she slid back into the stilettos and got back on the bed. She reached for his belt, undid it, and yanked down his zipper. The snake sprang up like a python ready to strike. But she was, too. The same lips that had smashed against his just seconds before now covered the tip of his penis. The same tongue that had thrust its way into his waiting mouth now swirled around the mushroom-shaped head before exploring the length of him and back again, teasing him as she took him in, licked him up and down, teased his sac, and used her hands to increase the pressure.

"Baby, untie me."

She shook her head in a way that caused her curls to dance around her shoulders and back. "Not yet."

She scooted down until her face was flush against his pelvis and continued sexing him orally. His groans and hisses let her know she was doing something right. The way his head turned this way and that, the way his hips raised off the bed, the way he pulled against his constraints.

You will never forget me, Dr. Randall Atwater. After tonight, you'll be addicted.

After several long minutes of intense attention to Randall's burgeoning erection, Jacqueline poised herself over it . . . and slid down.

Slowly, delicately, with vaginal muscles constricting and releasing as she went.

"Oh, baby." Randall's voice was hoarse as yet again he pulled on the restraints. "Oh my God."

She repeated the motion, once and again, becoming wetter with each trip down his long, thick dick. Placing her hands on his shoulders, she began to ride him, her bountiful breasts bouncing in front of a mouth searching for her nipple like one bobbing for apples. When he captured it he latched on, rolling his tongue around the pert areola, licking the tip of the nipple as he held it between his teeth.

Picking up the pace, she continued to ride, grinding her pelvis, twirling her hips, squeezing her walls until she felt him shiver. Her gyrations became wilder, faster. Her mouth went slack as she felt a powerful release coming on. She squeezed his shoulders as her booty bounced up and down, riding his dick like a horse on a merry-go-round, only with way more of a thrill.

"Yes. Yes. Yessss!"

She collapsed on Randall's chest. For several seconds she lay there, pussy twitching, legs shaking, head rising just enough to initiate a hot, wet kiss. He was still rock hard, which meant this was only round one in a match that would go several. She slowly freed him from the constraints.

"Do you like chess?" she cooed, stroking his hairless chest.

He wearily nodded. "Good." She slid off of him and got on all fours. Looking back, she taunted, "Your move."

Sunday morning. The night with Randall had been as amazing as Jacqueline had imagined it would be, and now, sitting in her bulkhead seat on her flight to Washington, she had five nonstop hours to replay each tantalizing moment. Before leaving, she'd shared snippets of the night's adventures with her best friend. Kris had once again stressed caution where her feelings for Randall were concerned, and Jacqueline agreed that falling head over heels was not recommended. But she'd never met a man who made her feel the way he did, and from his actions of this past week, she believed his interest in her was more than fleeting. The sparks between them were genuine and their erogenous fire burned bright and hot. His parting words to her were to keep in touch and he looked forward to seeing her again.

As the plane leveled off at a comfortable cruising altitude, Jacqueline fired up her iPad and settled in to work. But every now and then a memory of her times with Randall would make her pause and bring a smile. Maybe all the frogs she'd kissed had brought her to this handsome prince. If so, it had been more than worth it. Knowing the payoff was to end up with someone like Randall . . . she'd kiss them all again.

The Malibu meeting ended earlier than scheduled. Randall and his research partner, James, both caught a redeye flight. Several hours later, an exhausted Dr. Atwater spotted his driver and entered the town car. He didn't realize how tired he was until he woke up mere blocks from his home with his mouth slightly open and his iPad on the floor.

"Looks like you had a long week, Doctor," the friendly driver said, watching through his rearview mirror as Randall ran a hand over his face.

"Man, you don't even know the half."

"Well, we've almost got you home now. You can get a good night's sleep."

"That's exactly what I need. I can't wait."

They arrived at his stately residence, and Randall paid the driver, waving away his offer to take the luggage to the door. He inserted the key, opened the door, and was immediately greeted by family.

"Daddy!" His twelve-year-old daughter, Albany, bounded into the foyer and into his arms. "We missed you, Daddy. I'm so glad you're home."

Ten-year-old Aaron strolled around the corner. From the look in his eyes, he too wanted to jump into his father's arms. But it was obvious he thought himself too cool for that. "Hey, Dad."

"Hey, Son." They gave each other dap.

"Where's your luggage?" Aaron asked.

"Outside. Will you grab it for me?"

"Sure."

Randall stepped aside to make room for his son and heard a sultry voice behind him. "There you are."

He turned around and walked into arms that hugged him tightly, and lips that brushed his own. "We've missed you," she said to him as hand in hand they strolled into the living room, kids and dogs not far behind.

"I've missed you too." They sat. He immediately pulled her into his arms. "How are you, baby? How's my beautiful, loving wife?"

CHAPTER 12

"Come here." Randall lay stretched across their custom, king-size bed, having only taken off his shoes and loosened his tie. By the time he'd reached their master suite, the fatigue had returned full force.

"I can tell you're glad to be home." Sherri, his college sweetheart, climbed on the bed and nestled herself against him.

"I am. The conference was good, though. Me and James finally got a chance to catch up."

"How's married life treating him?"

"I've got to admit it. He looks good, Sherri, like he's lost at least ten pounds. Debbie must be doing something right."

"She's probably cooking, something that wifey number one felt was beneath her."

"Now, don't be too hard on the gold digger."

"Ha! I wonder what she's up to now."

"If I know her, trying to find another cash cow."

"Thank God for Debbie. She'll help restore James's faith in women. The few times we've talked, I've really enjoyed the conversation. I think I have her number in my phone."

"You should call her. In fact, we should make plans to do

an adults-only getaway. Maybe meet them in Vegas or somewhere fun."

"That sounds good." She repositioned her head in the crook of his arm. "Anything else exciting happen?"

A pause and then, "I did an exclusive interview for *Science Today*."

"Ooh, very nice. I take it that went well."

"Yes. She asked probing, intelligent questions, which allowed me the platform for informative answers."

"She?"

"Yes. Her name is Jacqueline Tate. She is a freelance writer for them as well as other medical and science publications."

"Hum. Is she pretty?"

"Beautiful, actually."

"Well, why don't you tell me how you really feel!"

"Hey, woman, you asked! But you don't have anything to worry about. Nobody can compete with you."

"Un huh. Whatever. I hope you behaved."

Even if she hadn't smiled, Randall knew she was joking. Aside from a single indiscretion early on in the marriage, he had never given Sherri anything to worry about. She trusted him completely.

Randall took off his tie, then slid off the bed to remove everything but his black Calvin Klein briefs. "Any updates on Mom Elaine?"

Sherri's disposition immediately changed. Her mother's health issues were a constant concern. "She's doing okay. There have been no changes."

"Then take comfort in that, baby. In this situation, stability is actually good news."

Sherri nodded, but looked at him with forlorn eyes.

He sat down, reached for her hand. "She's going to be fine, babe. We've got the best doctors in the country checking into her situation. Plus, I discussed her symptoms with my colleagues during our private meetings on Saturday and Sunday afternoon. One of the doctors is going to forward information he has on cranial infections and how they affect brain function."

She sat beside him. "You think her brain is infected?"

"Sherri, please don't get worked up. The truth is, I don't know. But because the doctors have yet to offer a solid diagnosis, I wanted to describe her situation to those present and see if it rang a bell on something they'd treated. The head of neurology at UCLA is now on my speed dial. I'm going to do everything in my power to make Mom well."

Sherri teared up as she moved in close to her husband. "You are such an amazing, incredible man. What would I ever do without you?"

He kissed her tenderly on the lips. "Thankfully, you'll never have to find out."

"Baby, I'm so sorry."

"About what?"

"That night . . . before you left."

"I told you over the phone not to worry about that."

"But I do worry, thought about it all the while you were gone! You're a good man, a wonderful father . . . and I need to be a better wife. I need to always take care of your physical needs, especially when you're heading out of town for a week!"

For a while, Randall said nothing. After all, one couldn't argue with fact. The home fires had been cooling for quite a while, especially since Sherri had become preoccupied with her mom. This wasn't the first time. After each child was born, it would be at least two months before Sherri again felt in the mood. Other times it would be Randall's nonstop schedule that kept them behaving more like roommates and less like lovers. Scarce sex wasn't good for any marriage, especially one that was nearing its fifteenth year.

"We've both been under pressure," Randall finally said, hoping to take away some of his wife's guilt.

"You've always satisfied me, given it to me whenever I needed it, whenever I asked." A single tear escaped her eye and headed toward her chin.

"Come on now, don't cry." He wrapped his arms around her. "You always make me happy, no matter what."

"You're too good to me."

"And you're good *for* me. I love you, baby."

"I love you too."

Sherri got on her knees and positioned herself behind Randall's back. Placing her hands on his shoulders, she began a massage. "Baby, you're tight."

"Am I?" He dropped his head. "That feels good."

They were silent as Sherri worked her magic. He'd gone to professionals, but Randall still felt that his wife's was one of the best massages around.

Sherri placed her fist against his back and ran it down his spine. After going back and forth a couple times, she firmly grasped the nape of his neck and used pressure to get out the obvious kinks. "Where to next week?" she asked, placing her fingers on his close-cropped curls and massaging his scalp.

"Nowhere if you keep making me feel like this."

"You like this, huh?"

"Almost as much as I like massaging something that you've got."

"Hum. We'll get to that next."

"Let's see. Week after next I'm in New York, then Chicago."

"The Big Apple and the Windy City."

"Hopefully not this time. Last time, I was there in February and the wind was no joke, not to mention the snow. I can't imagine April will be any windier than that."

"What's this conference about?"

"It's a symposium done in conjunction with the University of Chicago. There'll also be a special gala where several prominent Illinois doctors and donors will be recognized."

"Sounds nice."

"It will be. You should get Blair to watch the kids and come hang out with me."

"You never have free time during these things."

"You don't need my help to shop the Magnificent Mile."

"Sounds tempting, but it's pretty busy right through here, Albany with her cheerleading and Aaron with his sports and band. Plus, Albany now fancies herself a beauty queen and wants to enter a contest sponsored by a mall."

"She already spends half of her life in front of a mirror."

"Ha!"

"Do you think that's a good idea?"

"I don't know. We'll see."

Randall placed his hands on Sherri's, which were once again kneading his shoulders. "I feel much better, baby. Thanks. I need to hurry up and take this shower," he said with a yawn as he got off the bed. "I'm about to pass out."

When he finished his shower and came out of the bathroom, Sherri had turned off the lights and lit several candles. The soft sounds of Robin Thicke filled the air.

"Um, you smell good," she purred, turning to snuggle against him once he lay down. She ran a hand across his naked back and taut behind. "Feel good, too."

He pulled her close and kissed her deeply. "Baby, I'm so tired. If you let me sleep tonight, I promise I'll love you in the morning."

"I'll let you do anything you want." She turned so that she could spoon against him, and nestled herself in his arms. "I'm just glad to have you next to me. This bed doesn't feel the same without you in it. Know what I mean?"

Randall's soft snores were the only reply. Sherri smiled, raised his hand to her lips, and kissed it. *You work so hard for us, baby. Always providing for our family, taking care of our needs. Thank you.*

She lay there, silent and content, listening to the sounds of Robin and her sleeping husband. She'd loved this man for more than a decade, and when she'd spoken earlier she'd meant what she said. She was going to take care of him the way he took care of her. He was a good man, a providing man, a faithful man. He deserved that . . . and more

CHAPTER 13

"Girl, what are you doing still up? What's wrong?"

Sherri smiled at the incredulity in her best friend's voice. She knew that calling Renee at any time past ten p.m. Eastern Standard Time usually meant that there was a problem. And no matter that her former high school home girl lived in Vegas. Sherri knew she could call her at any time. "Everything's fine, Nay. I just couldn't sleep. Randall's home and I didn't want to wake him. So I'm here in the kitchen, eating popcorn and talking to you."

"Your mom's okay?"

"There haven't been any more episodes lately. But I still worry; her in Raleigh, with no immediate family nearby. That's part of what keeps me up at night."

"I feel you, Sherri. I'd probably be walking the floors myself. Have the doctors discovered what's going on with her?"

"No. They've run a battery of tests but still can't conclusively say whether it's dementia caused by Alzheimer's disease or something else."

"What is Randall saying?"

Sherri sighed. "He's been so busy. But while in LA he talked to a doctor there who might have some information."

"He still hasn't been back to check on her? Since a month ago?"

"He's a scientist, Renee, not a medical doctor. So while he has a lot of information on cause and effect and is actively working on a stem-cell-related cure for all types of brain malfunctions, he can't instantly fix my mom."

"I guess you're right. It would still probably make you feel better if he were working more closely with the doctors."

"He talked extensively with the team that was chosen to treat her. I have confidence in them." There was a pause. Sherri heard Renee rummaging through something. "What are you doing?"

"Girl, I'm looking for Rambo."

"Who is that? Or should I say *what* is that?"

"Either works. It's my dildo, and he's been more faithful than any man I've had lately."

"Whoa, sistah. That's a little TMI even for me."

Renee chuckled. "You asked."

"What happened to that guy you were raving about just, what, two months ago? The one who you said had you hitting notes like Mariah Carey?"

"Ooh, girl, don't remind me about Shannon's big dick."

"Why not? Sounds like you could use it right about now!"

"Only problem is, I'd have to stand in line behind half of Las Vegas!"

"He was cheating on you?"

"To his credit, we hadn't quite gotten around to the exclusive-or-not conversation. But I didn't know he was rocking two to three of us in one evening."

Sherri leaned back in the chair. This is why she loved her still-single-after-all-these-years friend. It made her remember what it felt like to be young and carefree, to enjoy the thrill of the chase, getting caught, and even having to throw an overzealous, uninteresting fish back in the ocean. But Shannon was fine. She'd seen his Facebook picture. Had she been single,

Shannon could have parked his shoes under her bed at any time.

"How did you find out he was multitasking?"

"Would you believe? The hair salon!" Sherri whooped, and Renee responded, "It sounds funny now, but believe me, when I heard the woman in the chair next to me talking about the date she'd had the night before, one that greatly resembled mine except Shannon and I had met for lunch, I was all ears. Flowers at the pickup? Check. Nice meal in a fancy restaurant? Check. Coming home and getting screwed seven ways from Sunday? Check and checkmate."

"Wait, girl. That sounds like the type of date had by millions of women across the country."

"It does, except for when she began talking about how he smacked her ass three times before coming and then hissed like a snake when he went over the edge. When she ended with the same phrase he'd used with me, 'Baby, that was better than front-row seats at a Lakers play-off game,' I knew we'd both played ball with the same bat, know what I mean?"

"Oh my God, girl. What are the chances that you two would be getting your hair done at the same time?"

"I know, right?"

"Did you ask her? I mean, did you confirm for sure that it was Shannon that she was talking about?"

"As if that lame-ass comment wasn't enough? But to answer your question, yes, I asked her. Discreetly though. I didn't want everyone in the shop to get all up in my info."

"So how'd you do it?"

"Passed her a note and included my telephone number. She called right away and gave me more information on that fool than a background check. Turns out she and him grew up together here in Vegas. He was her first, and still tunes her up two to three times a week, at least that's what she told me. She also informed me that he has several children by several women, all who still appear to be receiving baby-mama benefits—and I'm not talking child support, although I'm told he does that too."

"Wow, I hear about guys like this, even saw somewhere on the Internet where a man with, like, twenty-two babies by fourteen women was trying to get a reality show. Stuff like that just doesn't seem real. But I guess it is."

"Sherri, you've been married so long that you've forgotten how it is. But the truth of the matter is, a good man is hard to find, so much so that after month after month of being alone, sometimes a hard man is good to find and all some women are looking for. When you can't find that . . . you go buy Rambo."

"You're a good woman," Sherri said, her voice filled with sincerity. "Don't give up on the idea that what you want is out there. A good man may be hard to find, but when you meet him you'll know that it's been worth the search."

"You were lucky to find Randall before he blew up."

"What do you mean?"

"Girl, those of you who were smart enough to marry the man with potential instead of waiting and trying to snag the man with means were way ahead of the game. Once a man becomes successful and has reached the age of thirty without getting tied down? They act like they've dodged a bullet. By that age they've also learned how to play the single game."

"I still believe that there are plenty of men out there who want to get married."

"Why would they? Nine times out of ten they already have a child somewhere, so they're not worrying about a legacy. Ten times out of ten they've got their choice of women to warm their bed at night, take to the concert, get invited to Thanksgiving dinner, or what have you. Today's single Black man has it made in the shade, while we're out here just getting played!"

Sherri laughed. "You're silly. But seriously though, there's a good man out there for you, Renee. You just have to know where to look and, more importantly, what to look for."

"Meaning?"

"Meaning he may not look like Boris Kodjoe or be driving a Mercedes or wearing a Ralph Lauren suit."

"Well, what the hell do I want with him then?"

"He might not have a large bank account, but he could have a large appendage."

"Hmm, in that case . . ."

"Ha! I knew that possibility would make you think twice. But that he be well-endowed shouldn't be a high priority either."

"Please. If I'm going to be with the same pecker the rest of my life, you'd best believe he's got to be able to satisfy."

Sherri shook her head. "You've been talking to your great-grandma again. How is Miss Hattie?"

"Still as feisty at ninety-two as she was at twenty-two."

"Next time you talk to her, give her my love."

They talked for another half hour. Sherri yawned, looked at the clock, and was surprised to see that it was two thirty a.m. "Thanks for the conversation, sis, but I'd better run. Albany has cheerleading practice at seven."

"In the morning?"

"Girl, her schedule is busier than mine." She yawned again. "I think I can go to sleep now. Thanks again, girl. You're the only one I can call and know I'll feel better."

"Whatever, heifah. I'm the only one you know in the West, and can call this late."

"Well, there is that." They laughed.

"Speaking of the West, was Randall's good doctor friend at that LA conference?"

"Yes. I could tell Randall was glad they got the chance to hang out a bit."

"He's married, right?"

"Yes, for the second time. I've met the Mrs. and I must say . . . he picked a good one this time."

"The first wife wasn't?"

"Let's just say the first wife married his title and his bank account. When his practice suffered as a result of the economic meltdown, she caught the first thing smoking straight out of the marriage. Her loss, because James is the real deal. Just goes to show you, Nay, they're still out there. Just keep believing."

"Why didn't I know about James before he got remarried?"

"Uh, because this time two years ago, when he was available, you were head over heels for somebody named Troy, remember?"

"The bodyguard," Renee said with a sigh. "I knew my chances were slim with somebody like him. But the one time I got behind the velvet rope, I had to take my chances. And I have no regrets."

"Do y'all still talk?"

"No. I tried calling him, but after he married his Larger-Than-Life Superstar wife, all of his numbers changed."

"Can you blame him?"

"No, I guess not. He still chose the wrong sistah. She might be able to sing like a canary, but I bet she can't put her foot in a pot of greens or a peach cobbler from scratch."

"You're probably right." Sherri stood and stretched.

"Look, girl. Don't worry about your mom. God's got her, all right?"

"Okay."

"And don't ever forget how blessed you are to have a man like Randall. They don't make many like him anymore."

"Thank you, sistah. I won't forget."

She tiptoed back into the master suite and quietly, so as not to wake him, eased under the covers to go to sleep. Her head had barely hit the pillow when she felt an arm come around her middle and pull her close. Randall kissed the back of her neck and ground himself into her backside.

"I'm sorry." She turned to face him. "I didn't mean to wake you."

"It's okay." He kissed her and ran his hand across the top of her gown, tweaking a nipple when he found it.

"You want something?" she coyly asked, stroking his manhood until it felt like steel.

"Mm-hmm."

Without a word, Sherri threw back the covers, scooted down until her mouth was where her hand had been, and licked him.

"Oh, baby . . ."

"You like that?"

"You know I do."

"Just lie back and enjoy, big daddy. I'm going to give it to you real good."

And for the next hour, in different ways and different positions, that's exactly what she did.

CHAPTER 14

"Jack!"

Any other voice surprising her like this would have sent Jacqueline jumping through the ceiling. But the greeting from the only person allowed to call her anything but her formal name only caused a really big smile. She'd know the voice anywhere; couldn't remember a time when the woman in front of her hadn't been her best friend.

"Kris!" She left the foyer in the home of her childhood friend, and entered the sun-filled living room. "Phillip didn't tell me you'd be here! You didn't either."

They greeted each other with an enthusiastic hug.

"He didn't know," Kris said. "It was a last-minute decision."

"Wow! It's so good to see you!"

"Likewise, girl. But you know I had to come. Especially since my last phone calls went unreturned."

"Sorry about that, chickie. I know I said I'd get back with you. But Los Angeles was a whirlwind."

Jacqueline sat on the couch. Kris joined her. "Hmm . . . I wonder why." There was no mistaking the sarcasm in her voice, or the concern on her face.

"You know why. The reason can be summed up in two words. Randall Atwater."

Kris rolled her eyes. "Obviously you didn't take my advice on being cautious. So . . . you've shared bits and pieces before, but now I want to hear everything, from the beginning."

Jacqueline lay her head back against the couch's cushions to better relive each moment. "It started at the airport."

"The airport?"

"More specifically, we met at the taxi stand. I walked over with him checking me out the entire way."

"Are you sure that this meeting didn't happen on purpose?"

Jacqueline smiled but said nothing.

"Jack . . ."

"What?" Her voice was all innocence and light.

"Never mind. Go ahead. Tell me more."

"It was raining like crazy; more inches than the city had seen in years." Jacqueline sat forward, her tone conspiratorial. "I saw more inches than I'd seen in years, but I don't want to get ahead of myself." This comment finally loosened the worry lines from Kris's face and brought on a smile. "On top of that," she continued, "an accident had prevented taxis from arriving at the airport, causing long lines to form at the taxi stand."

Kris obviously wanted to quickly hear the whole story. "And?" she asked, impatience coating the word.

"After discovering that we were both headed to the same place, Randall secured a car service for us. We parted in the lobby, only to end up having dinner together that very night!"

"He didn't waste any time, I see. And why would he? You're gorgeous."

"I guess he thought so. The very next night he invited me to the Walt Disney Concert Hall to see the LA Philharmonic and LA Opera. He bought me these gorgeous gowns and shoes to match. We rode in a limo. It was so romantic, Kris.

And to his credit, as I've shared before, Randall was the perfect gentleman."

"Much to your chagrin."

"Girl . . . you know me too well."

"Of course I do. So you two didn't have sex?"

"I didn't say that."

"Right, you talked about inches. A comment, I would imagine, that comes from personal experience."

"After the concert was over, I didn't want the night to end. He escorted me to my room and then turned to leave. Before he did, I gave him a key card."

"Brazen hussy!"

"I couldn't even believe I did it! Felt like a fool, to tell you the truth. But the next night, while I was bathing in the tub, he used it. When I heard his voice I thought I was dreaming, but when I looked up . . . there he was."

Jacqueline continued to share their week together: his breakfast speech, her exclusive interview, attending his workshops, and, of course, their sizzling sexual trysts. "It was amazing, Kris," she finished, her eyes shining with excitement at the memory of it all. "More than I ever could have imagined or dared to dream."

"I can't believe you slept with the scientist!" Kris scooted closer to Jacqueline, her eyes mischievous. "Your comment about inches takes on a whole new meaning, namely that the guy came well equipped!"

"Not only had the equipment, but knew what to do with it. He was big but gentle, able to take control while making me feel that my needs came first. Does that make sense?" When Kris nodded, Jacqueline added, "He's everything I dreamt he'd be from the moment I saw him at the taxi stand."

"This is Kris you're talking to, Jack. Be honest. These feelings started way before the two of you met."

Jacqueline pulled her legs close and wrapped her arms

around her knees. "I'll admit that reading an article on Randall and then seeing his picture motivated my keen interest in stem-cell research. But I'd been involved in the medical and science communities before knowing his name. You know this." Kris nodded. "I'm not obsessed with him, per se," she continued, her eyes narrowing as she tried to make sense of the past week. "But I am terribly, incredibly infatuated."

"He sounds like quite the catch. I can't believe he's not married."

"I'm pretty sure he was married at some point. He has two kids."

Kris frowned. "Are you sure he's divorced?"

"Pretty much. He wasn't wearing a ring."

"Is that all the proof you've got? Are you kidding me right now?"

"It's all I need, for now," Jacqueline said with a shrug. "I'm ninety-nine percent sure that there isn't a missus. He doesn't seem like the type of guy who'd cheat."

"The next time you talk to him, make sure that's the first question you ask. If he's married, Jack, you're setting yourself up to get hurt badly."

"I understand why you'd say that. But you weren't there, Kris. You didn't see how we were together, how he looked at me, how he couldn't keep his hands off of me whenever we were together, or stay away . . . even when he knew he should and said he would."

"It's a rare man who turns down free sex, Jacqueline."

"Our being together was about more than sex! We talked about his passions and mine. He knows that I'm well versed in all aspects of his research. Believe me, I took a mini-course in Dr. Randall Atwater to make sure there was nothing about the field he loves that I didn't know.

"It paid off, Kris!" Jacqueline's voice was part passion, part pleading for her friend to believe her. "Randall couldn't believe how much I knew about his work and was pleased that he could speak in his language and I could understand. Obviously he's never had a woman who could do that before."

"That you know of. You need more information. If he's not married, you could be one of several women warming his bed."

"I'm not going to worry about that. I'm going to focus on him, take care of me, and study up for the next conference. One thing for sure; love is in the air. Who knows what the future might hold?"

CHAPTER 15

Randall eased experienced hands over Sherri's shoulders, kneading with methodical precision. He ran a hand over the shoulder blades and up around her neck. In a rare move, they'd slept in and let their nanny, Blair, get the kids off to school. Then they'd enjoyed another round of lovemaking. Lately, having back-to-back sex had not only been rare, it had been almost nonexistent.

"You were talking about me. Now look who's tight." He braced his knees on the mattress and placed a kiss at the base of her hairline. "Relax, baby."

Sherri took a deep breath. "I'm trying. And while I really appreciate this, darling, I'm the one who is supposed to be taking care of you."

"We'll get to that," Randall said, his voice low and purposely sexy. "I have no intention of forgetting what you promised me tonight."

"I believe that promise was made this morning?"

"I guess you're right. It was after midnight that I got a chance to hit that spot."

For a few moments, the only sounds in their master suite were Randall sometimes rubbing his hands briskly together to

warm the oil and R. Kelly crooning some of the couple's favorite songs from back in their dating and early marriage days.
When the next selection began playing, Sherri shifted her
head from one side to the other.

"Wow, that takes me back to good memories: the good old
days."

"Yeah, that was a runaway hit," Randall agreed. His hands
moved from her shoulders to the middle of her back. He used
his fist to reach the deep tissue and loosen the knots he felt
there.

"Mom loved that song. She heard me playing it in my
room one day and came in to listen. When it was over she
asked me who was singing, and then asked me to play it again."
They listened as R. Kelly's popular song offered faith, hope,
and the knowledge that one could do anything, achieve everything, if they believed. "We're going to have to hire live-in help
for her. Next to moving her to Virginia to live with us, or at
least close to us, that is the only thing that will give me total
peace. Knowing someone is with her, living there, and watching her every move."

"I spoke with that UCLA neurosurgeon about a serum
that I've developed from a specific plant's stem cells, one that is
very promising in reversing memory loss and decreased motor
skills in the elderly. Unfortunately, until it's been approved by
the FDA, no hospital in America will touch it."

"Then let's try it outside of America," Sherri answered.
"Canada is very progressive and you have colleagues there. I'd
fly Mom over the border in a heartbeat if it means that she'll
get better. I'll do whatever it takes to make her well."

"I know, baby," Randall said, immediately thinking of another Canadian and how her citizenship and other connections
might come in handy in this endeavor. "I'm as committed as you
are in seeing that happen. I'd like nothing more." He'd reached
the small of her back, his ministrations soft and gentle as he
massaged her there. His hands continued, slightly squeezing

her love handles before moving over her round butt and squeezing again.

Sherri turned over. The look of love was in her eyes. "Remember when we first began dating," she asked, rubbing her hands across his bare chest, "and I brought you home to meet Mom?"

"And I impressed her with my good looks and above-average intelligence?"

"Uh, not quite."

"Ha!"

"No, I'm just teasing. She liked you right away, especially when you showed up with flowers. None of my other boyfriends had done that."

"What do you mean 'none'? You make it sound like there were several, when to my knowledge there was only one!"

"Will you stop being the researcher and just listen to my story? Yes, before you came along I'd only had one boyfriend. But I had several dates and none of them ever brought Mom anything."

"Admit it, baby. From the very beginning . . . I was the man." He leaned over and kissed her, light yet promising.

"She couldn't get over the way you dressed: Hush Puppies paired with khaki pants, button-down shirts, and those Bill Cosby-style sweaters. "

"Hey, don't knock a man's style. I had to rock those sweaters with my wire-rims!"

"Okay, I'll give it to you," Sherri said as she moved over so that Randall could lie down beside her. "You did look cute in those horn-rimmed glasses."

"Not cute . . . handsome."

"Okay, now you're pushing it. You were just . . . ah!" Sherri reacted to being tickled. "Randall, stop!"

He did, and pulled her on top of him.

She kissed him, ran her tongue along the crease of his mouth until his lips parted, then darted her tongue inside. "You still look cute," she said, kissing him again.

"Is that so?" His hands went on a journey of discovery, luxuriating in the feel of her naked skin. Fourteen going on fifteen years . . . and he hadn't had enough.

Sherri rolled her hips, pressing her pelvis against his hardening manhood. "There's nothing about you that I don't like," she whispered into his ear, before nipping its lobe. "Absolutely nothing."

Soon, Randall's mouth found a nipple and Sherri's hand found his shaft. Leisurely moments of kissing, fondling, nipping, and licking gave way to panting and thrusting and a sex-scented room. There was something to be said for time, and how the longer one made love to one's mate the better they knew each other. Randall knew exactly where and when to touch, and Sherri knew just how hard to squeeze. Some nights they got frisky and talked nasty, but on this night—Sherri's return home after a quick trip to Raleigh—no words were needed. Their bodies communicated everything that each needed to know.

I love you.

I missed you.

I'm here.

I know.

They changed positions and for a moment, with Randall above her, they stared into each other's eyes. "I missed you, baby," he said at last, as he once again entered her and began to stroke. "I missed this."

"Me too." Sherri spread her legs wider, then lifted them up to grant him deeper access. "I'm sorry for not—"

"Shh. What's past is past. We're here right now. And I'm loving every minute."

"Ooh," she whispered, as he shifted his hips and hit her spot. "Me . . . too."

Their orgasms weren't seismic clashes of bodies where stars were seen and trumpets heard. Rather they were intense yet subdued, like a melody that's been heard over and again, but is still enjoyed every time. Randall gave one final shiver before resting his full body weight on Sherri: hip to hip, chest to chest, forehead to forehead.

"That was good, baby," she said, once she'd caught her breath.

"It's always good. I appreciate you, Sherri," he said, rolling off of her and then cuddling her to his side. "I know these last few months have been challenging: my rising profile, the increased travel and time away from home, the kids and their full schedules, this situation with Mom Elaine. I want you to know that I understand why you've been distracted. With the award and the newfound grant money and the like, I've been caught up as well.

"What time are the kids getting home today? I might take them to the mall or something, spend some daddy time."

"That would be nice. But Albany already has plans to go to the mall later on, with her study group."

"How much studying can you get done in a dressing room?"

"Trust me, I was skeptical as well. Until I found out that Melissa would be there with them."

"Ah, good. Lauren's mother will make them toe the line. That's one of the reasons I'm glad that she and Albany are best friends."

"Me too. Hopefully Lauren's study habits rub off on our daughter and not the other way around."

"I can't see Lauren becoming a fashionista. She's too much like Melissa for that."

"Practical, tolerates no nonsense."

"Exactly. What about Aaron?"

"He has track practice, but I'm pretty sure he's free after that. You might want to send him a text indicating your plans; otherwise he'll head straight to his room and the videogame that is rarely detached from his hand when he's home."

"As long as his homework is done and his grades remain high, I guess there are worse habits he could have."

"No doubt."

"All in all, we've been blessed. They work my nerves sometimes, but they're good kids."

"Things might change up during their teenage years, but I'm keeping my fingers crossed."

Randall kissed the top of her head. "All done." He eased out of bed.

She rolled her head and lifted her shoulders, grateful that she indeed did feel more relaxed. Watching Randall padding naked to the bathroom, she asked him, "Where are you going?"

"Into D.C. I have a meeting. Don't worry. I'll only be there a few hours."

"Please make sure that you're back by seven thirty. I'd like us all to have dinner together tonight. You know, like one big happy family."

"That sounds doable. I might even be able to pick Aaron up after his practice. I'll call and let you know."

Sherri slid on a robe and left the room, humming as she went to the kitchen in search of some much needed java. Snatches from the conversation with her friend Renee continued to play in her head, especially the part that reminded her of what she had—a good man.

She smiled as she reached for the coffee, thankful for the blessing that showered upstairs. *Yes, I've got a good one,* she mused, thinking of Randall. *That I do.*

CHAPTER 16

There wasn't anything like April in Washington, D.C.—air fresh from recent rains, leaves green from the same, sun shining brightly, and cherry blossoms everywhere. Randall inhaled deeply as he neared the corner of Sixteenth and P Streets to enter the administration building for the Carnegie Institution for Science. He was relaxed and ready to begin this new week. It was going to be great for many reasons, not the least of which was the fact that Randall would not be traveling. He'd be in town all week. He'd already planned an individual play-date with each of his children (which for Albany would take place in a shopping mall), and then on Friday looked forward to a date with his wife. The conference had been amazing, his company had received great exposure, he'd returned home to a family he loved more than life itself, and after talking to the doctors tending Mom Elaine, even felt that situation becoming more promising. Yes, life was good. He entered the building, remembering a time when being alive wasn't so great. Like when he lost his father. Then he thought of Sherri and his children and was brought back around to the blessings.

Life was good, and getting better.

He walked down the halls of a place that over the past ten

years had been like a second home. The Carnegie Institute for Science, an organization founded in 1902 and dedicated to scientific research, was where one of Randall's mentors had worked for years. After college and before founding his own company, Randall spent a couple years at this institute both interning with and shadowing his mentor, and working part-time for CASE, the Carnegie Academy for Science Education, specifically their First Light program, designed to encourage interest in science among D.C.'s schoolchildren. He learned a great deal from this patient teacher. Their discipline of choice differed—his mentor's focus was global ecology while Randall focused on plant molecular biology—but the basic facets of research remained the same. And while the biology arm of the institute was actually operated out of Stanford University in California, Randall came here often, as he had today, for phone- and video conferences, to take advantage of their well-stocked library and to tap the learned minds of the scientists who occupied its rooms.

Randall looked at his watch. *Fifteen minutes until my meeting. Cool.* Instead of turning right, he kept straight and headed for the library. Over the weekend, he'd remembered a book he once read here on interactive biology. As he recalled, there was a chapter that included a more in-depth study of plant cell anatomy, which broke down in a simple way how the knowledge of the similarities among plant cells and human cells, both being eukaryotes and having the same organelles, could be effective in finding better ways to use plants as medical cures. He specifically thought there might be something within the pages to jolt his mind into an awareness of how what he'd developed with plant stem cells could be used to affect the anomalies occurring in his mother-in-law's brain.

He entered the library, turned the corner . . . and there she was.

"Jacqueline?"

She smiled before lifting her head from the large volume she was perusing. "Hello, Randall."

It's a crying shame for a woman to look that good and still be single. Her conservative black pantsuit with a plain, cream-colored shell that reached her neckline and showed nothing, should not have been a turn-on. But Randall had worked out with Jacqueline and knew what lay beyond the suit jacket. Putting her hair in a ponytail accented her almond eyes, sleek nose, and pouty mouth, and made her look all of nineteen.. *And gorgeous.* Yes, he was married, but he was still a man. Thinking of his wife made him think of her brother. Jacqueline was just the type of eye candy he'd go for. Randall made a note to ask Sherri about his current relationship status. Randall agreed with Sherri that at thirty-two it was time for Nathan to seriously think about settling down.

Shaking off his initial surprise, he walked toward her with hand outstretched. "I guess I shouldn't be surprised to see you here. You did say you'd be in this area for, what, a couple months or so?"

"At least," she answered, playfully slapping away his hand in favor of a nice, warm hug, one that lasted longer than some would find socially acceptable when said hug involved a beautiful single woman and a happily married man. Randall pulled back. "It's good to see you," she continued, nonplussed. "Though I'm surprised."

Randall walked over to the towering bookshelf. "Why's that?"

"It seems you're always traveling. I just assumed you'd be out of town."

"No. I have the good fortune of not having to leave again until next Tuesday."

"Headed to New York and the science symposium?"

"You're going to be there too?"

"Yes. For the next few months, if there's a conference between here and Timbuktu that deals with science or medical technology, I'll more than likely be there."

"What are you here to research?"

"I've got an appointment with one of the teachers at First Light. I'm doing the prep work for an article I'll be submitting for the fall issue, on how programs like this impact the futures of those living in urban neighborhoods."

"That's excellent. I worked with that program for a few years and still contribute when I can. In grade school I had an excellent science teacher, who helped me a lot, but it is exactly the type of program that would have saved me as a child. I know the history, and am still in touch with some of the students who passed through here. So if you need additional material for your article, let me know if I can help you."

"That's a generous offer, Randall. I fully plan to take you up on it."

"You do that." Randall ignored her sexy smile, feeling that he was probably mistaking friendly for flirtation. They'd spent time together in LA. But there's no way a woman like Jacqueline would seriously be interested in a man like him. Sure, he was successful and financially secure. And when he put his mind to it, he cleaned up pretty well. Still, a woman like her could get anyone she wanted: professional sports player, influential politician, crooner topping the adult contemporary music charts. He turned away from her to peruse the aisles. "When we meet to talk about that, I'd also like to tell you about the Atwater Achievement Module, a science and math program for inner city kids."

"I can't wait to see you again and . . . hear all about it."

"Good to see you again, Jacqueline. Take care."

She watched him walk away—slyly, surreptitiously—from beneath her long lashes. He'd tried to hide his attraction to her, but she'd felt it anyway. It wasn't hard to detect since she'd been doing the very same thing. He'd turned the corner, but his scent lingered: that musky odor with a hint of spice and a touch of something citrusy. Memories of the last time she smelled that scent made her core clench: when he lay there, hot and sweaty, imprinting his name on her heart with his "equipment."

The next time you're with him, finding out whether or not he's married should be the first question asked. Jacqueline placed the book she'd been perusing on the table and headed for the aisle. Her happy mood faltered against the possibility that he might actually have a wife. Then, remembering the man who had wined and dined her in Los Angeles, she let go of every worry, every doubt. She'd been with a man who unequivocally showed her what real admiration looked like and how true passion felt. Before *meeting* him, she'd felt that someone *like* him was the perfect man for her. After their week together in the City of Angels, she was sure of it.

Looking left and right to make sure no one else had entered their area, she turned the corner. It was as though he'd been waiting for her.

"Randall."

Her eyes met his and never wavered as she walked purposefully toward him. She reached him and, wearing four-inch Michael Kors pumps, looked him directly in the eyes. She stepped closer. Their bodies touched. Eyes still open, she leaned in for the kiss, that inevitable meeting of flesh that had plagued her thoughts and hopes and dreams since boarding the plane at LAX. He opened his mouth to concoct a lame objection, but Jacqueline wasn't having it. She used the opportunity to plunge her tongue inside his warm cavity, slid her arms around his neck, and pressed herself against him.

"Jacqueline," he said, panting after several moments of deep, wet kisses. "I can't. People know me and . . . you might think this is a big city, but gossip travels like it's a small town."

"I can't help it, Randall." She allowed her hand to slide down the front of his shirt to the burgeoning bulge just below his belt. "I want you so badly."

"I want you too."

She felt his breath inside her ear and shivered, heard his words and became moist in hidden places. There had never been a moment in her life when she'd gotten this hot with a single kiss, a gentle touch. She was on fire, she wanted to tear off his clothes and mount him on the carpet. But the door opened and someone entered the library.

Sanity prevailed.

"Jacqueline?"

"Uh, yes?"

"You had a question?"

"Sorry, I got distracted." She watched the culprit who'd ruined their moment walk down the opposite aisle. "When will you be arriving in New York?" She'd stepped back a respectable distance from Randall, but her voice remained low.

"Leaving on Tuesday," he repeated.

"Do you like Broadway?"

"Every now and then, Sherri and I love to take in a show. But this trip is all business."

"Sherri?"

"Yes. My wife."

"So you are married."

"I thought I told you that in LA, when we talked about my children."

"You may have. I don't remember." Jacqueline worked hard to keep her voice light. Now was not the time for an ugly confrontation, and her emotions were running all over the place.

He looked at his watch. "It's time for my meeting. I've got to go." He reached out and squeezed her upper arm. "Enjoy your stay in D.C."

She squelched her urge to kiss him again and let a simple nod suffice. Similarly, she forced herself not to stare after him like a love-struck puppy. Someone could be watching, and considering what she'd just learned it would not be beneficial for anything to get out about them.

Kris's intuition had been accurate. Randall Atwater had a wife. She tamped down the urge to cry, or scream, or rant and rave. She forced away all emotion and forced herself to be calm as she returned to get the books she'd been perusing, checked them out, and left the library. *Randall is married. But he couldn't love her. That's not possible, considering the way he made love to me.* It hadn't just been with his body, but with his soul.

As she drove the short distance to where she was staying, a myriad of thoughts fought for dominance. One direction said that she should curse him out, slap his face, end the madness and cut her losses. But just the thought of doing so put a hole in her heart. A different take would be to follow his lead, see what happened, and let the chips fall where they may.

By the time she'd reached Phillip's row house, Jacqueline had made a decision. Right or wrong, there was something between her and Randall. She wanted to see where that something led. She wasn't ready to run away because of what very well could be a marriage of convenience. No, she needed to know more about the status of their marriage, and what she could do to hasten its end. The more knowledge she had, the better. Fortunately for her, gathering information was something in which she excelled. It's what made her such a great writer.

She'd just ended a call to Phillip's friend, Marco, the computer whiz, when Kaitlyn called. Minutes into a much needed chick chat, where she learned that Rosie had dyed her red hair brunette, Nicole had met a guy from Match.com, and Molly was pregnant, Jacqueline felt better. With the minor marriage detail omitted, she told Kaitlyn about Randall. As expected, Kaitlyn was thrilled that she'd met someone, and encouraged her to pursue this new love possibility. Jacqueline assured her that she would. Now, even more than before, she couldn't wait to see her lover, Randall, in New York.

★   ★   ★

So much blood. Everywhere. On the walls, on the floor, on her. She swallowed a scream, pushed it back down with the back of her hand, along with the evening meal that threatened an unwanted reappearance. Later, the scene would be described as ghastly, horrific. She would agree. Whoever did this had to be the most depraved of human beings, psychotic, narcissistic, mad.

Jacqueline stepped over puddles of blood and busted glass, stopping in front of a mirror. What she saw barely registered through the shock: clothes torn, hair matted, eyes glazed. Looking down, she saw long scratches along her arm, and blood oozing from jagged, broken skin.

Gasping, she looked down farther. How did a long pair of stainless steel scissors end up in her hand?

She looked up and asked the woman in the mirror: *What have you done?*

CHAPTER 17

The week had passed quickly. Randall hadn't left town, but he'd been busy every night of the week. There was no complaining on his end, however. Between a plethora of voice mails filled with media and PR requests, the dinner meeting with his employees at PSI, separate date nights with his daughter and son, and yesterday's feeble yet valiant attempt at eighteen respectable holes with his neighbor, it had been time well spent. But he'd saved the best for last. Tonight, a Friday-night date with his one and only. They'd decided to go out: dinner at Tosca's, an intimate concert featuring Esperanza Spalding, and a quiet night for two at the Four Seasons. Weeks like this continued to remind him of how blessed he was and, as attracted as any living man would be to her, why someone like Jacqueline would never be able to hold a candle to someone like the woman he married. The sight before him caused his brow to crease. Traffic was brutal and he couldn't wait to get home. The sooner he arrived there, showered, dressed, and packed an overnight bag, the sooner he could start the date with his girl.

He'd just turned his satellite radio from news to sports when his phone rang. "Hey, man. What's up?" he asked after reading the caller ID.

"Nothing much," James answered. "Just sitting here chilling, waiting for Debbie and Montell to get home."

"You're home already?"

"Yes, a surgery got canceled."

"I see. Big plans for the weekend?"

"We're going to a play tonight."

Randall hid a laugh behind a cough. "You?"

"Man, don't get me started, and Montell is more annoyed than I am. But the wife has insisted; some nonsense about family bonding and cultural expansion and wanting to spend time with her men. I told her, 'Heck, we could do that on the basketball court in the backyard!' "

"You really said that?" Randall's voice was tinged with humor.

"Yeah, and got bopped upside the head for my honesty. Tomorrow will be cool, though. We're driving into Manhattan for a day at some swanky spa."

"James, married life has turned you into a metro man."

"Hey, don't knock a mud bath till you try it." The men laughed. "What about you?"

"Date night. Sherri and I are going to hit the town and then spend the night at a hotel."

"Uh-oh. Watch it, player!"

"Got to keep those home fires going, you know how we do it!"

"For sure."

"Speaking of fire . . . guess who I saw today?"

"Who?"

"Jacqueline."

"As in Tate, the writer?"

"The one and only."

"Where'd you see her?"

Randall told him about that as well as the fact that she'd be based in D.C. for several months and would be attending several medical- and science-related conferences. "She'll be in New York next week," he finished.

James whistled. "Ran, you're a better man than me. I love Debbie with all my heart, but there is no way I'd be able to be close to that brown sugar and not try to get a taste." Randall remained quiet. "I don't see how you were able to have dinner with her and not try to sample some of her dessert, know what I mean?"

"Look, bro. I need to run. This is Sherri calling."

"All right, then. See you next week."

Randall thought about what his friend and colleague had said as he switched over the call. When it came to Jacqueline and the temptation to "taste her sugar," he knew exactly what James meant.

Sherri sang along with Janet Jackson as she shimmied into her brand-new dress. She was happy to be wearing the outfit she'd bought on a whim, and thankful that after only a week of exercising, eating smaller portions for dinner, and cutting out all snacks, she'd lost a pound or two. The formfitting dress, a blend of poly silk and elastane, hugged her curves; its bold geometric print, with a splash of flowers across her midsection, had a slenderizing effect and emphasized her hips and chest. She slipped into a pair of red Valentino scalloped pumps and immediately added three inches to her height, further helped by her new, spiky haircut. She loved her wash-muss-and-go look, but Randall preferred her hair long and had more than once asked her to grow it back out. While fluffing her locks, she gave the thought consideration and concluded, *Maybe I will.*

By the time she did one last turn in the mirror, "That's the Way Love Goes" had given way to another 90s smash hit, H-Town's "Knockin' Da Boots." She smiled, remembering how she and her then best friend used to sing this song like they knew what those boys were singing about. They didn't. Both were virgins. Didn't matter. They'd hole up in one of their bedrooms—music blasting if the parents weren't home—and sing as hard as someone with a recording contract. They fought over Shazam, one of the group's members, and which one he'd want if they met in person, but when it came to their high school sweethearts, the lines were distinct and clear. Her friend's heartthrob was Damien, a boy at her church with hazel eyes. He could sing like an angel, but had a little devil inside as evidenced nine months after he'd gotten his freak on in the church basement with another classmate. Sherri was gaga over Luke a senior when she was a sophomore, a football running-back standout who didn't give her the time of day. When she finally knocked boots, it wasn't with him but with Victor, a guy who'd come to Chicago from Alabama the summer after high school graduation. His dark skin, tall frame, and striking white teeth—combined with that Southern charm and Southern drawl—charmed her right out of her panties. They were deeply in love for a whole nine months, until both discovered that they weren't cut out for the long-distance relationship that Sherri's attending Howard University required. Emotionally, the breakup was brutal. Sherri didn't seriously date again until meeting Randall during her sophomore year. Quiet and studious, handsome in an understated kind of way, and very different from the gregarious and outgoing Robert or swagger-savvy Victor, Sherri knew almost immediately that Randall was the one for her. But man, oh man, how men like Robert and Victor had once made her heart go boom.

Somebody rockin' knockin' for real!

The sound of her cell phone brought her back from the walk down memory lane. She placed the call on speaker as she walked over to where her jewelry was stored. "Hey, Mom!"

"Hello, Sherri. Sounds like I caught you in a good mood."

"I am. Randall and I are going out tonight."

"Ooh! I like the sound of that. What's the occasion?"

"Nothing special. Just wanting to put some 'us' time inside of our busy lives."

"That's very smart, Daughter. Marriage takes work, but the payoff is worth it. Your daddy was my best friend. I miss him every day."

"I'm sure you do, Mom. I miss him too." She paused, thinking that it had only been three short years since her father had died unexpectedly at the age of sixty-four. They spent the next several minutes talking about him before Sherri got around to what she always did when talking to Elaine, her mom's health. "How are you feeling today, Mom? You sound good."

"Today was a good day, baby. Your mom feels like her old self."

"Good. How's Ms. Riley?"

"Neighbor is clucking over me like an old hen. Between her and Lady, I can't get any peace. I love her to death."

"Both she and Lady love you, too. I can't believe that dog is still alive. In human years it's what, eighty years old?"

"Near 'bout, and going blind. She's my constant and loyal companion, that dog. I wouldn't have survived Clarence's death without her."

"Give her a hug for me. I'll call you tomorrow."

Sherri finished the call and donned her jewelry. She walked out of the dressing room just as Randall stepped through the door to their suite.

"Dayum, woman!" Randall stepped back, placed his hands in his pockets, and eyed her appreciatively. Then he strolled over. "My name is Randall," he said, his tone low, his eyes still perusing every inch of her body. "What's your name?"

"Sherri," she shyly answered.

"Well, listen here, Sherri, as sweet as a berry." Sherri chuckled and batted her eyes. "Is there any way that I can get those seven digits, you know, call you up, take you out?"

"I'll give you my phone number," she said in a soft voice.

"But you don't have to wait and call me. You can take me out tonight."

"As fine as you're looking? I'd say let's skip the restaurant and the concert, head straight to the hotel and order room service!"

"As long as it took me to pull on this Spanx? Trust and believe I'm getting ready to show this body off!"

They laughed, hugged, and shared a kiss.

Randall began removing his shirt as he headed to the master bath. "I just need a quick shower," he said over his shoulder. "And time to ponder the exceptionality of your anatomy."

"You nut!" Sherri laughed at one of Randall's corny, oft-used lines. The first time she'd heard it was almost fifteen years ago.

It worked then. It worked now. This—she had a feeling—was going to be a very good night.

CHAPTER 18

Just over an hour later, Randall and Sherri enjoyed appetizers at their favorite Italian eatery.

"You always order that!" Sherri teased after listening to Randall request the polenta-crusted crab appetizer with broccoli rabe.

"It's always good," he countered.

"Let's see." Sherri scanned the menu. "I think I'll try the *cavoletti verdi.*"

They handed the waiter their menus.

"Pretty fancy name for a plate full of greens," Randall said.

"Maybe, but it sounds good, especially with the kale being organic. I'm trying to buy most of our food that way."

The sommelier delivered and poured their sparkling wine. "To what should we toast?" Randall asked once he'd left.

"To an amazing man," Sherri said, leaning in for a kiss.

"To an amazing woman," Randall replied, "and the awesome night we're going to spend together."

Love shone in their eyes as they enjoyed a sip. With her glass still upraised, Sherri's expression changed ever so slightly.

But an astute Randall recognized it. "What is it?"

"Not what . . . who. Don't look now," Sherri continued,

"but one of the most beautiful women I've ever seen in my life just entered the restaurant on the arm of an equally amazing-looking man."

"You say something like that and expect me not to turn around?"

Sherri watched as the restaurant manager approached the couple. "They must be celebrities. The manager just joined the maître d' to greet them."

Randall couldn't resist. He turned around and locked eyes with the vivacious vixen. "Oh wow," he mumbled.

"What?" Sherri looked from her husband to the woman and back again. The woman who was still staring in the direction of their table. "You know her?"

Randall nodded. "Remember the freelance writer in LA I told you about? The one who interviewed me for *Science Today*?"

"*That's* her?" Another nod from Randall. "No wonder when I called her attractive you corrected me. She is beautiful, as you said. Stunning, even. Gorgeous." Randall took another sip of wine. "Who's that guy she's with?"

"I don't know. Her boyfriend, I'd imagine."

Sherri eyed them as she too took a taste of bubbly. "Yes, you're probably right. She looks like a black Barbie and he could be her olive-skinned Ken." She continued watching the couple chat with the manager. "What do you think he is? Hispanic, Middle Eastern, dark-skinned white boy? I can't tell."

"And you think I can? As comfortable as I am in my sexuality, you won't find me turning around and staring a brother down so as to ascertain his heritage."

"Looks like you won't have to."

"Why do you say that?"

Another voice answered that question for him.

"Randall," Jacqueline said as she reached the table, "I thought that was you."

He stood and extended his hand. "Hello, Jacqueline. It's a small world. I'd like to introduce you to my wife, Sherri."

Jacqueline turned toward a bemused Sherri and stretched out her hand. They shook. "It's a pleasure to meet you."

Sherri nodded. "Likewise."

"This is Phillip," Jacqueline said, turning to the very handsome man beside her. "He's the dear friend who's been gracious enough to host my extended stay in D.C., and the one I'm helping with the website."

Introductions were made.

"Where are you two from?" Sherri asked.

"Canada," they answered simultaneously.

Phillip continued. "My father is from Romania originally. He saw my mother, a woman of color, and it was love at first sight."

"Are you a writer also?"

"No, Sherri," Phillip said with a laugh. "Not unless you count my rants on Facebook. My degree is in hanging out and having fun."

Jacqueline laughed. Sherri didn't get the humor. And Randall was as quiet as a sleeping church mouse.

"He's being modest," Jacqueline offered. "He's a business and branding genius, as his website will prove."

"How's that going?" Randall finally rejoined the conversation.

"Fine," Phillip replied.

"You're very pretty, Jacqueline," Sherri said, after having taken in her large diamond studs, formfitting dress (which looked quite different on a tall frame boasting about one finger snap of body fat), high-heeled sandals, flawless skin and makeup, and bone-straight hair that reached mid-back. "You look more like a model than a writer."

Jacqueline dismissed the compliment with a wave of her hand. "It's all my parents, I'm afraid. I didn't do a thing."

Sherri's brow rose. There was no way someone could be

that beautiful naturally. If those boobs weren't fake and that hair wasn't a weave, she'd pay for lying. But looking over and detecting Randall's discomfort, she chose to let it go. She also decided to ignore the pangs of jealousy that rose up unbidden, or how the slimming apparel she was wearing suddenly seemed smaller, cutting her stomach in two and taking away her air.

Thankfully, their appetizers arrived. "That looks delicious," Phillip said, placing his hand around Jacqueline's waist. "We'd best be moving along so that you two can enjoy your meal."

There were several seconds of silence after Jacqueline and Phillip made their exit from the area. Randall seasoned his food, and though her appetite was nowhere near what it had been, Sherri tasted the salad that included oranges, radishes, and burrata cheese.

"That was interesting," she said at last.

Randall looked over. "How's your salad?"

"The salad is delicious. Your friend is interesting."

"She's an associate," he corrected. "Not a friend."

"Thank God for her fine-ass date is all I'm saying. If she weren't hanging on his arm, and he wasn't all over her, I'd be worried."

Randall reached across the table and took Sherri's hand. "You have nothing to be worried about, ever. No matter how attractive some other woman may be, they'll never replace you."

"I'd assumed she was from LA. You didn't mention that she lived here."

"Actually, she's from Canada. She's only here temporarily, freelancing for a magazine and, like she said, helping that guy with his website."

"Sounds like you learned quite a bit about her. Who was interviewing who?"

"Just small talk shared through the week," Randall replied, with a shrug.

After that comment, the conversation shifted away from freelance writers to fun ideas for their summer vacation. Sherri wanted to go to the Caribbean, a place she'd dreamed of seeing but had never visited, while Randall thought it might be nice to let the kids decide. Through main courses of risotto with shrimp and roasted halibut, they acted like newlyweds, feeding each other bites from their plates and remembering lines from some of their new-jack-swing musical favorites. They passed on dessert, enjoyed the concert, and then arrived at the Four Seasons, where they performed creative feats with the warm chocolate sauce that accompanied the dessert delivered by room service. By the time Sherri and Randall entered their second round of lovemaking, thoughts of Jacqueline, or any other woman, were the last things on her mind.

Not so with the woman across town. Randall consumed almost every thought, except for when she was thinking of his wife. Having seen Sherri, she was more confident than ever that there was nothing going on in his marriage that was close to the intimacy they'd shared. The plans she was getting ready to execute would no doubt prove this to be fact. Having Randall all to herself was just a matter of time.

"Thanks, Phillip. I appreciate you letting me crash here, and for being my escort around town."

"No worries, kiddo. That's what friends are for."

"Speaking of, are you meeting up with Marco?"

"Heading over to his place to spend the night. He said you guys got everything set up."

"We did, in record time."

"When it comes to computers, he's the best. I'm going to run up and grab clean clothes. Don't wait up," he said with a wink, then bounded up the stairs.

Jacqueline followed him, entering the room at the other end of the hallway. Kris assailed her as soon as she shut the door. Ever since Jacqueline had told her about Sherri and her unwillingness to let go of Randall, her friend had been on edge. "Well? How was your evening out on the town? Do anything interesting, like meet a tall, dark, handsome, and unmarried man?"

"I did see someone who almost met those criteria," Jacqueline replied. "I guess three out of four of those traits isn't bad."

"Well, don't leave me hanging. Tell me about him."

"His name is Randall."

"Huh?"

"Kris, I couldn't believe it. Phillip and I went to dinner and there sat Randall . . . and his wife!"

"No!"

"Yes."

"Shut. Up!"

"True story."

Kris plopped on the bed, her face a mask of intrigue. "Oh my God, Jack. What did you do?"

"What any well-mannered person in that situation would. I went over and introduced myself."

"Damn, you've got balls."

"Phillip being with me made it easy. Of course she assumed that we were together." Jacqueline joined Kris on the bed. "In a way I feel sorry for her, probably married to a man before he was established professionally, only to find herself now with a stranger totally out of her league."

"Is that what you picked up?" Kris asked. "That they are an unhappy couple?"

"Oh, she seemed quite happy to be there. I could tell she'd worked hard to look the part of a professional's wife."

"Is she pretty?"

"Yes, in a down-home, soccer-mom sort of way. But she doesn't look like the type of woman that someone like Randall should have by his side."

Kris's eyes held a hint of mischief. "With his myriad of accomplishments and impressive social status, why, pray tell, do you think that any woman would be good enough for Mr.

Randall Atwater? Is there anyone who can breathe his rarified air?"

Jacqueline simply took a long, deep breath and exhaled.

"Okay, I get your point. But I'm still worried, Jack. You've been through so much pain and heartache in your life. Just be careful."

"Shit!" Jacqueline put her head in her hands. "Why are the good ones always married?"

"There are plenty of good men out there, Jacqueline, most of whom would date you in a heartbeat."

"You're probably right." Tears filled Jacqueline's eyes. "But it's too late for any of them, Kris. I know that I just met Randall. I know this is crazy. I know that I probably shouldn't do this. But he's who I want."

CHAPTER 19

Randall buckled his seat belt and then leaned against the roomy first-class seat. It was a good thing the past week and weekend had been relaxing, because his Monday had started out with a bang. His publicist had called with an opportunity for him to appear on *News Today*. Only thing was, he was replacing a scientist on a panel that would be interviewed live for a six p.m. show, giving them only two hours to scramble on a plane and make it to Atlanta in time for the show. He'd raced to the airport where a car service awaited, did the segment, and then headed straight back to Hartsfield-Jackson Atlanta International, where he barely made it onto the eight-thirty flight. Because he'd had to fly into Baltimore, he didn't arrive home until almost midnight. By the time he'd spent a little time with Albany, who was up cramming for a test, and packed his bags for New York, it was one thirty in the morning. Sherri had been fast asleep. The next morning, Sherri had gotten up early to chat with her mom, an early riser. Randall spent his usual forty-five minutes on the treadmill. They'd been able to share a quick conversation over the kitchen island as she'd quickly scanned and signed a release for Aaron to go on a field trip and Randall had gulped down a protein superfoods drink.

In other words, it was a typically chaotic morning in the Atwater home. Now, able to take a few sips from the cup of coffee he'd been given before the plane took off, he could relax for the first time in the past twenty-four hours.

New York City. The flight that had lasted little more than an hour had been uneventful. Now he sat in the back of a taxi taking in the sights of a city he'd always found a bit intimidating. Funny, since he'd grown up in a metropolitan area. During his childhood and even now, D.C. was sometimes a challenging city to navigate. But New York? It was a fascinating city, but for this conservative, contemplative brother, it was almost too much.

Ping.

Randall looked down at his iPhone. An incoming message. He tapped the message screen and didn't recognize the number attached to the text. He tapped the screen again.

Good morning, Dr. It's Jacqueline. Called last week. I want to include PSI in the piece I'm writing for Science Today. When will you arrive in NY? Maybe we can meet, and also set up a time to interview you at your company's offices. Let me know if you're interested, and what days/times work for you. J.

While gazing at the tall buildings and watching the people in midtown Manhattan scurry like ants, he thought of the freelance writer who from the second he saw her seemed to have invaded his world. There was no denying her intelligence, or beauty. He thought back to the dinner on Friday night, and her meeting Sherri. His shyness rose up when he saw her outside of a hotel or work environment, looking extraordinarily stunning in her tight mini and super-high heels. In LA, she'd been sexy in a conservative kind of way. Even when they'd met for dinner in LA, and enjoyed the ambiance of Inn of the Seventh Ray, her dress was understated. At Tasco's he'd seen what he felt was her true public persona, the head-turning vixen she was when not on the clock.

Randall liked just about everything about Jacqueline. There were many male colleagues with whom to discuss his work but few females to engage. Not only was she beautiful and intelligent, but she was funny too. *I'm glad Sherri met her,* he thought as he tapped the screen to reply to her text message. *That way it doesn't appear as though, when it comes to her, I have anything to hide.* His thumb moved quickly across the pad.

HELLO, JACQUELINE. BUSY PAST WEEK. EN ROUTE TO THE TOWERS NOW. YES, LET'S MEET. I'LL CALL LATER. RANDALL.

"Ran, my man!"

He looked back from the car he'd just exited in front of The Towers of the Waldorf Astoria, and smiled. "Perfect timing, huh?" He tipped the driver, passed his luggage to the bellman, and walked back to where James was getting out of a taxi. They shook hands. "I thought you were going to check in last night, take advantage of some quiet time to finish your research paper."

"Had a change in plans, bro. My mother-in-law unexpectedly came into town."

"Ah," Randall answered in a tone that suggested that no more needed to be said.

"I saw the segment last night on *News Today.* Good job."

"Thanks, man."

"Not bad at all from a dude who grew up in the sho'nuff hood."

"Everybody wasn't lucky enough to grow up like the Huxtables."

"We weren't quite like that," James countered.

"No? Physician father, attorney mother, four perfect children, the white picket fence. What would you call it?"

"Someone else's family."

"Ha!"

The men checked into their rooms and decided to meet for a drink in the hotel's Peacock Alley before joining two of their colleagues for a dinner meeting, which would also be at the hotel.

"This is beautiful," James said as he stretched his long legs in front of him and nursed a tumbler of scotch. "I've always loved New York. Fell in love the first time I came here, a wide-eyed dude fresh out of the Iowa cornfields. Lived on Long Island for ten years and am still as enthralled as when I first arrived."

"It is a special city," Randall agreed as he sipped his Arnold Palmer. "I know this is your home turf, but maybe Sherri and I can just come here for the four of us to hang out."

"I wouldn't mind that. Debbie and I rarely get into Manhattan unless we've been invited to some event or are entertaining guests. Showing you two around would be fun.

"Randall, how is your mother-in-law, man?"

"She's doing better. The doctors are still trying to come up with a proper diagnosis so that they can better know how to treat it." He told James about Miss Elaine's most recent episode, when she left food cooking on the stove without realizing it. "Sherri is in regular contact with Mom Elaine's neighbor, Ms. Riley. But she's understandably very concerned. We're looking into hiring a live-in assistant to help take care of her."

"Sounds like a good idea." James took a moment to look out on the magnificent view from this location, including the popular Chrysler Building landmark. "I know you've been working on a cure, and that's been causing you some aggravation. Sherri knows you're trying, Ran, and that if there is any way possible for you to help her mother, you'll be on it."

"It's very frustrating," Randall admitted. "I've never liked feeling helpless and I definitely don't like seeing my wife in such pain. She and Mom Elaine are very close. It will be the end of Sherri's world to lose her."

"It may feel like it for a while," James said. "But she'll still have the kids. And you."

Randall paused to read a message that came through on his phone. His smile was evidence that whatever he'd read had lifted his mood.

"Good news?" James asked.

Randall looked to see who was around him, then leaned forward to speak to his friend. "There's something I need to tell you, James. It needs to stay between us."

"Okay."

"It's very important that you not leak so much as a word to anyone, especially Debbie. I can't take a chance on Sherri finding out."

James frowned. "Am I going to find it difficult to keep this secret?"

"Perhaps. But it's driving me crazy not to tell somebody. Because you're like a brother—I know I can tell you. But believe me, you are the only one who can know."

CHAPTER 20

Jacqueline tapped her finger against her chin, trying to decide between the little black dress that she'd just purchased at Nordstrom and a Calvin Klein striped maxi that fit her body like a glove and had a peekaboo slit up the side. Thinking of who she'd be keeping company with this evening, she finally decided on the black dress.

Thirty minutes later she walked into the restaurant, purposely late. She wanted to make an entrance, for Randall to be waiting when she arrived so that he could get the full effect. She wore black except for a colorful necklace and earrings made from various chunky stones paired with a wide bracelet. Her hair was pulled back into a ponytail that cascaded from the top of her head. Her heels were five-inch-high Louboutins. When she reached him and spoke, his eyes spoke volumes. His reaction did not disappoint.

"Wow, Jacqueline," he said as his eyes drank their fill. "You look fantastic!"

"Thank you," she gushed, sitting in the chair next to him. "Sorry I'm late. I got caught up on a call with the office."

"It's okay. Gave me a moment to soak up the theater district atmosphere." Randall looked behind her. "Where's the young man from Columbia University, the one who you said would be joining us."

"Evan isn't here?"

"No."

Jacqueline sat down in the seat next to Randall. "Let me text him." She did, and then placed the phone into her small clutch. "Randall." She placed a light hand on his forearm, noting the softness of the tailored black jacket he'd paired with a white shirt and jeans. "Thank you so much for agreeing to join me and see the show. Phillip was beside himself for having to renege on coming up to spend the weekend with me, especially knowing I'd scored first-row seats."

"What happened?"

"Give me a moment." Jacqueline turned to get the bartender's attention. He walked over right away. "A white wine spritzer, please," she requested. She turned to Randall. "You?"

Randall held up his near-full glass of club soda with a lime twist. "I'm good."

"Okay." Jacqueline fixed him with a dazzling smile even as she crossed her legs and not-so-innocently exposed a good deal of thigh. "Where were we?"

"I was asking about your boyfriend, and what he's working on that kept him from spending time with someone as lovely as you."

She lowered her eyes. "I appreciate the compliment. Regarding Phillip, one of the investors for his website came into town. And he's not my boyfriend, remember. We're just really good friends."

"From the way he looks at you, he wants to be much more than that." Jacqueline's response was a simple, coy smile. "What is his occupation, the one that requires a degree in partying and having a good time?"

Jacqueline laughed easily. "Sorry that you remember that comment. He's a dear but can be so quirky at times." The waiter brought her drink, which she promptly held up. "To *Les*

Misérables." Clinking glasses, she continued, "Have you ever seen it?"

Randall shook his head. "The last Broadway play I saw was with Sherri and the kids, three or four years ago. I loved it though: *The Lion King*."

"That's one of my favorites! I love *Les Misérables* as well. It's a very different type of play."

"Oh, you've seen it before."

"Once. A traveling cast came through Toronto. I loved it and said if I ever had the chance to see it on Broadway, I would."

Randall checked his watch. "It's almost time for the show to start. Has Evan texted you back?"

Jacqueline pulled out her phone. "He can't make it," she said, after checking the screen. "Sorry, doctor, but it looks like it's just the two of us."

"What's that on your phone?" He pointed to a silver disc on the back of her cell case.

"It's something that someone who uses the phone as much as you do needs. It's a radiation shield that lessens potential brain damage from constant cell phone use. I'm surprised that you don't have one already."

"That's because the results of studies about this potential hazard have been mixed."

"Still, better safe than sorry, right? In fact," Jacqueline reached for her purse. "I happen to have an extra one; I get them free from a friend of Phillip's who works in the electronics industry. In fact, I have two. Give one to your wife." She passed them over.

Randall studied the thin, lightweight device, about the size of a dime. "I guess it wouldn't hurt to try it. Thanks, Jacqueline."

"You're welcome. Hand me your phone and I'll show you how to attach it."

They continued conversing while finishing their drinks

and during the short walk to the Imperial Theatre on West Forty-Fifth. Not once did they talk about the conference, science, or PSI. Jacqueline found Randall fascinating, and he felt she was a breath of fresh air. He'd forgotten all about Phillip and finding out what Jacqueline's boyfriend did for a living. By the time he'd joined the lead character, Jean Valjean, on his journey through legal struggles, grace, and the search for redemption, Randall wasn't thinking about much of anything save the play he'd just experienced and the woman beside him—including the message from Sherri he'd listened to during the intermission and his promise to call her as soon as the show ended.

"Thanks again," Randall said as they stood waiting for a taxi. "I didn't know what to expect, didn't think that I'd enjoy it, based on the title. But there was such depth to the story. It was really good."

"So I take it you didn't see the film adaptation with Hugh Jackman and Anne Hathaway?"

"I'm afraid not."

"It's out on DVD. I think you'd enjoy it as well." She looked up and down Forty-Fifth Street, still bustling at almost eleven p.m. "This city is so exciting," she exclaimed.

"I agree."

"I'm not ready to go back to the hotel. Join me for a light snack?"

Randall looked at his watch.

"Please!" Jacqueline inched closer. "I won't keep us out past midnight . . . promise."

"I could use a bite," Randall agreed.

"Perfect."

Shortly after the theater manager made his recommendation, the two settled into a table at B. Smith's on New York's popular Restaurant Row. Jacqueline was excited. As the manager described the restaurant and its iconic owner, she remembered reading about Barbara Smith, the pioneering, transformational lifestyle expert whose home collection was the first by an African-American to be featured at the retailer Bed Bath & Beyond. Now, as she looked around at the stylish décor, she knew that the bedroom was not the only area in which Ms. Smith's tasteful design sense prevailed. She shared all of what she knew with Randall.

He sat back and crossed his arms, a slight smile on his face as he stared at her.

"What?"

"You're a very intriguing woman."

"How so?" She took a dainty sip of water.

"You're brainy enough to hold a fairly in-depth conversation about various sciences. Now you're going on about . . . what was it . . . divets?"

"Duvets," Jacqueline corrected.

"You didn't finish your degree yet are making quite a name for yourself as a freelance writer. And while you clearly could take advantage of wonderful genes and pursue a career as an actor, model, or the like, you're grinding it out in the rather geeky world of science. Your parents must be very proud." He immediately noticed a change in Jacqueline's demeanor. "Did I say something wrong?"

"No," Jacqueline answered with a quick shake of her head. "I'm sure my parents would have been very proud. Had they lived to see me in this moment."

"I'm sorry. They're both . . . gone?" She nodded, her eyes still downcast as she reached for the glass of Riesling that the waiter had earlier set at their table. "If you don't mind my asking, what happened?"

When she looked up, her demeanor had gone from vivacious vixen to vulnerable little girl, and a flash of something else in her eyes that Randall couldn't quite name. "They died in a fire when I was ten years old."

This time it was his turn to reach out and place his hand on Jacqueline's arm. "I'm so sorry for your loss."

She nodded and attempted a smile.

"Thank God I still have my mother, but I lost my dad when I was fourteen," he added.

"Right, you told me during a conversation in Los Angeles."

"He was my hero and a wonderful man. I miss him every day."

"Do you mind my asking what happened to him? I wondered about it in LA but felt it impolite to ask. If you'd rather not . . ."

"No, it's okay. It was a classic case of being in the wrong place at the wrong time." Randall looked up and waved away the waiter. Neither had picked up their menu to decide what they wanted to eat. "My brother and I wanted Oreo cookies. He went to get them. Put on his ever-present Redskins cap, and headed out the door. Told my brother Antoine and I that he'd be right back. Those were the last words I ever heard my dad say."

"What happened?"

"A botched robbery; some young punks trying to hold up the local convenience store. Dad knew the owner, a hardworking Korean who'd been in the neighborhood for as long as I could remember. When he saw what was going on, Dad tried to intervene. Got shot in the back. Funny thing is, my dad died but the store owner, Mr. Koh, lived. To thank our family, he promised to help me and my brother graduate from college. And he did."

"In a sad yet poignant way," Jacqueline whispered, her eyes suspiciously shiny, "your dad helped too."

"I never looked at it that way," Randall said.

"As devastating as it was to lose them, my parents helped me, too. Both had substantial life insurance policies that have allowed me to pretty much do what I want without financial pressure. I left college my senior year to follow a boyfriend to Italy, his home country. He was a biochemistry grad and is responsible for my initial interest in the scientific and medical fields. So when things didn't work out with him and I returned to Toronto needing a job, an opportunity presented itself and I made the best of it."

"Do you have siblings?"

Jacqueline paused a long time before answering. "It's just me."

"I'm glad to know that Phillip is in your life," he answered. "It's not good to try to make it through this world alone."

"I don't only have Phillip to call friend." Jacqueline's smile brightened and she picked up her menu. "Now I have you."

Her heart soared when Randall did nothing to correct her. During dinner, not once did he mention his wife. And the best part? When they arrived back at The Towers of the Waldorf Astoria, Randall spent the entire night in her room, in her bed. How could this be wrong when their love was so perfect?

CHAPTER 21

Sherri turned in the department store mirror so that she could see how the dress fit in the back. The time last week that she'd spent with Randall, culminating in their Friday night date, had reignited something in her, and honestly, seeing the gorgeous woman who'd conducted the LA interview had made her want to step up her game. It was a shame to love a man as much as she did him, even after nearly fifteen years. But Randall had it like that. He'd kept himself in shape, ate properly, and aside from a gray hair or two still looked almost as he had in college. Sherri looked pretty much the same too. She longed to lose the twenty extra pounds that still lingered ten years after giving birth to Aaron, but thought that all in all she didn't look bad for a thirty-seven-year-old sistah with two kids, one who was about to hit her teens. She had a cute, round face, the breast augmentation that she'd had after breast feeding made her girls nice and firm, and her butt—the part of her anatomy that Randall swears made him turn in his bachelor card—was still nicely rounded. *Still, girl, you need to get back in the gym and lose that tummy.* She turned to the side. *I should call Elle and take her up on her offer.* Elle was a woman who lived on their block. They'd met a couple years ago when Elle's dog, in serious heat and on a mission, wanted to do the nasty with their dog Atom. Sherri had suggested that a spaying was in order, and Elle had agreed. The day of the surgery, Sherri went over and delivered gourmet doggy treats. The two women became friendly, and while their schedules didn't allow for a lot of girl time, they enjoyed each other's company. The last time they'd talked, Elle, who'd just had her first child a year prior, suggested they begin a workout regimen. Sherri had promised to think about it. Now, as she left the dressing room and went in search of the department that sold Spanx and other body-trimming apparel, she knew that she needed to do more than think. She needed to act.

Two hours later, Sherri pulled into her driveway. She was glad to see that the nanny had arrived. Blair, a cheery recent college graduate with a degree in child development, who also served as the children's tutor, had decided to take a year off before going for her master's. Next year she'd leave for Massachusetts to attend a small college with a great program in child education. Sherri missed her already.

"Hey, guys," Sherri said as she entered the kitchen and saw Blair and Albany at the breakfast nook with a slew of books and a bag of chips between them. "What are we studying?"

"Algebra." Albany's tone and expression broadcast that she was none too pleased.

"Better you than me," Sherri replied. "I barely made it through basic math."

"She's doing fine," Blair assured them, reaching for a chip as she did so. "As soon as we nail how to factor polynomials, she'll have it made."

"Whatever you say, Blair. I don't speak that language. Where's Aaron?"

"Over at Hunter's house. They're having some type of tournament with stupid video games." Albany noticed the bag. "What did you buy me?"

"Girl, as quiet as it's kept, life isn't all about you. I bought me a new dress." She pulled out the formfitting black-and-tan dress with the geometric print she'd tried on at the mall. She'd purchased it after discovering that it looked just right with a dose of new Spanx.

"That's cute, Sherri," Blair said.

Albany's face was in a frown, no doubt because the dress wasn't for her.

"When your dad returns, he and I are going on a date."

Albany frowned. "Another one?"

Ignoring her, Sherri turned to Blair. "Do you think you'd be able to spend the night one day next week?"

"Sure, no problem. Just give me a heads-up a day or two in advance. There's nothing I do at home on my laptop that I can't do here."

"You're a godsend, Blair."

"What else is in there?" Albany was still fixated on the Loehmann's shopping bag.

Sherri reached inside it. "These." She twirled the dainty sandal this way and that.

"Okay, Mom. I have to give it you. Those shoes are tight."

"I'm glad they meet with your approval, Tyra."

"Ooh, does that mean you're going to let me try out for *America's Next Top Model?*"

"If the show is still on the air when you turn eighteen, you can do what you want."

"Mom!"

Sherri placed her purchases back in the bag. "Tonight's dinner is on the fridge," she said. "Mexican, Thai, Italian, whoever delivers."

"Why? Where are you going?" Albany asked.

"If I get in touch with Elle, it might be to a gym."

She got in touch with her neighbor. They didn't make it to the gym. Instead, they tortured themselves in Elle's newly renovated, open-space basement which housed their new custom gym. Some guy named Shaun T, with his insane behind, had made her use muscles she hadn't known she had, muscles that tomorrow would probably let her know how much they hadn't appreciated it. Heck, truth be told, they'd been complaining from the get-go, as soon as she sat on the floor to stretch. "You'll love it!" Elle had said about the workout video. Wrong. Right now she hated it, and Shaun. So did her muscles.

Once home, Sherri took off sweaty clothes and eased into a tub filled with steamy hot water. She'd been in the water for about fifteen minutes when the phone rang. It was a number she didn't recognize, so she let the call go to voice mail. As soon as the message indicator sounded, she listened to her one new message:

"Sherri, hello. This is Debbie, James's wife. You don't recognize my number because I changed it when I got a new phone. Long story. Tell you later. Anyway, it's been way too long since we talked, so I thought I'd give you a call. My number probably registered on your missed calls, but just in case, here it is again. It's five-one-six—"

Instead of listening to a number she knew had been captured, Sherri hit redial and then put the call on speaker before placing the phone on the ledge beside her and leaning back against the bath pillow. "Debbie! Sorry about that. You're right. I didn't recognize your number."

Debbie laughed. "I figured as much. I said to myself, 'I know Sherri is looking at the number and sending me to voice mail.' Ha!"

"You know it. I'm glad you called because I had sure planned to call you. Randall mentioned you after spending time with James in Los Angeles. Said we were overdue for a grown-folks-only get-together, going somewhere fun like Atlantic City or Vegas."

"I vote for Vegas, get me off of the East Coast. I almost surprised James with an impromptu visit when he was in LA."

Sherri's head lifted off the pillow a bit. "That's a great idea! Why didn't you do it?"

"Mama stuff. You know my son plays baseball."

"You probably told me, but I don't remember. I barely can keep up with my own children's extracurricular activities."

"I hear you, sis. But, yes, Montell plays for his high school team and they're doing some practice thing that's city-wide, where scouts from several colleges will be coming to check them out. So I had to give up my plans for having a wild time on the West Coast and report for mommy duty."

"I'm sure Montell appreciates you."

"Did I tell you that he is sixteen? Kids that age don't appreciate anything but money in their pocket, food in the fridge, me playing taxi driver when they need a ride, and oh, let me not forget designer clothes, one-hundred-dollar sneakers, and the latest iPhone and video games, thank you very much."

"You're right about that," Sherri said with a chuckle. "Albany turns thirteen in December and you'd think she was getting married. She's asking for everything but a car!"

"They grow up fast. How old is Aaron?"

"Ten going on twenty-one. But he's my quiet one. Albany is the hellion."

"Both of mine are out of control."

"Debbie."

"Yes?"

"Have you and James discussed having a child together?"

"Yes, and we also agreed that hell would have to freeze over first."

"Ha!"

"His son is grown and mine are almost out of the house. As soon as the last one leaves, hubby and I are going to screw in every room in the house."

The women laughed as Sherri reached to pull the stopper

up. "Girl, I'm about to shrivel up and turn into a raisin. I've been soaking this whole time, hoping that my body forgives me for trying to keep up with that crazy *Insanity* video. Not that I kept up with any of it, not even close!"

"So you've started working out? Good for you."

"Yes, everybody hasn't been blessed with your kind of genes, the kind that allows you to eat anything, not break a sweat, and gain absolutely no weight."

"Funny you should mention that. I'm actually trying to put on a few pounds."

"See what I mean?" Sherri stood and reached for a towel. "On that note, let me get out of here and go check on the kids. Aaron should be home now and I have to make sure he's eaten. That boy will stay on a game all day, even if his stomach is growling."

"Okay, Sherri. It was nice talking to you. And, hey, just because I can't surprise James in LA doesn't mean you can't pack a bag and come to New York. I know Randall is here with James."

"It's been about a year since I've been to Manhattan. I'm definitely going to think about it."

"Either way, let's talk again soon and make plans for all of us to do a weekend somewhere."

"That sounds good, Debbie. We'll talk soon."

Sherri rubbed her body down with some lotion that Elle had suggested. Her husband was also a doctor, one of the reasons they clicked so quickly, and he specialized in rheumatology. The lotion, she said, would help relax the muscles and keep the tissue pliable as well.

After checking on the kids and answering a few e-mails, Sherri settled onto their large TempurPedic mattress with the latest tabloids—her guilty pleasure. She wanted to see who was being lied on about being pregnant, sleeping around, getting arrested, doing drugs, or other acts of foolishness. But her mind kept wandering. She kept thinking about what Debbie said about surprising Randall in New York. She knew he had meetings over the weekend, but they wouldn't last all night. The more she thought about it, the more she believed that it was exactly what she needed to do. Sherri placed down the magazine and reached for her iPad.

CHAPTER 22

Deciding to surprise Randall had been the easy part. Now Sherri stood in the middle of their humongous walk-in closet, clothes strewn everywhere, trying to decide what to pack into her carry-on. This weekend, their housekeeper was going to earn her pay.

Come on, Sherri. It shouldn't be this hard. After all, she was going to be in New York for less than forty-eight hours, taking the first flight out tomorrow morning and returning Monday night. Technically, she only needed two outfits. Maybe three—something dressy should they decide to dine at a fancy restaurant. Since she'd begun working out, and following her conversation with Debbie, she'd become more conscious of herself as wife versus mother. It was time for a wardrobe makeover.

Not that Randall was neglected, nor had Sherri let go of her looks. She was the wife of a prominent member of the science community, and she was heavily involved in community and social events as well as her children's school activities, so she normally dressed in business casual. Unlike her neighbor, Elle, or her fashion-forward daughter, Sherri didn't necessarily follow the fashion trends. While home, she usually donned fashionable leggings and a slightly oversized top. If out running errands, she'd pair the ensemble with wedgie sandals or stylish flats. She'd had to buy a pair of tennis shoes to join Elle in her workouts, and she still possessed the classic pumps and tailored suits she wore during her brief career in education. The pumps, she could still comfortably slide into. The suits? Buttoning those jackets would require her to get just a little more insane with Shaun T, her man on the side.

After an exasperated sigh, she picked up her phone, scrolled down her contact screen, and tapped a name. She was glad that Debbie picked up.

"Hello, Deb."

"Hey, Sherri! I was just thinking about you."

"Oh yeah?"

"Yes. Are you going to surprise Randall?"

"As a matter of fact, yes."

Debbie squealed like a schoolgirl. "Ooh, I'm so happy. That's what I wanted to hear."

"Why, are you coming in from Long Island?"

"I hadn't planned to, but now I might. I was just thinking about how romantic surprising your husband would be."

"I think so too. That's why I called you. I haven't joined Randall on one of his business trips in ages, and cannot figure out what to take."

"No worries, chickie, you've called the right number. First of all, do you have some of those stretch jeans, the design that should be in every woman's closet?"

"Where do I get those?"

"Oh Lord."

Sherri smiled; she could just see Debbie rolling her eyes.

"Go to any department store; even T.J. Maxx, Marshalls, or Ross may have them. Definitely put a pair of those in your carry-on, along with a sexy top and some heels to go with it. Heels, not flats. We want this to be a grown-up, sexy weekend for the two of you."

Sherri reached for a top that she'd only worn once, an off-the-shoulder yellow sweater with a subtle swirl print. Still listening to Debbie, she walked over to the shoe section and pulled out a pair of navy ankle boots with gold studs.

"Okay, I think I have the outfit I'll wear on the plane, for when Randall first sees me. This top makes me feel sexy, and I think I know where I can get those stretchy jeans."

"Good. Now, you'll need to pack a slinky dress, preferably one that looks as ratchet as possible."

"Ha! I only know what that word means because of Albany. I said someone looked hoochie in front of her friends and she almost choked."

Debbie laughed. "Oh yeah, girl. Hoochie went out when the new millennium came in. Teenage kids are good for something, huh?"

"One or two things," Sherri agreed as she eyed the black dress she had worn to a New Year's Eve party two years ago. It was simple yet sexy. Randall had barely kept his hands off her all that night, and they had made love real good after coming back home. *With the Spanx, I think I can pull it off.*

She tossed it into the carry-on, along with two comfortable yet stylish maxi dresses, another sweater, a pair of black stilettos, a pair of flats (if she was going to shop she was going to be comfortable), and several pieces of fancy lingerie.

"I think I've got it together," she said, going into the master bath to put various toiletries into her cosmetic case. "Haven't done this in a while. Guess I just needed someone to talk me through it."

"You'll be fine," Debbie assured her. "Did you remember perfume?"

"Yes."

"Makeup?"

"Of course."

"Fragrant douche?"

"Girl! Stop!"

"Look, I'm just keeping it real." They laughed. "I've got to

run. But keep me posted on how things go, okay? Call me
when you get here. I'll come in if I can. No matter what, have
a great time!"

"Thanks, Debbie. I plan to do just that."

The next morning Sherri didn't need the alarm to wake
her, even though it had been set for six a.m. Her flight was
scheduled to leave from Ronald Reagan Washington National
Airport in Washington, D.C. at nine o'clock and arrive in New
York's JFK airport at ten fifteen. She figured that even if Randall's work consumed most of his day, she could still get in
some good shopping, maybe even take in a Broadway matinee.

Sherri made quick work of her shower and dressed fast as
well. *These really are flattering*, she thought as she viewed herself
in the new stretch jeans. She'd always had a nicely shaped rear,
but the pants made it look smoother. The three-inch sandals
elongated her frame, and she was thankful that her hairdresser
was able to make a change in the schedule and fit her in. The
short, tapered style worked with Sherri's round face, and regular facials paired with her just-waxed brows made makeup almost unnecessary. Satisfied that she looked like a tempting
chocolate morsel for any man, let alone her husband, she
closed her carry-on, grabbed her cell phone, keys, and oversized Coach bag, and left the master suite.

She reached the hall leading to the kitchen and was surprised to see lights. "Blair! Good morning. I didn't expect to
see anyone up."

"Good morning, Sherri. I'm an early riser, take after my
mom. Even on the weekends I'm usually up before eight
o'clock."

"Good Lord!"

"But I'm usually in bed by ten . . . like my grandma."

The women laughed. Sherri walked over to the island,

picked a banana and apple from the fruit bowl, and placed them in her bag. "I don't have to tell you that for a young adult, this is unusual behavior."

"Trust me, my college roommates let me know it every chance they get." Blair looked at Sherri's carry-on. "Do you have everything?"

"I believe so. What I don't have, I'll buy."

"Don't worry about the kids, Sherri. I'll be extra observant and make sure they're safe."

"Blair, if it weren't for the fact that I believe so strongly in higher education, I'd put in a serious bid to keep you in our family."

"Thanks, Sherri. I appreciate that. I look forward to getting my master's but will miss you guys just the same."

"You have both my and Randall's cell. I emailed you copies of our flight itineraries, hotel information, along with the household and children's schedule. If you need anything, or have any questions, don't hesitate to call."

"Stop worrying, Sherri. And get out of here before you miss your plane."

"I guess I should." She walked back over to give Blair a light hug. "Thanks for everything."

As she navigated the light traffic on the George Washington Memorial Parkway for the short trip to long-term parking, Sherri's thoughts whirled. She was 99.9 percent sure that Randall would be delighted that she'd decided to do something spontaneous. Since having the children, it seemed that their lives had been planned to within an inch of Outlook, and his increasingly busy travel schedule only added to the chaos. Their last vacation had been a year ago, and had included the children and her mother as well.

Realizing they hadn't spoken that morning, Sherri decided to call Miss Elaine when she reached the gate. After parking the car, taking the shuttle and arriving curbside, she headed for the security checkpoint. Halfway to her destination, her phone rang. She immediately recognized the number: her mother's neighbor.

"Hello, Ms. Riley. I must have thought you up. I'm at the airport and was going to call mom as soon as I got to the gate. How is she?"

"We had a little episode."

Sherri stopped. "What's wrong?"

"She's home now, so I want you to stay calm. But Elaine walked off this morning."

"Walked off!" Sherri's raised voice caused heads to turn. She lowered her voice, but knew that lowering her escalating blood pressure wouldn't be as easy. "What do you mean, walked off?"

"When I called this morning she didn't answer, so I went over. The door was unlocked and she was nowhere to be found. I called the police and we found her after about ten minutes of searching."

"And you're just now calling me?"

"Child, I don't want to get you all worked up, but I felt this was something you needed to know."

"Where is she now?"

"She's in her bedroom, lying down. We're trying to get her to go to the hospital, but she swears that she's okay."

Sherri turned and headed to the Delta counter, ready to book a flight to Raleigh. "Thanks for everything, Ms. Riley. Just watch her until I get there. Tell Mom that I'm on my way."

Jacqueline walked down the hotel corridor, purposeful and confident. She'd looked at the agenda and knew that Randall didn't have a session until that afternoon. A quick look around the restaurants and lobby area had suggested he hadn't come down for breakfast. Their schedules had both been packed and aside from their Broadway date, not much intimate time had been shared. But if he'd ordered room service, as she suspected, this was about to change. Nearing his door and wearing nothing beneath a chic, wrap dress, Jacqueline's breasts tingled at the mere thought of what she had planned. Soon, she'd be wearing nothing but a smile.

CHAPTER 23

Randall stepped through the door of his spacious colonial-style home in the Mt. Vernon subdivision on the Potomac. He'd done a rare thing: left a conference early. It couldn't be helped. After getting Sherri's phone call about Miss Elaine, he knew that staying another night in New York wasn't an option. So he'd checked out of the hotel and boarded the first available flight back to Virginia.

He set down his luggage and walked into the living room. "Aaron! Albany! Anybody home?"

A shriek was proof that Albany had heard him. "Daddy!" She liked to think of herself as a woman, but this daddy's girl had no problem running and jumping into his arms. "How was New York? Did you bring me back anything?"

"You'd want something from New York?" Randall teased. "I can't think of anything from there that I could buy you."

"Are you kidding?" she asked, following him into the master suite. "They've got all the fashions there, and all of the designers too. You could have brought me a Louis Vuitton, some Manolo Blahniks, something!"

"Why would I bring Louis or Manolo to the house? You know you can't date until you're sixteen."

"Dad!"

Randall chuckled as he reached into his carry-on and pulled out a gift bag. "Here you go, baby."

"Thanks, Daddy! Ooh," she said after quickly relieving her father of the purchase and rushing to open it. "What did you get?"

"Whatever it is, you don't need it." Aaron strolled into the room eating a sandwich. "Hey, Dad," he said around a mouthful of roast beef.

"You know your mother would kill you if she saw you eating like that. Where is your napkin, or better yet . . . a plate?"

"Dang, Dad. I'm not three. I know how to not get anything on the floor." They all looked as a mayonnaise-covered piece of lettuce dropped to the floor. Aaron's expression was innocent and endearing as he looked up. "Oops."

"Uh-huh. That's exactly what I'm talking about."

"Hey, I'm just trying to make sure our housekeeper stays employed. You know, doing what I can for the economy and all."

"Shut up, boy." Albany had removed the colorful bangles from the bag and was now placing them on her arm. "You're not doing a thing but making a mess." And then, "Thanks, Dad. These are pretty cool. But on my birthday, can you fly me and a friend out to New York? Let me and Lauren go on a shopping spree?"

Randall gave Albany a look. "Go on and get your money together, girl. If you can pay for the plane ticket, hotel room, taxi fare, and food and still have money, you have my permission to go and shop till you drop!"

Albany's face matched her whine. "Daddy. All of that is supposed to be included as part of my gift!"

The children continued chatting with their father, with lots of teasing and endless questions about his trip to New York. It was clear that they hadn't heard about their grandmother. Randall decided to keep it that way until he knew more. After giving Aaron his gift, a wireless, wearable video cam, and telling them that yes, they could go and show their friends, he retired to the master suite. He removed his travel clothes and was headed to the shower when he decided to call Sherri instead.

She picked up on the second ring. "Randall, are you home?"

"Yes, baby," he answered, hearing the angst in her voice. "Just got in. Don't worry about anything here. How's Mom?"

"We're waiting to find out. Ms. Riley and I finally convinced Mom to go to the hospital."

"Good. Was she lucid?"

"It's so strange, Randall. When I arrived, I found the same Mom I've known for thirty-seven years, except for one thing. She was aware of being away from the house, but she didn't remember leaving."

"Hmm. Interesting."

"I asked her what the last thing was she remembered before Ms. Riley and Officer Lang found her at the park. She said she remembered pouring herself a glass of water. I walked into the kitchen and saw a glassful of water on the island. She never drank it, Ran. She poured the water and then, for whatever reason, she walked out of the house with absolutely no awareness. I'm so scared," she continued, her voice a near whisper and laced with unshed tears.

"Do you need me down there?" Randall asked. "Blair is still here and my bags are still packed. I can be on the next plane to Raleigh."

"No, that's okay. You would be a big comfort, as always, but until the tests are finished and we talk to the doctors, there's really nothing else to do."

"I don't know, baby. I don't like the thought of you dealing with this alone."

"I'm not alone." He smiled, and he imagined her doing the

same. "Ms. Riley is not only Mom's neighbor, she is heaven sent. I was pretty upset when I arrived here, but she talked me off the ceiling. I also spoke with Nathan, who is on standby to fly in from Atlanta, depending on what the doctor says. Of course Lady is Mom's shadow, and follows her everywhere."

"I feel better knowing you've talked to your brother. How is he doing otherwise?"

"He sounded good; tired though. I guess he and some of 'his boys,' as he calls them, just got home after having tried to drink up half of Dallas."

"Ha! That boy is getting too old to act a fool."

"Try to tell him that. He's thirty-two going on thirteen! Part of the reason is that Mom spoiled him. He's a mama's boy through and through, and like you, I had to stop him from jumping on the next plane." A pause and then, "You must be exhausted."

"I'm pretty beat; was getting ready to jump in the shower and then I'll probably take a brief nap."

"Okay, sounds good. I'll call you as soon as we know anything."

"Call me in an hour either way. I want to stay posted on what's going on, okay?"

"Okay. I love you, Randall."

"I love you too, baby. And try not to worry. Everything is going to be okay."

He ended the call, turned on his laptop and opened the folder labeled Cytology, marked as such so that Sherri wouldn't go near it. Setting up this folder had been James's idea, suggested after Randall, in confidence, had shared the tricky situation he faced. He moved all of what he didn't want Sherri to see into this folder, and further secured it with a password code.

After a long, hot shower, Randall lay naked on top of the designer comforter. His thoughts meandered from the conversation he'd had with James in New York to the challenging situation befalling Miss Elaine in North Carolina; from the love of his kids to the support of his colleagues, and finally to the tempting times he'd spent with the freelance writer, Jacqueline Tate.

The woman was intriguing, no doubt about that. If he hadn't been headed to the airport when she'd stopped by his hotel room—smelling nice, looking good and suggesting the salacious—who knows what might have happened.

CHAPTER 24

"Which suit should I wear?"

It was Tuesday following the three days Jacqueline had spent in New York with Randall. An emergency phone call had prevented her from conducting a second interview there, and prevented the impromptu morning sex romp she'd planned. A conversation with James revealed the call was from Randall's wife, making Jacqueline none too happy. She'd texted her disappointment to Randall, who'd suggested she come to PSI, interview him at his company's headquarters. She'd quickly agreed. That they were back in D.C., close to his home, was no longer a concern. Being in his office would work to her advantage. For Jacqueline, the time spent in New York had only solidified what had begun in LA. She knew that between her and Sherri, she was close to tipping the love scales in her favor and wanted to do everything absolutely right, down to the last earring and choice of purse.

Kris sat on the bed in front of her, having seen her in the beige suit and now eyeing the bold red choice. "I like that one," she finally answered.

Jacqueline looked down at the single-button suit with its

dipping cleavage and skirt that brushed her knee. "Are you sure it isn't . . . too much."

"Not at all. That boring world of photogenes and chromosomes could use a dash of excitement, something stimulating to wake up what I'm sure is a drab, tasteless office filled with men of equal flair."

"I'm not sure." Jacqueline continued to eye herself in the mirror. "I want to be taken seriously."

"Believe me, you will be."

"Okay. I'll wear the red." She flashed Kris an appreciative smile. "Thank you for being the best BFF a girl could ask for. You've always steered me right."

"And today will be no exception. Okay, next question. Have you been able to reach Phillip?"

Jacqueline flopped on the bed. "Finally, and yes, he received my e-mail. Thank God for that man. I don't know how I would have been able to pull this off without him."

"You haven't yet," Kris chided. "But I agree that Phillip will make it easier. Even though you've said he's not your boyfriend, Randall's wife has to feel better seeing him with you, knowing he's around."

"You're right about that!"

Kris cocked her head to the side as she watched Jacqueline pull a brush through her thick tresses. "How long do you plan to stay here, at Phillip's house?"

"Because he spends so much time with Marco, he says it doesn't matter. So probably for the rest of the time I'm in the states."

"I'm not trying to be Debbie Downer, Jack, really I'm not. But what do you think is going to happen when you go home to Canada? Do you really think this affair can continue long distance?"

"Maybe, maybe not. If I have my way, by the time this freelance gig is over, it'll be time to change my zip code to one in District of Columbia or in Alexandria, Virginia. Permanently."

★ ★ ★

Sherri paced the master suite, where she'd retreated to make this call. She'd tried to convince herself otherwise, since returning from Raleigh two days ago, but there was no denying the obvious. Randall was acting strangely. She couldn't put her finger on it; at first she had felt that worry for her mother was clouding her judgment. After he'd returned from LA, they seemed to be moving in a good direction, putting some of the spark back into their marriage. But since returning from New York, he was definitely preoccupied. And now this? Having been unsuccessful in convincing herself that this was all in her head, it was time to entertain another opinion. The first person she'd thought to call was Renee, but given her single friend's low view of relationships in general and men in particular, she rang Debbie instead.

"Hey, Sherri!" Debbie's cheerful voice rang into a bedroom whose gloom was not only due to the morning rains.

"Hello, Debbie. Do you have a minute? I need a second opinion because I'm about to get all worked up."

"Sure, I'm stuck in traffic anyway. What's going on?"

"Probably nothing. But hear me out anyway. I noticed this morning that Randall is dressing differently than usual for a regular day at work."

"What does he usually wear?"

"Either jeans or khakis and a button-down or polo."

"What is he wearing today?"

"Jeans, but paired with one of his nicer blazers and the nice loafers instead of his regular Jordans or other casual shoes."

"Okay."

"I asked him why he was dressed up. He said because of an interview he was doing with *Science Today*." Sherri paused after this declaration.

"So far, so normal," Debbie finally replied into the silence. "Why are you getting upset?"

"The freelance writer conducting the interview, their second in almost as many weeks. Her name is Jacqueline Tate and . . . well . . . let's just say Halle Berry would become background standing next to her."

"A real average-looking chick, huh?"

"Exactly."

Debbie laughed. "You've met her?"

"At dinner during date night a week or so ago, she showed up with a man as handsome as she is beautiful on her arm."

"Her man?"

"It looked like it."

"So he has an interview with a pretty woman who's involved with a handsome man and spruces up a bit. Come on, Sherri. How long have you been married to that man?"

"We're celebrating our fifteenth anniversary in August."

"Then you've known him long enough to know that this doesn't mean anything except that he is as normal as any other red-blooded male. He's like a peacock, trying to spread his feathers solely to impress. Unless the interview is taking place in a hotel room instead of his office, I wouldn't read too much into his actions."

"That's how I felt . . . at first."

"And then?"

"Debbie, I know that man almost better than I know myself. I can gauge his moods, guess his attitude . . . heck, I can almost tell if he has a fever simply by looking at him. Something is going on with him. Something he isn't sharing. So no matter whatever or whoever I can feel something amiss deep down in my gut."

There was silence as Sherri walked over to the sitting area she'd redecorated just last year. She sat on one of two oversized chairs that faced the room's fireplace and two of its three windows. The rain matched her mood.

"Sherri?"

"Uh-huh?"

"This is a personal question and you don't have to answer, but has Randall ever been unfaithful?"

"Once, a long time ago."

"Oh."

"It was during the second year of our marriage. We were both young and stupid, not understanding that marriage is about compromise, not competition. I was the strong, independent sort, focused on my own career. He wanted a doting wife. Let's just say there was a certain secretary at the place he worked, who paid him the attention he craved. It lasted a month before I found out. He ended it immediately, and Mom talked me out of getting a divorce. We finally got the counseling that should have preceded our marriage, learned to communicate better, and basically just grew the hell up. We've had our share of challenges, but he hasn't given me another reason to doubt his faithfulness since."

"Then don't doubt it, Sherri. Trust your marriage, and trust your man."

CHAPTER 25

Randall stood as Jacqueline walked into his office. He was growing more accustomed to her beauty, but seeing her still took a little bit of his breath away. "Hello," he said, coming from behind his desk. "And welcome to my humble abode."

"Thank you," Jacqueline said, taking his outstretched hand.

"Have a seat." He walked behind his desk and sat as well. "Can I get you something to drink? Tea, coffee, juice, water . . ."

"Nothing for now, thanks." She looked briefly around the office and then back at him. "I have a confession," she said with the slightest of smiles.

"What?"

"The PSI offices are quite impressive. I'm completely blown away. For some reason I assumed they'd be drab and plain; a bunch of cubicles, too much fluorescent lighting, metal file cabinets, messy desks. But what I've seen so far is exactly the opposite. Are those marble floors in the lobby?"

Randall shrugged. "I have no idea. Sherri is the reason my offices look the way they do. She picked out all of the colors and materials. My company just wrote the checks."

"Oh. She's an interior designer?"

"No. Her master's degree is in education. But HGTV is her favorite TV network and she has a natural talent for color and fabrics and such. So she asked me what different types of rooms I needed and then worked with a decorator to give me that . . . in a tasteful way."

"They did an excellent job."

"Thank you."

Randall handed Jacqueline a pocket folder made of fine, cream-colored linen. The company logo was embossed on the front in silver block letters. "You've probably done your research, but here is an overview of our company: history, staff bios, accomplishments, and goals." He briefly paused as she rifled through the papers. "Feel free to take that with you. We have approximately an hour until my next meeting. I thought we'd start with a quick tour of the facility and then return here so that I can answer any questions that you have."

"Sounds like a plan," Jacqueline said cheerfully as she placed the folder into her large Coach bag.

He stood. "Shall we?"

"By all means."

From his corner office they walked down a short hall with two offices on each side. Randall explained the positions of those they passed, his voice respectfully low in the quiet environment. They passed a small yet functional break room before heading down another hall where all of the rooms had been turned into one type of lab or another. The last door they reached was not only closed but locked, housing biometric thumbprint technology. Randall placed his thumb against the keypad and waited until he heard the door unlock.

They stepped inside a room that was twice the size of the other laboratories. There were easily recognizable instruments, such as petri dishes and microscopes, along with machines that looked as though they could have been used on the Starship Enterprise.

Jacqueline stopped to look around. "I have no idea what I'm looking at."

"That's probably a good thing, as most of what's going on in here right now cannot be reported." At her questioning look, he continued. "This is where we're doing the plant stem cell work."

"I'm honored that you would bring me here."

"I just wanted you to see the place where so much of what we discussed in LA happens." He did a quick walk around the room, explaining the types of plants being used in the research and explaining the function of some of the machines. They were in the stem cell lab less than ten minutes, and after completing the basic tour of offices and rooms that made up PSI, ended up back at the door to Randall's office.

He looked at his watch. "We have forty minutes left for your questions. Are you sure you don't want anything?"

Jacqueline smiled, looked at the nearby open office door, and replied, "That water looks refreshing. I'll have a glass if you will."

He walked over to where a pitcher of ice-cold lemon water sat on a silver tray, along with a set of glasses. After pouring them both a drink, he nodded his head toward the small conference table on the far side of the room. "Let's sit there for the interview. A little less formal." He closed the door to his office and then joined Jacqueline at the table. "Okay, Jacqueline," he said, his expression unreadable. "Let's begin."

When she'd first arrived, Jacqueline had balked when Randall chose a handshake over a hug. But then she'd reminded herself that they were on his turf, with his partners and staff, a number or all of whom knew his wife. She understood why he'd be standoffish. Unless his divorce and remarriage were handled absolutely perfectly, he could lose a lot of credibility and social standing. They'd both better stay cognizant of what was at stake.

This was on her mind twenty minutes ago, but now, with Randall having closed his door, and knowing they had at least thirty minutes of alone time, her thoughts were on something else entirely. She sat down and watched his long, bold strides as he walked back over to join her at the conference table, took in his sporty attire and clean-shaven face, and imagined him naked, hovering over her, right on the table. He wasn't a classically handsome man, one who would typically grace a magazine cover or walk a runway. But his skin was dark brown and smooth, his lips pleasingly plump, and the glasses he wore gave him a scholarly, sophisticated air. That, combined with the confidence that seemed to ooze from his pores, and he became the sexy scientist indeed. Her heartbeat quickened and the room grew as warm as her private parts. He sat down next to her. She asked several questions. He answered them succinctly. She asked for a refill of her glass of water. When he passed her to get it, she thought she'd swoon from the scent of his cologne.

It brought back memories.

She looked at him and imagined the lips that were forming his next question touching her lips, neck, breasts, and thighs. Imagined the scratchiness of his mustache as it brushed up against the sensitive skin just above her honeypot. She leaned over, silencing his talk of inventing more innovative and less intrusive ways to save lives, with the softest of kisses.

"Jacqueline . . ."

She kissed him again.

"Not now," he whispered, even as he kissed her back, giving her a little tongue for her troubles.

"I've missed you," Jacqueline murmured as she got up from

her seat, hiked up her skirt, and straddled him. "Is the door locked?"

"Mm-hmm." His voice, deepened by desire, hummed against her chest as his face pressed against her knit top, her nipples straining to be touched, tasted.

She shimmied out of the jacket that blocked his progress, lifted her top and eased down the sheer thin mesh that held her girls in check. Randall immediately took advantage, sucking a hardened peak into his mouth and swirling it with his tongue. Jacqueline threw her head back as she gripped Randall's shoulders and suggestively rotated her pelvis against his hardening manhood.

"My appointment," Randall eked out between licks and nips on her tits. "I've got to—" Jacqueline reached between her legs and stroked his rigid shaft. "Ahh."

Easing off of his lap, she dropped to her knees, made quick work of unbuckling his belt, pulling out his penis and getting down to business. *Um, this tastes so good, feels so good. I can't get enough. I can't wait to have it inside me to . . .*

"Sorry for the interruption, Jacqueline, I had to take that call. Now, where were we?" Randall sat down at the table, closed his eyes and gave his head a shake.

"Randall, are you all right?"

"Felt a little light-headed just now. Guess the busy schedule is taking a toll on a body that is not as young as it . . . once was."

"No worries. You've answered all my questions. My work here is done." After one last piece of business, Jacqueline gathered her things, stood and looked around a room that was in perfect order. "Thanks for inviting me to your office, baby. I'll see myself out."

Jacqueline exited the office and closed the door behind her. She strode confidently to her silver sports car and hopped inside. Everything with Randall had gone better than expected. Knowledge was power, and the internet was her friend. She was a geek and technology a wonder. Amazing how creatively cameras and recording devices could be hidden these days. Almost anything could be caught on tape.

Smiling, she entered D.C.'s afternoon traffic. "Almost anything."

CHAPTER 26

Days had passed and Randall was still puzzled. One minute, he'd been talking to Jacqueline. The next minute he was being shaken awake by his assistant, thirty minutes late for an important conference call. Sure, his schedule had been hectic and sleep elusive, but he'd never passed out like that. Ever. After making a note to call the doctor first thing Monday morning, he turned to the other situation consuming his thoughts.

It had been a long time since Randall had kept anything from his wife; years since he'd had a secret. In doing so he felt nervous, uneasy, and a little bit sneaky. They'd been married almost fifteen years, enjoyed their share of triumphs, weathered their share of storms. Through it all, she'd been his constant companion, cheerleader, supporter, and friend. They shared almost everything. Which is why keeping what he was currently doing from his wife was so incredibly difficult. Would the end justify the means? He felt it absolutely would. But still, not telling her was hard.

He rocked the office chair he'd occupied for the past thirty minutes, having gone there at just after six a.m., even though it was the weekend. He hoped Sherri wouldn't wake up until he'd finished the phone call and could slide back into bed with his absence unnoticed.

"Dr. Atwater?"

"Yes, I'm here." Upon hearing the voice on the other end of the line, Randall clicked over from the *Science Today* web page highlighting Jacqueline's bio and back to that of Chase Bank.

"Thanks for waiting. Are you still online?"

"Yes, I am."

"Okay. If you refresh your page, you'll see that your new checking account has been successfully opened and is now operational. From here you may deposit, withdraw, and transfer monies, all online. As you'll see from the web page, you can also pay bills, wire money—"

"I can wire money directly from the account, all online?"

"That is correct. In addition we offer QuickPay, which allows you to make or receive payments directly from and into your account as well as send an overnight check if a paper trail is desired."

At this little tidbit, Randall remained silent. The last thing he wanted was a way that the upcoming transactions could be tracked. At least not easily, and not by someone who shouldn't know what was happening. Namely, not by his clever, detail-oriented, and extremely astute wife.

"If you'd like, Dr. Atwater, I can look up the nearest branch in your area where you can visit and talk with a representative personally."

"That won't be necessary. I've already researched that information. But I do have one question about transfers to accounts outside of this bank. Is it . . ."

The door opened. Randall looked up. Sherri entered the room.

"Okay, thanks for the help. I'll keep you posted on what I find out about additional funding."

While hanging up he closed the tabs on his computer until Outlook was the only thing on the screen.

"What are you doing up so early?" Sherri asked with a yawn as she plopped down in the chair facing his desk.

"Couldn't sleep."

Sherri's brow creased. "Really? So you now snore when awake?"

"I don't snore," Randall scoffed, knowing full well he did and also knowing that the sooner he got Sherri off the subject of why he was up early and on to another topic, the better.

"Who was that on the phone?"

Well, so much for changing the subject. "Just work, honey."

"This early? And on a Saturday?"

"It's a guy from Switzerland who I met in New York," Randall explained, having seen an e-mail from the gentleman with whom he'd actually had a conversation about funding. Just not this morning. "He'd sent me an e-mail." That it had nothing to do with money and everything to do with the best slopes in the Alps was something Randall felt Sherri didn't need to know. "So I gave him a call."

He deleted a few e-mails, moved those the bank had just sent him to the cytology file, and then closed his computer. "So, Mrs. Atwater," he began, leaning back and crossing his arms. "What are you doing up at the crack of dawn?"

"I'm always up early. Oh, but you wouldn't know that since you're rarely seen on the weekend before ten a.m."

Randall noted her teasing tone but perceptive eyes. "I think that's an exaggeration."

"Perhaps."

"Hey, did you see that disc I put on your phone?"

"That silver thingy? You did that? I thought it was some designer mess from Albany. I meant to ask her about it but was asleep before Blair and the kids got back from the movies."

"No, it's supposed to divert cell phone radiation away from your brain. While in New York last week, somebody gave it to me." He held up his phone. "I have one, too. See?"

"Hmm. We need to get one for Mom and the kids."

"Okay."

Sherri reached over for a magazine at the edge of Randall's desk. He quickly picked up the envelope that had been hiding beneath it.

Sherri noticed. "What's that?"

"Confidential information," Randall quickly responded. "Something from the science office." At her confused expression, he continued. "Government, Department of Energy. My company may be close to a breakthrough that will have national and international implications." Randall placed the envelope into his desk drawer, turned the lock, and discreetly deposited the key into his cargo shorts pocket. "As more of the details fall into place, I'll be able to share."

He stood. "Have you brushed your teeth yet?"

"Why? Have you?"

"Yes," he said, coming around the desk to stand before her. "And I don't want mouthwash to meet morning breath, know what I'm saying?"

"Whatever." Sherri stood and wrapped her arms around his neck. They enjoyed a brief kiss before she pulled her head back to look into his eyes. "Is everything okay?"

"Sure. Why wouldn't it be?"

"I don't know. But you've always been pretty easy to read, and I get the distinct impression that something is going on with you."

"I just told you, Sherri." Randall surprised himself with the ire in his voice. Keeping secrets was hard work! "It's the stuff I'm working on with the Office of Science and Technical Information."

"You just said it was the Department of Energy!"

Randall broke the embrace. "Really, Sherri? You're going to question me as though I'm lying to you?"

Sherri's temper quickly rose to match his. "Well, if you are, the least you can do is keep them straight!"

"The parent agency is the Department of Energy. The Office of Science and—Wait a minute, I'm not one of your children. Why in the heck am I trying to explain myself to you?"

"That's a good question," Sherri said, crossing her arms and glaring. "Is there anything else that you need to explain?"

Randall looked at Sherri a long moment. "You know what," he said, his voice low and devoid of anger, "obviously one of us woke up on the wrong side of the bed. Maybe someone got their period, I don't know. But I do know I'm not going to begin my day by arguing with you. If you want to calm down and do something together, fine. If not, I'll go to the course and get in eighteen holes."

"You do that," Sherri said, still on fire. "And while you're at it, stick the nine-iron up your bald-faced lying ass."

CHAPTER 27

Sherri walked out of the office, and had it not been for the spring hinges that made it impossible, she would have slammed the door. She started for the kitchen but, believing that the desire to break something might be too hard to squelch, went to the master suite instead and headed straight for the closet. After making quick work of pulling on a pair of sweats and sneakers, she placed house keys, earbuds, and her cell phone in a pouch, ran into the kitchen just long enough to retrieve a bottle of water, and left the house.

She started walking without a destination in mind. It really didn't matter where she went as long as it was away from Randall. She pulled out her phone, attached the earbuds, and tapped the music screen, scrolling until she found the folder titled "Walking." Soon the upbeat sounds of McFadden and Whitehead blocked out the outside noise. In time, she hoped their positive message would work on how she was feeling on the inside as well. Securing the pouch around her waist, she engaged her arms, allowing them to swing freely as she did a semi-fast walk down the block. One of the early risers in their gated community was walking his dog. Another was jogging and yet another—who fancied herself to be the next Martha Stewart and tended the beautiful flower garden that framed their front lawn—snipped away at some unfortunate weed that didn't belong. "Martha" attempted to wave and speak, but Sherri averted her gaze and kept it moving. She didn't feel like talking to anyone. She needed space and time to focus on her feelings; why she'd gotten so upset just now and instigated her and Randall's very uncharacteristic argument.

Face it, girl. You don't need time to figure out your problem. Her name is Jacqueline and the problem is you're jealous of her, insecure because of her, and suspicious that your husband is, wants to be, or has been with her.

Sherri took a deep breath. Just this inner acknowledgment had taken a toll. She increased her pace, enjoying the increased heart rate, the rush of air from her lungs, and the slight discomfort in her fast-moving legs. Her friend Elle had been faithful, but after the first couple times, Sherri and Mr. Shaun T had had a parting of the ways. Her body was letting her know that stopping before really getting started had probably not been her best move.

But focusing on her body took her mind off her suspicions.

Is that a good thing? She slowed a bit, remembering the conversation she'd had with Debbie, just after meeting Jacqueline Tate.

Has he ever been unfaithful?

Aside from his singular indiscretion all those years ago, she'd never doubted her husband. True, he mostly worked around men, and the women in the field didn't intimidate her, but there had never been a time when she felt this uneasy. Even when he'd cheated, she'd not had a clue. Not at first anyway. Back then, she'd been the last to know, and only found out because of a sympathetic woman in Randall's office who hadn't liked her being in the dark.

Trust your marriage, and your man.

Sherri knew this was sound advice. So why was she finding it so hard to take heed? She reached inside her pouch to retrieve her vibrating phone. Looking at the caller ID, she welcomed the much needed distraction. "Good morning, Nathan."

"Is it? By the sound of your voice, I can't tell. When I called the house and Randall said you'd already left, I thought something had happened with Mom, but he assured me she's fine."

"Have you called her?"

"No."

"You need to call her more, Nathan. Or better yet, make a few visits."

"I know, Sis. I'll do better." A few seconds of silence and then, "So what are you doing up and out so early?"

"Decided to get a little exercise, take a walk."

"A walk or a jog?"

"Walk, Brother. Unlike you, I'm not in the same shape as when I was nineteen."

"Sherri, I am not in that kind of shape." A pause and then, "My body feels like it's all of twenty-one."

"Oh, excuse me!" They laughed. "You're up early too."

"Yes, I'm participating in a barbecue cook-off."

"When did you start cooking?"

"Not cooking, Sis, barbecuing. Don't put me in the kitchen, but when it comes to meat and a grill, I can hold my own. It's a fundraiser to send the kids we mentor to college."

Sherri began walking again, a little slower this time. "We?"

"I was asked to join a prestigious group here: the One Hundred Black Men of Atlanta. I didn't tell you?"

"Not that I remember."

"Several of the guys at the club where I work out are

members. I figured that since I don't yet have my own, I'd do what I could to help someone else's child."

Sherri pulled the phone away from her ear. "Wait a minute. Is this Nathaniel Duane Carver I'm talking to, or has an imposter reached me?"

"Don't go making a mountain out of a molehill. And to answer the questions I know are in your mind: No, I'm not engaged. No, I'm not seriously dating anyone. And, no, nobody's pregnant with your niece or nephew."

"Are you sure about that? Because unless you're celibate . . ."

"I'm sensible. I don't take chances. I don't take risks."

"And again I say, unless you're celibate there's . . ." Sherri paused as she looked at her phone. "Hey, Brother, this is Mom's neighbor, Ms. Riley. I'll call you back." She clicked over, stopping abruptly in the middle of the path. "Ms. Riley? How are you doing? Is everything all right?"

"I'm doing fair to middling, and your Mom is okay."

Sherri audibly released the breath she'd been holding and began walking again. Instead of turning right and heading back toward the house, or left toward the golf course, she went straight, to an area where more grandiose homes and a community clubhouse stood. "Then what can I do for you this morning?"

"Now, I don't want you to panic . . ."

Sherri stopped again. *Too late.*

"But I called to talk about the full-time assistant you mentioned for your mom, and whether you'd found somebody."

Sherri's gait was slow as she began to walk again, eyeing the mostly cloudy sky and the slivers of sun peeking out. "Why, Ms. Riley? What's going on?"

"One, your mother continues to be forgetful. She hasn't wandered off again, but she couldn't remember where she parked the other day, and while conversing she repeats topics we've just discussed. Then, there are the headaches. I don't feel comfortable leaving her alone for too long. And, two, that's what I'm about to do. Leave."

Sherri's heart dropped. "Where are you going?"

"St. Louis. My oldest grandchild just had a baby, a bouncing baby boy."

"Congratulations, Ms. Riley. I'm sure you're quite proud."

"I am."

"How long will you be there?"

"That's the thing, Sherri. Taking care of a child is a lot of responsibility for a twenty-year-old who is also working and going to school. My daughter is already overloaded handling school, a full-time job, and a special-needs child. So I'll be gone for a good little while. Eventually, I might move there."

"I'm sure your daughter will like that. I've been trying to get Mom to move for years."

"I think she holds on to that place because it reminds her of Clarence. She says he was never as happy as when they left Chicago and moved here."

"She always wanted to go back to where she was born. Daddy was a southern boy, so it all worked out."

"I won't be too happy about leaving. But my children need me. So, do y'all have somebody in mind who can come and watch your mama?"

"Not yet but don't worry. We'll step up our efforts to get someone right away. When will you be leaving?"

"I told them I wouldn't leave until Elaine had someone to watch her; I'm hoping in the next month or so, to stay for a couple weeks. Then, depending on how I feel about a longer stay in the Midwest, I'll make the move permanent. But if that happens, it will be more toward the end of the year."

"We'll get right on it. Thank you so much, Ms. Riley, for everything. Mom talks about you all the time. You're a good neighbor and a wonderful friend. We really appreciate you."

"It's my pleasure, darling. Your mama's not just a neighbor; she's my friend, too."

Sherri ended the call, scrolled the screen and tapped the redial button. "Hey, Nathan," she said once her brother had answered. "It's me again. We have to find live-in help for Mom, and we have to do it now."

CHAPTER 28

Randall ran a hand over the lapel of his tuxedo as he walked into the dimly lit grand ballroom at Chicago's Peninsula hotel. He remembered a time when putting on a monkey suit felt as foreign as Tanzania, and entering a formal setting could bring on the nerves. But tonight he was calm and self-assured, knowing that he stood shoulder to shoulder with everyone in this room, and that he belonged. He adjusted his cuff links as a heavily Russian-accented voice caused him to turn around.

"Dr. Atwater. Dr. Atwater!"

"Yes?" Randall reached for the hand outstretched before him.

"I am Dr. Varennikov, from the European Medical Center group in—"

"Moscow, Russia," Randall finished, as recognition dawned and he shook the doctor's hand more heartily. "You're a leading authority on brain-related diseases, and sent a note after reading an article on my work. It's a pleasure to meet you."

"I was delighted when, upon looking at the schedule of speakers, I saw your name along with that of Dr. Chatterji and others whom I admire."

"Well, the feeling is mutual, sir."

Before long another Russian doctor joined them and soon Randall was surrounded by colleagues interested in his research and those whose work he admired. Some of them, especially the international contingents, had brought their wives, who were introduced as well. It made Randall think about Sherri and the few words that had passed between them since the past weekend's argument.

He'd tried to make it right. Had returned from an invigorating game of golf and apologized for his outburst. He'd tried to relieve her suspicions about the snippet of conversation she'd heard. Potential additional research funding, he'd explained, possibly that might help properly diagnose her mother's illness. Talk of Mom Elaine tended to pacify her somewhat, but Randall knew she still had questions.

"Are you sure there isn't anything you're hiding from me?" she'd asked him.

That he'd said no with a straight face just underscored how committed he was to making sure that nothing was revealed, that she didn't know a thing about the details of his covert actions until the time was right. Keeping this particular situation a total secret would simply be better for everyone. And since the doctor had given him an all clear during Monday's physical, he didn't tell her about the strange sleeping-in-the-middle-of-the-day episode either. He just hoped that at the end of the day, when everything came to light and the reason he'd lied had been revealed, she'd be able to forgive him and life could go on.

For the first couple days of the week, Randall had left for work early and come home late. By the time he arrived, Sherri was either in another part of the house reading or watching TV, or already asleep. He'd interacted with the children mostly—with Blair, their nanny, and with Atom and Dizzy, their shepherd dogs. He'd left a note in the master bath before catching the plane on Wednesday. It was simple: I love you. She'd texted her response: Me too. That's the only interaction they'd had since Wednesday. Today was Friday, and he'd be going home on Sunday. *When I get back there,* he thought as he watched a few couples take the dance floor, *I'll fix this lack of communication between us. I'm the reason it's happening, and I'll make it right.*

"We've got to keep meeting like this." Jacqueline had sidled up to Randall without his knowing and now whispered into his ear, from behind him.

He turned, the scowl on his face turning into a smile once he saw her. He started to speak but stopped as he took in the formfitting maxi and the deep-plunging neckline where a strategically placed teardrop necklace highlighted her generous globes. He allowed a moment for his eyes to travel down to her shiny stilettos and up to the bone-straight hair cascading around her shoulders before meeting her eyes and speaking again. "Isn't the phrase *stop* meeting like this?"

Jacqueline shrugged, happy to see how Randall's eyes kept darting to her cleavage. "I prefer my version." She shifted until she was standing directly in front of him. "You look quite handsome tonight. The tux works for you."

"Thank you. You look nice as well, although, quite frankly, I'm surprised you're here."

"Why's that?"

"You've been to what, two or three conferences and expos in the past few weeks, meeting many of the same doctors, scientists, researchers, and engineers. I'd think you'd have enough for several in-depth articles for a variety of magazines."

"What are you trying to say, Randall?" she asked, closing the distance between them. "That you're growing tired of my presence?"

"Not at all. I'd never begrudge the company of an intelligent woman who can speak my sometimes boring language. I guess not knowing much about the life of a writer makes me curious, that's all."

"You know what I'm curious about?"

"What's that?"

"If a man of your intellect can also get down on the dance floor."

Randall chuckled. "I do okay."

"Oh really? Let's see."

In that moment he became aware that the band had gone from playing classical music to instrumental pop. "I really probably shouldn't, I don't want to embarrass you or myself."

"Trust me," Jacqueline said as she linked her arm through his and turned toward the dance floor. "That isn't going to happen. Just follow my lead, handsome, and we'll do fine."

Sherri nestled deeper into the great room's wraparound couch, ready to enjoy a peaceful Friday night and an episode of the new *Arsenio Hall Show.* She and her BFF Renee had just today talked about how good it was to have him back on late-night TV, how he picked up where he left off, and how it hardly seemed that more than a quarter of a century had gone by since last seeing him in the late-night spot. She liked how many of the guests were stars she'd grown up with and artists she enjoyed. Mostly, she knew that for at least an hour she'd be able to stop thinking about Randall and how unfairly she felt she'd treated him earlier in the week, before he went to Chicago.

"Girl, why are you trying to create drama where there is none?" Renee had asked, when during an earlier phone call Sherri had detailed their latest argument. "So the man doesn't want to talk to you about his business, so what? Is he providing for you?" *Yes.* "Is he supportive of you and what you want to do?" *Yes.* "Has he given you any solid, valid reason to believe he's not being faithful?" *Not really.* "Uh, that would be a no. Listen to me, Sherri," she'd continued, her voice filled with compassion mixed with concern. "You've got a good man, and take it from this single woman out here trying to find one, they aren't as plentiful as they used to be. It sounds like you have too much time on your hands and not enough to keep that mind of yours occupied and that imagination from working overtime. You're creating a problem that's not even real. When that man comes home, you need to have a good meal, a hot bath, and a wet pussy waiting, and let him know how much you missed him, and how much you love him. You know I love you, sistah, and you know I support you, but that's real talk right there."

"But what about Jacqueline?"

"What about her? Didn't you tell me he told you about the interview; didn't try and hide that he'd met the woman in LA?"

"Yes, he told me."

He'd also admitted that he thought she was beautiful. And he'd been right. But during the chance meeting at the restaurant in D.C., Jacqueline had had eyes only for her date, a man who looked like he'd stepped right off the pages of a fashion magazine as well. She'd been cordial and professional, and hadn't shown any romantic interest in Randall at all. But still, Sherri had judged her.

Muting the TV during a commercial break, Sherri chided herself. "You've messed up royally, girl," she mumbled. "It's time to get it back together."

"Get what together?"

Sherri jumped. "Albany! Girl, you scared me. I didn't hear you come in the house, let alone this room."

"That's because you were a million miles away." Albany plopped on the couch, munching on an apple. "Thinking about Dad and why you're mad at him?"

Sherri's head snapped around. "Who says I'm mad?"

"Please, Mom. You guys try to hide it from me and Aaron, but we can always tell when you guys are fighting."

"Oh really?"

Albany laughed. "It's so obvious." She reached for the remote.

Sherri grabbed it first and placed it on the other side of her, away from Albany's hand. "I'm watching this."

"Who is it?"

"Arsenio Hall."

"Who's he?"

Sherri gave her daughter the side eye. "You don't know who that is?"

"Nope."

"I guess you wouldn't, but at one time he was very, very popular, and made history as the first African-American to host a show on late-night TV."

"Must have been before I was born," Albany responded in the kind of bored voice that only a thirteen-year-old can possess. "I'd rather watch TeenNick."

"Why are you home anyway? I thought that after the movies, y'all were going bowling."

"Plans changed." Albany turned to look at her mother. "Why are you mad at Dad?"

"I'm not mad at him, honey. We just had a little misunderstanding, that's all."

"But y'all barely talked for two whole days. Looks like more than a little misunderstanding to me."

"That's because you're a child who knows nothing about relationships. Now back out of your parents' business and stay in the child's lane where you belong."

"But your marriage is my business. If y'all get divorced, it will affect my life!"

Now it was Sherri's turn to shift so that she could face her child fully. *Why in the world would Albany even consider such a thing as Randall and I separating?* She had no idea but knew it was time to find out.

"Honey, every couple has their ups and downs; every family. Do you and Aaron always get along?"

"No, but that's different!"

"How?"

"Because he's my younger brother and they are always pains in the butt."

"Ha! Can I tell you a little secret?" Albany nodded. "Sometimes, so are daddies and husbands. And sometimes mommies can be a pain. But that doesn't mean that we don't love each other, just like it doesn't mean you don't love Aaron when the two of you fight. Daddy and I love each other very much. So you can get the thought of a divorce right out of your head. Because the four of us—you, me, Aaron, and Dad—are a family. And no one is going anywhere."

Jacqueline tossed her hair away from her face, smiling as she mounted Randall like a thoroughbred and began to ride. "Ooh, baby, you feel so good inside me. Does this feel good to you?" He nodded. "Do you want me to come for daddy?" Another nod. "I can't hear you!" she sang out.

"Yes, Jacqueline. Come for daddy!"

"Okay, I'll do it. I'll do it. Now, now, now!" She increased her pace, her breasts bouncing up and down, her smile wide as she heard the mattress springs creaking with the intensity of their lovemaking. "I love you, Randall! I love you!"

Jacqueline went over the edge, her body jerking with the force of her release. She flopped on the bed, body sweaty, breath labored. And in this moment she knew. It wasn't enough to see Randall sporadically, to enjoy only clandestine meetings in luxury hotels. She wanted everything, all of him, and to know that there was someone named Sherri standing between her and this desire mattered not at all.

Because she was Jacqueline "I'm a Survivor" Tate. And she always got what she wanted.

CHAPTER 29

"Sherri!" Randall set his carry-on in the foyer and went in search of his wife. "Baby, where are you?"

"In here."

He followed the sound of her voice, walking down the hall, past the formal living and dining rooms and into the large, airy kitchen. "There's the love of my life," he said, picking her up when he reached her, twirling her around. "I'm sorry for last week, baby. I probably should have—"

"Shh." Sherri placed a finger against his lips. "Don't even go there. It was me, creating a problem where there wasn't one. All this worrying about Mom has me crazy. And you've been nothing short of amazing." She noticed the flowers that he held behind his back. "Like now," she said softly as she reached for the enormous bouquet of exotic blossoms. "These are beautiful, especially the orchids." She closed her eyes and sniffed deeply. "My favorite. Let me get a vase . . ." She turned to leave him.

"That can wait," he interrupted, pulling her back. "This is more important." He lowered his head and captured her lips in a slow, heartfelt kiss, rubbing his tongue across her lips until she opened them and then plunging inside.

Sherri placed the flowers on the island beside her before wrapping her arms around his neck to deepen the exchange. This was her husband, her man, the only man she'd ever truly loved. That she was crazy enough for even a second to mess up this good thing was beyond her. There was no way she'd ever let anyone or anything come between her and this man!

"Where's the chef?" Randall mumbled as his mouth left hers and he ran his tongue up the side of her neck.

"Gave him the day off," she breathily replied.

"But the food . . ."

"I thought I'd cook tonight. Braised ribs . . ."

"My favorite." He ran a hand across her already hardening nipples, his eyes dark with desire as they looked into hers. "Are you still . . . ?"

She shook her head. "It stopped this morning. I've douched and showered and the kids are gone."

"Then what are we still doing talking in the kitchen?"

"I have no idea, because what I want to do to you involves some edible massage oil and a nice big bed."

A little more than an hour later, Randall and Sherri were back in the kitchen, making plates of braised ribs, scalloped potatoes, and sautéed kale.

"You made these?" he asked, biting into the succulent tenderness while en route to the table.

"They're good, huh?" Sherri put down her plate on the table then went back for the glasses of tea she'd poured. "I cooked them for hours."

"Low and slow, just like I like it." The sound of his voice and the look in his eye told Sherri he was talking about more types of meat than were on the plate. "It's so good to be home."

Sherri returned to the table. "I'm glad you're back. The house never feels complete when you're away, and even less so when we're fighting."

"It's crazy because when I recalled it, I can hardly even remember what the fight was about."

"I know, right? It doesn't matter," Sherri said, reaching over and taking his hand. "We're back on track and that's what's important." She took a bite and chewed thoughtfully. "I had an interesting conversation with your daughter though, while you were gone."

"Where are the children?"

"They went with Blair to a play at her church."

"I can see Albany wanting to go, but Aaron too?"

Sherri nodded. "She showed them an excerpt on YouTube and they both wanted to see it."

"Wow, Albany and Aaron on the same page? Wonders never cease. So you had a convo with the oldest, huh? Anything I want to know about?"

"Maybe not, but you should anyway." At Randall's raised brow she continued. "She knew we were fighting and is scared we'll divorce."

"What?" Randall stopped eating and put down his fork. "Where the heck did she get that notion?"

"My thoughts exactly. I assured her that this was not the case." Sherri shared the rest of their conversation. "Turns out that one of her friends at school is having to deal with her parents divorcing. It's a contentious situation and the children are being dragged in, with both the mother and father seeking full custody."

Randall shook his head. "Not good."

"I guess the girl shared her sadness and frustration and got Al thinking."

"I don't like that it upset our daughter, but unfortunately, divorce is a reality of life."

"That's what I told her."

"Do you think I should talk to her?" Randall asked as he picked up his fork and speared a chunky piece of rib. "Reassure her that you and I will be together at the old folks' home, side by side in rocking chairs, sneaking into each other's rooms so we can get our groove on?"

"You might end up in an old folks' home. I am going to be independent and self-sufficient until the day I die." They laughed. Sherri took a sip of tea. "I appreciate the offer, but maybe we should just keep what I've shared between us. She may have thought she was speaking to me in confidence, and I'd hate to break her trust. A little PDA and a lot of laughter between us and she'll be okay."

"How's Mom Elaine?"

She told him about Ms. Riley's upcoming trip and eventual move to St. Louis. "We're working to find a qualified live-in assistant ASAP, one with whom Mom will feel comfortable, and get along."

"I wish your mom would move up here."

"You and me both; suggested that again just yesterday. She won't budge. So Nathan and I are doing what we have to do, including making more trips to personally check on her welfare. He's going there this weekend."

"That's good. What about you?"

"I'll probably make the next trip when the kids get out of school."

When Blair returned home with the children, Sherri gave her the night off so that the family could enjoy some private Atwater time. They pulled out the old board games and before the night was over, the house was once again filled with laughter. Sherri and Albany whipped up a batch of cookies and Randall and Aaron surprised the girls by volunteering to join in the fun. After everyone retired for the night, Randall and Sherri went for round two, making love low and slow . . . just the way Randall liked it. They talked well into the night, happy that in all their years of marriage, no disagreement they'd had ever lasted too long.

★   ★   ★

"Any conferences this week?"

It was the following morning. Sherri and Randall were in the master suite, both getting ready to head out for the day.

He tapped her on the butt as he came out of the shower. "Where are you headed?"

"Down the street and over to the park. There's a nice jogging trail there that Elle and I have been half running, half walking for the past few days."

"Are you losing weight?"

"I may have lost a few pounds."

"I thought so. You were lighter last night when I smacked it, flipped it up, and rubbed it down."

Sherri turned and placed her arms around him. "That was so bad," she said, giving his lips a quick peck. "But you did take care of business last night, so I can't even complain." She turned back to the vanity and reached for the toothpaste. "What about you? Out of town again?"

"Not until next weekend, a conference in Vegas. Hey, maybe you should think about joining me there."

"Really? You're going to have downtime?"

"There'll be some free time. This is a smaller conference, a meeting of the minds really, with a consortium of doctors, scientists, and researchers from across the globe. We'll be watching presentations from a series of companies offering cutting-edge technology to help us do our job. I'll be busy during the day but free most evenings. In the meantime, you can hang out with Renee, try your luck at a table or two."

"I could check Blair's schedule and see if she's free next weekend. Or better yet, I hear that Vegas is becoming more and more kid friendly. Maybe I'll pull Albany and Aaron out of school and bring them along. Their grades have been stellar; they've earned a break."

"That sounds like a plan," Randall said as he sidled up behind Sherri and wrapped his arms around her. "As long as it doesn't interfere with any test-taking. And as long as you understand that we have a lot more personal business to handle. The kids will have to have a room of their own."

The following week, the Atwaters descended on Sin City. They booked two suites at Aria Las Vegas—one for Randall and Sherri, and one for Blair and the kids. The meeting began on Monday, so Sherri decided that she and the kids would join him the weekend before so that they could enjoy time together as a family. It was agreed that Blair would fly back with the kids on Monday so they'd only miss one day of school. Sherri would stay and enjoy her days in Vegas with Renee, and her nights with her man.

CHAPTER 30

Jacqueline waved her hand at the handsome man across the lobby, quickening her strides to close the distance between them. She threw her arms around him. "The days couldn't go by fast enough," she whispered. "I'm so happy to see you again!"

"Jacqueline!" An obviously uncomfortable Randall reached up and disengaged Jacqueline's arms from around his neck, looking around as he did so. "What are you doing?"

"Sorry," she responded, seeming genuinely contrite, even as her eyes sparkled. "I just saw you and got so excited. You made me forget that we're in a public place."

"Dr. Atwater," the front desk employee called out, holding a small envelope. "Here are the new keys to your suite. So sorry that the first ones didn't work and for any inconvenience this may have caused."

"Uh, no, it wasn't any trouble. No worries at all." He turned back to Jacqueline. "I assume you're here to report on the latest technology."

Jacqueline's smile turned sultry. "Among other things." She watched as he continued to look around, and then at his watch. "Are you expecting someone?"

"It's good to see you. But I have to go. I have some business to take care of back in my suite."

Randall turned and left Jacqueline where she stood, without looking back.

Jacqueline stood calmly as she watched Randall cross the lobby to where the elevators were located. *What in the world is wrong with him? He's acting like a scared rabbit.* She turned to the front desk, saw a preppy-looking young man standing at the end of it, and walked over.

"Hello, handsome," she said, leaning on the counter so that the cleavage she was boasting, thanks to her tight knit shirt, was front and center.

"Good evening, ma'am," the young man stuttered, wondering why his comment had caused the patron to frown. "Welcome to Aria. Are you checking in tonight?"

"No, I'm here for a job application."

"Oh, I'm sorry, let me, um . . ."

"I'm just kidding, darling." Jacqueline reached into her oversized bag and pulled out her wallet. "I'm here to check in. Jacqueline Tate." She handed over her driver's license and a credit card.

The worker visibly relaxed as he took her cards and began a task that he'd handled literally hundreds of times, making small talk as he located her reservation and began entering additional information. "Is your visit business or pleasure?"

"A little of both," she purred.

"This is a city that can handle both, that's for sure."

"Indeed," she continued, leaning closer to the worker and lowering her voice, "especially when the pleasure is a clandestine affair involving a colleague. One that we have to keep very hush-hush."

"Oh." The worker swallowed, and a telltale shade of crimson began creeping slowly from his neck to his chin. "Well, you know what they say. What happens in Vegas—"

"Stays in Vegas," Jacqueline said, laughing as she finished the sentence. "Listen, I'm wondering if he's here yet. Can you please let me know if Randall Atwater has checked in?"

"Sure, I can do that." The young man clicked a couple keys, and then nodded. "Yes, he's checked in."

"Alone, correct?"

"Uh, sorry, ma'am. But we can't provide any details on our guests."

"I know it's against protocol. But you could save us and possibly your employer and this hotel huge embarrassment if you tell me. I'm not asking for specifics, you understand, no names or anything of that nature. I just want to make sure that he checked in alone."

"I'm sorry, Ms. Tate, but I simply can't provide that information. If you'd like, we have courtesy phones and you can call his room."

"Did I ask you about courtesy phones?" Jacqueline snapped. "Don't you think I've stayed in enough hotels that I know how to use a phone if I need one?"

"I'm sorry—"

"You sure are. Now shut up and get me checked in before I really lose my temper and report you to management for being incompetent."

"Yes, ma'am."

"And stop calling me ma'am!"

"Yes, ma—uh, yes, Ms. Tate."

Jacqueline reached her suite, so glad that she'd invited Kris to tag along on this trip. Relaying what had just happened in the lobby made her angry all over again.

"Calm down, Jack, you're overthinking."

Jacqueline turned away from her view of the Strip. "You might be right. But what if I'm not? He acted so weird when I approached him; jumpy, nervous even."

"He's a married man who you hugged in the lobby! How did you expect him to act?"

"Like a man who's been screwing me seven ways from Sunday, that's how. Like I'm the woman he wants to spend his life with, the woman of his dreams! He's a genius, but at the end of the day, Randall is also a nerd, a scientific geek. I'm a geek, too, but I'm also his fantasy. I'm the girl in school he wanted but could never have."

"He has you now."

"Go ahead, chick. Be sarcastic. Because you're right. He has me. I have him. And I'll do anything to keep him. He does *not* want to find out how far I'll go." Jacqueline whirled away from the window and joined Kris on the bed. "She has to be here. It's the only thing that makes sense. But you know what? I don't care. In fact, maybe it's time to take things to a whole other level." She jumped off the bed and headed for the closet. "It's time for me and Randall to have an honest conversation. After that, I'm sure he'll do the right thing."

"What's the right thing?" Kris asked.

Jacqueline turned, eyes blazing. "Leave his wife. Be with me. Simple as that."

Sherri put on her sunglasses as she stepped from the elevator into the hotel lobby. She looked around, opening her purse and reaching for her cell phone as she did. She stopped just shy of the revolving doors and scrolled her contacts for Renee's number. "Hey, girl. Where are you?"

"Parking the car. Where are you?"

"In the lobby."

"I'll be there in a sec."

Within minutes, the two best friends were strolling Aria's exclusive shopping area, oohing and aahing about overpriced items that neither needed. But that didn't matter; shopping was simply the backdrop to their being able to spend quality time together and catch up on each other's lives.

"Let's go in here," Renee said over her shoulder as she walked into a shop. "Look at these shoes!" Sherri followed her into a boutique called Terrenes, skeptically eyeing the five-inch high heel Renee held aloft. "Aren't these fantastic?"

"Yes," Sherri replied sarcastically. "For a photo shoot."

"Most definitely." Whether or not Renee caught Sherri's sarcasm was anyone's guess. "These would go perfectly with the dress I bought at Ross last week."

"Ha! Girl, you're a mess."

"Why?"

"How much are those shoes?"

"Six hundred," Renee said after glancing at the tag.

"And how much was your dress?"

Renee's smile showed her pride. "Got it on clearance for $19.99."

"You don't see the humor?"

"I don't see your point. I'm not one to worry about labels, honey. As long as it looks good on me, I'm fine." She gave a talk-to-the-hand motion to Sherri as she turned to the sales clerk. "Do you have these in a size eight?"

The women continued shopping for another hour before deciding to grab a bite to eat. "There're a couple restaurants in the hotel," Sherri suggested.

"No, girl. We're going to get you off the strip. Show you how the locals do it."

"Sounds good to me."

"Do you want to take your shopping bags to your room?"

"Sure." Sherri started toward the hotel entrance before reconsidering. "On second thought, I'm hungry. I'll just put them in your trunk so we can keep it moving."

"Sounds like a plan."

★ ★ ★

Jacqueline stepped into a skintight white mini, eyeing herself critically as she looked in the mirror and zipped it up on the side.

"What do you think?"

She watched as Kris tapped a finger against pursed lips. "Very hot, Jackie."

Jacqueline exhaled. "I hoped you'd think so." She turned to check out her firm derrière, which was on full display in the tight-fitting dress. "You don't think it's too . . . trashy?"

"Perhaps, but in the classiest sort of way." Jacqueline laughed. "I think it's a great choice," Kris continued. "After seeing you in this, Randall won't think twice about divorcing his wife."

Jacqueline bent over, ran her hand through the long locks that today were worn in their naturally curly state, and then straightened and flipped the hair back from her face. The result was a wild mane full of body, which added to a look that screamed femme fatale.

"You look fabulous, Jack. But are you sure about doing this right now?"

"Kris! Why are you asking me that? I've made up my mind!"

"Not whether you should do it at all, but whether you think the timing is right—now, unannounced, in the middle of the afternoon? Or would it be better to make an appointment, or catch him publicly? If his wife is with him, Jack, there'll be a scene."

"I overheard him say that he was headed for his suite and a conference call. I also heard talk about the men perhaps meeting for dinner tonight, and one of the doctors said that the bulk of the presentations will happen tomorrow and many attendees are leaving tomorrow night instead of Wednesday. If

Sherri's there, I'll deal with it. But one way or another, Randall is going to know the truth of how I feel about him . . . about us."

"Good luck," Kris said, giving Jacqueline a thumbs-up. "You deserve to be happy. I mean it."

CHAPTER 31

"Is that it, guys?" Randall sat back against the plush brown sofa and placed his feet on the matching ottoman. Two researchers from his company asked a few more clarifying questions to ensure their directions were clear. He answered them. "All right then, team. I guess that's it. Thanks again for all your hard work. Dan, keep me posted on our request for special clearance. I want you to call me as soon as that comes in."

"Will do, boss."

Randall's head turned toward the knock on his door. He stood. "Thanks. Listen, I think my wife may have forgotten her key card. I'll see you guys soon." He disconnected the call and reached the door just as the person knocked again. "Did you forget your k—" When he saw who stood in the doorway, Randall's tone and demeanor completely changed. "Jacqueline? What the heck are you doing here?"

Jacqueline pushed by him. "That's the second time in as many days that you've asked that question," she said lightly, though there was no smile in her voice. She turned and crossed her arms. "I'm beginning to get annoyed."

"Make that two of us," Randall said, once the shock of her brazen entry had worn off enough for him to react. "First you grope me down in the lobby and now you show up in my room? Your actions are highly inappropriate, Ms. Tate. I'd like you to leave."

"Ah. Ms. Tate, is it?" Jacqueline slinked over to where he stood and ran a fingernail down the side of his face.

Randall recoiled.

"I think we're way past formalities, don't you?"

"All right, Jacqueline, if you insist. I'll ask just once more before calling security. What are you doing here? Specifically, why have you come to my room? Wait a minute. How did you even know my floor?"

Instead of answering, Jacqueline walked over to the bar area, opened a Fuji water and poured a glass. "I don't know what has you acting so . . . weird. Normally you're laid-back and ready for fun. What's going on?"

"Laid-back? Ready for fun?" Randall looked behind him to see who she was talking to, convinced it wasn't him. Then he headed for the door. "Look, I don't know what game you're playing, but it's about to be over. You need to leave." He opened the door. "Now."

In answer, Jacqueline headed for the bedroom. Randall was right behind her.

"This is an amazing view," she said, taking in the nearly all-glass walls that offered a 180-degree view of Vegas. She crawled on the bed, unzipped her dress, and exposed her newly-waxed wonder. "But I think this view is better."

He quickly turned his head away from the sight of her labia. "Have you lost your mind? Zip up your dress! And get the hell out of here! I'm not going to ask again."

Jacqueline laughed, got up from the bed and did as asked. "Okay, I get it. It's the middle of the day and you still have meetings. It's just that we haven't talked since yesterday in the lobby. I haven't had the chance to feel those magical lips on mine."

This statement was met with a blank stare. But his complacency didn't last long. "That's it. You're leaving." He walked toward the hotel phone.

"Randall, no!" Jacqueline rushed over to keep him from punching the front desk button. "Please. I know Sherri's here. Which makes what I have to say, and what you need to hear, even more important."

"You have my cell number," Randall calmly replied, wrestling the phone away from Jacqueline and placing it back on the receiver. "Leave my room and send me a text."

"You've got to leave her, Randall. I'm in love with you."

For a moment, time stopped. Jacqueline held her breath, gauging Randall's reaction. Randall paused to wonder what he'd really just heard.

In love with me? "Impossible."

"I know how you feel about me. It's in your eyes, on your face, every time we're together."

Randall scowled.

Jacqueline hurried on, blocking his potential objection. "Yes, it's crazy. We've known each other for such a short time. But you've got to know that I consider you more than a friend."

"How do you figure? We talked over dinner, you interviewed me a time or two. You're not a friend, you're an *acquaintance* who doesn't know me at all."

"What about LA?"

"What about it?" Randall asked, his voice growing uncharacteristically loud.

"When we had dinner," she said, taking one step toward him.

"It was just dinner, Jacqueline; great food, good conversation, nothing more."

"Until we made love." She took another step. "There, New York, Chicago . . ."

"That's it. I don't need security." He placed a firm hand on her arm and began walking her to the door. "You're leaving. Now!"

"No!" She twisted her arm out of his grasp and stepped out of his reach. "I'm not going anywhere. I will *not* be ignored or disrespected just because your wife is in town, and treated as though you haven't been screwing me from expo to conference, from state to state!"

Randall took a deep breath, his voice low and calm as he responded. "Jacqueline, I don't know what you're talking about. I don't know who you're sleeping with. But it's not me. There is *nothing* going on between us."

With shopping and lunch over, Renee pulled into the valet area of the Aria hotel. She and Sherri waved away the bell captain and removed Sherri's shopping bags from Renee's trunk.

"Are you coming up?" Sherri asked as they entered the hotel. "Or do you want to wait here while I put these away and then hit the casino?"

"No, I want to come with you and use the bathroom." They crossed the lobby and reached the elevator, Renee taking in every square foot. "I'll probably not ever be able to stay in a place this nice."

"I told you what you need to do." Sherri pressed the button for the elevator.

"What?"

"Stop being a cougar. Find an older man with a genteel nature and a healthy bank account."

Sherri's phone rang.

"Sorry, sis, but I don't see that happening. You know how much I love a bad boy."

"Hello, Blair," Sherri said into the phone, holding up a finger to shush Renee. "Have you guys made it home okay?"

The elevator arrived. Renee took a step inside but Sherri stopped her. *I don't want to drop the call,* she mouthed. Renee nodded and stepped out of the elevator. "Go ahead," she said to the gentleman holding the door open. "Thanks."

"That sounds good," Sherri said. "Call and let the pet sitters know you're back. They will bring the dogs home." She looked in the direction that Renee had pointed and shook her head at the young, buff brother her thirty-something friend admired. "Uh-huh," she said into the phone. "Just make sure the kids do their homework. You guys can order takeout, whatever you want." She nodded as Blair responded. "Right, the housekeeper comes on Tuesdays. She knows the routine, so just let her in and let her do her thing." Once again, Sherri pushed the elevator button. "I'll check in periodically, but call me if you need me. Okay, bye."

"Wait a minute," Renee said, as once again the elevator door opened. "I want to check something out real quick."

"Is *something* young, male, and breathing?" Sherri asked with an expression that suggested that she already knew the answer.

"Don't judge me," Renee said, moving in the direction of her interest. "You know I like to shop."

"Jacqueline, please, I don't want to argue." Randall's denial of intimacy between them had sent Jacqueline into a tirade, and seeing her about to come totally unglued, he quickly decided to try a different tactic. "There's obviously been a misunderstanding." A major understatement, but right now he'd say almost anything to get this crazy woman out of his suite. "I'm open to talking to you so that we can work it out. Just not here. And not now."

"Because Sherri's here."

"Yes."

"Well, isn't that just cozy. A family affair. It might have been quite nice to meet your children, considering how close I've become with their father."

"Please, Jacqueline. I don't want any problems."

"Who are you trying to protect? Me or your wife?"

"My reputation," he quickly answered, believing that mentioning how much he loved his wife was not the best idea. "A scandal making the news could jeopardize careers for both of us."

This seemed to get through to her. She nodded subtly. "I guess you're right. Given what I know, I'd have to agree that now is not the time. But when?"

"When we get back to D.C. I'll call you. We'll do lunch."

She walked over and stood in front of him. "Promise?"

He reached for her arm, more gently this time, and began guiding her toward the door. Reaching it, he opened it tentatively, stuck his head out, and looked the length of the hallway. "Would you mind taking the stairs?" he asked her. "Just a couple floors," he hurriedly added when a protest seemed imminent. "I don't want you and Sherri getting into it. At a conference of this magnitude, that type of drama is the last thing I need." Randall heard the elevator ding. "Go! Please hurry!"

Jacqueline leaned in to kiss him full on the mouth. Randall stepped back, barely avoiding her fiery red lipstick. She covered her anger at the affront with a great big smile. "You'd better call me when you get back to D.C., Randall. Or I'll be upset. And trust me. You do *not* want to make me unhappy."

She walked quickly toward the exit sign, looking back for one final wave. She'd barely turned one corner when Sherri and Renee came around another.

Randall turned his head and rubbed a heavy hand across his mouth. He prayed that no lipstick had touched his face.

"Who are you looking for, pizza delivery?" Renee teased as they neared him.

"Who are you looking for?" Sherri asked, no joking in her voice.

"I thought I heard a knock." Randall was still rattled. "I thought maybe you'd forgotten your card key." He moved so the ladies could go inside, quickly looking around as he followed them in for any sign that Jacqueline had been there.

A sign other than his still rapidly pounding heart.

Sherri took two steps and stopped dead in her tracks. "Do I smell perfume?"

Renee turned around, sniffing as she retraced her steps. "Hmm, I smell something."

Sherri turned to her husband. "Randall?"

"Randall, what?" he asked, his hands in that trademark what-the-hell pose. "I don't smell anything. And I sure as hell don't wear perfume."

"Is it me?" Renee walked over and placed her wrist under Sherri's nose. "Earlier I tried on this, the new one by Versace."

After a careful look around the room and another one at Randall, Sherri relaxed. "Maybe so."

"Girl, this suite is amazing! Look at the view!"

Thankfully, Renee's comment shifted the topic. When Renee went into the bathroom, Sherri answered a text from Aaron. Randall, who was not much of a drinker, walked to the bar, poured a shot, slammed it back, and scrunched his face against the burn.

Once out of the bathroom, Renee joined Sherri who'd walked into the bedroom, leaving a shell-shocked Randall in mental disarray. His mind whirled from the last several minutes. *What the hell just happened?* Accusations of adultery? Jacqueline Tate professing love? *What is going on?*

CHAPTER 32

"Urrggghhhh!" Jacqueline shut the hotel room door and then kicked it for emphasis.

Kris came from around the corner. "What happened?"

"I'm so pissed right now!" Jacqueline exclaimed. She walked over to a table and swept its contents on the floor. "I can't believe he's treating me like this!"

"Calm down, Jack."

"I don't want to calm down! I feel like hurting somebody." Her eyes were crazy wild as she looked around her. "If I could get my hands on Sherri right now, I'd—"

"Wait—you saw her?"

"No, but she's here."

"Oh, man." Kris's concern was evident. "What did Randall say when you arrived?"

"Asked me what I was doing there, as if he didn't know. I paid over three hundred dollars for it, but he didn't even notice my dress!"

"Okay, Jacqueline. I get why you're upset. But come on, the man's wife's here. Granted, you didn't know for sure, but now that you do, you have to understand why he did what he did."

"He wants to be with me, Kris. Even now, even with her here. I could feel his desire. I could see it in his eyes!"

"All the more reason why he wouldn't want to cause a scene right now." She paused, giving Jacqueline the chance to entertain a different perspective. "If he is in love with you, as you believe, their home life is probably the pits right now. Can you begin to imagine how his wife must feel? They probably aren't having sex; I doubt he even shows her any affection. She probably threw a tantrum just to come on this trip."

"He didn't have to bring her," Jacqueline countered, but there was less venom in her voice. "He knew I'd be here."

"He knows what you should remember: that you two have the rest of your lives. He's a high profile scientist, Jack, who knows how damaging a divorce can be to his public persona and private career. He has to handle everything correctly, has to work out things with his wife just so. He won't want to do anything to make the proceedings any more acrimonious. He'll have to shovel out a ton in alimony and child support as it is."

Jacqueline walked over to the couch and sat, her face scrunched in a frown. "He acted as though we hadn't been together, like I was crazy and making all of this up."

"Girlfriend, don't you get it? He was terrified that his wife would come back to their room and find you there. Denial was his only choice!"

"I guess."

"Did he say he'd call you later, that you two would talk and he'd explain everything?"

"He wants to have lunch when he gets back to D.C."

"Then that's what you'll do. He was married when you met him, tied down when you two got together. You knew it would be awhile before he could take his love public, maybe even a year or more before he could divorce so the two of you can tie the knot. Patience, chick. That's what you have to practice right now. Use that, and confidence, knowing that when all is said and done, you'll be the beautiful bitch with the handsome husband. Leave the role of the nagging, insecure woman to his soon-to-be ex-wife."

Sherri looked around the room, taking in the warm, soothing ambiance of Sage restaurant in the Aria hotel. She admired the use of browns and bronzes, and the thoughtful use of purples and creams. Spending the day with Renee had been a stark reminder that life was different for those with money, and status was something she'd begun to take for granted. And her incessant paranoia had almost messed things up again. Earlier, upon reentering their suite, she could have sworn she smelled perfume. Her mind had immediately gone to the possibility that Jacqueline had been there. Pure nonsense. For all she knew the woman wasn't even at this conference. Starting tonight, this moment, Sherri vowed to be more observant of and appreciative for what she had, the life she lived, and the man she'd married. All were huge blessings in her life and she vowed to be more thankful.

"Honey, this setting is beautiful."

"Hmm . . ."

"Thanks for bringing me here." She looked up, continuing to admire the chandeliers and columns. "The interior designer tried to talk me into getting a chandelier for our bedroom. I couldn't see her vision, but now . . . I'm thinking it just might . . . Randall? Randall!"

"Excuse me, baby. What did you say?"

"Did you hear anything I just said?"

"I'm sorry. My mind wandered for a minute."

"Is it work? Have the meetings gone well?"

"They've been enlightening. But I don't want to talk about work right now." He reached across the table and grabbed her hand. "I want to enjoy the most beautiful woman in the room, the woman who I was lucky enough to persuade to say yes, and become my wife."

"Ah. . . . that's sweet, baby. I'm pretty lucky too."

"You think so?"

Sherri smiled, placing her chin in her hand as her mind traveled to yesteryear. "Remember those early days, baby, right after we got married? That tiny ground floor apartment and the neighbors who screwed nonstop?"

"If they weren't fucking, they were fighting," Randall said, his voice low and filled with mischief. "I think they got a kick out of the notion that their antics could be heard."

"Then I'd see her in the parking lot in her conservative suit and sensible pumps, heading to her job at the courthouse. She was so proud of being a paralegal. I'd give her a look like 'uh-huh, I heard you,' and she'd act all innocent and nonchalant."

"What was her name?"

"Erma. And the man we heard, the one who she eventually married, his name is Wally."

"How do you know?"

"Ran into her several years later, when I was teaching first grade. She walked into the class with a child who looked just like him. I took one look at the little angel and said, "I guess hard work paid off."

"Ha!"

The sound of tinkling laughter caused Randall to tense up. He tried to hide his discomfort, but it was written all over his face.

Sherri immediately noticed the change. "Honey, what is it?"

"Nothing."

A woman passed their table. Randall averted his eyes, causing Sherri to turn around. She glimpsed the back of a tall, slender woman in a sleek print dress, with dark hair piled in a loose ponytail on the top of her head. When she turned back to Randall, he'd visibly relaxed.

Several seconds passed before Sherri spoke. "Do you want

me to sit over here and stew all evening, or do you want to tell me exactly what is going on?"

He sighed, reaching over to fiddle with his water glass. He picked it up, took a long swallow, and sighed again. "I don't want to upset you."

"Your silence is already pissing me off." Sherri turned again, searching for the woman. She saw her sitting several tables away; an olive-skinned woman with strong, dramatic features. At first she thought that it might be Jacqueline, but the woman's face was rounder, her nose more pronounced than the woman who'd previously caused Sherri so much chagrin.

She turned back to Randall once more. To be sure, she asked him, "Is that Jacqueline?" He shook his head. "I didn't think so." She continued to study her husband. "So why did you act so nervous just now?"

"Honestly, because I thought it was her."

"Is she here?" He nodded. "But that's what she does, right? Cover these types of conferences?"

"Yes." Randall took another sip of water, wishing he had something stronger to drink.

"Then why would seeing her make you upset?"

"Something strange happened today, baby. It was very unnerving. I now want to tell you what I couldn't share earlier. But please stay calm when I do. Because there is absolutely no truth to what she believes."

"Who, Jacqueline?"

A pause and then, "She came to the room."

"When?" The frown popped up on Sherri's face so fast she couldn't even hide it.

"Earlier today, just before you and Renee returned from shopping."

"So I was right! I *did* smell perfume . . . and it was hers."

"Trust me. I was as shocked and angry then as you are now."

"How'd she know our room number?"

"I don't know. But she knocked on the door and I thought it was you, thought you'd forgotten your key card."

Sherri sat back and crossed her arms. The waiter approached. She waved him away and refocused on Randall. "I'm listening."

"I opened the door and she barged in. I was so shocked that at first . . . I just stood there. Then she started talking crazy and—"

"About what?"

"Long story short . . . she came to the room to tell me that I need to leave you because she's in love with me." He waited for a response.

"I'm listening."

"Sherri, I swear I don't know where all this is coming from."

"You had to do something to make her feel that divorcing me was an option."

Randall shook his head. "Nothing that I haven't done with other business associates: the interviews, a couple of meetings, dinner—"

"Dinner?"

"Yes, Sherri. She and I had dinner together in LA. But that was it! We shared a meal in a public place, and continued an interview that had begun earlier that day. It was totally innocent, baby. You've got to believe that."

"What I believe," Sherri said, shaking her head, "is that you have no idea how a woman thinks. Where did you have dinner? McDonalds?"

"No." Randall's voice was low, subdued.

"Some kid-friendly buffet?" He shook his head. "I bet it was at an upscale establishment just like this, with a romantic atmosphere and a little privacy to boot. How am I doing?"

"That . . . pretty much describes it."

"Was it only the one time?"

"Dinner with just the two of us? Yes. But we've, you know, shared small talk at other conferences."

"You've seen her in other cities besides LA and D.C.?"

"For the past few weeks, she's been at every conference. But that's not unusual. There are several reporters I know on a first name basis."

"Yes, but did you take them to dinner?"

"That wasn't wise. I see that now."

"This doesn't make sense." Sherri's eyes narrowed as she pondered what she'd just learned. "Women don't just fall in love after sharing a single meal. You had to have flirted, hinted, done something . . ."

"Damn." Randall ran a weary hand over his face. "We went to a play in New York." Sherri gave him the kind of look where no words were needed. "She told me that Phillip had planned to join her in Manhattan but had to cancel at the last minute. She had an extra ticket to a play, one where another associate, a young man named Evan, was to join us as well.

"She arrived alone. I asked about Evan and after texting him, she said he couldn't make it." Sherri snorted. "And the PSI visit. Because of the cover story on me that she was writing for *Science Today*, I'd thought her seeing the offices was a good idea."

"I bet she did too."

"Sherri, I swear to you on my life. I did nothing to make her think I was interested."

"You never flirted, never teased, never looked at her with those baby-boy eyes?" Randall shifted uncomfortably. "Of course you did."

She let out a huff and then, taking in the true devastation on her husband's face, softened her voice. "What did you say when she told you she loved you?"

"Basically, that she was crazy. I assured her that not only had absolutely nothing happened between her and I, but also that you and our children were here, in Vegas! Then I told her to get out of the room before I called security. Before opening the door, baby, I didn't look to see who was out there. I assumed it was you!" He rested his forehead against his fingers, all appetite gone. "I sure hope she got the message and stays the hell out of my life."

"That would be the best thing," Sherri said, calmly picking up her menu and beginning to read. "But don't count on it."

CHAPTER 33

Randall groped for his phone, eyes still closed, and silenced it once again. "I'm sorry, baby," he grumbled.

"Was that her again?" Sherri asked, her voice filled with sleep.

"Yeah."

"What time is it?"

"Five thirty."

"Why don't you just turn off your phone?"

"Can't. There are too many important calls from overseas I'd potentially miss."

Five minutes later the phone rang again. A frustrated Randall threw back the covers and got out of bed. "Might as well start the day," he grumbled, "since it looks like my chance for peaceful sleep is over."

"I still think I should answer the phone. I have a few things to say to Ms. Jacqueline, trust and believe."

"I know you do, Sherri, and you have every right to want to confront her. But you should have seen her. She acted . . . off. I don't know how else to say it. Let me handle this, baby, talk to her when we get back home—"

"Talk to her? Seriously? Oh, hell no!"

"I've got to try to get her to see reason. Obviously there's been a big misunderstanding. But one thing I've learned in my time with the media: You don't want to piss off someone with a pen. Just one meeting, Sherri. I'll apologize for anything I did to give her a wrong impression and try to . . . calm things down."

Sherri nodded but didn't respond.

"I'm going to take a shower."

"Okay." She smiled, watching Randall's still firm, toned ass as he walked around the corner and into the bathroom. As soon as she heard the water running, however, her whole mood changed. He'd asked her not to, but she'd made him no promises. She reached across the bed, grabbed his phone from the nightstand, and scrolled the screen for missed calls. Without hesitation, she redialed the number.

"Good morning, handsome," Jacqueline purred into her ear. "About time you called back."

"Jacqueline." Sherri's voice was as cold as an Alaskan winter. "This is Sherri, Randall's wife. You know, the one who you feel he should divorce?" Silence. "He told me about your little declaration of love when you stopped by our suite yesterday. So let me tell you this. There is already one Mrs. Atwater, and there will not be another. You got that? I can appreciate your being interested in someone as handsome, intelligent, and successful as my husband. You're not the first sorry skirt to go chasing after him and you won't be the last. But when it comes to wives . . . I'm it. Do you understand? Hello? Hello?!" She looked down and saw that the call had disconnected. "Conniving whore," she hissed under her breath. "Hanging up was your best bet."

Sherri got out of bed and walked over to her purse. She retrieved her phone, recorded Jacqueline's number into her contacts, and placed Randall's phone back on the nightstand. It would have been foolish for her to return to bed; there was enough adrenaline pumping through her right now to run a mile. So that's what she decided to do. She pulled out some workout gear and headed for the hotel's exercise room. Before leaving, however, she texted Renee.

THE YOU KNOW WHAT HAS HIT THE FAN. I'LL CALL YOU LATER.

Jacqueline sat, deceptively calm and still. Outwardly she barely moved, but inwardly her mind was racing.

It had been twenty-four hours since she had endured Sherri's cocky takedown in Las Vegas, and she was still seeing red. When she got off the phone, she'd smashed a vase to smithereens and worn a new groove into the hardwood floor, then she'd turned on her computer and began doing a variety of searches: Randall Atwater address; Sherri Atwater address; Atwaters Alexandria Virginia; Atwaters Virginia; Dr. Atwater address; and on and on. Finally, she pulled up the PSI website, and within minutes—using the techniques Marco had shown her—had cracked the security code and gained full access. This did little good. There was no hidden data on where the Atwaters resided. Knowing that staying in Sin City was futile, she'd quickly checked out of the hotel and boarded a plane.

Now she sat brooding in a rental car, in the parking lot of the office building where PSI was located. She'd dressed casually, jeans and a simple navy blue tee, her hair and part of her face hidden behind dark glasses and a baseball cap. She sat there, waiting, observing the comings and goings, waiting until a glimpse of genius came to her, until she had a plan.

She sat there for two hours, waiting for she knew not what. Finally, she saw a perky blonde cutting across the lawn heading to the parking lot, deep in conversation with a handsome brown-haired gentleman dressed in a polo shirt and jeans. Jacqueline immediately recognized her as Randall's executive assistant, the one who sat directly outside his office whom she had been introduced to when she'd toured the place. *On her way to lunch, no doubt,* Jacqueline thought as she continued to watch her. *If you're going to make a move, Jacqueline, you need to do it now.*

With a half-baked plan and nerves of steel, Jacqueline casually exited her car. She'd purposely parked in the back of the parking lot, next to a row of service vehicles. Keeping her head down, she made her way to the building's front door and, attaching herself to a group of businessmen, stepped inside the building after one had used his card to gain access. She headed directly for the elevators and, instead of stepping in with the same group of men, opted to wait for the next one, hopefully empty. A car arrived and opened. She hurried inside. Pushing the button to the top floor, she still had no idea how she was going to get past the receptionist, past the occupied offices with doors often open, and into Randall's office. She just knew that it was going to happen. One way or another. She pushed the button to close the door. Just before it shut, someone entered. *Dammit!* Pulling out her phone, she busied herself with the illusion of texting, so that keeping her head down would not look suspicious.

"Jacqueline?"

Her heart stopped at the mention of her name. She slowly raised her head. "Evan?" Her face broke into a friendly smile. "Oh my goodness. I haven't seen you since the conference in New York. I thought you lived in LA."

"I do."

"What are you doing on this side of the country?"

"I'm doing a six-month internship with Dan Cole, one of Dr. Atwater's colleagues."

"Really?"

"Yeah. After a brief meeting with Dr. Atwater in New York, he suggested I send my resume. I did. Dan called me, just last week. What about you? Do you work in this building?" As he said it, Jacqueline noted him taking in her attire.

"Oh no," she said, offering up a flirty laugh. "I'm off today, but came over to pick up some information from Dr. Atwater. It's for the article I'm doing on him."

Evan frowned. "I thought he was at a conference in Vegas."

"He is," Jacqueline quickly countered. "I'm getting this from his secretary."

The small talk continued as they reached the impressive embossed doors to Randall's company. The receptionist looked up, and upon seeing Evan pulling out his key card, took no note of the woman beside him. They entered, passed the lobby, and started down the hallway.

"It was nice seeing you, Evan. I'm in a hurry though, so let me run. Enjoy your time in D.C."

"Hey, maybe we can . . ."

Whatever he said or was going to say, Jacqueline didn't hear. She was on a mission, and Evan's purpose had been served.

Two days later, Blair looked up from her cell phone as the doorbell rang. "Hold on, Kirk," she said to her boyfriend. "Somebody's at the door." She reached the door and looked through the peephole. Seeing a casually dressed, plain-looking woman wearing thick glasses, she opened the door.

"Yes, may I help you?"

"Hello, Blair. Housecleaning," the woman said in a heavily accented voice.

"Excuse me?"

"I with housecleaning service. I'm here to clean house."

Blair looked beyond the woman to the street, searching for the regular housecleaner's black Honda Accord. "Where's Lucia?"

"Sick," the woman said, keeping her eyes downcast. "The company sent me to work for her." The woman held up a bucket filled with cleaning supplies. Propped up next to the front door were a broom and a mop. "I do a good job."

"Why did you bring all that? Didn't the company tell you that the supplies are kept here?"

"I like to use my own. Special cleaning." Jacqueline had no intention of leaving anything bearing her fingerprints behind.

The woman smiled, and Blair noted that her teeth were badly stained. Taking in her scruffy clothing and battered tennis shoes caused a wave of sympathy to wash over the young, caring adult. She smiled back sincerely. "Sure. Come on in."

Blair stood aside so the woman could enter. "What's your name?"

"Ruth."

"Nice to meet you, Ruth. I'm Blair."

The housecleaning employee stopped just inside the foyer. Her eyes darted from one place to the other, before settling on the floor. "This beautiful home," she said.

"Yes, it is." Sensing the woman's discomfort, Blair tried for small talk. "You have a lovely accent, Ruth. Where are you from?"

"The islands."

"Oh! I love the Caribbean. I've been there several times. Which one?"

Instead of looking at her directly, the woman stared just beyond Blair's shoulder. "Where you travel?"

"Let's see." Blair began counting on her hands. "Jamaica, Grand Cayman, Puerto Rico—those all on one cruise—and then the Bahamas, Barbados, and Aruba."

"I'm from Belize," Ruth quickly responded.

Blaire frowned. "Isn't Belize in Central America?"

Ruth shrugged. "All island to me." She looked at her watch. "This big house. Best get started."

"Sure, I'm sorry. Did they tell you what to clean?" The woman shook her head. "No problem. I'll show you around."

Ten minutes later, the two ladies stood in the Atwaters' master suite. "I think I'll start here," Ruth said, reaching for the furniture polish. "Thank you."

She turned her back, a clear sign of dismissal. Blair left the room.

Jacqueline counted to ten and then pulled out the pouch from where it had been hidden beneath her bulky clothes. It contained a lock pick kit, several motion-activated mini-cams equipped with night-vision lenses and high-frequency recorders, GPS trackers, and an item that would serve as Jacqueline's calling card. Thanks to her visit to Randall's office, and with the help of a code-breaking recovery stick, she'd also been able to capture the totality of what was on his office computer, information that had been blocked by his company's elaborate computer security system. Contained in that information were both the household and family itineraries. This document, along with conversations she'd heard courtesy of the disc recorders on their phones, apprised Jacqueline of the family's movements and schedule, including that of their cleaning personnel. After today there would be nothing inside the Atwater home that she couldn't see, and little she couldn't hear. She hadn't lied to Blair. This was a big house. She needed to be thorough. And work fast.

After donning thick, latex gloves she stripped the bed, emptied the hampers, scrubbed the master bath until it sparkled, and dusted until not one speck remained. Methodically, she "cleaned" every room in the house, testing equipment as she went. She took the trash out through the garage and left a tracking "gift" beneath each of their cars.

Four hours later, and she was done. She quickly gathered up her supplies and placed them by the door. Then she went back upstairs and walked into the master suite one final time. She'd almost forgotten to leave her calling card. Taking one last look around, she headed for the foyer. The job was done. It was time to go.

Halfway down the stairs, Jacqueline heard voices. Her heart almost stopped beating inside her chest. She held her breath, straining to hear the voices and what was being said.

"So your practice got canceled?"

Oh, Blair's voice. What a gullible girl. She let out a shaky breath.

"Yes, but Coach said that we . . ."

Jacqueline didn't wait to hear the rest, just hoped that Blair and the little rug rat she guessed was Randall's son were somewhere out of sight of the front door. She'd get her stuff, run the hell out the door, and hope no one saw her between there and the block or so to the rental car, parked beyond the community gates. Blair would know she was gone when a search failed to find her. Good-bye wasn't necessary for folks you'd never see again.

It crept closer, the fire. Slowly, surely, flames licking her ankles and taunting her hem. She stepped back.

"Help me!"

She stepped forward. "I'm coming to get you. Hold out your hand!"

Another step. Stainless steel scissors, gripped, dripping blood.

Two more steps. And then a scream. But that's not what stopped her, what kept her planted where she stood. What paralyzed her was the odor that rushed toward her on the waves of the wind: smells of boiling beer, feigned ignorance, gin-soaked blankets, and acrid, burning flesh. Or was the repulsive stench that of once raw chicken, covered in sweat?

Jacqueline awoke to the sound of her rapidly beating heart.

CHAPTER 34

"Good afternoon!" Randall entered his office with a new kind of pep in his step, offering the company receptionist a hearty smile. The Jacqueline fiasco notwithstanding, the trip to Las Vegas had been a good one, providing a breath of fresh air to his marriage, which he and Sherri both realized had been long overdue. After the conference, they'd stayed two extra days, most of them in bed. By the time he returned to Virginia, thoughts of Jacqueline were few and far between, and that time he'd mysteriously fallen asleep in his office was a distant memory.

Randall greeted his executive assistant, then walked into his office singing a tune. Firing up his laptop, he quickly scrolled through the day's e-mails and checked Outlook for appointments and messages. Seeing that there was nothing urgent, he called his number-two man. "Dan, it's Randall. I'm in the office. You got a minute?"

Within minutes his good friend came through the door. A study in contradictions, this sixty-something brainiac from Bern, Switzerland had curly black hair, looked not a day over forty, and had already retired from two careers. After losing his wife to breast cancer, he'd taken Randall up on a jokingly delivered offer to "come over to America and do something great." With his expertise on the brain and Randall's skill in the lab, it looked as though these two close friends were poised to do just that.

"Good afternoon, good Doctor," Dan said, his soothing voice laced with the merest of accents. "How did you find the city of sin?"

"Full of temptation." Dan's brow rose. "Fortunately they all came courtesy of my wife."

"Ha! So Sherri joined you? Smart girl." Dan looked around before lowering his voice. "How are the plans coming for . . ." He let the sentence hang in the air.

"Moving forward, Doc. Thanks for asking." Randall glanced at someone passing by and changed the subject. "How did it go while I was out? Did I miss anything interesting?"

"No, not really. Except there was one interesting article that landed on my desk: a report written by a Nigerian doctor about a plant native to Africa, grown and only available in a five-square-mile area. Evan uncovered it and sent me a copy. There's probably one in your mail as well."

Randall went back to his e-mails and put Evan's name in the search engine. The article that Dan spoke of appeared at the top. He starred it. "I'll be sure to read it later. Thanks." He leaned back, lacing his fingers behind his head. "Anything else?"

For the next thirty minutes the two men chatted, their conversation passing easily from science to golfing and from medicine to sports. Both were huge Redskins fans, though Dan professed to still be learning the game. A phone call interrupted their casual conversation. Dan went back to his office and Randall spent the next few hours reading, returning phone calls, and checking his mail. He was just about to head to the lab when the intern walked by.

"Evan."

Evan stepped back. "Hello, Dr. Atwater."

Randall waved him in. "Glad I saw you. Interesting article you found on the African cacti."

"It looked like something that might be useful to your work, sir. Dan agreed."

"Both of you were right. I'd like you to keep digging, forward anything and everything you find on the subject, including contact information for any of the personnel connected to the study."

"Hey, if you go to Africa, can I tag along?"

Randall's face was one of amused surprise. "You'd want to?"

"Absolutely. I'd love to be a part of a scientific or medical breakthrough."

"I appreciate your hard work while you're here. You're heading back to Cornell for your junior year, correct?"

"That's correct."

"Well, you're doing well here, so keep in touch. When it's time to find employment, we just might be able to work something out."

"Thank you, sir. I appreciate it."

"You're welcome." Randall began shuffling papers, a sign that the conversation was over. "All right, let's get back to work."

Evan began walking toward the door. "Oh, Dr. Atwater?"

Randall looked up. "Yes?"

"Have you spoken to Jacqueline since returning back home?"

The hairs on Randall's neck stood up. "No," he replied, as calmly as his suddenly tense nerves would allow. "Why would you ask?"

"I ran into her yesterday when she stopped by the office."

"What office?" Randall queried with a crease in his brow.

"Uh, this office." Sensing Randall's unease, Evan hurriedly added, "She was getting the paperwork you left for her, the information you gave your secretary for her to pick up? Thought she might have called you about it."

"Oh, right. The papers. Thanks for letting me know she got them, Evan. Now, could you please close the door on your way out?" Randall watched him leave, and as soon as the door latch clicked shut, he picked up the phone and dialed the security firm protecting their building. He forced his voice to remain calm when the call was answered. "Yes, this is Dr. Atwater. There's been a breach in our office security. I need to speak to the captain, and I need to speak to him now."

Sherri reached for another grape as she studied the information on her iPad. She was happy, excited, and a wee bit nervous. Going to Vegas had been just what the marriage doctor ordered, and the stunt that Jacqueline pulled had been a blessing in disguise. She believed that Randall had been faithful, and a long sistah-girl chat with Renee had helped her refocus on that fact. It had also led to a conversation she'd had with her husband on the plane ride back to D.C. She'd been pleased at Randall's reaction when she'd mentioned returning to the workplace, if only part-time.

"You gave up a lot to support me," he'd said, reaching for her hand and squeezing. "The kids are growing up, the business is doing well. If that's what you want to do, if it will make you happy, then . . . go for it."

So here she sat, having Googled and Binged and called former associates to try to get a bead on the education climate today. When she'd left her career, she'd been on a fast track to becoming a principal, then a president, and eventually a college dean. Those days and dreams were behind her; the desire to reach those heights had passed. But the genuine love of teaching remained inside her, the joy in giving back still stirred her soul. *Maybe I should research alternative options for sharing knowledge.* She sat back, popped another grape, and thought about academics within detention centers, prisons, and centers for people at risk. *Randall and I are so fortunate. Our children are receiving the best education that money can buy.* She stood and walked to the plate-glass window that covered most of the back of the great room. She took in the perfectly landscaped yard with its cabana and pool. *They have every tool at their disposal, everything needed to ensure success.* Thinking back to her and her husband's challenging childhoods increased her interest in this new possibility: going outside of her tony environment and using her education to help those who needed it most. A smile scampered across her face as she felt a conviction about this direction, felt goose bumps of excitement cover her arm. She thought of her mom, the woman who'd inspired her love of teaching, and decided to give her a call.

"Mom, guess what?" she began by way of greeting, placing the phone on speaker as she walked around the room.

"Sherri? How are you, baby?"

"I'm fantastic!"

"Oh? Why's that?"

"Randall and I just returned from a short vacation, during which I decided to return to teaching. I'm going back into the classroom, Mom."

"Well, now. This is a surprise. No wonder you sound so happy. And Randall approves?"

"Yes. He said that if it made me happy, then I had his full support."

"That's wonderful, Sherri."

Sherri paused, listening closely to see if she heard anything amiss in her mother's voice or breathing. "How about you, Mom? Is everything okay?"

"I'm fine, girl!" Sherri heard the frustration in her mother's voice. "I keep telling everybody that. And I'm still angry at Constance for suggesting I need someone taking care of me full-time. I can take care of myself."

"Ms. Riley only does what she does because she loves you." Sherri's voice was soft as she shared this truth. "As you probably know, she's going to St. Louis soon, and may be moving there. We all want you safe. Nathan and I have been look-

ing at in-home care agencies and are close to choosing one to
find your nurse."

"Hmph."

"Maybe you don't need a full-time nurse. But you do need
a companion, besides Lady, okay? Think about it, Mom.
Wouldn't it be nice to have someone to share breakfast with,
join you for your walks, or engage in a game of gin rummy?
Someone to take you shopping or sit with you at church?"

"Got my own friends in the congregation, and I don't
need babysitting."

"I know." Sherri worked hard to keep the smile out of her
voice. "But you're all that Nathan and I have. If anything happened to you, and we could have done something to prevent
it, we would never forgive ourselves. So will you consider it?
For us? Let us send a couple women over and just see how you
like it?"

"I guess so, Sherri. Sometimes I do get scared at night,
wondering if something happened how long would it take for
someone to find out."

This statement tugged at Sherri's heart. "You could always
come up here and live with us, Mom. We've told you that for
years."

"It will be a cold day down under before I share another
woman's kitchen. Even my daughter's. That's just asking for
trouble."

"Then it's settled. As soon as Nathan and I have selected an
agency, and they provide a couple candidates, we'll let you
know." Sherri heard the doorbell. "Mom, I need to go. Someone's at the door. I love you."

"Love you too, baby."

"Bye."

Sherri's thoughts were running from classrooms to companions as she walked to the door. Even so, her heart was filled
with happiness. She had a loving husband and a beautiful fam-

ily, a marriage back on track, and now, the opportunity to return to the career that she loved. How could life get any better
than that?

One look through the side-pane, and she had her answer.

"Jacqueline . . . Tate, right?" She shook her head sadly, and
crossed her arms. "You are an unhappy, jealous, and pitiful
woman, with a hell of a lot of nerve coming to my house."

CHAPTER 35

Jacqueline removed her oversized, Jackie Onassis–inspired shades. She was as cool as a winter breeze, dressed in a simple yellow halter-dress and Lanvin ballet flats. No one in the world, especially Blair, would believe that this same woman had arrived on this doorstep as a tackily dressed cleaning woman just two days ago. "Hello, Sherri. May I come in?"

Sherri stepped out onto her front porch and closed the door behind her. "Absolutely not." She looked across the street and noticed a neighbor walking his dog and another one driving by, waving as she passed. Sherri waved back, and used the same smile she'd pasted on for the sake of that driver to keep herself from punching Jacqueline straight in the mouth. But she loved this neighborhood and had no plans to move. Holding in the rage might cause a heart attack or stroke, but she would not give this woman the satisfaction of making a scene. "How did you get through our security gates?"

"The same way I got into your husband's bed," Jacqueline replied, casually inspecting her nails before looking at Sherri. "Determination."

Resisting the urge to curse, Sherri walked over to the seating area hidden from the street by an ivy-covered lattice. "Is that so?" she asked, as she sat and inspected her nails as well. Inside her head, however, were visions of Jacqueline's head meeting pavement as Sherri dragged her from the porch to her car . . . by her feet.

Jacqueline joined Sherri in the sitting area. "Sherri, I came here in hopes that we could talk peacefully, sensibly, woman to woman. I don't know you, and wish you nothing but the best. Honestly, I do. I believe you love Randall and the idea of a picture-perfect family. But life happens, and when it does, we have to adjust. Randall and I didn't mean to fall in love with each other . . . but we did."

Sherri turned so that she was facing Jacqueline directly. "You seem like a smart girl, so there are a few things I'm going to tell you. But I want you to listen carefully because I'll only say them once. If you ever get up the nerve to ring my doorbell again . . . we won't be talking." She ignored the smirk on Jacqueline's face and continued. "Randall and I have been married for over a decade, in fact, almost fifteen years. We are not only spouses, but best friends. There are no secrets between us."

"Are you sure about that?"

"I knew about you from the beginning, Jacqueline, when you set up the interview in LA. I know about the romantic dinner, the subsequent coincidental meetings in various hotels, and how you tried to incite suspicion by showing up at the door to our Vegas suite. None of this has been spontaneous, in my opinion. No, you planned this shit.

"I'll admit it. The scent of perfume that wasn't mine almost got me out of character. Almost, but not quite. I trust my husband.

"Randall was right about one thing. You are beautiful. But from your recent actions, including being on my porch right now, it's obvious that you're not too smart." Sherri stood. "I'm going to go inside my house and call the police. Shortly after that, I'll be heading to the police station with a copy of your picture and a request for a restraining order. I will also alert our homeowners association and the guards at the gate about the trespasser who somehow got past them and on to my street. And I'll make sure that they keep the surveillance footage of your entrance, just like I'll keep the footage captured by our *personal* security cameras of you on my porch right now." Sherri nodded toward a camera discreetly tucked between two beams. "Now, get off my porch and out of our lives. Use your assets to get your own man, and stop this foolish, impossible attempt at trying to take mine."

It had taken all Sherri had to remain calm, but Jacqueline's smug look had her anger rising to the boiling point. She knew if she didn't get away from this woman soon, things were going to get ugly.

"Goodbye, Jacqueline." She turned and walked toward the door.

Jacqueline stood and walked to the steps. "Sherri," she said, turning back after taking the first step down. "Since Randall tells you everything, will you let me know when he tells you where he found my panties? Albany came home early from her day trip with Lauren and I had to, uh, leave in a hurry. It was quite the romp we had in your bed. You know how insatiable he can be. I was wearing them when I came here. But not when I left. So they've got to be somewhere around that gorgeous, mahogany, custom-made four-poster."

She took two more steps and turned once more. "Those TempurPedic mattresses really are amazing." With a flip of her hair over her shoulder, she bounced down the steps.

Sherri followed, ready to go with this nervy heifah for fifteen rounds.

"Hey, Mom!"

The sound of Aaron's voice stopped her. She turned to see him walking toward her from the opposite direction of where Jacqueline now fled. His best friend, Hunter, rode a skateboard alongside him. She tried and failed to put a smile on her face.

"See you later, Aaron," Hunter said, once they'd reached the Atwater sidewalk.

"All right, man." Aaron fell into step beside his mother as they neared the porch. "What's wrong?"

"Nothing." She opened the door and walked in, then held it so that Aaron could follow.

"Who was that woman?"

Darn it. He saw her. Sherri had been so hoping that he hadn't. "Nobody important."

"Looks like y'all were arguing."

"Well, we weren't! Okay?!" Immediately regretting her outburst, Sherri took yet another calming breath. "Just a little misunderstanding, that's all."

"About what?"

"Not now, Aaron. I'm not in the mood!"

"All right. Geez." Aaron walked toward the kitchen and Sherri headed for the privacy of the master suite.

Once inside, she closed the door and reached for the home phone. "Girl, I'm so glad you answered," she said to Renee, "because I need to ask you a serious question."

"Sure, anything," Renee replied.

"If anything happens to me, will you raise my children?"

"Oh my God, Sherri, why would you ask me that?"

"Because I can't raise them from prison, and if that witch Jacqueline shows up at my front door again, that's exactly where I'll be."

Randall pulled into the garage and turned off the engine. His hands stayed on the wheel, clutching it tightly. He was still trying to figure out what the hell had happened, and how what he thought was a casual friendship had turned into Jacqueline acting like a love-starved fool! And coming to his office without his knowledge or permission, on the pretext of picking up papers? *For what?* This knowledge, after what she had pulled in Vegas, left him with a very bad feeling. The office. *Wait, she was there that day, right before I fell asleep. Could she have . . . ? No, I don't think so. That notion is too far out, even for her.* He sat there, rigid, as questions continued to plague him. Why had she gone back to the office? What was she looking for? What did she want? "James warned me about her," he mumbled, reaching for his briefcase and iPad case. "I should have listened."

He entered his home through a hallway that led from the garage to the kitchen. The first thing he noticed was that it was quiet. Too quiet for a weeknight at the Atwater house. The second thing he noticed was that there was no food on the stovetop, no delicious smells wafting up to tickle his nostrils and tantalize his senses. Given the events of the day, the bad feeling in his gut worsened. "Sherri."

Loosening his tie after placing his briefcase and iPad on a table in the hallway, he mounted the stairs. "Baby, where are you?" He entered their room. Sherri was standing near the foot of the bed, arms crossed, foot impatiently tapping the floor.

Her demeanor stopped him cold. "Baby, what's wrong?"

"Don't." She held up her hands, as if blocking his words from reaching her body. "Don't even stand there trying to look as if you don't know what's wrong."

"How'd you find out?" Randall was genuinely confused as to how Sherri could know about Jacqueline's visit to the office.

"How do you think I found out? She came over here, Randall. That woman had the nerve to bring her ass to my house!"

"How in the hell does she know where we live?"

"You tell me. And while you're at it, tell me how she knows the style of our bed and the type of mattress."

CHAPTER 36

"Sherri," Randall began in a pleading voice as he walked toward his wife. He stopped a couple feet away from her, dissuaded from going any further by her frown as much as anything else. "I swear to God, I don't know what's going on here. A week ago I saw her in Chicago and she was cordial but professional, and then we got to Las Vegas where she acted like she'd lost her damn mind!"

"People don't just 'go crazy' all of a sudden," Sherri replied, using air quotes for emphasis. "And you still haven't answered how that woman knows the style of our bed."

"I. Don't. Know."

"Have you brought her to this house, Randall?"

"Of course not!"

"Have you slept with her?"

"No, Sherri, I told you that there was nothing going on with her and me."

"You've told me a lot of things: that you had dinner in LA," she began, counting on her fingers. "That she interviewed you in your suite, instead of the restaurant or the lobby or anywhere a man with an ounce of sense would have conducted it. That you went to a Broadway play together."

"There was supposed to be a group of us. The others didn't show up."

"How convenient." She sounded anything but convinced. "You're spending time with a woman who's obviously enamored of you, and then acting surprised that she got caught up!"

Randall walked over to the bed and wearily sat down. "I admit that we flirted around, but you know that about me, babe. I may toss a compliment out or give a wink, but it's never more than that. Yes, all of what you just pointed out is true. I did all of those things. But I wish you could have been there to see the innocence of those meetings. Even while we were together in the suite's *living room* . . . nothing happened. We sat in two chairs with a table between us. Once the interview was over, she left the room. And never came back—in any city, at any time."

"And you didn't go to her room?"

"Sherri . . ."

"Look. Don't get mad at me because I'm asking questions. It's because of something you did that we're in this mess."

"That's just it. I haven't done anything."

Sherri shook her head, walking to the door. "Well, I guess if that's true, you don't have anything to worry about."

Still angry, Sherri went downstairs to find Blair. She found her doing homework at the breakfast nook. She sat down. "Blair, I need to ask you something."

"Sure, Sherri." Blair put down her book.

"Did anyone come by here while Randall and I were gone?"

Blair thought for a moment. "No, no one except the delivery guys. We ordered takeout both nights, as you suggested."

"The people who delivered the food were guys?" Blair nodded, so Sherri asked, "And no one else that you know of came in the house?"

"Uh-uh. Oh, wait, except the housekeeper."

"That's not unusual. Lucia comes here every week."

"It wasn't Lucia."

Sherri's head shot up. "It wasn't? Then who was it?"

"A substitute named Ruth. Lucia was sick."

Sherri tried to remain calm as she reached for Blair's iPad. "Can I see this for a minute?"

"Sure."

Sherri went to a search engine and typed in a name. She clicked on images and soon saw the face that she'd wanted to slap just hours ago. She turned the iPad around. "Is this her?"

"Who?"

"The woman who came to clean the house."

Blair burst out laughing but quit as soon as she caught Sherri's unsmiling face. "I'm sorry for laughing, Sherri, but, no. Ruth looked nothing like this woman. This woman is gorgeous!"

Gritting her teeth, Sherri ignored the comment. "What did Ruth look like?"

"She was really plain: short hair, no makeup, glasses and really stained teeth. Oh, and she had an accent. She's from Belize."

Sherri exhaled, but her relief was short-lived. If Jacqueline hadn't sneaked into the home unnoticed, how did she know theirs was a four-poster bed? A lucky guess? That was a possibility, but one that Sherri found highly doubtful. Randall swore he'd never sexed her. For now, she believed her husband. But where there was smoke, there was fire, and Sherri vowed to herself to not stop digging until she found the source of the flame.

Jacqueline stood back and admired her handiwork. All those years watching Phillip fiddle with computer hardware and software, and the recent crash courses with his partner, Marco, had definitely paid off. Setting up the network had been easier than she thought, especially since, not wanting anyone privy to her actions, she decided to tackle the installation alone. Now seven screens sat glowing before her, showing all of the key areas of the Atwater house. She'd just overheard Randall and Sherri's heated exchange. When Sherri disappeared from the bedroom camera and reappeared in the kitchen, Jacqueline reached for another knob and turned up the volume. She listened intently.

"What did Ruth look like?"

"She was really plain: short hair, no makeup, glasses, and really stained teeth. Oh, and she had an accent. She's from Belize."

When Sherri's conversation went from questions about the cleaning lady to the next day's activities, Jacqueline relaxed. "You're so stupid," she spat at the TV screen. "So easy to manipulate. Anybody with an ounce of intellect would have called the cleaning company, confirmed the substitution. That's why this stuff is so easy." She continued to mutter as she turned her attention back to the screen where the Atwater master suite was displayed. "All it took was a phone call and five hundred dollars and I was able to stop good old Lucia at the community gate."

She watched Randall pace from one side of the room to the other, stopping at various points while deep in thought.

"Are you thinking about me, baby?" Jacqueline asked, her fingers searching for and finding nipples that she slowly rubbed into hardened peaks. "I bet you are. I'm thinking about you too. I know you miss me. And the very next time I get the chance to see you, I'm sure you'll show me just how much."

CHAPTER 37

Sherri looked across the peaceful-looking pond with a sense of irony, considering her life was anything but.

"Sherri," she heard Renee say into her earbud, "you still there?"

"I'm here."

"I asked if you really think he's cheating?"

"I don't want to, but that's the only explanation that makes sense. I've thought about this until my head hurts, and no matter how I try to rationalize it, everything points to Randall cheating on me. With Jacqueline. In our home." Renee remained quiet. "Think about it, Nay. What woman do you know who'd go to another woman's house and confront her about a man if there wasn't something to her accusations? And that she talked about our bed, right down to the TempurPedic mattress—well, that is just something I can't ignore."

"But except for that one indiscretion, Sherri, Randall has never lied to you."

"Not until lately. If you'll remember, it was only a month or so ago I was telling you about a strange incident that occurred when I happened upon him in his office early one morning. Remember how I said he was talking to someone about money or a bank statement or something, and then stopped when I walked in?"

"Right. And he said it was business."

"Exactly. Just like he told me his interaction with Jacqueline was business. Until it wasn't."

"I'm so sorry this is happening, Sherri. What are you going to do?"

"I'll tell you what I'm not going to do," Sherri said, rising up from the bench and beginning the short walk back to her house. "I'm not going to stand back quietly if I learn my husband has been unfaithful. If I find out Randall was with her, Renee, no matter whether it was once or a dozen times, things in our household will definitely change."

As she walked, Sherri thought back to the conversation she'd had with her daughter, when she'd so confidently assured Albany that in the Atwater family there would be no divorce. That every set of parents had their differences, but her parents' union was solid as a rock. Sherri hated to admit it, but she couldn't lie to herself: this rock had a crack in it . . . a big one.

The phone was ringing when she reached the patio door. She hurried inside to the kitchen and pushed the speaker button on the phone on the counter. "Hey, Brother," she said after seeing Nathan's name on the caller ID. "What's going on?"

"I found an agency that I believe fits our needs where Mom is concerned. Do you have a minute?"

"Of course."

"Okay, go to this website." He gave her the name of a top-rated agency in North Carolina. "Check out their information and if you agree that they're a fit, can you give them a call?"

"Sure."

"Good. I have meetings all afternoon. But keep me posted on what you find out."

"Will do. Thanks, Nate."

"You're welcome, Sis. Love you."

"Love you back."

After returning a few calls regarding her career search, and meeting with the chef regarding the night's menu, she returned to her suite upstairs. Getting comfy on a chaise in the sitting area, she pulled out her iPad and read the information on the agency website that Nathan had suggested. The company had been around for twenty-five years, had stellar reviews and a good Better Business Bureau rating. She picked up the phone without hesitation and dialed the number. With her own life spiraling like crazy, it felt good to find an area where she felt in control.

"Hello," she said once her call was answered. "My name is Sherri Atwater. I'm calling to possibly hire a full-time, live-in assistant for my mom." She put the call on speaker and reached for a bottle of water. "Yes, she lives there in North Carolina."

"What is her medical condition, ma'am?" the woman asked, her voice calm and reassuring, her Southern accent pronounced.

Sherri gave her a brief rundown of what had been happening with her mother. "She has good and bad days," she finished. "But because the neighbor who's been our eyes and ears will no longer be there regularly, my brother and I will just feel better knowing there is someone else in the house."

"Could you give me your mother's information so that we can schedule an on-site visit for the initial screening?"

"Sure, it's Elaine Carver and her address is five-five-seven-two . . ."

On the other side of town, as Sherri relayed this information, Jacqueline sat looking at and listening to the camera she'd placed in the Atwaters' master suite, carefully making note of everything that she heard. She didn't know why, couldn't think of a reason why information on some old lady in another state might be important. But one thing being a writer had taught her was to always gather as much information as you could, no matter how seemingly trivial. She'd practiced it throughout her short career, and more than once it had paid off. She thought that now might be one of those times.

After saving the document to her computer, and determining that nothing of interest was happening on any of the other six screens, Jacqueline rose, stretched, and walked from the guest-bedroom-turned-spy-headquarters into Phillip's modern, seldom-used kitchen. True to his word, he'd only been there a day or two since letting her stay with him. Having met Marco, she understood why. He was as beautiful as Phillip, with stark black hair and deep blue eyes. Too bad they were gay. If more men like them were available to more women like her, she might not have to chase married guys.

Not seeing each other hadn't interfered with Jacqueline's ability to help him finish his website. After helping her with the initial design, Phillip would send requests for promotional material as well. She'd write a couple variations of what he requested and send it back. Her part in their website project was almost complete.

She stood in front of the open fridge, eyeing her options. In all of her running back and forth to electronics, furniture, and office supply stores, she'd forgotten about food. She looked at her watch. Four thirty, not exactly the time she wanted to tackle the streets of D.C. She grabbed a bottle of soda from the refrigerator before moving to the cabinets, where she was rewarded with a can of minestrone soup. She poured the contents into a bowl and set it in the microwave. After finding a box of crackers, she placed them, the piping hot bowl of soup, and a bottle of water on a tray and walked into the living room. She'd just sat down in front of Phillip's fifty-five-inch television when her phone rang.

"Dr. Atwater? Are you sure you have the right number?"

"Jacqueline, we need to talk."

"It's too late for that. You said you'd call when you returned from Vegas . . . promised me that we'd have lunch."

"Your showing up at our private residence changed those plans."

"How is Sherri? Are she and the kids all right? What about those cute little doggies. I hear shepherds are a great breed."

"How do you know about our dogs?"

Jacqueline winced behind her clumsy snafu. "I guess you forgot that you told me about them just like how you forgot that we shared a bed."

"I don't know what I did to cause you to do this, but I want to apologize," Randall said, his voice sounding authoritative and sincere. "If you think I led you on, if my flirting was inappropriate, whatever the reason this . . . misunderstanding . . . has occurred, I want you to know that I never meant to hurt you or mislead you. I'm sorry that you feel ours was anything but a professional relationship and that my taking you out to dinner was anything more than saying thanks for a great interview."

"A thank you, huh? Prematurely perhaps; the article hasn't even been finished, let alone published."

"I need for us to come to a resolution in this matter so we can make this right with my wife."

"Ah, so that's it. I was sitting here wondering why on earth a person who lied about calling me, lied about wanting to talk to me, and had me barred from an office building would contact me now. I have my answer. Because you're unhappy that I shared our romance with your precious wife."

"That's just it, Jacqueline. There is no romance. There never was."

"Liar!"

"Jacqueline, please . . ."

"You slept with me! And you loved every minute of it."

"Jacqueline, you've got to stop this. We've never had sex."

"Just because you're regretting it, Randall, doesn't mean it isn't so. I had you all to myself for six glorious nights in LA, and the few other times we've gotten together since then isn't enough for me. I'm sorry, but it isn't." He remained silent. She continued. "You're denying our love. Are you also denying that you find me attractive?"

A long pause and then, "You're very attractive, Jacqueline. I told Sherri as much."

"Well, tell me this. If Sherri wasn't in the picture, if you were a single man, would there be a chance for me?"

"I don't see the benefit of talking about what isn't and what can never be. I'm calling to apologize, and to ask you to tell Sherri that you lied about our sleeping together in my home. And you need to tell her how you knew what type of bed is in our room."

Jacqueline's laugh was genuine. "When I said four-poster, Randall, you should have seen the look on her face!" Silence on the other end. It was obvious that she and the mad scientist didn't share the same sense of humor. "Tell her it was just a lucky guess. I figured it was either a four-poster, platform, or canopy, and hey, anybody who loves a good night's sleep owns the country's number one bed."

"Jacqueline, you are smart and talented, with a great personality. You could have your pick of any single man out there. I'm married. I love my family. And I need you to tell Sherri what you just told me. I need you to tell her the truth."

"Sure, Randall."

Another long pause and then, "Really? You'll tell her? I can do a conference call right now."

"I'll tell her that lie when you tell her the truth about us." Then she disconnected the call.

Soup and soda forgotten, she reentered her "lab." She fired up the screens showing views of various areas of Randall's home and turned up the volume on all of the microphones. She did this and thought about what Randall had said. More importantly, she thought about what he didn't say but she knew he was feeling in his heart.

He wanted her, there was no doubt. If he weren't married, if Sherri was out of the picture, then Randall would choose to be with her. Of this, she was certain. Jacqueline leaned forward, watching as Sherri talked on the phone to her brother. But she only half listened. There was only one thing on her mind: being with Randall. And there was only one obstacle in the way of their happiness: Sherri. Jacqueline was determined that in the not too distant future, this minor inconvenience would be moved out of the way.

CHAPTER 38

"I called her, man." It was six thirty in the evening, and Randall was still in his office. Someone watching might have speculated that he was hiding out, afraid to go home. He chose to use the term "strategizing."

"Aw, man," James replied. "Do you think that was a good idea?"

"Honestly, James, everything is so crazy. I don't know what to think right now."

"What happened when y'all talked?"

"I can't tell whether she's just good at lying or she really believes it, but she swears we slept together, man, and that's just bull."

"Are you sure?"

"Don't you start going there too, man. I seriously need somebody in my corner right now."

"I'm on your side, bro. Trust me on that. But y'all were hanging pretty tough in LA, which is why I warned you about it. Is there any chance, any chance at all, that you drank a little too much, went a little too far . . ."

Is that possible? Randall thought for a moment. He'd never been able to hold his liquor, which is one reason he didn't drink that much. *Could I have drunk too much of something and effed that chick?*

"No! I'm 150 percent sure that I never had a sexual encounter of any kind with Jacqueline. We didn't even so much as share a passionate kiss. Nothing."

"Then I don't know what to tell you, man."

James fell silent. Randall got up to pace his office, looking out on a waning sun in the late June sky. He watched people caught up in their own dramas: walking or driving by, talking on cell phones, waiting at bus stops, living their lives. He wondered if anybody was dealing with anything remotely as crazy as the scenario that had entered his life. He doubted it.

"Let me ask you something, Randall."

"Shoot."

"Do you know anyone who knows Jacqueline, I mean, outside of a professional environment?"

"No. Like I said, I've only dealt with her professionally." Randall came back to his desk and sat behind it. "Except for that night when Sherri and I ran into her at the restaurant. She was with her friend Peter. No, wait. His name is Phillip. I don't have a last name though. Why, what are you thinking?"

"Between your profile in our community and the magazine articles, there's a lot of information on you out there. But what do you know about her?"

Randall sat up. James had a point. Besides the fact that she was beautiful, intelligent, and freelanced for the magazine *Science Today*, he didn't know much.

"You know what, James? I think you're on to something. I don't know anything about her, and it's time I did."

"Debbie, Nathan is calling. He probably has news on Mom's assistant."

"Okay, keep me posted."

"Will do."

It had been just over a week since Sherri and her brother

had begun the process of finding an assistant for their mom, and just two days since she'd returned from her visit. Because he was single and lived a little closer, Nathan had the more flexible schedule and had taken the lead in the assistant search. Sherri was grateful. Her home life was a mess. She and Randall were talking, but barely. There had been no more sightings of Jacqueline, but Sherri couldn't help but feel that they were experiencing the calm before the storm. If not for the seriousness of the situation, handling the details of her mother's care would have been a relief. She clicked over, hoping for good news and, as she did most of the time, put him on speaker phone.

"Hey, Nathan."

"Sherri, I've got good news."

"That's what I was hoping you'd say. What's going on?"

"Well, I talked over the phone with two women today. Both sounded nice, and very capable of handling taking care of Mom."

"I'm listening. Tell me more."

"One is an older woman. She's a retired nurse who lost her husband two years ago to cancer. She has a daughter who lives in Missouri, and she belongs to a church in town. Then there's a younger woman, Wanda. I really like her, Sherri. She has a kind, sweet demeanor with a quirky sense of humor. She might be the kind of personality to bring some joy into Mom's life."

"Is she a nurse also?"

"She's a certified home caregiver who took care of her grandmother for two years before she passed."

"How old is she?"

"Thirty-four."

"Married?"

"No."

"Dating?"

"She says no."

"Hmm, I don't know, Nathan. I don't want to bring any type of drama to Mom's front door." The irony of what she'd just said wasn't lost on Sherri. Although Nathan was five years younger, the two of them were very close. But she was too angry and embarrassed to share with him the hot mess that had recently rung her doorbell. Hopefully, if or when she shared it, the incident would be far behind her.

"If you'd like, I can go back next week to help out with the interview process."

"That would be great, Bro. It would ease my worrying and make Ms. Riley feel okay about leaving town."

"I think all of us will breathe easier knowing someone is there with Mom."

"All right, then. Let's do it. Let's set up the interviews, have you and Mom conduct them, and see who she picks. Keep me posted, okay? I'm dealing with a few family matters but will plan another trip there next month, while Ms. Riley is in St. Louis."

"Family matters? Is everything all right?"

"Everything's fine."

"Albany isn't pregnant? Aaron hasn't joined a gang?"

"Boy, you're crazy."

"Just checking."

"I appreciate that. I love you, Nate."

"Love you too, Sis."

Jacqueline sat back in her bedroom-turned-computer-command center, having heard every single word shared between sis and bro. An idle finger tapped against the desk as various scenarios of what to do with the information flitted through her mind. Finally, with a plan crystallizing, she turned off the computer, reached for her purse and headed out to meet the document-making contact she'd found online. Soon, it would be time for another trip.

CHAPTER 39

A few days later, Jacqueline entered the modest yet well-kept North Carolina neighborhood, having driven the approximately two hundred and seventy-five miles in roughly five hours. She'd turned off her personal GPS-equipped cell phone and purchased a throwaway, relying on directions obtained from a library-owned computer in inner city D.C. She drove slowly, glancing around surreptitiously, checking to see if anyone was up and about, anyone watching, anyone who could later identify the car that she drove. Not that it would have much mattered. The hookup in downtown D.C. had lived up to his reputation and been well worth the exorbitant price. The driver's license bearing the name Anna Mae Miller looked authentic, and the employee at the small used car lot had accepted her cash payment and the additional one thousand dollar "incentive" to lose the paperwork with barely a blink of an eye. With full-access to Sherri's computer, she was well aware of Wanda's appearance, and had already made a trip to a second-hand store to match the woman's horrible taste. Looking down at her hastily-scrawled directions, she turned on to a quiet street.

"Seventeen thirty-five . . . ," she mumbled, slowing the car to better read the house numbers. "Here it is." She stopped in front of a gray-painted home with stark white shutters. The lawn looked recently mowed, and pink, purple, and yellow flowers set in wooden pots swayed in the early morning breeze. White curtains framed the windows facing the street. When Jacqueline saw one of them move ever so slightly, she reached for her props, straightened the ruffles on her chin-high blouse, and opened the car door.

"Yes, may I help you?" The young woman who answered the door was pleasant yet curious.

"Praise the Lord, sister," Jacqueline said in a Southern accent so authentic she could fool someone born and bred below the Mason-Dixon Line. She raised the Bible obtained from a secondhand store—the same one where she'd gotten the wig, blouse, long skirt, and shoes—clutched it to her chest and began the spiel she'd practiced all the way down I-95. "I'm so sorry to bother y'all so early on this beautiful, blessed morning, but my church is raising donations to feed the homeless and we're canvassing the neighborhood for canned goods, staples, just whatever you feel able to provide."

"What church is this?"

"It's a new congregation that just started, Rise Up and Walk Ministries. It's a ministry devoted to the downtrodden."

"Sure, I'd love to help. Come on in."

Jacqueline's eyes took in everything as she entered, including the mail slot in Wanda's front door. *Excellent.* She wouldn't have to worry about letters piling up in a box outside. Following the unsuspecting woman into the living room, Jacqueline recalled how after securing the ID she'd returned to the house and stumbled onto the second part of her plan.

It had been early morning two days before, when she'd been flicking through the channels and happened upon a religious station. She'd paid close attention to the story and its message, and knew from what she'd heard Nathan say about Wanda that the story of helping others would ring close to home. From the way she saw the young lady's expression change at the mention of her imaginary ministry, she knew that her deception had worked like a charm.

"Could I have some water?" Jacqueline asked as soon as the woman had shut the door behind them.

"Sure," the woman answered. "Or I could get you a tall glass of sweet tea."

"That would be great, my sister," Jacqueline said softly. "By the way, I'm Vickie. What is your name?"

"Wanda," she said, coming back with hand outstretched. "Wanda Smith."

"It's a pleasure to meet you," Jacqueline replied, shaking Wanda's hand.

"Likewise." Wanda went into the kitchen and soon Jacqueline heard cabinets opening and ice cubes dropping into glasses. She tossed down the Bible and folder filled with blank paper she'd brought, then quickly reached in her purse for a small packet containing white powder. When Wanda appeared in the doorway unexpectedly, she hid the packet in the palm of her right hand and reached for the glass with her left.

"Thank you, Wanda." She took a sip. "This is good."

"You're welcome. Goodness, where are my manners. I have some Danishes in there as well. They're not from scratch, just the bake and serve variety, but you're welcome to one."

"I left the house without a bite of anything this morning. A Danish is an answer to my prayer for food."

Wanda smiled, her eyes shining with the joy she felt in helping another human being. She set her glass down on the coffee table between her and Jacqueline. "Have a seat. I'll be right back."

Jacqueline sat down and as soon as Wanda rounded the door to the kitchen, she quickly emptied the contents of the packet into the second glass of tea. Looking around for something to stir the concoction with and seeing nothing, she reached into her purse and used an ink pen to help the fatal dose of tasteless poison dissolve. The same day she'd gone to the public library for driving directions to Raleigh, she'd researched various types of poisons, and then used a stolen credit card to both purchase the powder online and have it shipped overnight to Phillip's address. She'd hated to potentially involve her friend, but time was of the essence and there'd been nowhere else close by to send it. She'd figured it was a risk worth taking. If what the research said was true, it would only take about thirty minutes for Wanda to fall asleep and, unless the same guy that helped the Bible dude came to her rescue, she wouldn't wake up. Jacqueline snickered at the thought but sobered when Wanda reentered the living room carrying a saucer of rolls.

"These look delicious," Jacqueline said as she reached for a napkin and the rolls Wanda offered. "Thank you."

"It's no problem at all. It's rare that I get to break bread with anyone, so I'm delighted." She took a sip of tea and watched with pleasure as Jacqueline took a few bites from the Danish. "Let me go in here and see what canned foods I have." She stood and almost drained her glass before walking into the kitchen. "Whew! I didn't know that I was so thirsty!"

"So you don't get many visitors?" Jacqueline asked from where she sat in the small, comfortably decorated living room.

"No." Wanda spoke from her kitchen, where she searched her cabinets. "I moved here to take care of my grandmother. She died about six months ago."

"Sorry for your loss."

"I miss her but she's in a better place. Aside from a few people at church, I haven't made many friends."

"No boyfriend?"

"Ha! No, girl. It's just me and the Lord."

Good, it will take a while for someone to miss you, Jacqueline thought. "Hallelujah!" she said.

"What about you?" Wanda asked. "Are you married?"

"Only to my work," Jacqueline replied. "But I believe that I'll be married soon."

"Me too!" Wanda reappeared in the kitchen doorway with cans of corn, diced tomatoes, pinto beans, and green beans in her hand. "Until recently, I didn't think I was ready. But just last night I prayed for God to send the perfect man. I believe he will."

As the two women continued to chat, Jacqueline rose from the couch and walked over to lean against the kitchen door frame as she watched Wanda fill up a small box with canned goods, boxed noodles, and a couple boxed soups. About twenty minutes after finishing her large glass of iced tea, Wanda slumped against the kitchen counter in her small, square kitchen.

Jacqueline didn't move. "Wanda? Sister, are you all right?"

"I feel woozy," she replied, as she tried to right herself by the kitchen sink. "My stomach feels . . . my head. . . ." She looked at Jacqueline with a curious expression on her face. "Help me, sistah."

Jacqueline nodded but allowed several seconds to pass before crossing the floor to where Wanda half stood, half slumped against the counter. "Just relax, Wanda. You're a little dizzy, that's all. Everything will be all right." Her voice was soothing as she watched Wanda's eyes close and her body relax. Wanda slumped to the floor.

"Rest well, Wanda Smith. Now you're with your grandma, in a better place."

After laying Wanda on the tiled kitchen floor, Jacqueline stood to her full height and looked down on her. She waited a full five minutes, continuing to check her pulse and place a finger under her nose until she was sure that the woman was dead. Then she got busy.

First, after putting on a pair of surgeon's gloves, she closed the blinds in the kitchen and on the windows facing the kitchen entryway. She wanted to close them all but thought that it might seem suspicious to a nosy neighbor. She took the items from the box, placed them back in the cabinets, and then placed the empty box under the sink. After pulling out a garbage bag she'd brought with her, she placed the glasses, saucer and everything else she'd touched inside it. Using a sponge and industry-strength cleanser she'd also brought along, she wiped down the coffee table, counters and all of the cabinets, taking no chances that a trace of her remained. *It's a good thing I watch* Investigation Discovery, she mused, as she tied the bag with a rubber band. *Otherwise I might make a crucial mistake, like using a trash bag from this house, one that could be traced back to the store where it was bought.* Jacqueline sneered at the thought that if someone found and traced the origin of this bag, it would be to whoever purchased trash bags for the company PSI.

Cleanup done, she dragged Wanda into the bathroom, positioning her so it would appear that the poor soul had fallen. Finally, she cracked the code on Wanda's computer and after spending an hour memorizing pertinent information—date of birth, social security, and driver's license numbers, family members, past employers, nursing history, and time at the agency—she downloaded everything from the computer on to a small, portable hard drive, just in case there was something else she'd need.

Jacqueline looked around in satisfaction, walking from the living-dining space to the kitchen, then into one of two bedrooms in the humble abode. She looked at the homey patchwork quilt laid across the queen-size bed, the knitted afghan folded at the foot of it, and the needlework on the decorative pillowcases. Her heart clenched. She grabbed her chest as her knees buckled and unexpected tears sprang to her eyes. Images flashed before her in quick succession, like a movie on steroids: a hodgepodge of faces, various places, and then . . . she and another little girl with a kind old woman, the three of them walking through a park, two people arguing, a frightened little girl hiding in a closet, an adult standing over her holding a belt in one hand and a bottle in the other, cuddling up in an older woman's lap, and finally, being taken from a burning house, all alone, wrapped in a bedspread with a design similar to the one on the needlework on Wanda Smith's bed.

Falling to the floor, her sobs muffled against the sleeve of her blouse, she murmured, "Grammy, I miss you. Mommy and Daddy were bad when you left. Why did you leave me, Grammy? Please come back! Don't make me go with them. She's mean and he scares me. They made me lose Sissy. They took her away! I'll be a good girl, I promise. I'll never be bad again. Never." she whimpered. "Ever," she cried. "Please come back. Please!"

A telephone rang, seemingly from miles away. It jostled Jacqueline out of a trancelike state. She became aware of the unfamiliar surroundings. *Where am I? What am I doing on the floor?* The ringing stopped. She shook her head, trying to rid herself of the mental cobwebs as she looked around the room. She looked behind her at the nondescript hallway and then back at the neatly made bed. *How long have I lain here?* Slowly, the memories from earlier came rushing back, especially the smile on Wanda's compassionate face. *Somebody killed her. That nice woman is dead.* Tears came to her eyes as she thought of the woman who'd offered her tea and a Danish. "Why did she have to kill you, Wanda?" she asked in the voice of a small child. "Why did you have to die, too?"

And then another voice, from within. *It's not your fault, Jacqueline. Sherri made you do it. She made you kill the nice lady because she wouldn't leave Randall. She refuses to leave your husband, Jacqueline, and Wanda was helping her! Wanda and Sherri are very bad girls!*

"Yes," Jacqueline whispered, rising to her knees and then to her feet. "And bad people die."

An hour later, Jacqueline left the house, got into her rental car, and drove away. She drove to Durham, found a park, and put another part of her plan in motion. Pulling out her iPad, she wrote several e-mails, then sat back and read her handiwork. "Perfect," she murmured under her breath. "You should become a writer."

At a public library, she printed out a copy of the emails, along with copies of text messages that she'd forwarded to her email address. She placed the papers in a pre-stamped envelope and dropped it in postal service mail box. After going to a theater and watching three movies back to back to back, she returned to Raleigh to implement the idea that had come to her in the middle of a boring comedy.

Under cover of darkness and her all-black clothes, she walked the relatively short distance from the main road where she'd parked her trusty gray Toyota back to Wanda's home. Careful that no one was watching she knocked, waited as if someone was answering the door, and then quickly let herself in. She moved Wanda's body from the bathroom to the trunk of the brand new Ford Focus parked in the garage. Locating a piece of the dead woman's luggage, she filled it with personal effects and then sent an email from Wanda's computer to the dead woman's brother in Michigan. "Doing God's work in Africa," is basically what it said. Her plan carried out, she hurried back to the car and headed for her next destination: a motel just ten short minutes away from the home of Elaine Carver.

CHAPTER 40

Except for the sound of stainless steel utensils scraping plates, it was so quiet you could hear a pin drop. This was not exactly the scene one would expect from a dinner featuring four live persons including a teen and a pre-. If it was quiet because of how Chef had thrown down on the linguini, that would have been one thing, but this somber scene was brought on by something different. A definite pall was in the air. Albany had even brought her phone to the table, a definite no-no, and was texting away without repercussions. Something was definitely amiss.

"What's wrong with everybody?" Aaron finally asked, pushing away his plate and sitting back in a huff.

"Mad because your breath stinks," was Albany's immediate off-the-cuff answer.

"Cut it out, Albany," Sherri snapped, finally becoming aware of her daughter's texting. "And put down that phone."

Randall cleared his throat. "Your mom and I have a lot on our minds, Son." Sherri snorted. Three pairs of eyes turned in her direction. She kept hers glued to the veggies on her plate, the ones she'd been moving from one side to the other for the past ten minutes. In an attempt at normalcy, she looked at her son. "How did baseball practice go today?"

Aaron shrugged. "All right, I guess. I want to play first but Coach has me out in center field."

"Every position is important, Son."

"Yeah, but the first baseman gets in on all the plays!"

"It's summer, Aaron. There's a lot of other things you can do besides baseball."

"Like what?"

"Swimming, tennis, bowling—"

"Bowling! No, Mom, that's not cool."

"You can get a job," Randall offered.

Albany's eyes widened. "That's not cool either, Dad."

"The food is delicious, baby," Randall said, venturing a conversation in Sherri's direction. After days of minimal conversation about only what was absolutely necessary, and otherwise passing each other like virtual strangers, this was the first time he'd openly tried to engage in real talk. He hoped that the children's presence would prevent Sherri from telling him to go straight to hell. "Did you make it?"

She looked at him with a dead-on stare. "No."

"It's good," he said, clearing his throat again. "Do you like it, Albany?"

"It's all right. I like her lasagna better."

After another excruciating ten minutes, Albany asked if she could be excused from the table. Aaron followed her. Sherri stood and began gathering the plates. She reached for Randall's. He grabbed her wrist, looking up at her with a pleading look in his eyes. "How long are we going to go on like this, Sherri?"

She pulled her arm away from him. "I don't know."

That evening, talk was all but missing in the bedroom. Randall kept trying to find a conversation with Sherri that would last longer than five seconds, but without success. When she said she was going downstairs to watch a DVD, he'd actually been grateful for their earlier decision to leave electronics out of the bedroom. Because honestly, he didn't know how much more of her silent treatment he could take.

The following morning, Randall left the house on a mission. He'd spent the time that Sherri had been out of the bedroom on his iPad, and contacting a couple close friends for information that he'd have to be sure remained confidential. By the time he logged on this morning, the information that he'd requested had shown up in his in-box, and after an e-mail to the referral his New York colleague had provided, Randall was ready to move full speed ahead.

While at a stoplight, he programmed the phone number from the e-mail into his car phone and waited for the call to be answered.

"Evans Investigations."

"Hello, Douglas Evans, please."

"Yes, and who's calling?"

"Mr. Waters," Randall answered, using the code name that Mr. Evans had suggested to ensure his anonymity. "He's expecting my call."

Shortly afterwards, Randall heard a raspy voice he felt could have been scripted for that of a private eye. "Doug Evans here."

"Doug, it's Randall Atwater."

"Oh yes. Hello, Doctor. I've been expecting your call." A short pause and then, "What can I do for you?"

Randall took a deep breath before he replied. This was a big step. He hoped it would pay off. "You can find out everything you can about someone who's been harassing me."

"Someone in the workplace?"

"Indirectly. It's a freelance writer whose interest in my work seems to have turned into a personal obsession. I want it to stop."

"What's this writer's name?"

"Jacqueline Tate."

"Have you crossed the line with this person?"

Randall was thrown by the investigator's candor. But given what he was asking the man to do, he felt it fair, and knew he'd do whatever it took to get his life back to normal. "Ours was a professional relationship," he responded. "I haven't crossed the line."

"What other information can you give me about her?"

Randall shared what he knew.

"Wow, I just pulled her image up online. She's a beauty."

"Beauty and brains don't always equal a sound mind, or good character."

"What exactly do you want to know about her?"

"Everything you can find. This woman came to my home, verbally attacked my wife, and accused me of having an affair. She did other things, like break into my office, all of which re-sulted in restraining orders for me and my wife. She knew in-formation that was unsettling, namely, what type of bed was in our master suite."

"Any chance she's been in your home?"

"Absolutely not, which is why I'm determined to know how she obtained this information. I need to know everything about her. Do you think you can do this?"

"I can't guarantee what I don't know," Doug said, "but I can tell you this. I'll find out everything out there on this Jacqueline Tate, and pass on this information. What happens from there is up to you."

"That's as much as I can ask for. Thank you, sir."

"Don't thank me yet. Thank me after I produce."

Randall's smile was tentative yet hopeful as he hung up the phone. Maybe the playing field would now become level. Maybe he'd learn as much about Jacqueline as the woman seemed to know about his family and him.

CHAPTER 41

Sherri settled into a chair in the living room, wearing a genuine smile for the first time all day. "Hey, Nate. What's going on, Brother?"

"Aw, nothing shaking but the leaves in the trees." A pause and then, "But I did meet a cute little honey over the weekend."

"Family material?"

"Dang, why is it that you women tend to rush to judgment? I said I just met her two days ago. That's not enough time for me to find out her favorite color, let alone decide whether or not I should propose or if she'd be in the running to be the mother of my child."

Hearing his words, Sherri had to laugh. "I apologize. I'm turning into Mom, asking you the same types of questions she fired at me continuously until Randall gave up the ring."

"To be honest, Sis, lately I've entertained thoughts of settling down. Not only because I'm not getting any younger, but because I feel the goals I have set for myself would be accomplished more easily with a nice, strong woman by my side. That said, I don't know that I've met her yet. When I do, you'll be one of the first to know."

"I appreciate that, Brother."

"I do have news, though."

"About the in-home caretaker?"

"Yes, Wanda."

"What about her?"

"I like her, Sis. Mom spoke to her on the phone. She's a breath of fresh air, professional yet down-to-earth, a Southern girl who seems to love what she does—take care of people."

"Family material?" Sherri joked.

"Ha! Maybe, big sis, but not in the way that you think. Don't get me wrong. She's a pretty enough girl, in a plain sort of way."

"But not bougie enough for my brother, huh?"

"Don't act like I'm shallow, it's not like that. In fact, my focus was so tuned in to her and Mom's interaction that I wasn't thinking about much of anything else."

"And Mom liked her?"

"Sis, they've already bonded. Mom clearly enjoyed Wanda's personality and Wanda is clearly interested in enhancing Mom's life. I told her that I was very pleased with the agency's selection and that until further notice, she could consider herself hired."

"Well, who am I to argue? You've got my vote. I'll call and talk to her over the phone tomorrow and make plans to meet her in person very soon."

Later that evening, Sherri and Elle worked out in Elle's home gym. "You're getting better, lasting longer," Elle said, after they'd finished working out on the elliptical and Stairmaster machines respectively.

"Yes, I think I'm beginning to feel some results. Going up and down the stairs, I find I'm not as winded and I've started jogging instead of just walking the dogs." She looked over at Elle, whose stomach showed no signs that she'd carried a child. "Still trying to lose the stomach flab, though."

"You might want to make another date with Shaun T."

"I can see his workouts have you toned."

"A friend of mine has lost over forty pounds."

"Maybe I'll give him another try. But not tonight." Sherri hung her towel around her neck and walked over to her bottled water.

Elle sat on a nearby chair, drinking water too. "What else is going on?"

"I heard some good news today. My brother met the woman who's going to be my mom's in-home assistant. He likes her. She starts right away."

"That's great news, Sherri. I know that her neighbor leaving was a real concern."

"Yes, it was."

"Is your mother feeling better?"

"Whatever is happening with her is really weird. She'll go for weeks feeling fine and then have an episode. It's frustrating that the doctors can't pinpoint the cause."

"It's often a process of elimination. That's why they call it *practicing* medicine."

"Spoken by a doctor's wife," Sherri announced to the room.

"Hey, practice makes perfect is what I always say. I'm glad to hear your mom has someone there with her, to keep her company if nothing else. You're lucky to still have her around, Sherri. I miss mine every single day."

"I can't imagine what I'd do without her, Elle."

"Hopefully it will be a long time before you have to."

Jacqueline stood back and looked at her handiwork. For the last hour she'd been making herself at home in her new space—the guest bedroom at Elaine's house. Nothing in the home was to her liking or taste, too over-the-top with the country theme. But in the short time she'd been here she'd managed to place a camera in Elaine's room and another one in the living room. She'd rearranged the furniture in the guest room so that her computer desk faced away from the door. She'd also changed the door knob to one that locked. Old people tended to be nosy. She couldn't chance her patient snooping around and finding things she shouldn't. With one last look around and then in the mirror, satisfied that she looked appropriately average, she ventured back upstairs.

"Miss Elaine?" Thinking about how her country twang would sound to her friends back home almost made her laugh out loud.

"In here, Wanda!"

She walked into the kitchen, where Elaine was pulling a chicken out of the oven. "Mm, that smells delicious."

"It's not much, but I figured you might be hungry."

"You really shouldn't have bothered."

"Been a while since I had someone to cook for, so it was actually kind of nice."

Small talk continued while Jacqueline helped Elaine place bowls of mashed potatoes, green beans, and a plate of rolls on the table.

"I've got some lemonade in the fridge."

"I'll get it," Jacqueline replied. She returned with the pitcher and two glasses, sat down, and began dishing up food.

"Wait, child. We have to bless it first."

"Of course."

"You want to offer prayer?"

"No, Miss Elaine," she hurriedly replied. "You go right ahead."

After saying the prayer and preparing her plate, Elaine said, "So, Wanda, tell me a little more about yourself."

Pulling from the information she'd gleaned from Wanda's computer, Jacqueline told Elaine about growing up in Alabama and spending the summers in North Carolina, where her grandmother lived. "When she got sick, I moved here to take care of her. It was the best decision I've ever made. I miss her tremendously, but am so thankful that I got to spend that quality time with her before she died."

"I'm sure you were a blessing. That had to be a sacrifice. How old are you, Wanda?"

Jacqueline gave her the age on Wanda's driver's license.

"Don't you want to get married, have children?"

"One of these days, I guess, when the right man comes along."

"Choosing a husband is a big decision. You're right to take your time. I think that's why there are so many divorces today. Women latch on to the first man who proposes, don't take the time to see whether he's really the one or not. That and the fact that they don't pray on the decision and wait on God for the answer."

"You're absolutely right, Miss Elaine. There is this one man I like and I think he likes me. But there's something separating us."

"What, a woman?"

Jacqueline cut her eyes at Elaine before she could think. The woman's accuracy was unnerving.

"No, ma'am. Distance. We, uh, live in two different states."

"Is that all? Hmph. That's a problem easily solved. Why don't you just go where he is?"

"I want to, Miss Elaine, would do so in a heartbeat. But not without a commitment."

"You know what, baby? Tonight, I'm going to say a prayer for you, that God will this man will see the light so that he'll ask for your hand in marriage."

"Sure, Miss Elaine. Maybe your prayers will get through. Mine seem to be stuck somewhere between here and heaven."

"Child, there is nothing too hard for God. You just keep the faith and don't you worry," Elaine said, spooning up another serving of her fresh green beans. "I know that God answers prayer, and it just might be sooner than you think."

Jacqueline smiled and changed the subject by commenting on Elaine's homemade rolls. But the irony wasn't lost on her that the man Elaine was praying would become her husband was currently her son-in-law.

CHAPTER 42

Randall navigated the streets of Washington, D.C. on his lunch hour, glad for the diversion of pedestrians and horns. "James, how's it going, man?"

"That's what I was going to ask you." James's concerned voiced boomed through Randall's automobile speakers. "It's not like you not to return a phone call."

Randall nodded, belatedly remembering the message his friend had left earlier in the week. "I apologize, man. A lot going on."

"Talk to me."

"Aw, man," Randall said with a sigh. "Where do I start?"

"Debbie always says the beginning works pretty good."

"You know the beginning. In fact, you warned me in the beginning."

"You know I'm not one to cut you with 'I told you so,' but I thought that woman was trouble from the moment I saw her."

Randall turned down the music and filled him in on the most recent events. "I couldn't believe she had the nerve to come to the house. And then guessing correctly that we sleep on a TempurPedic mattress? That was the final straw, right there. Sherri didn't speak to me for over a week."

"I'm surprised y'all are talking now."

"Just barely. I've been sending Sherri love letters all week, little e-mails letting her know how I feel. Those, and the daily gifts of flowers, chocolates, and in-home massages, finally wore her down. I think the teardrop necklace I have for her tonight, plus what I have planned for our anniversary, will finally put this mess to rest, man. Things got so bad, I almost told her."

"About her anniversary gift? No, man. Let it be a surprise. Speaking of . . . how's that working out?"

"Very well, especially considering that everything has had to happen by phone, internet, and a local contact."

"She's going to be shocked beyond words."

"I hope she appreciates all it took to make it happen."

"Trust me, she will. What about Jacqueline? Have you seen her around?"

"No, and I hope to never see her again."

A short while later, Randall walked into his home and heard the sounds of Bobby Brown. He smiled, hopeful. Sherri normally only played her 90s music when she was in a good mood. He walked through the house, finally finding her in Albany's bedroom.

"Hey, baby."

She turned from where she was going through the CDs on her daughter's shelf. Randall saw something he hadn't seen in a while . . . her smile. "Hey," she said.

"Find any contraband?"

"No, but that doesn't mean anything. With everything available on YouTube and all other kinds of websites, there's no telling what our children are listening to."

He walked over. "I've missed touching you, baby. Can I get a hug?" She obliged him, and when she would have pulled away, he held her tighter. "I want us to get back to where we were, Sherri, before all this madness happened."

She hugged him tighter. "Me too," she said at last.

He stepped back. "I love you and our children more than

anything in this world; more than science, more than my career. I would never do anything to jeopardize what we've built together. If you believe anything about me, please believe that."

"Look at this from my perspective, Randall. What if some dude came to you and told you what type of bed we slept in? Do you think you'd just dismiss what he told you because I said it wasn't true? Would there be no doubt at all in your mind, no wondering if the possibility of my cheating existed? I'll tell you the answer. No, you wouldn't. You'd question me. You'd think about it. You'd have to digest my explanation and cool down from being pissed off. There's no way you'd calmly accept whatever I told you."

"But you believe me now?"

"To be honest, it's still a struggle. But aside from that comment, I can't find anything else to support her story. You've given me no reason to be suspicious, no proof that what she said could be true. The more I've thought about it, the more I agree that it could have been just a lucky guess. It is a very popular mattress, and there are only so many types of beds."

"I tell you one thing. She won't have another chance to come between us. I've instructed the guards at our building and my employees that if they see her to call the police. We've both followed through with restraining orders. So if she comes here again, she'll get locked up. I'm sorry for all of the pain my knowing her has caused us. Had I known this would happen, I never would have offered her that ride."

"But you didn't know," Sherri said, giving him a peck on the lips. "It was a random act of kindness from a thoughtful man. It's just about time for dinner. I'll go call the kids."

She moved out of the room and they began walking downstairs. "Just so you know," he said, placing his hands on her hips as he followed her, "that little kiss you gave me didn't even qualify as an appetizer. Tonight, I want a gourmet meal."

"This past week without has given you an appetite?"

"Baby . . . you don't know the half."

They retired to their room not long after dinner. "Join me in the shower?" he asked soon after he'd closed the door.

"Okay."

Randall walked over to the iPod. Soon, the sounds of an R & B ballad filled the room. Quietly they undressed and walked into the en suite. The water was turned on and soon, so were they.

"Come here." Randall pulled Sherri into his arms, kissing her thoroughly, deeply, all the while massaging her shoulders and back. His hands dropped to her buttocks and he kneaded them gently. They swayed to the music coming through the bathroom speakers, began doing a slow dance under the stream.

He reached for the soap and a loofah. Gently, as if she were porcelain, he washed her, allowing his tongue to follow where the sponge had been. He blew on her hardening nipple before sucking it into his mouth. She hissed, dropping her head back as his hand slid down her stomach to her heat. He rubbed against her folds until they parted. She spread her legs to offer better access. For Randall, it was an open invitation. He dropped to his knees to RSVP—nipping and licking and kissing her there. Her nub hardened and he took it into his mouth, stroking her with his finger, intensifying the pleasure. She placed her hands on his shoulders and ground herself against him. She'd missed this, being with her husband. Being loved by her man.

"I want you inside me," she whispered following this revelation. "I want you to make love to me, Randall."

"That's exactly what I plan to do," he said, his eyes hooded with desire as he took the sponge and washed his thick erection.

"But first . . ." She got on her knees and quickly pulled him into her mouth, cupping his balls and squeezing just right.

He grew longer, harder. "Baby, I can't wait. It's been too long."

He didn't have to. They made quick work of drying off each other and then moved the party to the bed. She got on all fours and he entered her from behind. He stroked, and plunged, pulled out, and plunged again. Tickling her nub with his finger, he continued to love her, teasing her breasts, squeezing her cheeks, kissing her everywhere that he could. They changed positions and then changed again. She rose up to meet him stroke for stroke, their skin slapping together in a frenzied rhythm, then slowing to a tender beat.

"I'm coming," Sherri whispered, right before going over the edge.

Randall quickly followed suit. "Thank you, baby," he said after he'd caught his breath. "That was wonderful."

"Maybe I should let you go a week without more often."

He got up to retrieve the diamond necklace. Now was the perfect time to surprise her. "Girl, don't even joke like that. I don't ever want to be without my honey pot again."

CHAPTER 43

"Let's go, kids!" Sherri stood in the mudroom of her home, happier than she'd felt in a while. The time she and Randall had enjoyed the night before had been just what they needed. A year ago, if someone had told her that this time in her life would be more topsy-turvy than a theme-park roller coaster, she would have begged to differ. But the truth of the matter was her life had never been more chaotic. She hadn't been totally satisfied with her prior humdrum existence, but she definitely wanted to get off of this crazy merry-go-round. Today, for the first time since she'd heard the name Jacqueline Tate, she felt hopeful for her marriage, her family, her future.

She laughed as she heard Albany and Aaron bounding down the stairs. "I beat you!" Aaron said with his usual competitive exuberance. "Get back, girl, and watch how an expert operates!"

"I'll watch how you—"

"That's enough!" Sherri interrupted, laughter punctuating her words. The children's bickering was just another sign of the household's return to normalcy, and she was determined to milk it for all it was worth. "If y'all don't straighten up, I'm going to tell your father."

"Ooh," was the stereo sound delivered by daughter and son.

"Yeah, y'all act like you're scared, but if I discuss the possibility of relieving you of your allowance . . ."

"Uh, okay, Mom, let's talk about this," Aaron said, as diplomatically as if he were running for office.

"Mom, we wouldn't want to bother Dad with such trivialities," Albany added. "He works too hard for us to get him upset."

As the children preceded her into the garage, Sherri locked the door and pushed the unlock button on her keychain. Within minutes she had backed the SUV out of the garage and was heading down the street. It had been so long since the family had been together to celebrate one of Randall's accomplishments. She wanted everything to be as perfect as it could be. She glanced over at Albany, satisfied that her jeans were contemporary yet stylish and her blouse was age-appropriate. They'd had their share of fights over wardrobe, so she was glad that had not been an issue today. Aaron tended to dress like his father, and today's look of jeans and a T-shirt boasting PSI's logo was no exception. For a second, Sherri questioned whether or not she should have sported a T-shirt with the company's logo in orange and beige, but looking down at the tan sundress that she'd paired with multicolored flat sandals and a large brown belt, she felt appropriately dressed.

They reached the building where the Atwater Achievement Module's science fair was taking place. Randall, along with the students who helped to tutor the kids, had made sure everything had been set up in top-notch fashion. All of the equipment was the latest, and the best money could buy. There were microscopes and centrifuges, Petri dishes and other items scattered about. Sherri saw Randall and waved.

"Come on, guys. There's your father."

"Hey," he said, giving her a quick kiss before greeting his children.

"This looks cool, Dad," Aaron said.

Albany didn't respond. She was too busy trying to look cute for a handsome boy eyeing her from across the way. Randall and Sherri both noticed it and rolled their eyes. "Glad you came to the science fair now, Albany?"

She shrugged and changed her focus. "It'll be okay, I guess."

"Go ahead and handle your business," Sherri said to her husband. "We don't want to keep you from what you should be doing. Just came over to say hello."

"I'm glad you did. I want you to meet the guy who runs the program when I'm out traveling. Kids, you can go check out the exhibits."

"Make sure your phones are on and available," Sherri added. "I don't want to have to come looking for you."

Sherri met some of the people connected with Randall's program and then joined the others in walking around. Among the children and teens in attendance she watched with humor as her children tried to set themselves apart as "the man of the hour's ultimate seed." The more they heard their dad's name mentioned, or saw the work of his students displayed throughout the room the more they interacted with the participants—especially Aaron—to show their special connection to what was happening that day.

Afterwards, the foursome headed to a popular restaurant for dinner. They settled into a booth and, once the waiter came back from dropping off menus and water, placed their orders.

"Today was fun," Aaron said, looking through some of the brochures he'd acquired.

Sherri smiled and placed her chin in her hand. "I enjoyed it too. Kind of reminded me of how we used to hang out when y'all were little. Now everyone's so busy with their own activities. I think we should do this more often. Don't you, Albany?"

"Yes," Albany said while texting on her phone.

"Put that phone down."

"Why? We're not at our dinner table."

"We're at a dinner table; they all count."

She huffed, but put down the phone.

"Did you get Tay's number?"

"Huh?"

"Don't huh me," Randall said, sitting back and looking at his daughter with humor. "I saw y'all talking just before we left. He's a good kid. Smart too."

"That your new boyfriend?" Aaron asked. He looked at his parents. "She has a new one every week."

"I do not."

"Yes, you do."

"Okay, y'all, stop fighting," Sherri chided.

"I'm just glad y'all aren't fighting anymore," Albany said.

"Mom and Dad were fighting?" Aaron asked his sister.

"You didn't notice all last week when they kept talking to us but not each other?"

"What were y'all fighting about?" Aaron asked.

"Grown folks' business," Sherri replied. "But we kissed and made up, didn't we, baby?"

Randall winked as he responded, "We sure did."

CHAPTER 44

Jacqueline waited for several moments, wanting to be sure that the light dose of sleeping medication she'd mixed with Miss Elaine's evening meal had taken full effect. So far her searches had proved fruitless, but she still wanted to know if there was any information that her "patient" had on Randall, Sherri, or the kids that could prove useful. She tapped lightly on Miss Elaine's bedroom door before opening it and walking to where the older woman lay peacefully sleeping. Looking down at her for several seconds, Jacqueline experienced a range of emotions; some, like caring and a tiny built of guilt, felt like foreign objects in her body. A memory slammed into her mind—another woman: old, kind, and wise, just like Miss Elaine. *Grammy.*

She looked at the nightstand beside the bed, and before she realized what was happening, picked up the pearl-handled brush that had been placed there. She sat on the bed and slowly, tentatively, reached for Miss Elaine's curly silver locks and began gentle strokes. Tears formed in her eyes as faded memories of happier times swirled in her mind, the pictures fuzzy and distorted, but the feeling of warmth unmistakable.

She'd been happy once, had felt cared for and loved. *That's the feeling I want to have again*, she thought, brushing away tears as after one last stroke she replaced the brush on the nightstand. *That's what I want to feel again with Randall by my side.*

She stood and idly walked around the room picking up first one thing and then another. Miss Elaine's was not a cluttered house. Most items had a place and were in order, so it didn't take Jacqueline long to realize that nothing of value to her was in this room. She walked back into the living room, reached beneath the coffee table, and pulled out two large photo albums. She made quick work of looking through the pictures, some old, faded, and in black and white, others very recent. She paid particular attention to several pictures featuring Sherri and her brother, Nathan. He looked professional, and attractive. Another time, another place, and Jacqueline would have loved a closer get to know. But it was too late. Randall had her heart.

These thoughts were making her melancholy, an emotion that Jacqueline didn't handle well. So she went down to her room and picked up her phone, choosing to be productive instead. Following the advice that Marco had provided, she went to her message box, entered a variety of codes, and within minutes was sending text messages between her phone and Randall's. A devilish smile formed as she thought of how very clever was the job she performed. According to Marco, Randall would not know that a thread of additional messages had been added to the first one, unless he scrolled beyond the initial text. Since Jacqueline hadn't been in contact with him directly in over a week, and had only sent a text that one time on the way to New York, she doubted that Randall would have an inkling of what she was doing. Until it was too late.

She sought and found the initial text and the test message she'd sent right after Marco's tutorial. She reread the first one that she'd sent Randall:

GOOD MORNING, DR. IT'S JACQUELINE. CALLED LAST
WEEK. WANT TO INCLUDE PSI IN THE PIECE I'M WRITING
FOR SCIENCE TODAY. WHEN WILL YOU ARRIVE IN NY?
MAYBE WE CAN MEET, AND ALSO SET UP A TIME TO
INTERVIEW YOU AT YOUR COMPANY'S OFFICES. LET ME
KNOW IF YOU'RE INTERESTED, AND WHAT DAYS/TIMES
WORK FOR YOU. J.

Settling back against the couch, she read his response.

HELLO, JACQUELINE. BUSY PAST WEEK. EN ROUTE TO
THE TOWERS NOW. YES, LET'S MEET. I'LL CALL LATER.
RANDALL.

Then she read one of the "conversations" she'd created.

HEY, IT'S ME. I KNOW YOU TOLD ME TO WAIT UNTIL YOU
CONTACTED ME, BUT I JUST WANTED YOU TO KNOW THAT
I'LL BE OUT OF TOWN FOR A WHILE, TAKING CARE OF
BUSINESS BACK HOME. I'LL MISS YOU AND THINK ABOUT
YOU EVERY DAY.

The only thing that was better than the message she'd
written as herself was the one she'd concocted to look as
though it came from Randall's phone:

HEY, BEAUTIFUL. I MISS YOU LIKE CRAZY, ESPECIALLY THAT
SEXY BODY LYING NAKED BENEATH ME. YES, WE NEED TO
LIE LOW FOR NOW BUT WHAT'S A FEW WEEKS WHEN WE'LL
SOON HAVE A LIFETIME? I'LL CONTACT YOU SOON. MIGHT
BE TIME FOR A QUICK TRIP TO THE OTHER SIDE OF THE
BORDER.

"That was good, girl," she muttered, sliding her thumb
over the words. "Let's see, this was sent last week. What should

I say to up the ante a bit?" She thought for several seconds and giggled at what she was getting ready to do, then let her thumbs fly across the keys.

Grammy stood there, serene and enchanting, gazing at her with soft brown eyes.

"Grammy?"

"Yes, child."

"Grammy, you came back!"

"I did."

"I'm so happy! Is Sissy here, too?"

"Yes, child. Come with me."

Jacqueline eased away from the wall and began to walk toward her, watching the ground to avoid glass and blood. When she looked up, Grammy was gone. But she was there, the other woman, this one mean and ignorant and smelling of gin.

"You're a very bad girl," she said, raising a hand that clutched a thick, black belt.

"No, Mommy!"

She protested, but still the belt came down: once, again, countless times.

Jacqueline awoke to tears wetting her face. She sat up, clutching a pillow against her chest, working to quell her erratic breathing and calm the wretched fear.

With you, Randall, there will be no more nightmares.

Repeating this thought, she turned on her side, and fell into a dreamless sleep.

CHAPTER 45

A few days later, Sherri was on the Internet when she heard the front door open. "Good afternoon, Sherri. It's just me."

"Hi, Blair."

"I got your mail."

"Oh, good." Sherri walked out of Randall's office and over to the table. "I've been waiting on an answer to my proposal about teaching part-time at the alternative school across town. They said they'd mailed me something." She flipped through the mail and stopped when she got to a padded envelope. "This may be it."

There was no return address on the envelope, but the address label looked professional enough. She opened it and pulled out the contents. There was a short, typed note on a blank sheet of paper, and several more papers beneath it.

> *Dear Sherri:*
> *So you think I'm the one who is lonely, jealous, and pitiful? Maybe this will convince you that your husband loves me and I am not crazy.*
> *Sincerely, Mrs. Jacqueline Atwater*

She moved on to the other pages. There, in black and white, was a series of text messages and emails between Randall and Jacqueline, another after another after another. *I don't believe this shit.* She looked at the headings and noted that the dates went back a month or more, most sent to Randall's work e-mail address, and some to his phone. Some were short, mere terms of endearment or declarations of love. Others were more revealing. *I'll try to get away tonight,* one of them said. And another: *Baby, you know I want to be with you and I will. But I can't leave Sherri while her mom is sick. She goes to North Carolina next week. We'll be together then.*

Eyes widening at this comment, Sherri hurriedly went to her Outlook calendar and checked the dates against when the e-mail had been sent. Sure enough, it was sent on a Thursday, the week before she'd gone to see her mom. She swallowed, closed her eyes, and felt sick to her stomach. She wanted to cry, or scream, or break something. But she was so numb that she could not move. *This cannot be happening,* she repeated over and over. But it was.

She reached for the phone. Renee answered on the second ring. "What's going on, girl?"

"I've got proof."

"Hold on a minute," she said, her voice lowered. "Let me close my door." After a couple seconds she came back to the phone. "Okay, what's going on?"

"I just got a package."

"From who?"

"Who else? That bitch, Jacqueline!"

"What was in it?"

Sherri told her, and read some of the exchanges.

"This is crazy," Renee finally said.

"This is what I feared the most; that that bitch was telling the truth and Randall was lying."

"Wait a minute, Sherri. Are you sure those are real e-mails?

I wouldn't put it past that scheming heifah to just type some stuff and mail it."

"They look real to me, with Randall's work e-mail address. It looks like she just printed them out."

"This is messed up." Silence, and then, "I'm so sorry, but I've got to go into a meeting. But listen, don't do anything drastic until you know for sure about those e-mails. Talk to Randall and really listen to his side. Okay?"

"Okay."

"I love you, girl. Call me later."

"I will."

She heard him when he came in. They were alone. She'd had Blair take the kids to the mall, thinking things might get ugly. It might get loud. But now, four hours had passed since she'd opened Jacqueline's package. Enough time for her to have calmed down. Enough time for her not to rip Randall's dick off as soon as they both were in the same room.

"Sherri?"

She took a breath, listened as his footsteps grew silent. He'd left the hardwood floors of the living and dining rooms and was now coming up the stairs.

"Baby," he said when he reached their suite, "didn't you hear me calling you?"

She answered without looking at him. "I did."

"Oh."

Imagining the look on his face caused her heart to crack. She knew him so well—every expression for every emotion. But then, considering the messages he'd written to Jacqueline, she doubted if she'd ever known him at all.

Randall walked over, his face showing concern. "What's the matter? Why are you sitting here in the dark?"

She said nothing, just handed him the contents of the mail Jacqueline sent.

For a moment he was silent. "What the hell?" he finally mumbled, almost to himself. He scanned the other papers before crumbling the papers and throwing them on the ground. "This is bullshit, Sherri. I didn't write that crap!"

"I didn't want to believe it. But you can't argue with black and white."

"It's obvious she created these to make it look as though we were corresponding. But I swear to you, baby, other than one or two times when I responded to a professional question, I've never e-mailed that . . ." Randall ground his teeth together, so angry that he was glad there was distance between him and Jacqueline right now. He wasn't a violent man and had never hit a woman. But right now, if he saw Jacqueline, he'd knock her smooth out.

He picked up the papers, smoothed them out, and peered at them closely. Then he went over to his briefcase and came back with his cell. Sitting across from Sherri, he put the call on speaker. "I'm going to call my tech guy," he told her. "Find out how Jacqueline could have done this because as God is my witness, this was set up."

A half hour later, Randall and Sherri had moved their conversation downstairs to Randall's office. Using the office phone, he called his tech guy, who said that indeed an e-mail account could be accessed from a remote location and explained how, by using her computer or phone a person could create a false chain of text messages and e-mails. Sherri finally said she believed him, but honestly, Randall felt it was more because she was tired of dealing with the whole situation.

His wife wasn't the only one. He was more than tired too. So he excused himself for a moment and went down to his office. There was someone he needed to call.

"Listen," he said when the call went to voice mail. "This has got to stop. Your trumped-up e-mails didn't work. My tech guy was able to explain your stunt in five minutes. I'm on my way upstairs to sleep with my wife. If you contact us again, in any way—e-mail, text, phone, whatever—you will regret it. The authorities will be contacted, as will human resources at *Science Today*. This isn't a warning. It's a promise. For the last time I'm telling you in no uncertain terms. Leave me and my family alone."

CHAPTER 46

Just when Jacqueline was ready to climb the country walls, a woman named Constance Riley returned to Raleigh. Since "Wanda" had mentioned the need to take a couple days off, the old biddy said it would be a pleasure to watch her neighbor. It was exactly the answer that Jacqueline needed. Obviously, her package to Virginia had arrived days ago. The conversation between Sherri and her sidekick, Renee, had told her that. Randall talked to James, but not often. Yet a niggling feeling told her that something was going on. Something she didn't know about. So between getting Randall's threat and (while in North Carolina) having no remote access to the feeds from the cameras in the Atwater home, she couldn't get back to D.C. fast enough.

Not wanting to be seen driving the gray Toyota, she drove to the airport's long-term parking lot and then took a cab to Phillip's place. She paid the cab driver and on the way up the walk, felt it again, an unsettled something in the pit of her stomach.

She'd had this feeling before, when her school had informed the social workers of her bad behavior, and they had put a team on watch to observe her. This had led to almost one year in a girls' home, where she'd met and become fast friends with Kris. Kris, the only person ever to truly have her back.

Looking around but seeing nothing out of the ordinary, she walked as casually yet quickly as possible up the sidewalk to the front door, slid her key into the lock, and walked inside. The singer Adele was playing on the stereo. "Kris?"

"Hey!"

Jacqueline immediately relaxed. Something about Kris's disposition always worked to calm her nerves. "Hey."

Kris paused, checking her out carefully. "What's wrong?"

"I don't know. I felt funny just now, when I walked up the sidewalk to the house."

"Probably nerves brought on by paranoia. I wouldn't make a big deal of it, if I were you."

"Did anyone come to the door?" Jacqueline asked, obviously unconvinced.

"Huh?"

"A delivery man, anyone soliciting anything, mail delivery, a stranger. Did anyone ring our doorbell or come to the house?"

"No, Jacqueline! Really, girl, you need to chill."

Jacqueline ran a hand through her thick, soft tresses, picked up the mail from the table in the foyer, and walked into the living room. "Where's Phillip?"

"He and Marco went on vacation. They'll be in Europe for over a month. That's why I decided to stay."

"Oh, that's right. He sent me an e-mail. I'm glad you're here." She walked into her room and looked around. The feeling she had wouldn't go away. She looked at her watch, reached for her phone, and called Phillip. Placing the call on speakerphone, she began to undress.

"Phillip! I'm glad you answered."

"I almost didn't. Marco and I are headed to the beach."

"Where are you?"

"Barcelona."

"I've never been there."

"You'll have to visit. It's a beautiful place." She heard Phillip muffle the phone, then come back to her. "I hate to rush you, Jacqueline, but—"

"No, it's okay. I just wanted to ask you a question. Did anyone come by here before you left?"

"Like who?"

"I don't know. Someone asking about me, maybe?"

"No."

"Did you have friends over, or maybe a repairman?"

"No, Jacqueline. Why all these crazy questions? What's going on?"

"Nothing. I just couldn't find something that I thought I'd left on the table in my room, that's all."

"Oh, you're back in D.C.?"

"Just for a couple days."

"Are you staying somewhere else now?"

"Uh, just helping out a friend in New York. Look, I have to run, Phillip. Give Marco a hug for me. Have fun and be safe!"

"You too, Jacqueline."

She hung up the phone, and after a quick shower she poured herself a glass of wine and settled down in front of her monitors. She rolled back the tapes and for the next two hours got caught up on the happenings around the Atwater home front. She heard the argument, saw Sherri confront him with the papers, and laughed when Randall balled them up and threw them on the ground. Her smile disappeared when they left the room, went downstairs, and she could no longer hear them.

"Where'd they go?" She searched the other screens. All of the monitored rooms were empty.

Obviously, when she'd posed as the cleaning woman, there was a room she hadn't gone in, one she hadn't set up for her surveillance.

This was a problem.

When she turned back to the screens, she found herself eyeing a situation that was even worse than not knowing what she didn't know. Randall and Sherri had returned to their bedroom. And they were making love.

"That's enough," Jacqueline mumbled through gritted teeth, as she watched. "He's mine!"

Jacqueline turned off the screens and marched out of the room. There was something she needed to do, but she knew even this may not be enough to send Sherri packing. So far nothing she'd done was enough to separate them. That was unfortunate for the good little wife. Because when the opportunity ever presented itself, Jacqueline would take care of Sherri . . . for good.

CHAPTER 47

Sherri walked into the kitchen, grateful that the house was empty. Both of the kids were busy with activities and Randall had texted her to say he'd be late. With this information, she'd informed the chef that he wouldn't be needed and moved her appointment with the masseuse to another day. She needed time alone to digest what she'd just discovered. To think about the secret bank account that Randall had been hiding, the one with information she couldn't access. Given the runaround she received when she called to inquire about it, she believed that the balance was a substantial amount.

He'd lied to her. That morning when she'd walked into his office and caught him on the phone, she'd asked what he was discussing, had thought she'd heard something about finance. He'd blown her off and attributed whatever she'd heard to business. Then later, when he continued to act funny, she'd asked him point-blank if there was something he was hiding, if there was anything at all he wanted to share with her. He'd turned the tables by blowing up, acting as though he was the one who'd been wronged and had a right to be angry. So much so that she questioned her actions, allowing Renee and Debbie to convince her that she was rushing to judgment, finding problems where there were none. Now, things were different. Now she knew for sure that there was a secret bank account. This was a serious problem. Because if he'd lied about this, what else had he lied about? Sherri was afraid that she knew the answer. Confirming it was just a matter of time.

Walking into the kitchen, her mind was racing. For the life of her, she couldn't get what had happened to make sense. Even if Randall were having an affair, they already each maintained separate spending accounts. Why would he have to place money into yet another account at a totally different bank? As she was reaching for the orange juice, an answer surfaced, one so shocking that she almost dropped the glass bottle.

Is he going to divorce me? Is he preparing to leave me and the children and he's lining his ducks up in a row?

For the next two hours, she gave herself a headache trying to figure out the mystery, solve the puzzle. She wore a path in the plush upstairs carpet and felt the knot when it formed at the base of her neck. She heard the garage door and sprang up from where she'd been sitting. She walked over to where she'd thrown the letter that told of the account. She stood there, shoulders heaving, breath coming in spurts. She'd promised herself that she would remain calm, cool, and collected. She almost pulled it off.

"You lied to me, and this time you won't be able to explain it away!"

"My God, Sherri. What has she done now?"

"Would you believe that for once I'm not mad at Jacqueline? No, Randall, this one is all on you."

She advanced, paper in hand. "The bank where you have your secret fund made a mistake, and instead of sending this to your office they sent it out to your home address. You still don't have anything to tell me, still have nothing to hide?"

Randall reached for the paper she handed him. He looked and saw that indeed the notice was from the bank where he'd set up the account to handle a very special project. He'd wanted it to be a surprise. But he wanted his marriage more.

"It's not what you think," he began, then cleared his throat and spoke more confidently. "I'd wanted it to be a surprise."

Sherri said nothing, just stood there listening, looking as though she could kick his butt into next week.

"Come with me." He turned and walked toward the bedroom door. When he saw that she wasn't following, he added, "You said you wanted to know what I've been up to, right? What secret I've been keeping from you? Then come on." He didn't wait this time.

Sherri hesitated a moment before she followed. No doubt she didn't want to know what he'd been hiding from her, didn't want to acknowledge the situation that could very well mark the end of their marriage. But this horse was already way out of the barn, so she had no choice but to ride it. She took a deep breath and followed Randall into his office downstairs.

She watched as he walked over to the wall safe tucked behind a picture. Funny, but she'd never thought to look there.

"You're right, Sherri. I did lie." He tossed a folder on the desk. "This is why."

She looked at the folder and then at him. Something about his demeanor unnerved her. Suddenly she wasn't sure she wanted to know what was behind door number three.

"What is it?"

"Go ahead. Look at it. I was going to surprise you, but . . ." He shrugged and turned his back on her and looked out the window.

Tentatively, Sherri picked up the envelope and looked inside. There were pictures of the Bahamas, with an area circled. Leafing through the papers, she saw architectural drawings and maps, and what looked like some sort of deed.

"What is this?" she asked again. This time her voice held no accusation but was rather soft, almost pleading.

"What was supposed to be a surprise for our fifteenth

wedding anniversary." He slowly turned around. "I secretly ne-
gotiated the purchase of your very own island in the Caribbean, Sherri. Where I've also had a vacation beach house built."

"I'm sorry, Randall. I thought . . ."

"I know."

"Please forgive me."

"Already done."

She walked into his open arms. "Will we ever get back to
normal, where we trust each other completely again?"

"I sure hope so. Maybe our healing can begin on the island."

"I'd like that, baby. This is the most incredible gift. I can't
wait to go there. Will it be done by our anniversary date at the
end of August?"

"I knew you'd feel that way. It's one of the reasons I
wanted it to be a surprise. I just found out that due to delays,
the house won't be ready until November."

She stepped back and looked at him. "Perfect! We can go
there for Thanksgiving."

"Sounds like a plan. Happy anniversary, baby."

"Happy anniversary."

For a moment they were happy, just like in the good old
days, the days before Jacqueline.

Unfortunately, the moment would be short-lived.

CHAPTER 48

Randall must have stared at the e-mail link a full five minutes before he opened it. He'd threatened her freedom and livelihood if not left alone. Now, with an e-mail sitting in his in-box with her name attached, he felt anxious, had a sense of foreboding, because somehow when it came to his life, everything this woman touched went from sugar to shit.

You've already received racy e-mails, with naked pics of her attached. E-mails and text messages that were also forwarded to Sherri. All it can be is more of the same. It can't get worse than her legs gaped open in front of a camera lens, right?

He opened the e-mail. Immediately he noticed that instead of an attachment, she'd sent him a link. He paused, his finger hovering over the mouse, his mind whirling with what the change could possibly mean. Did she send a virus, hoping to corrupt his computer, maybe even somehow damage company files? Randall almost laughed at the thought. Here he was, worried about the state of his company, when she'd already made his home life a living hell.

Pushing the speaker button on the company phone, he sat back wearily as he waited for his IT guy to answer. Brandon was only twenty-two years old, but when it came to anything involving computers, he was a beast. The son of an employee who'd been at the company for only a few months less than the ten years he'd been in business, he'd quickly snapped up the young whiz fresh out of college and hadn't once regretted the decision. Within six months he'd cleaned out a variety of bugs, spyware, cookies, and the like and had increased the speed of the company network by 15 percent. Likewise, he'd installed a security system with a firewall he swore was akin to what they used in the White House. Still, President Obama may have dealt with a terrorist named Osama Bin Laden, but he'd never dealt with one named Jacqueline Tate. Randall wanted Brandon's assurance that it was safe for him to click on the link and view what had been sent.

"Hello, Dr. Atwater."

"Hey, Brandon. Quick question for you. I just received an e-mail with a link attached, and I'm concerned that there may be a virus attached. Can you check it out for me?"

"Sure. Just forward it to my e-mail and I'll give it a test."

"Uh, it's a personal note on my personal laptop, so I'm going to need you to come to my office."

"Okay, no problem. I'll be right there."

Randall tried to busy himself by looking at a report that had just been sent over and checking his calendar for upcoming appointments, but it was no use. His mind was singularly focused on Jacqueline and how to stop the havoc she was wreaking on his life. When his friend James called, he hurried him off the phone. "Hey, man. I'm in the middle of something. Let me call you back."

At that very moment Brandon walked in, so if James had a comeback, Randall didn't hear it. He'd already hung up the phone.

"Come on in, Brandon, and close the door." The young man entered. "Let's go over to the conference table," Randall said, picking up his iPad and heading for the other side of the room. The two men sat down. He slid the computer in front of Brandon.

"Did you try to open it?" Brandon asked.

Randall shook his head. "I didn't want to take a chance on opening up a virus."

"You don't have to worry about that, Dr. Atwater. The security system I put on your devices won't allow a virus to get in." He moved his finger, then paused before opening the file. "May I?"

"Go ahead."

Brandon clicked on the link. It was a video. Randall became immediately concerned. He reached for the iPad and paused the video. "Okay, Brandon, thanks. I'll let you know if I need anything else."

"Oh, uh, okay. Thanks, Doctor."

Randall waited until Brandon left the office and closed the door behind him. Then he looked at the iPad, staring at the picture that had been paused, wondering why he was scared to push the play button. Currently, the picture looked innocent enough; just an off-white-looking wall. After staring at the frozen picture for another several seconds and realizing he was acting like a scared little boy, he angrily swiped at the face of the iPad, releasing the pause button.

Then he sat back, crossed his arms, and waited. His relaxed posture didn't last long. In fact, his heart dropped from his chest to his toes when the camera began moving and a familiar room came into sight. *What the hell . . .* It was his office. He sat up, leaned forward, repositioned the computer, and swore he must be dreaming. There was no way that he was seeing his office on the screen, from a link that had been sent by the woman he despised. *Is this what she was doing when she broke into my office?*

The answer almost knocked him out of his chair.

The picture became shaky as someone laid down the camera. Its lens was pointed to his desk at first, and then over toward the large pane windows. *What is going on?* Then the camera was picked up and placed on some type of stand. Once again it focused, and this time it was on the conference table—where he sat with Jacqueline astride him.

"Fuck!" Randall jumped up, bumping his leg on the edge of his desk. His eyes bulged out of his head, he placed a hand on each side of his face and thought he was going crazy. He had to be going crazy. Stark-raving mad. That is the only explanation for why he was seeing himself on the screen. In this room. With Jacqueline's breasts exposed.

"Where are her clothes?" he asked the screen, even as he watched. He was one of the lightest sleepers that he knew. "So how is this happening without me waking up?"

Didn't matter how, he soon reasoned. If this video got leaked to the public, it would be a PR nightmare. In the next few seconds he realized that his horrible ordeal had only begun. The more he watched it, the more he knew that his professional life was the least of his worries. If Sherri ever saw this, their marriage would be doomed.

At that very moment, his phone rang. *Sherri.* He reached over to answer the call and see what she wanted. But he had a sneaking suspicion that he already knew.

CHAPTER 49

Two days had passed. Nothing had changed. Sherri knew he was watching, could imagine the look on his face without turning around. Randall. Helpless. He didn't feel this way very often; this she knew. That her actions were causing him this pain did not make her happy. But it didn't change the course of her actions. She was hurting too.

"Is there anything at all that I can say? Anything I can do?"

She'd known the question was coming. Randall's was an analytical, problem-solving mind. It was probably driving him crazy that he couldn't find an immediate solution to this problem.

"I just need space," Sherri said, walking past him to the closet to pull out more clothes. "I need time to think, to process all that's happened."

Randall walked over to stand beside Sherri. Close enough to touch her, but he didn't. "I don't see how space right now will bring us closer together."

Finally, Sherri turned to face him. "Perhaps not, but it's what I need."

Randall watched helplessly as Sherri walked into the master bath and placed a variety of toiletries in a tote bag. "None of it's true, babe," he finally said. Silence. "We're thinking with our emotions," he continued, probably encouraged that he didn't get shut down flat out. "I mean, think about it. I'm a rational person; I think everything out. Right? So why would I develop a relationship with someone, tell you about her, introduce you to her, and then keep up a written dialogue with that person on my personal laptop? I have computers at the office. Wouldn't it make more sense for me to keep something that I'm trying to hide out of my house?

"And using that logic, wouldn't it also stand to reason that I wouldn't invite the other woman to PSI headquarters to have sex, surrounded by employees and colleagues and my executive assistant right outside my office, in the middle of the day?"

"Dicks are dumb," Sherri said, remembering the line from a blog that her friend Renee had sent her. Who was the blog's author? Mary something or other. *Mary B. Morrison. Yeah, that's her.* At the time Sherri had received it, she'd thought it entertaining reading but nothing that related to her. What a difference a couple months made. "Granted, you're intelligent, but most of the time in these situations, men think with the wrong head."

"Sherri, I'm telling you—"

"I know, Randall," Sherri snapped, losing patience. "You're telling me, and you've told me the same things forever. But stop for just one minute and look at this situation from my perspective. Stop and listen to yourself. You say you're not having an affair, yet I get a video emailed to me of a woman in your office, kneeling, with your dick in her hands! Now, in light of this irrefutable evidence, even Mother Teresa would have reached her limit, even Jesus himself would have said hell to the no."

She walked over to her dresser and began pulling out underwear. Slowly, she lifted out a lacy, white thong, at least two sizes too small for her. She turned to Randall. "This isn't mine."

"What do you mean, they're not yours?"

Since Randall tells you everything, will you let me know when he tells you where he found my panties?

"I can't, Randall. I. Just. Can't." Sherri pressed her fingers against her temples. She felt a doozy of a headache coming on. "If you're smart, you'll let me leave now," she finally said, tossing her underwear in before closing the hard plastic suitcase. "Don't bother calling. I don't know when will be the next time that I want to talk to you."

She took the luggage off the bed and placed it near the door. Then she walked out of the master suite without looking back.

Randall watched her leave, feeling a part of himself leaving with her. He'd heard from the private investigator and knew that they'd tracked down where Jacqueline lived, with a man whose description sounded like Phillip, and were waiting for the perfect opportunity to get inside the row house and search it out. But time was running out, both on his patience and on his marriage. He didn't have a thug, gangster, or burglar bone in his body but he might have to take the matter of finding out the truth about Jacqueline into his own hands. A part of him wanted to run after his wife, do whatever it took to keep her in Virginia. But he knew that nothing he said right now would matter, plus he didn't want to make a scene in front of the kids.

CHAPTER 50

As soon as she reached her room, Jacqueline slammed the door shut and pulled off her wig. "Dammit!"

"What's going on, girl?"

In her frustration, Jacqueline had almost forgotten that Kris had showed up in Raleigh late last night. "That old coot is starting to get on my nerves," she said, plopping down on the queen-size bed. "Going on and on about cooking and her stupid flowers. And I have to sit there and act interested, happy to help her."

"Help her how?"

"The woman's loony; can't remember where she puts things."

"That doesn't sound good. How sick is she?"

"Who cares? I've got bigger problems to worry about."

Jacqueline had been thrilled to learn that Sherri was coming to visit her mother. It was exactly the chance that she'd been waiting for. Then came the last conversation she'd monitored, the one that had put a wrench in her plans.

"Have you figured out what you're going to do yet? I know you want to get rid of her, but what about the others?"

"Geez, I don't know." Jacqueline ran a harried hand through her hair as she sat up, then stood and began to pace the room. "It will be my pleasure to take out Sherri, but that she is no longer coming alone has definitely thrown a hitch in my plans."

"What about the mom?"

"What about her?"

"Are you going to let her live?"

Jacqueline thought about it, heaving a sigh. "If she's lucky."

"When is the last time you talked to Randall?" Kris asked.

"Not since he threatened to contact *Science Today*."

"Do you think he'd really call them?"

"No, but Sherri would. She's pressuring him, believe me. He's not acting on his own."

"What if he is?"

"He's not! He loves me, and that's all that matters."

"Of course, Jacqueline. You are right. So . . . Sherri is coming tomorrow. What's the plan?"

Miss Elaine hummed softly as she walked among the gardens in her large back yard. Near the back patio were her flower gardens, filled with irises, leopard plants, larkspur, asters, and geraniums. It had been weeks since she'd felt this healthy. She credited that sweet girl Wanda, with her pleasant nature and attentive care. *Hard to believe that loneliness may have been part of my illness*, she thought with a chuckle as she bent to smell a flower. Now she'd admit that this may have been true. She'd fought Sherri's notion of her needing someone living with her but already felt that if Wanda had to leave for some reason, especially with Constance spending so much time in St. Louis with her children, she didn't know what she'd do.

She straightened and looked behind her. The vegetable garden was in full bloom and could rate in any farmer's mar-

ket. Greens of several varieties—cabbage, spinach, peppers, lettuce, onions, tomatoes, squash, and okra—all raised their leaves
to heaven as if as thankful for the afternoon sunshine as Miss
Elaine herself. She gazed at the garden patch lovingly as she
neared it, remembering the years that she and her husband
would share conversation as they picked weeds.

"Looks like we've got a few," she mumbled, reaching between the okra stems and pulling up errant weeds. She continued walking and snatched a few more. Normally, she paid a
neighborhood child to come over a couple times a month and
weed the garden, but today, for the first time in a while, Miss
Elaine was thankful to feel able enough to do it herself. "Let me
go get my hat and my gloves and my weeder . . . ," she said to
herself as she walked toward the backdoor. "And I'll be all set."

She entered the house, crossed the kitchen, and went down
the hallway toward the basement stairs. Another project lovingly overseen by her husband, they'd been proud to turn the
unfinished underground area into one that now boasted a
guest bedroom, large, airy den, and storage room. Crossing the
den toward the storage room, she paused at the sound of a
woman's voice. It was strong and animated.

*Funny, that doesn't sound like Wanda. There's no Southern ac-
cent.*

Miss Elaine took a couple more steps, until she heard the
next comment. "Don't worry about her finding out, Kris. You
can stay here as long as me."

She turned around. *Who's this talking about staying in my
home?* It couldn't be Wanda. That sweet child would never do
something as presumptive as that. But someone was in her
house and since they were in the guest room with Wanda, she
had to know them. *They're probably just over for a visit.* Miss
Elaine stood there, listening.

"Her flight arrives at one fifty," she heard the woman saying. "She's renting a car and will be here by two thirty. Somehow, I need to get her separated from her mom and the kids, give her the shot, and then make sure we're all together when the poison takes effect."

Miss Elaine's eyes widened as she heard this. Surely she couldn't have heard correctly. *Maybe they're talking about a movie or something, or a book that they've read.* Any other thought was simply too foreign for the kindhearted mother of two to comprehend. Again, there were voices. She leaned forward instinctively, trying to hear what the Kris woman was saying. She couldn't hear the other woman and decided to move closer.

Wait a minute. This is my house. Let me go in here, talk to Wanda, find out who's visiting and exactly what's going on. She started to announce herself and then for some reason changed her mind. Instead of calling out Wanda's name as she'd started to, she became even quieter, walking on tiptoe toward the door that was only slightly ajar. She reached it, raised her hand to knock, and then froze at the next words spoken.

"With any luck she'll be dead before nightfall. And then Randall will be all mine."

Miss Elaine clamped her hand over her mouth to keep from crying out. She took one step backward and then another, trying to convince herself that she'd really heard what she knew had been spoken. Who was the woman talking to? Was her name Kris? And where was Wanda? Too many questions without enough answers. *Let me go and call Sherri. Warn her about what's happening. And then I'll call the police and get these people out of my house.*

She reached the first step and cringed as it creaked. Funny, but she'd never paid much mind to it before. Then again, she'd never had to sneak around in her own home. She waited a few seconds, not realizing that she was holding her breath as she did. She turned and looked toward the almost-closed door to the guest room. It was quiet, but no one came to the door to investigate the sound. She hoped they hadn't heard it as she went up the stairs as quickly and quietly as she could. Once she reached the top, she raced toward her phone where it lay on the kitchen counter. Her hands began to shake as she dialed. *Come on, baby. Please, Sherri. Hurry up and answer your phone!*

Jacqueline stopped in mid-sentence. "Did you hear that?"

"What?" Kris answered.

"That sound?"

Kris followed Jacqueline's gaze to the door. "No, I didn't hear anything."

"Hmm, maybe I'm just being paranoid."

"You?" Kris said in a playful, sarcastic tone. "Never!"

Jacqueline laughed and then just as quickly her smile flipped and she rushed to the door. Yanking it open, she looked left and right before focusing on a plant situated on a table by the stairway. The leaves were swaying, which meant one thing. Someone had just walked by it.

She looked at Kris in sheer frustration. There was no time to don her Wanda façade. "Darn it! We may have just gotten busted. I'll be right back."

Jacqueline took strong, determined strides over to the stairway and then, bypassing the first step that she knew creaked, quickly snuck up the remaining stairs. As quiet as a mouse, she tiptoed down the hallway, sticking her head around the doorway, trying to locate the whereabouts of Miss Elaine. In the end she only had to follow the voice.

"Sherri, baby, pick up! This is my third time calling. Oh Lord, I hope you haven't gotten on the plane and turned off your phone. You need to . . ." Miss Elaine's voice tapered off as she felt a presence behind her and felt a hand slowly closing around the back of her neck. She turned around.

Hang it up, Jacqueline mouthed.

Miss Elaine complied as she looked at Jacqueline in confusion. "Who are you and what have you done with Wanda?"

"Sit down, Elaine," Jacqueline said, giving the older woman a little shove as incentive to move. "I'm going to tell you a story and it might take a while. But I want you to listen closely and do exactly what I tell you. The life you save may be your own."

CHAPTER 51

Randall stood as the private investigator came into his office and closed the door. "Lay it on me, Doug. What did you find out?"

"A lot. You need to prepare yourself. It's pretty far-out."

Randall sat. "I can't believe it's any more incredible than what's already happened."

"It is. Trust me." The detective laid a folder filled with pictures on Randall's desk. "Those are pictures from where I just left. The home of Phillip Bochinsky."

"My God," Randall said as he began to flip through. He picked up one picture to study it. "Looks more like a computer lab."

"Those are monitors that I believe are attached to cameras placed in your home." Randall's head shot up. "You mentioned that she knew what type of bed you slept in and seemed to know your every move. I believe this is how.

"There was a master control missing, which prevented me from turning on the computers or monitors. But don't worry. I already have a friend at the station working on a search warrant so that everything in that room can be legally confiscated."

"Those cameras are the least of my worries. Somehow, just the other day, she emailed this to both me and my wife." Randall walked over to his computer. "As much as I hate to show it, you have to see this."

Doug walked to where he could see the screen. Randall pushed play on the short video clip of them Jacqueline had taken.

"My God."

"It's not what it looks like," Randall quickly offered. "I have absolutely no recollection of this happening. But I clearly remember the day she came by my office. One minute we were talking and the next minute I was being awakened by my assistant, late for a conference call. She said she'd been trying to wake me for several minutes. I was groggy the rest of the day."

"She drugged you, most likely. How long ago did this happen?" Randall told him. "Unfortunately, any evidence has probably disappeared by now."

"It's likely that she's monitored your family's every move, at least while you're home. With your permission, I have a guy prepared to come and sweep your office for electronics. That tape confirms that this office is also bugged. Perhaps your car as well."

Randall continued to look through the stack of information. "What type of woman would do something like this?"

"A very troubled one, who from the looks of it may have done far worse."

"Like what?"

"Jacqueline Tate grew up as Jamie Barnes, in poverty, in a small country province in Canada. Her parents were abusive: mother, physically; father, sexually. When Jamie, or Jacqueline if you will, was ten, her parents died in a fire. It was officially ruled as an accident though the authorities believed otherwise. They just couldn't prove it."

"Are you saying that she killed her parents?"

"And a sibling, from the looks of things. Early records allude to a younger sister but after the fire, all traces of her vanish. As the lone survivor, Jacqueline was the sole beneficiary of a very large insurance policy."

Randall sat back in his chair, shell-shocked. "She told me a version of this story. I felt compassion. My heart may have gone out to a murderer."

"She was sent to an orphanage until she was sixteen, and there were a couple stints in mental institutions after that, until she left the system at eighteen years old. I uncovered a friend in Canada, a woman named Kaitlyn. She knew Jacqueline was troubled, but described her as very good person who'd gotten some very bad breaks. I found a few other people who knew her; an elderly neighbor is watching her cat."

"What about the job with *Science Today*?"

"That's legit. For the most part, her professional resume checks out, and nothing else stood out until recently. She was suspected of the theft of several designer dresses and shoes in LA, but the items were all recovered by housekeeping staff at the Ritz."

Randall stood, and began to pace the room. "Where is she now?"

Doug shook his head. "More than likely, after sending that tape, she's lying low, waiting for the fallout to dissipate. Because of the hidden cameras she undoubtedly knows that Sherri has left you and is in North Carolina. She's probably under the impression that with your wife out of the picture you'll now see the light. You have to understand that while this seems totally ridiculous, you two being in a relationship is completely real in her mind. For all intents and purposes, you are her husband.

"Oh, and there's one more thing." Doug reached into his pocket and pulled out a slip of paper. "Among her things I found an address and phone number for a woman named Wanda Smith. Do you know her?"

"That's the caretaker living with my mother-in-law."

"I tried calling the number and it keeps going to voice mail."

"Why would she have the name of Mom Elaine's caretaker?" He stopped, an incredible thought coming to his mind. He raced to the phone, to call Sherri.

Doug watched as Randall tapped the screen and placed a call that went to voicemail.

"Sherri, please call me. This is an emergency. Call as soon as you get this message. I love you."

He placed the phone on the desk and continued to pace. Doug walked over and picked up his phone. He snapped off the silver disc. "Who gave you this?"

Randall turned and looked. "Jacqueline. It's helps to prevent radiation from . . . no."

Doug nodded as for Randall, realization dawned. "She's got connections. This is sophisticated. It's a camera, recording device and tracker, all in one."

"Dammit! There's one on Sherri's phone, too." He snatched his phone from Doug and called his mother-in-law. That call too went to voicemail. "I've got to get a hold of somebody in North Carolina. Make sure they're all right. I'm starting to get a very bad feeling about this, Doug. A very bad feeling."

CHAPTER 52

The cell phone beeped in her ear, causing Sherri to look at the caller ID on the dashboard. *Randall again. I need some space. Why doesn't he get it? He really needs to leave me alone!*

"Daddy keeps calling, Mom," Aaron said from the backseat. "Why do you keep ignoring his calls?"

"Is your seat belt on, Aaron?"

"You're changing the subject, Mom," Albany interjected. "But I want to know too."

"Your dad and I are having a disagreement," Sherri calmly replied, knowing that her kids deserved some type of explanation. "I need a little space to think things out. Plus," she continued, trying to brighten her tone, "I want to meet the woman taking such good care of Mom."

"You promised me that you and Daddy wouldn't get divorced." Albany clearly wasn't even buying the woman-caring-for-mommy story.

Sherri started to answer with a firm denial, but she stopped herself. Truth was, with all that had gone down in the past couple weeks, she no longer knew what would happen. They'd been in their twenties the one and only time she knew Randall had cheated. Then, given their brash, thoughtless choices and immaturity and the fact that Albany had barely been a toddler, his indiscretion had been easier to forgive. But now? Things were different. It would be difficult to have their parents split, but Sherri thought her children strong enough to survive it. She and Randall cared enough about the children to maintain a civil relationship, and money wasn't an issue. So now, instead of finding reasons why she shouldn't leave the marriage, she was looking for reasons why she should stay.

"I don't want y'all to divorce," Aaron said at last.

"That's enough!" Sherri hadn't known she was so close to losing it until the gasket was blown. "I don't want to hear any more talk of divorce. What's happening now is between me and your father." Glancing in her rearview mirror, her heart softened when she saw the concerned look on her young son's face. "Marriage isn't always easy, guys. Arguments happen. And much like I have to send you two to your respective rooms to keep you from bashing each other, sometimes your dad and I need our space too.

"I love your father very much," she continued, putting a comforting hand on Albany's leg. "We've been together for half my life. And we both love you rug rats to pieces. Don't worry about us. We'll be all right."

As Sherri finished talking and turned up the radio for the short drive from the airport, she tried very hard to believe the words that she'd just told her children.

Jacqueline walked around Miss Elaine, who sat shivering at the dining room table. "That wasn't a smart move you made," she told her. "You just put your beloved daughter in jeopardy."

Miss Elaine looked at her and spoke through her fear. "I don't want anybody to get hurt, baby. Not my daughter, and not you. There's still time for you to avoid what is sure to be a travesty. If you leave now, just walk out of here, I won't say a word. I promise. And you'll still have the chance to not mess up your life."

"Oh, you'd stay quiet, would you? Only for as long as it took you to dial 9-1-1. No, I'm afraid that there's no turning back from this road I've gone down. But being with Randall is worth it. Once he and I are together, everything that I've had to do to make that happen will be justified."

"Baby, where are your parents?"

For a moment, a glimmer of humanity shone in Jacqueline's eyes. "Six feet under. Deadly house fire. They burned to a crisp." A satisfied smirk crossed her face as Miss Elaine flinched at the description.

After a second, Miss Elaine responded, "You have my sincere condolences. How old were you?"

"Ten."

"That had to have been terrible to deal with, losing your family so young. Are you an only child?"

Jacqueline stared at Miss Elaine. No response.

"I was an only child," Miss Elaine continued. "And while I lost my father in my teens, my mother was around until I turned fifty-two. I must admit that since then I've had my share of lonely times. Baby, there are people out there who can help you."

The sincerity she heard in the older woman's voice was something Jacqueline wasn't used to. A part of her wanted to crawl up in the woman's lap and be rocked liked a baby. An unexpected emotion arose in her chest: compassion.

There was no time for that.

"I don't need help you old wench," Jacqueline spat, smacking Miss Elaine on the side of the face. I need Randall. If your daughter weren't so delusional about her marriage, if she would have just cooperated, I would have him by now. But since she's insisted on being stubborn . . . here we are. She ran the butt of the gun across Miss Elaine's shoulders and when she saw them straighten had to admire the woman's spunk. In another lifetime, if she'd been blessed with a good mother instead of the monster who'd birthed her, she would have wanted one like the one sitting before her, the one who seemed to love her daughter so much.

A black SUV pulled into the driveway. Both Jacqueline and Miss Elaine turned at the sound. "Looks like it's show time," she said as she straightened her glasses and adjusted the wig. She'd looked at herself a thousand times and was 99 percent sure that Sherri wouldn't recognize her. At least not right away. A good five or ten minutes, enough time to get them tied up and drugged. After that, she'd have to play it by ear. Sherri was definitely going to meet her maker, but she hadn't decided what to do with the rest. This was unlike her. Normally everything was so thought out. But time had run out and the family had arrived. She'd have to use her instincts and take her chances. There was no turning back now.

"Remember what I told you. Don't mess up. There's still a chance that some of you may survive this. But one word to your daughter and I'll shoot them without hesitation, and make you watch."

Turning the corner and seeing her mother's car, Sherri breathed a sigh of relief. She'd arrived at the Raleigh-Durham International Airport to several missed calls and messages from Randall and a strange one from her mother that had her stomach in knots. For the life of her, she couldn't think of anything Randall could tell her about Jacqueline that would change the fact that she didn't presently want to be around him. She was headed to where she wanted to be. From the time she'd taken the shuttle to the rental car to this moment, she'd hit redial to her mother's number. All she got was voice mail. When she'd called the number to the in-home caretaker, those calls had gone to voice mail too.

"Her car is here," Albany said, stating the obvious.

"Yeah, she's home, Mom." Aaron added.

"I'm glad to see that," Sherri admitted, noting that another car, one she assumed belonged to the caretaker, was also in the driveway. She calmed down a little bit, but not too much.

The kids were out of the car before it had barely come to a stop. "Grandma!" Albany shouted, running to the front door. Sherri's smile was genuine as she brought up the rear. Nothing could make her feel better like parking her feet under her mother's table, preferably in front of a plate of homemade meatloaf or black-eyed peas and ham. She thought about having the kids pull the luggage out of the car. But then again, like them, all she wanted right now was to feel her mother's arms around her. Right now this was the priority. Luggage could wait.

Sherri's smile faltered a bit when she rang the doorbell a second time without an answer. But then her mother opened the door with a smile on her face. Right away, Sherri got the feeling that it looked rather forced. *She's probably not feeling well*, Sherri decided. *I'll feel much better after Wanda and I have a heart-to-heart.*

"Grandma!" The children rushed in and enveloped their grandmother.

"How's my babies?" Miss Elaine asked.

"We're good," Albany said.

"I don't smell cookies," Aaron commented, a relevant observation considering that fresh-baked cookies almost always awaited them when they visited.

"I didn't get a chance to get them ready for you," Miss Elaine said, still standing at the door. "Maybe we'll make some later."

This comment was followed by Miss Elaine giving Sherri a look that told her something was definitely wrong. But what could it be? "Mom, why are we standing here in the doorway?" Sherri stepped in and gave her a heartfelt hug. "Are you feeling all right?"

"I'm a little tired," Miss Elaine said as she turned and

walked down the hallway toward the living room. "Y'all come on in and sit down."

Sherri turned to the children. It was time to get them out of sight so she could find out what was going on with her mother. "Y'all, go and bring in the luggage for me." She gave Albany the keys. "And no fighting."

As soon as the kids were out of sight, Sherri turned to her mother. "Okay, Mom, out with it. What's going on?"

"Oh, baby, don't worry about me. I just got up too fast, that's all. I was so excited, and it made me kind of dizzy."

Sherri stood. "Well, let me get you a glass of water."

"No!"

Sherri looked at her mom with a frown.

"I mean, just come and sit down. I've been so worried about you and Randall. I want to know how y'all are."

Sherri looked toward the door and heard the kids coming back in. "We'll talk on that later," she said with a nod in their direction. "Where's the nurse? Where's Wanda? That's who I want to meet."

A dowdy woman with a short fro and glasses entered the room. "Here I am," she said, her head downcast as she approached Sherri. "It's nice to meet you."

Sherri eyed the woman a moment, trying to identify why she was filled with unease. But then again, for the past few months her entire world had been turned upside down. Paranoia and confusion had become her companions. She forced herself to relax and held out her hand. "Nice to meet you. Thanks for all you're doing for my mom. She's raved about you."

Wanda walked to the other side of the room and sat down on the couch. "How was your flight?"

"Uneventful." Continuing to battle against the discomfort she felt, she shifted and tried to be more polite. "Have you traveled much?"

"No, ma'am," Wanda said, her accent even more pronounced than usual. "I'm scared of flying, matter of fact. When I go to see anybody, Greyhound is my preference. Keep my feet on the ground, know what I mean?"

"Wanda." Miss Elaine cleared her throat. "I want to bake the kids some cookies. Can you please go to the store for me and get some chocolate chips?"

Sherri could have sworn a frown scampered across Wanda's face, but it was so fast that she immediately thought she'd imagined it.

"Oh, Miss Elaine, there's no need for that. I just saw some in your pantry."

"Oh, did you? Were there butterscotch chips in there too? And peanut butter?" To Sherri's confused look, Miss Elaine added, "I'm in the mood for variety. Want to make several different kinds and take some to church." She stood, walked over to where her purse sat on a side table, and gave Wanda a twenty dollar bill. "That should cover it," Miss Elaine said. "If you could go now, please." Belatedly, she realized the kids weren't in the living room. "Albany! Aaron!"

"I think they went out back," Sherri said with a wave of her hand. "Probably playing with the dog." When she turned back, Wanda had slipped out unnoticed. "Wow, Wanda sure left fast."

This time, Miss Elaine didn't try to hide her franticness. "Sherri," she whispered, hurrying over to her daughter. "We've got to call the police! Dial 9-1-1."

"Mom, you're scaring me. What's going on?"

"Don't ask me, baby. We don't have time. That woman is crazy, and she wants to hurt you bad."

"The nurse?"

"Baby, just call them. Call them now!"

"Mom, please, calm down. I'm not going to call the cops until you tell me what happened."

"She brought a woman in here and was sharing her plan to

hurt you." Miss Elaine was talking rapidly, wringing her hands. "I tried to call and warn you, but she caught me. She wants to hurt you, baby. And she wants Randall for herself."

"Wanda?" This comment caused Sherri's gut to clench. She thought back to the message on her cell phone, the one from her mother that had ended abruptly. What she'd hoped had been a dropped call hadn't been dropped after all.

"Her name ain't Wanda. I don't know who she is. That's a wig she's wearing and somebody else's clothes. I looked into the room and saw the real woman. I don't know what's going on, but it isn't good."

An eerie scenario began spinning in Sherri's head. *No, it isn't possible. There's no way.* She knew it wasn't possible, imagined the police chiding her for making an unnecessary call. But she'd deal with those consequences when she faced them. Better safe than sorry, her mother had always told her. Now, erring on the side of caution was the name of the game.

"Okay, Mom. Go get the kids. I'm calling the police right now!"

CHAPTER 53

"I wouldn't make that call if I were you."

The deathly calm of the voice behind her and its eerie familiarity made Sherri slowly turn around. When she did, she almost had a heart attack. A crazed-looking Jacqueline stood just inside the doorway to Miss Elaine's living room: a wig in one hand, a gun in the other. She wasn't standing alone. She dropped the wig, pushed Miss Elaine into the room, then put her hand on Albany's shoulder and the gun to her head. Sherri's hands balled into fists as Jacqueline slowly stroked her daughter's hair. She watched fear mix with tears in her daughter's eyes.

"Let go of my daughter."

"Shut up! You're in no position to make demands." Jacqueline pushed the muzzle of the gun against Albany's head. "Drop the phone."

Sherri reluctantly took her finger off of the dial and tossed the phone near Jacqueline's feet. "All right, there's the phone. Now, let go of my child."

Instead of letting go of Albany, Jacqueline pulled her flush against her chest, pointing the gun at Sherri. "Where is the boy?"

Everything had happened so fast that Sherri hadn't had the time to consider Aaron's whereabouts. *Did he have a chance to run away? Run and alert a neighbor?* Sherri hoped so because knowing that Ms. Riley was out of town left her with few alternatives.

Jacqueline cocked the trigger. "Where is he?"

"I don't know!" Sherri screamed, instinctively holding up her hands in front of her. "Aaron!" The same woman who just seconds ago had hoped her son was down the street seeking help now prayed to see his little chocolate head come around the corner.

"Ten, nine, eight," Jacqueline began, walking farther into the room and trying to keep her eye on Sherri, Miss Elaine, and the door. "Seven, six, five . . ."

"Aaron, get in here!" Sherri gauged the distance between her and Jacqueline, and wondered whether if she lunged she could reach her before the lunatic got a shot off. In the split second she had to decide, she chose against a sudden move at this juncture. She'd never forgive herself if she somehow caused harm to her child.

"Four, three, two . . ."

"I'm here." Aaron stood in the doorway, his hands raised above his small, lean frame.

He seemed surprisingly calm, and in this moment Sherri realized just how much he resembled his father in both looks and demeanor. *If Randall were here*, Sherri thought. *But he isn't. Which means getting us out of this impossible mess is up to me!*

"Get over there." Jacqueline sneered at Aaron, now aiming the gun at his close-cropped head. "Where is your phone?"

"In my pocket," Aaron answered.

"Take it out. Slowly . . . ," she added when he lowered his hand to reach into his pocket. "And don't try anything heroic, young man. You're not your father, so don't do anything that will make me hurt you before it's time."

Before it's time? She's going to kill my kids? Sherri wondered how Randall could have slept with this bitch and not have seen she was crazy.

"Listen, Jacqueline, whatever you want, I'm sure we can work something out. Money, possessions, whatever it is. Just please don't hurt my family."

"Family?" Jacqueline asked, as if she were chatting with an interview subject instead of the woman toward whom she was aiming a gun. "You and your family are the only things standing in the way of what I want."

"I tried talking to her." Miss Elaine's words were for Sherri, but her eyes never left the gun.

"Shut up, old woman!"

Without even thinking about it, Sherri took a step forward.

Jacqueline's focus went immediately from Miss Elaine back to Sherri, the gun aimed at her chest.

Sherri stepped back. Her mind whirled. Her heart pounded. She had to save her family but had no idea how.

"Sit on the couch, all of you." She pushed Albany towards them. When no one else moved, Jacqueline shouted, "Now!"

Miss Elaine hurried over to the couch. "Baby," she said as she reached the couch and sat on the end, "you don't have to do this. That's what I've been trying to tell you. Randall doesn't want this family. He and my daughter are getting a divorce."

Sherri barely stopped herself from looking at her mother like she'd lost her mind. Fortunately, she caught on immediately and began speaking as she too sat down on the edge of the cushion. "I'm surprised he hasn't told you," Sherri continued, trying to sound and act with a calmness she did not feel. "Why do you think I left and came down here to be with Mom? It's because Randall kicked us all out of the house."

Jacqueline suddenly seemed uncertain for the first time since this madness began.

"Call and ask him if you don't believe me," Sherri said, knowing that if Jacqueline took her eyes off of her for more than two seconds, it was about to go all the way down.

"You're lying," Jacqueline said at last.

"I only wish I were. If anyone had told me that Randall would divorce me, I would never have believed them. We tried to talk him out of it, but he says he has something with you that he doesn't have with me."

"What's that?" Jacqueline asked, as the arm holding the gun lowered ever so slightly.

"Rapport. He said that he can talk to you about anything. If he brings up anything about his work at home, I don't have a clue."

A smile of satisfaction crept onto Jacqueline's face. Sherri held her breath, watching her closely, waiting for a moment, a second, when she thought she could jump her and wrestle away the gun.

The moment came immediately when a most unexpected yet welcome sound was heard in the distance: sirens.

Caught totally off guard, Jacqueline turned her head toward the hallway leading to the door. That was all the distraction that Sherri needed. She leapt from the couch, her eyes glued to the gun. Jacqueline turned just as Sherri reached her and slammed into her, knocking them both to the floor. In the background she heard screaming but couldn't tell if it was Albany, Aaron, her mother, or all of the above. She didn't have time to look around or figure it out. She had bigger fish to fry.

"Give it to me," she growled, twisting her adversary's wrist as she tried to knock the gun loose. She was on top of Jacqueline, and given Jacqueline's height and lean build, would normally have been the weaker of the two. But there was a different kind of strength available to a mother bear trying to protect her cubs. The Incredible Hulk would have been no match for Sherri right about now.

That didn't mean that Jacqueline wasn't going to try to give as good as she got. She rolled them over, trying to sit up and aim the gun at the same time. Sherri still had ahold of her wrist, and felt her fingernails breaking flesh.

"Let go of the gun," Jacqueline spat out between clenched teeth.

"Get the gun, Mommy!" Albany cried.

Aaron had other ideas. He ran up to Jacqueline, grabbed two large handfuls of her luscious thick hair and pulled with all his might. "Get off my mom!"

It was the opening Sherri needed. She balled her hand into a fist and punched Jacqueline in her face, so hard that Jacqueline's head snapped back. In that moment the gun popped out of her hand, landing a short distance away from where the women continued scuffling. "Let go, Aaron," Sherri said as she delivered another blow. "I got this."

They rolled, and once again Sherri was on top. "Albany! Get the gun!" Her daughter jumped up like a rocket and picked up the weapon. "Give it to Mom," Sherri said, huffing.

"Give it to me, baby," Miss Elaine implored.

"Aww!"

Jacqueline had taken the second that Sherri's attention was diverted and bit her hand. Now Sherri was really pissed off. She grabbed handfuls of hair on both sides of Jacqueline's head, wound the thick tresses around her hands and began to beat the woman's head against Miss Elaine's hardwood floor. "You crazy witch!" she began, slamming her head down with every phrase. "Randall told you to leave us alone. But your ass has a listening problem. You gonna learn today!"

"Police! Open up!"

Aaron jumped up and ran to the front door. Soon heavy footsteps sounded down the hall as four uniformed officers entered the living room. Two had drawn their guns. "Freeze!" one of them said, pointing his gun at Sherri.

"She attacked me, Officer!" Jacqueline cried, scrambling up as another officer pulled Sherri away from her. "She just tried to kill me!"

Everyone in there began talking at once.

"She's lying, Officer."

"She tried to kill us!"

"This is my house, sir, and that woman shouldn't be here."

And then a most unexpected voice, one that had everyone but the officer with his gun trained on Sherri and Jacqueline turning to face its owner.

"Don't shoot, officer. That's my wife!"

"Daddy!" Albany shouted before she and Aaron ran into Randall's arms.

CHAPTER 54

"Baby!" Randall rushed to Sherri's side and snatched her up in his arms. The kids were right behind him. "Are you all right?" Sherri nodded, still breathing heavy and ready to fight. He turned to Albany. "You're safe now, baby," he said to Albany, kissing her forehead. "You're safe, my man," he said to Aaron, kissing him as well.

Sherri was squeezing Randall tighter than he squeezed her. "Randall! She tried to hurt our babies, Randall. She almost killed my mom! Mom!"

"Shh, baby, calm down." Miss Elaine came back through the screen door, having watched the police car that held a handcuffed Jacqueline until it turned the corner and was out of sight. With what she'd just witnessed from this Jacqueline character, she wanted to be sure the woman was gone. "It's okay. Everything is okay now."

Randall ran a nervous hand over his close-cropped hair. He grabbed Sherri again in a tight embrace. "That woman has serious mental issues," he whispered into her ear. "You are not going to believe what I found out!"

Everyone became quiet when they heard the front door open. Two officers walked in. "Are you all right, ma'am?" the older one asked Sherri. She nodded. "Are you well enough to make a statement? It won't be necessary to come down to the station. We can take it right here."

Sherri began walking over to the couch in her mother's living room. The gravity of what had almost happened suddenly overwhelmed her and her knees buckled. Randall was immediately at her side. Once he'd settled her on the couch he looked at the younger officer and jerked his head, gesturing for them to talk away from the family.

"Is there any way we can do this tomorrow?" he asked, once they were out of earshot. "My family has been through a lot."

"I understand, Dr. Atwater. But the longer we wait to take the statement, the more they might forget. It won't take long, we promise. We'll talk with your wife, your mother-in-law, and the children, and then be on our way."

"No. You will not talk to my children. They're traumatized enough as it is."

The older officer, who'd heard Randall's last statement, walked up to join them. "I agree with Dr. Atwater," he said, giving Randall a compassionate pat on the back. "If it's okay with you, sir, we'll have their questioning done by a child psychologist. We can set up an appointment a couple days from now."

Randall nodded. He and the officers walked back to the living room. They spoke first with Miss Elaine and then, while she entertained the children, they took Sherri's statement. After the officers had spent another thirty minutes or so documenting the crime scene, Randall turned to walk them to their patrol car.

"Wait," Sherri said as they prepared to leave. "How did you even know to come here? I didn't think the 9-1-1 call went through."

"We got a call from a young man named Hunter." All eyes turned to Aaron.

"I hit him up on FaceTime before she made me come out here," he said with a tiny smirk of satisfaction on his face. "My boy took it from there."

Randall followed the officers out. When he came back inside, he went over to Sherri and her mother on the couch, holding each other tightly. He sat down on the other side of Miss Elaine and hugged her as well. "You all right, Mom?"

Miss Elaine looked over at Albany and Aaron, who were staring at her intently. "I will be," she said at last. "We all are going to be just fine."

That night, Randall, his family, and Miss Elaine left her home and stayed in a hotel. The memories of what had taken place in the house were too raw for any of them to want to stay there. After getting Miss Elaine and her grandchildren settled down in the bedroom of the suite, Randall and Sherri lay in the sleeper sofa in the living room, talking in whispered tones.

"You're not going to believe what the private investigator told me, baby. It's right out of a movie script."

"Are you serious? After what I dealt with tonight, I'll believe anything."

"She had an entire surveillance network set up in our house."

"What do you mean?"

"She got into our house somehow, or hired someone to get in. As soon as we get back, I'll have it swept, but according to the investigator we'll find at least seven cameras hidden throughout our house. She had TV screens showing different rooms, including our bedroom."

"What?"

"Yes, and listening devices as well. That's how she found out about everything: my schedule, your outings, Mom Elaine needing in-home care. He found a whole network set up in her room at Phillip's house: computers, monitors, and other devices. He's seized her phone, which he believes will contain a mountain of evidence. Along with all of the electronics, he said he found wigs and other types of disguises. The investigator said it was one of the most elaborate setups he'd ever seen."

Sherri sat up against the headboard, pulling the sheet around her. She stared straight ahead and after a moment, her whole body began shaking.

Randall immediately sat up and wrapped his arms around her. "It's okay now, baby. We're safe."

"Are we?" Sherri asked, turning to him. "Can we be sure that they are going to charge that woman and lock her up where she belongs?" They were both quiet a moment, neither completely sure that this would be the case. Suddenly, Sherri grabbed Randall's arm and squeezed.

"What, baby?"

"She's been in our house." The weight of this realization hit Sherri square in the chest, and she was so upset that she threw back the covers and jumped out of bed. "She's been in our house," she said, her voice rising. She looked over her shoulder at the closed bedroom door and brought her voice back down. "That's how she knew about what kind of bed we had. That's how the panties got in my lingerie drawer. She was in our house, Randall, maybe even while we were there. Maybe when we were asleep!"

This possibility shook Randall as well. "I wish I could disagree with you, baby, but it's the only thing that makes sense." He looked at her, raw emotion showing in his eyes. "Sherri, I'm so sorry I put our family at risk. If I'd had any idea that she was a raving lunatic instead of an award-winning freelance writer, I would never have offered to split cab fare. In fact," his eyes narrowed and his face twisted into a frown. "I now find it suspect that she arrived at the same time I did, and sidled up behind me. Don't you?"

"I wouldn't put anything past her," Sherri acknowledged. "No doubt that woman is one of the most calculating creatures that ever walked this planet."

"I'll do whatever it takes to make sure she isn't able to do this to anyone else: write to the judge, talk to the lawyers. She crossed the line by trying to hurt my family. I'm going to make sure she stays in prison for a very long time."

EPILOGUE

Three months later

The driver turned off the narrow two-lane road into an entry-way guarded by a tall, wrought iron fence. Atop the fence were two diamond-shaped plaques bearing the words "Château Sherri," and beneath this was a huge red bow.

Sherri's hand went to her heart as she turned to her husband. "Honey," she whispered as her eyes filled with tears. "I can't believe you did this. It's so beautiful."

Randall grabbed her hand and placed it to his lips. "You're worth this and so much more, baby. Plus, you haven't seen anything yet."

"I sure don't see nothing," Albany pouted, mad that she'd lost Internet access several miles back.

"Yeah, where's the house?" Aaron asked.

Miss Elaine sat forward and looked at the kids. "Both of you be quiet and enjoy this beautiful scenery. Don't you see your parents trying to have a romantic moment?"

"Ugh!" Aaron scrunched up his face and turned away from his parents.

Albany chuckled. "How do you think you got here, fool!"

"OK, Albany," Sherri admonished, too happy and excited to put much chagrin in her voice. "That's enough."

Randall opened the gate with his remote, and the car passed through the private archway. The quaint, paved lane was framed by tall, leafy trees. It was just days before Thanksgiving, but here on their private Bahamian island, everything was vibrant and green. As they drove along the winding road, some of the branches hung over the lane, creating a canopy so magical that the typical bickering between siblings totally ceased. Everyone was quiet, taking in the hilly countryside, beautifully landscaped with seasonal flowers and blooming trees. As they rounded a curve, Sherri gasped. Before her lay a fairy tale: a beautiful, tan, castle-style home with turrets and balconies, every tree surrounding it boasting white mini-bulbs. The setting looked like a fairy tale in wonderland.

"Oh my goodness!" She turned to Randall. "Is this really mine?"

Randall laughed, intoxicated with the happiness that shone in her eyes. "All yours, baby. Château Sherri."

Sherri unabashedly wiped tears from her eyes. She had always loved the Bahamas but for a long time had joked about wanting a château in France. Her husband had done the impossible and given her the best of both worlds. A château on the island, with an unobstructed view of blue water and white sands below.

This was the gift that Randall had been working so hard to give her, something she had always wanted. This was the secret. Looking at what seemed to be a dream right before her very eyes made her even more sad that she had doubted him, justification or no.

"I'm sorry, baby," she said, fresh tears forming in her eyes. "If I'd known that you were doing all this . . ."

Randall reached over and gave Sherri's thigh a loving

squeeze. "We're not going to talk about that, remember? Family, where did we say we were going to leave the events of the past?"

"In the past," Albany dutifully responded.

Aaron made a face. "Where else would we leave them?"

"Clearly the intellect," Miss Elaine said, winking at Randall as she gave her grandson a pat on the head.

"Hey! I got a signal!" Albany held up her cell phone. "I got a signal!"

Sherri twisted her lips in sarcasm. "I guess that means you'll live."

While the driver unloaded their myriad of suitcases, the family explored the home. It was a wonderfully designed four-bed, three-bath home with a fireplace, vaulted ceilings, and two master suites. After an extensive tour narrated by a proud Randall, the family enjoyed a light repast prepared by the hired chef, went to their respective bedrooms, and welcomed sleep.

Two days later Randall, Sherri, Albany, Aaron, and Miss Elaine sat around a table laden with traditional American Thanksgiving fare. The chef they'd hired had outdone himself. The turkey was tender and shining with glaze, surrounded by stuffing and yams, mashed potatoes, green beans, and fresh cranberry sauce. In the short time they'd been there, the family had totally acclimated to their vacation home. The children went swimming every day and were learning to surf. They'd also befriended the elderly neighbors and were learning to ride horses. Miss Elaine was totally in love with the home's solarium, and when not out walking with her grandchildren, spent many hours there reading, doing needlework, and listening to classical tunes. Randall and Sherri mostly enjoyed each other, spending considerable time in their lavishly appointed master suite.

"There's enough food here to feed an army," Miss Elaine

commented after the chef had set down the last dish and left the room.

"For the next few days, that will be us. We've given the chef the rest of the day and the next two off. He won't be back until Sunday, to cook brunch."

"I'm ready to dig in," Aaron exclaimed, reaching for a serving utensil.

"Not so fast," Sherri said, staying his hand. "This is Thanksgiving, and we have much to be thankful for. So let's each of us state at least one reason we are grateful."

Randall looked at Aaron. "Son, since you're in such a hurry, you can go first."

"Aw, man."

Sherri shushed Albany's chuckle. The rest of the room remained quiet.

"We're waiting," Sherri prodded.

"Um, okay." Aaron sat straighter and fixed his tie. "I'm thankful for my family and for being on this, my own private island!"

"My island," Sherri corrected.

"Whatever, Mom. I love our vacation home."

Randall nodded. "Albany?"

"I'm thankful for my family and that Grandma is feeling better. And . . ." She swallowed, as if battling with her emotions. "I'm glad that Mommy and Daddy are still together and that Jac—"

Albany stopped cold as Sherri shot her a look. Her daughter was about to utter the name that had been banned from the family.

"I'm glad that woman who tried to kill us is in jail."

"Where she belongs," Aaron added with a scowl.

"God don't like ugly," Miss Elaine said, her voice a soothing balm on tense emotions. "And vengeance belongs to him. So let's spend this day focusing on what's good in our lives. A few months ago, I didn't know how I'd be feeling come Thanksgiving, or if I'd know it had arrived. But every day I'm feeling more like my old self, and for that I'm very grateful. I'm lucky to have a daughter like you, Sherri, and a son who couldn't have been more perfect had I birthed him myself." Miss Elaine's eyes became glassy. "Thank you for being so good to my baby. This is one of the best times I've had in my life."

Sherri dabbed her eyes with the tip of her linen napkin before she spoke. "I'm so happy my heart is about to burst, because the very best things I have in life are around this table. I'm over the moon to be in the Bahamas, my favorite place on the planet, and in our very own home! I can't wait to share it with Nathan and our good friends. Besides my family being safe, I'm most thankful that the doctors finally found the tumor that was causing all of your problems, Mom, and that the laser surgery, along with medication, has helped you back to a normal life.

"Randall, I can't imagine what it would have been like to spend the past fifteen years without you, and I'm looking forward to many more. I love you, baby."

They shared a quick kiss before Randall spoke. He wasn't much of a religious man, but no one questioned it when he asked them to bow their heads. "God, I just want to say thank you for everything this year: nice profits for my company, being able to purchase this home away from home for my wife, the health of my mother-in-law, and the safety and well-being of my family. Sometimes I take the life I have for granted, but today I, um"—he stopped to clear a throat that had become raspy with emotion—"thank you."

Late that night, Randall and Sherri cuddled on an oversized wicker chair under a blanket. They were on the château's rooftop, one of their favorite places in the whole space, looking up at a bright, full moon.

"I knew it, but I still can't believe it," she said, an involuntary shiver going up her spine.

"That Jacqueline has been charged with the murder of Wanda Smith?" Randall sighed, pulled Sherri closer. "I can. When they found Wanda Smith's body a week after the arrest, I knew Jacqueline had done it. Without a shadow of a doubt."

"Do you think it's finally over, Randall, really over?"

"Yes, baby. It's over. And I meant what I said in that hotel in Raleigh. I will do everything in my power to make sure that woman remains behind bars for the rest of her life."

"I love you, Randall."

"I love you, too."

They sealed these words with a long, hot kiss.

"I'll never get enough of you," Randall whispered to Sherri after coming up for air. "It's like the more I've had in the past few months . . . the more I want."

"I feel the same way." Sherri ran a lazy hand under her husband's sweater and around the top of his jeans. "One thing that came out of . . . the incident . . . I've never appreciated or loved you more. If this is what you've done for our fifteenth anniversary, I can't wait to see twenty, thirty, heck by number fifty you'll probably buy me the moon! Seriously, baby, this is the best gift you could have given me. It's absolutely perfect."

"Mm"—Randall repositioned his wife so he could kiss her more soundly—"just like you."

Frank, the transport officer, glanced in the rearview mirror for the umpteenth time, curiously watching the prisoner he'd picked up at the mental health facility. She'd been talking non-stop since settling herself into the backseat of the van, as though instead of going to prison she was going home.

He reached Duke Raleigh Hospital, his last stop before heading to NCCIW, the North Carolina Correctional Institute for Women. His partner, Greg, was leaning against the wall of the hospital, near the entrance, and pushed off as he approached.

"What's going on?" Frank asked as soon as Greg had gotten in, buckled up, and they headed out of the hospital emergency drop-off area. "Where's your charge?"

"She tried to make a break this morning," Greg replied, jotting notes in a log book. "Cut herself up pretty badly. They're going to keep her for a few more days."

"That's one way to avoid the inevitable," Frank mumbled. "Guess we've only got this one." He looked over and noticed Greg's frequent looks at their prisoner in back. He chuckled but remained silent.

"They released her from mental?"

"Yep."

"And we're taking her to prison, to be integrated in general pop?"

"Uh-huh."

Greg looked behind him, more blatantly this time. The woman stopped talking, gave him a cold stare, and then resumed her conversation in a much lower tone.

"She's talking as though there's somebody there."

"I guess in her mind there is," Frank said, pausing as he made a left-hand turn. "Somebody named Kris. She's been talking to her nonstop ever since I picked her up."

"You've got to be kidding."

"Nope. Been having a full-fledged conversation with her imaginary friend."

"Too bad she's cuckoo for Cocoa Puffs," Greg said, turning around and giving her a wink. "Because she doesn't look half bad."

"When her eye isn't blackened and her lip's not busted, she's probably a real beauty."

Behind them, Jacqueline sat back and crossed her legs. Her look was one of supreme confidence as she looked at the empty space beside her. "Did you see that?"

"What?" Kris asked.

"The guard, and the way he's looking at me."

"I don't know why you're surprised. He's a man, isn't he?"

"Yes," Jacqueline replied, her smile sinister. "He sure is."

"Are you thinking what I'm thinking?"

"That getting out of this place is going to be easier than we think?" Kris nodded. "I just have to find out which of the guards is the most helpful, and then I'll make my move."

"And go back to Randall?"

Jacqueline's smile disappeared. "No way. He made his choice. I thought he was smart, but he isn't. He'll rue the day he did this to me. Him and his bitch wife too. It's time to set my sights higher, focus on the man who's going to get me out of this mess, who'll be my knight in shining armor. Someone strong and manly." She nodded to the burly guard driving the van. "Maybe like him."

Kris looked, and smiled. "And then what?"

"Then I'll wield my charm, of course," Jacqueline said, laughing confidently. "And if he's married, I'll make damn sure that his wife isn't an issue by taking care of her first. The next time, without a doubt, will be the *perfect* affair."

The Shady Sisters Trilogy continues with
The Perfect Deception
Available December 2014 wherever books and
ebooks are sold

CHAPTER 1

A beautiful couple walked up the immaculately landscaped entrance to a large home located in a tony Alexandria, Virginia suburb. The woman was nervous. It was Thanksgiving, which, for various reasons, was one of her least favorite holidays, second only to Christmas. More importantly, it was the first time she was meeting the family of her beloved, an amazing man with whom she'd enjoyed a whirlwind courtship for the past six months. Today was important. Her man truly loved her. She could tell. Life had turned out better than she could have dreamed when she'd spotted the handsome stranger among a crowded Atlanta happy hour crowd and made a bold move. If she played her cards right and impressed the family, who knew what type of sparkly bauble Santa might place under the Christmas tree?

He knocked on the door and after a short moment, it swung open.

"Nathan!" An attractive woman dressed in black stretch pants and a colorful sweater opened the door.

"Hey, Sis!"

"Come on in!" she said, stepping back so that the couple

could enter the massive foyer with the high, vaulted ceiling and chic chandelier.

The siblings hugged before Nathan Carver turned and beamed at the woman with a hesitant smile standing by his side. "Sister, this is Jessica Bolton. Baby, this is my sister and best friend, Sherri Atwater."

A genuine smile lit Sherri's face. "I've heard so much about you," she said after a light hug. "You're as pretty as my brother bragged that you were."

"It's a pleasure to meet you," Jessica replied, her eyes darting behind them to the hallway from which jovial voices traveled.

"That's my crazy family," Sherri explained. "Along with a few of our friends. They're pretty lively but no one bites."

Nathan put his arm around Jessica and gave her shoulder an affectionate squeeze. They started down the hall. Halfway down, a handsome man rounded the corner and walked their way.

"I thought I heard voices." He reached them, and gave Nathan dap and a shoulder bump.

"Hey, bro." Again, there were introductions all around.

"Where are you from?" Randall asked Jessica, once they'd been introduced. "Your face looks familiar."

Private by nature, Jessica arched her brow in surprise. "Me?" She quickly added, "I live in Atlanta but am from California." This was basically true. She had lived in California for several years before her divorce.

"Southern California?" Randall inquired as they continued down the hall into the great room where the adults had gathered.

"Northern. Oakland."

They entered the great room where Nathan's mother, Elaine, was recounting a funny incident from when Randall and Sherri first began courting. Listening was Randall's mother, Barbara, her male companion, his brother and sister-in-law, Sherri's best friend, Renee and her cousin, and Randall's business partner, James, along with his wife.

"It was thoughtful for him to buy me a bouquet," she finished. "He went on about how he'd searched the city for just the right type of flowers he thought I'd like. I didn't have the heart to tell him that the price tag was still on it from the store where he worked part-time, along with the receipt that was time-stamped to show he'd bought them right after his shift!"

Various responses echoed around the room, laughter sprinkled among them. "Come on, Mom Elaine," Randall said as he entered. "Haven't I lived that one down by now?"

"Yes, but it's worth retelling." She'd answered him but her eyes were on Nathan and his lovely date, as were all other eyes in the room. "Hello, son."

"Hey, everybody," Nathan said with a general wave to the room, before crossing over to give his mom a hug. "Hello, Mom." He reached back for Jessica's hand to bring her forward. "Mom, this is my friend, Jessica. Jessica, my mother, Elaine Carver."

"Hello Mrs. Carver." Jessica's outstretched hand reached Elaine's, which had also come up. "It's wonderful to meet you."

"Nice meeting you, too, darling. Congratulations on making it to a family function." With a side glance at Nathan she continued, "It's been awhile since Nate has invited a guest."

Jessica split her smile between Nathan and Elaine. "Well, I'm doubly honored."

Nathan then addressed the room. "Everybody, this is Jessica."

With a slight giggle she waved, "Hi everyone."

"You'll get to know their names as the day unfolds," he said, still holding her hand. "Introducing them all at once would only confuse you."

"Yes, and by the time I'd met the last one I would have forgotten the first one's name."

"Exactly."

"What are y'all drinking?" Randall asked, as he walked over to the bar.

And with that, conversation resumed, more drinks were poured, soft music played and Nathan and Jessica made their way through the rest of the personal greetings.

"This is a beautiful home," she said, once they'd circled the room and once again stood near its entrance.

"Come on, let me give you a quick tour."

He was a perfect guide as they navigated the large yet cozy abode. Upon seeing the tastefully decorated rooms and a grouping of plaques, certificates, and photos that filled almost an entire wall in the downstairs office, Jessica was even more impressed with her honey's in-laws than when he'd told her about them. Randall, his brother-in-law, was a prominent scientist who'd won awards for his ground-breaking research. That in itself was a lofty achievement but the picture of him standing alongside President Barack Obama in what appeared to be a room at the White House placed the man under whose roof she stood in very high company. The day was already overwhelming and now she felt intimidated, too.

Nathan immediately noticed her change in attitude. "What's wrong?"

"Nothing."

"Tell me about nothing."

She smiled. His sensitivity and astute observatory skills were just two of the many things that she loved about him. "Your family is so . . . accomplished."

"You already knew that."

"Yes, but to be here, to meet them. I just hope that I'm not . . ."

"Trust me, you're not whatever you're thinking. Yes, there are those in my family who are highly successful but we don't judge people based on awards and degrees. We're more interested in a person's character, their integrity, their family values." He reached over and pulled her into his arms, gave her one kiss, and then another. "So you don't have anything to worry about."

Jessica nodded, and entwined her arm in his as they walked toward French doors that led to a solarium. She knew that Nathan meant what he said when he told her not to worry. He'd meant to be soothing. Little did he know that it was exactly what he said and how he and his upstanding family felt that worried her most of all.

CHAPTER 2

"What do you think?"

Dinner was over, and various family members had broken off into smaller groups. Nathan and his sister Sherri were in the kitchen, sitting at the island, eating more pieces of sweet potato pie that neither needed.

"She's cute, I'll give you that." Sherri took a sip of cold milk. "But she's so quiet, Nate, and"—she paused, searching for the right word—"somewhat reserved. Not the type of woman you usually date."

"She is different from anyone I've dated in the past. In the end, that's what drew me to her."

"How did you guys meet?"

"I told you, remember? We met at the sports bar in Buckhead where I like to hang out."

"Was she a friend of a friend, someone's sister . . . ?"

"No. She was at the bar, alone. We'd noticed each other throughout the evening and at one particular point, when my friends and I were in a heated debate she walked up and said, 'I don't know what you guys are arguing about but you win.' Looking at me."

Sherri gave her brother a look. "Really? You win? That was the line that drew you in?"

"It wasn't so much what she said as the way she said it: straight-forward, serious, with the merest twinkle in her eye."

Sherri finished her pie, pushed back the plate. "And then she whipped out the card containing her phone number."

Nathan shook his head. "And then she walked back to her barstool and pulled out her phone. Basically ignored me."

"And waited for the bait to take hold."

"Perhaps. But considering the types of bold and aggressive women out there and the insulting ways I've been approached, it was refreshing." Nathan finished his pie as well. "See, you've been out of the game too long to know what it's like out here right now. Married for going on sixteen years and with Randall for what, three or four years before y'all tied the knot? Hell, I think the Cabbage Patch Doll was all the rage the last time you had to flirt with someone not your husband. That or the Model T." He dodged Sherri's punch. "I'll admit that men in Atlanta have women coming at us every way and every day; beautiful, successful, educated women. It's easy to get jaded, to tell you the truth. Which is probably why I found Jessica's simplicity refreshing. She's never tried to impress me by being anything other than herself."

"Where'd she go to school?"

"She didn't."

"No degree?" Nathan shook his head. "Wow."

"If you'll remember, your dual-degreed brother was temporarily unemployed not so long ago."

"Only because your company down-sized and could no longer afford you. And only because you could afford to be selective in choosing your next job, which is netting you a cool six figures." She looked around, lowered her voice. "Does Jessica know this? Does she know that you own your own home, and how much you're making?"

"Sherri . . ."

"I know your nose is wide open and all, but I'm just throwing up the caution sign, that's all. That's what big sisters do."

"I know a gold digger when I see one. You should know that better than anyone."

Sherri nodded, knowing exactly who Nathan was talking about. A woman he'd met online last year had wormed her way into his home and bed long enough to try and steal his identity along with his bank accounts.

"You're normally a good judge of character, baby bro, and normally I wouldn't be overly concerned. But given what happened to me and Randall last year . . ."

"You have every right to be skeptical, and I have every intention of listening to your advice. I'll do a background check before things go much farther. I'll be careful, Sherri. But it's been a long time since I've felt about someone the way I feel about Jessica. That's why I wanted her to meet the people most important to me."

Sherri stood and hugged her brother. "I want nothing more than to see you happy, Nathan. I'll be keeping my fingers crossed that this one works out, and that Jessica will be everything you desire . . . and more."

On the other side of the tastefully-appointed home, and one level up, a conversation similar to the one Nathan and Sherri were having was happening with Jessica and Sherri's best friend.

"Nathan is like a brother to me," Renee said as the two ladies watched the dancing flames in the sitting room's fireplace. "He's one of the good ones. So if you mess with him, then you're going to have to deal with more than his family." Her tone was light, she chuckled even, but there was something in her eyes that suggested she was as serious as a brain tumor.

Jessica's response was guarded. "I see."

Renee's eyes narrowed a bit as she eyed the attractive woman with flawless brown skin, luscious lips, mesmerizing eyes, and hourglass figure. It was easy to see why Nathan would have been intrigued by the package. However considering the type of women he usually dated—vivacious, outgoing, and attractively confident—Renee had yet to understand why he'd fell so hard for the contents inside the pretty wrapping. Determined to find out, she decided to try and lighten the mood.

"How did the two of you meet?"

"At a sports bar."

"You're into sports? I like a good game, too; mainly because of the fine men playing them." This time her light laughter elicited a brief smile.

"Honestly, I barely know a lay-up from a field goal. But I like the establishment's ambiance. Plus, they make the best martinis, spinach and artichoke dip, and spicy wings that I've ever tasted."

"I love a great martini. I'll have to make sure and visit it the next time I'm in Atlanta. You do live in Atlanta, correct?"

"I do." Jessica paused and took a sip of the spiced tea that the two ladies had been drinking, except that Renee's had been enhanced by a shot of brandy. "Renee, it's understandable that you'd be curious about the new love interest of one of your dear friends. But I'm an extremely private person and quite honestly, your interrogation is making me uncomfortable."

Renee reared back. Her voice raised a notch. "Interrogation? Girl, that's a strong word for simple chit-chat. It was not my intention to pry."

"I'm sure it was not, so please don't take this personally." Jessica stood. "It's not you. It's me. It was nice meeting you but if you don't mind, I'm going to find Nathan. It's been a long, full day and I'm just about ready to turn in."

With that, Jessica left the room. Renee watched her exit, her mind whirling with questions from front to back. Renee's life had pretty much been an open book. There was very little of herself that she didn't share with those around her. So on one hand, Jessica had every right to not answer Renee's questions. But on the other hand, the young woman's response had left her feeling uncomfortable, and she didn't know why. Yes, she was very attractive. Yes, she seemed nice enough. But there was something about her that made Renee's brow crease. She slowly sipped her brandy-spiced tea and tried to figure out why.

She was still pondering the conversation moments later, when Sherri walked in. "Hey, sis. What's got your face all scrunched up?"

"An interesting conversation I just had with Nathan's friend." She put emphasis on the last word. "Are they gone?"

Sherri rushed over to her best friend and sat beside her. "Girl, yes. And I couldn't wait to come talk to you and get your take. What happened?"

Renee told her. "I've replayed the conversation in my mind. I am direct and very forward, as you know. But she should know that nobody in this house, the house of the sister of the man she's dating, means her harm. I just found it a bit odd that she was so guarded, that's all."

"I thought I was the only one who saw it like that. Throughout the day—while hanging in the kitchen, when she and Nathan were chilling in the solarium, after the guys had come back from playing ball—I went out of my way to engage her. She was nice enough, and seems genuinely taken with my baby bro."

"Who wouldn't be?"

"But, like you said, there's something about her that . . . I don't know . . . just gives me pause." They were both silent a moment. A log broke, causing the fire to pop and flare as the wood rearranged itself in the large hearth. "Do you think it's because of what happened to my family last year, all of the drama and mayhem caused by you-know-who?"

"Could be," Renee said with a sigh, an involuntary shudder accompanying the memories of that unspeakable event. "None of us will ever look at strangers quite the same way again."

"That's very true. You know what? I'm not going to turn into a paranoid skeptic. Nathan is an intelligent, astute man. So I'm going to trust his instincts and give Jessica the benefit of the doubt until or unless she does something that causes me to think otherwise."

"I don't know, girl. A man's thinking isn't always straight when he's using the other head. And trust me, one look at that girl's cute bubble booty and you already know. His other head is getting a work out."

"Nay, really? I needed that information? That's my brother we're talking about."

Renee's answer nonchalantly. "All the more reason to say what you already know."

The women continued talking well into the night, their conversation going from Nathan to Renee's latest beau, to Sherri's new, part-time teaching job to Randall's upcoming trips. In the back of both of their minds, however, was the topic that had begun this latest chat. The guarded, private Jessica . . . and what was up with that.

CHAPTER 3

She had failed the family test. The signs weren't glaring like they'd be on a school paper, when one expecting a gold star instead received red marks and a minus sign. They were subtle, like the way Sherri gave her brother a big bear hug while offering Jessica a brief squeeze and tight smile. Or how Sherri's friend, Renee, looked rather dubious when told it had been good to meet her. Nathan's mother, Miss Elaine, was definitely the kindest of the bunch, and probably the nicest as well. The men, especially Nathan's brother-in-law Randall, had been cordial but kept their distance. The other wives and girlfriends seemed distant at best. Not that she cared about them. The ones she wanted to win over were Miss Elaine and Sherri, and in this instance one out of two wasn't good enough. Especially given what was at stake, what she'd promised both herself and others. Especially given that Nathan was head and shoulders above any other man she'd ever known.

Having watched his family interact, she could only imagine what they must have thought about her actions, could only guess at the conversations that took place after they'd left. It was obvious to anyone watching that Nathan had grown up in a loving, trusting environment, where sharing one's thoughts and feelings was expected, even encouraged. Jessica's child-hood home had been filled with secrets and silence. From early on, she'd learned to shield her thoughts and guard her privacy. For her, personal conversations did not come easy. Old habits died hard.

If only I hadn't . . .

Jessica jumped up from the couch and walked to the window of her second-floor condo near Five Points. Of all the things she'd been thinking about since the weekend she'd spent with Nathan—first with his family in Virginia and then with his D.C. friends—what could, should, and would have been wasn't part of the process. It was Sunday evening. After being practically inseparable from Nathan for four straight days, some of the happiest of her life, she was back home. It had been less than an hour, but already felt like days. For the first time in a very long time she felt bereft and very alone.

A song came on the radio. Jessica smiled. It was one of Nathan's all-time favorites, or so he'd told her the first time they'd heard it together, the night after meeting him at the sports bar. Jessica walked back to the couch, plopped down and grabbed a pillow as her mind drifted back to the night she'd spotted him across the room.

There ought to be a law.

That's what Jessica thought as she looked across the crowded restaurant and beheld a table filled with caramel and chocolate testosterone. She lazily sipped a pomegranate martini, swinging a stiletto-clad foot as she watched them: laughing, scoping, sipping, too. They were all handsome but one stood out, and for more reasons than one. He was tall, at least six feet, which although she was only five foot three, she preferred. Nattily dressed, his eyes were expressive and his smile was easy. The group of four men was in a lively discussion. The one she watched spoke little but when he did, the others listened attentively to what he had to say.

A couple of times their eyes had met. After hearing snatches of conversation as she passed their table on her way to the bathroom, she stopped and boldly made her move. At her declaration of his superior position, Nathan had nodded with a casual smile. One of the guys blatantly flirted. But she'd walked away from the table as quickly as she'd come, had returned to her seat and become engrossed in something online. She'd finished her drink and believed a rendezvous with the handsome stranger a lost cause until she'd reached the door, felt a hand on her shoulder, and turned to find that same sexy, self-assured smile that had drawn her to his table now on display just for her.

They'd gone to dinner the next night, and dancing the night after that. The following weekend they'd enjoyed a neo-soul concert and the weekend after that they'd enjoyed each other. Nathan was a skillful, thoughtful lover, which she'd expected. What she hadn't expected was to develop real feelings for him. Nor had she expected such feelings to be reciprocated.

No, that hadn't been a part of the plan at all.

Her ringing cell phone brought Jessica out of her musings. Seeing the name on the Caller ID only further muddled her mood. "Hey."

"Hey, girl. What's wrong with you?"

"Nothing. Just thinking."

"About what?"

She hesitated. "Nathan."

"That's why I'm calling. How was Thanksgiving?"

"Fine. He has a nice family." This elicited a snort from the other end. "I know you might not feel that way, but it's true. His mother treated me kindly and his sister, too."

"Sounds like everything is working according to plan, working out just the way we'd hoped. His taking you around the family is a sure sign that he's falling for you, that he trusts you. Once you gain a person's trust, anything can happen."

"It's not about trust. It's about love. I believe I'm falling in love with him."

A sarcastic laugh and then, "What's love got to do with anything? No, don't answer. I'll tell you. Nothing. Absolutely nothing."

"Being around his family showed me what I've never had but always wanted; I used to talk about it. Remember?"

"Yes, you always were the dreamer, the believer in fairy tales. But this is life, not a story book, and blood is thicker than water. You remember that."